ALL THE WAY HAPPY

Kit Coltrane

carina
press®

Recycling programs
for this product may
not exist in your area.

ISBN-13: 978-1-335-44798-2

All the Way Happy

Carina Press
22 Adelaide St. West, 41st Floor
Toronto, Ontario M5H 4E3, Canada
www.CarinaPress.com

Printed in U.S.A.

To that child in the cold bedroom,
the window stuck open,
the rain coming down—this is for you.

You made it out.

This novel includes some descriptions of neglect and abuse, and healing from childhood trauma is a crucial theme of the text. There are also mentions of drug use and suicidality. Jack and Theo are navigating love, loss and adulthood as they cope with foundational trauma. If this is challenging to read, be gentle with yourself. The words will be here if and when you are ready.

ALL THE WAY HAPPY

Prologue

He was thirty-seven. Fuck. He was thirty-seven.

When he ran away from everything—from Baltimore, from his family, from blue eyes and guilt and casual schoolboy violence—he ran far. He got his first shitty apartment in Cork, Ireland, and he tried to live on the razor edge of a knife, in the dangerous dance of his own self-destruction.

He had a dodgy upstairs neighbor, Cathal, and windows which didn't shut all the way, and the water wasn't ever quite warm enough, but it was—it was his.

He'd cashed out the small trust fund that hadn't been impacted by what his father—what had happened, and the first thing he bought was an old record player and a stack of LPs. Music was what kept him going. The kind of music that his parents had never let him listen to, ugly and wailing and wild, soft and heartbreaking, stupid and silly and utterly perfect.

Led Zeppelin blared out when he smoked his first spliff (courtesy of that same upstairs neighbor, who was quite sketchy indeed, but with an apartment full of exotic birds and a too-kind heart). Tiffany sang about being alone, and he danced in front of the bathroom's cracked mirror while he cut his own hair. Long locks shorn, revealing an angular, violent beauty.

He listened to the Clash and thought about his father, about imposing his own brand of anarchy on his stilted and tight-fisted childhood, that man he had worshipped and the man who had hated him. He threw things and threw up at two in the morning, the fast food he'd grabbed after a night at the clubs coming up looking not all that dissimilar from the way it went down.

Stevie Wonder sang about falling in love and he tried, he really did, not to think about sky blue eyes and black hair.

And then there was David Bowie.

The feeling of sunrise in Cork—the way the air was damp and fresh, shaking, all too aware of the panic of nighttime, liminal and lined with edges of gold—went best with Bowie. Some mornings he listened to "Heroes," and he thought about what he had never been. On other mornings, he put on "Let's Dance" and drank cup after cup of shitty instant coffee before heading down across Saint Patrick Street to scrub the sticky floors of the club he'd been writhing in four hours before.

Rainy days and it was "Bring Me the Disco King," and he thought about taking a knife to the inside of his arm. When the flat was freezing with cold in a wet way which felt like falling into the sea, he played "My Death," which was Jacques Brel, but Bowie lived and died it. And "Wild Eyed Boy From Freecloud" was what he played when he first took another man into himself and wanted to scream out to his father and his past and those blue eyes.

He'd had enough of silence.

But most of all, that first year was marked by an almost orgiastic adherence to Bowie's sepulchral warning—the desired brevity of his life, an anticipated early end by twenty-five.

He didn't think he would make it, not even that far. He figured there was nothing much to live for at eighteen, anyway, other than one more drink, one more fuck, a few more cups of coffee, trad nights with American exchange students grinding in the corners, balancing on the rock wall across from The Thirsty Scholar at three in the morning and itching, always, to jump into the water and melt the fuck away.

And now, at thirty-seven, he was still very much alive—his blood pumped through him, and his brain was sparking in manic fury and discontent, and his skin felt like ice. He had a job, a respectable one, and he had a smooth face which no one could read. He had an ex-wife and a child, an aging mother who had never really loved him but who was maybe trying her best now. He was usually sober. He played music at an acceptable volume.

He was back in his childhood home. Managing it, and his money, and making it all look good.

As the Beaumonts had always done. At least until his father had fleeced half of Baltimore. But he was reclaiming that name, that heritage, even as he hated it.

And every little part of him, the broken bits, the whole bits—every breath which reminded him of cigarettes at midnight—every time his mother looked at him with a vague, muted disappointment—every time he saw blue eyes in the street or in a bar or the Gwynns Academy alumni newsletter—every morning when he didn't wake up in that shitty flat with Cathal and the parakeets upstairs and the old record player and the LPs which skipped—

Every single cell in his body longed, desperately.

Silently.

He was thirty-seven.

He wanted to burn the world down.

Chapter One

The first time Jack Gardner met Theodore Beaumont, he was staring at a rack of blue blazers, knowing that his mother could never afford them, and doubting every decision which had led him here, to Gwynns Academy, the most exclusive—and expensive—preparatory school in Baltimore.

All Jack had ever worn were hand-me-downs, clothing used by others, and the crisp lines of the Gwynns uniforms were foreign to him, nearly strange. The stitching was impeccable, the cloth a deep navy blue, and the school's crest was in gold and red embroidery, and he had never had anything so fine, so costly, so clean. Starched white shirts and pleated trousers and striped gold ties were the other elements of his soon-to-be school's uniform, and he wondered if this—this outfit, this costume, this mask—could ever hide the little boy who'd never really had enough to eat.

The school shop bustled with other students and their perfect families—ice-blonde mothers with pearls, and fathers with platinum tie tacks, and kids who looked like their copies, utterly at ease, expectant of nothing other than this, the chore, the way the world was, spending money without a thought. Jack was already out of place—school hadn't even started yet.

He caught a glimpse of himself in the full-length mirror and wanted to look away, but he couldn't. He saw his skinny frame, knobby knees covered by too-large shorts, a collarbone as thin and delicate as a bird's wing exposed by the stretched-out neck of his black T-shirt. His hair was thick and messy, impossible to tame. The only feature which might have been attractive were his blue eyes, piercing. He tried not to worry so much about how he looked. That wasn't why he was here.

He could see the rest of the school shop behind him in the mirror, crammed tight with the uniforms and notebooks, lacrosse gear, Shakespeare and Yeats and mathematical texts, the smell of fresh paper and glue, and all of those shining people. At the register, one of the other children stood with a stack of clothes, seeming bored, elegant, casually stunning, and cold. His mother was next to him, chatting with another mother with rich black hair, and his father typed away on his cell phone. Jack couldn't help but imagine the sort of life they must have—galas and fundraisers and meals out, clothing and jewelry and shoes without holes.

He held a blue jacket under his chin, trying to imagine the next four years, what he would look like. Who he might be. His fingers delighted in the soft material, but—

"For fuck's sake, Jack. We can't—go look at the used pile." His mother's face was pinched and still somehow disinterested. She had tucked herself in a corner, maybe in an attempt to go unnoticed, but she stood out here just as much as he did. She didn't fit.

He'd learned not to blush, not to show shame. He turned away from the mirror and dug through the pile of used uniforms.

The blond boy at the counter slanted his eyes over, looked at Jack from his scuffed sneakers to his frayed collar, and Jack could feel his eyes like glaciers on his neck. The boy smirked. "This school's really been lowering its standards, Mother."

His mother turned from her conversation, glanced at Jack and his mom, and pursed her lips. Half an unkind smile, and then her tanned skin smoothed out into a blank haughtiness. "Be nice, Theo." She turned back toward the other parents, unbothered. Dismissing Jack—and maybe her own son—as if he were of no consequence.

A sigh from the boy, unnoticed. "If I must."

Everything that Jack had ever hated about himself was visible on the other boy's face. An unpleasant face, a jeering face. That child had seen right through him, right down to the root, and he had found him wanting.

And that boy—Theo—was everything that Jack yearned to be. His skin was pale, clear, white enough to show the blue tracery of his veins, and his hair was perfectly coiffed, and he wore a five-thousand-dollar watch, and he could afford to be cruel. Could afford to go to Gwynns without a scholarship, without working himself down to the nub, competing and scrapping and begging, *Please, see me.*

Jack gathered up two jackets, two pairs of trousers, three shirts, one tie. His mother dug in her handbag and looked at him as if he were a terrible burden. This was a big day, an important day—he didn't want to admit his mother's resentments. He could look at that later; his mother's attitude wouldn't go away.

Jack got in line, keeping a significant distance between himself and that boy, Theo, who was tall and lithe and perfect, who smelled like vanilla and gin, who was sparkling. Who belonged here, effortlessly.

No one could ever miss Theo Beaumont.

Jack hated him at once.

"For fuck's sake, Will."

Jack, if pressed, would admit with a sheepish grin and a tilt of his head that Gwilim Linwood Alistair—Will, now, since all of his kids were determined to have normal names, despite his best efforts—was his favorite child. He was quiet, a dreamer, with all of his father's sarcasm but none of his insecurity, and Jack maybe felt a bit bad about the name, but it was too late now.

He looked exactly like his dad. But he was better.

Though, admittedly, just as absentminded. Christ.

Johnny, of course, had set herself up in her room with little fanfare and a careless hug for each of her parents—a very clear "go away" signal—and was already prepared for her junior year. She'd been through the routine before. And she was never quite as—distractible as Will.

Jack looked at Will's Gwynns Academy blazer, forgotten in the back of the car. Meg, as pretty as ever but twice as worn out, strapped Amy into her seat belt, and gave Jack a *that's your kid, you idiot* stare.

He sighed. "I'll run it in, all right? Maybe check in with Charlie, catch a cab home."

"Mm."

He handed over the keys and leaned down to press a kiss to his wife's freckled cheek, and then they had that moment which many soon-to-be divorced people must have—oh, shit.

Not his wife. Not anymore.

Jack turned away, walked out of the parking lot and back to the mica-flecked granite of the school gates, school uniform in hand, and he tried not to think about what was coming next. The signing of the papers. Finding a new place to live. Splitting up the hours, the days—Will and Johnny at school, for now, but where would Amy live, and would he get to see her enough, and would they all hate him, maybe, for tearing down a marriage which must have looked, from the outside, unbreakable?

They'd settled Will into his dorm room, posters on the walls, bookshelves jammed with science fiction paperbacks and thick textbooks and all that literature they were paying a ridiculous amount for teachers to shove into his head. Jack jogged back through campus, passing the old Japanese maple he'd climbed and hid in for so many hours as a teenager, and the running stream he'd fallen into while skipping study hall, and the lacrosse field where he'd shed so much blood. Parents and their children were still milling about, and despite the long years between his youth and adulthood, Jack was full of excitement and dread and that old longing, a kid at the candy store, a child without a home. He barely looked around him, eager to get into the dorms and out without being noticed, and he ran right into the back of another parent.

Juniper. Sandalwood. Vanilla.

Fine, combed wool. Ice-blond hair.

Oh, shit.

He was going to throttle Will.

Theo Beaumont turned, elegant, still. He was wearing a perfectly tailored suit, tie loosened around his neck and top button undone, a gold watch, shined shoes. Jack suddenly felt underdressed and unfashionable, just as he had twenty years ago.

He'd spotted him in the distance—of course he had—while getting Will into his dorm, though he'd tried not to think about it; he had a son, too, in Will's year, with the same chilly looks but a big toothy grin. They'd been filling out forms at the reception desk, designer luggage handed over to be carried up by school staff, and Jack had turned away, face hot. He didn't want—he had really tried not to look—he forced himself not to even though, God, he needed—

Now Jack couldn't look away. Theo's hair was long again, no longer asymmetrical and uneven, and his skin was still flawless, enriched by the few fine lines showing the decades between that summer after their senior year and today. His eyes held a hint of warmth—maybe he'd been softened by fatherhood, by marriage—but they were gray and frosted as he regarded Jack. Despite the subtle differences, he looked—it was still him, unequivocally. Still Theo—still so beautiful.

Nothing had changed.

Jack hadn't talked to Theo in nineteen years.

And everything had changed since then.

"Gardner."

"Um, hi. Sorry, I—" Jack felt like he'd been hit with a blast of ice. He was frozen to his spot, here on the red brick lane, in the shade of pear blossom trees, the thick wet scent of Baltimore in September.

He looked so much the same. He even smelled the same.

Jack was, very quickly, losing the plot.

Theo rolled his eyes. "Is there a reason you're holding a Gwynns jacket?"

Jack looked down at his hand, eyes catching on gold stitching. Looked over at the dormitory building. Looked at Theo. He opened his mouth, but nothing came out.

"Oh, for God's sake." Theo rolled his eyes again, somehow more dramatic, and waved a hand. "Just go in, would you?"

"I—"

"The dorms are quite nice, now." His casual tone was forced in a way that only Jack would be able to notice.

"Yeah, I—"

"I think they have your picture up there, somewhere. Sure to be a thrill."

Still kind of a bastard, it seemed. Jack grimaced, embarrassed. "I wish they hadn't done that."

Theo scoffed. He was unbelievably good at scoffing. "You're the only person I know who could be ashamed of such a... significant donation."

"Yeah, well..." He trailed off, uncertain. He really was

uncomfortable with people—people thinking about—"I hate that they—"

"I remember." Theo looked him over, eyes just as sharp and critical as ever, and then his face softened, just a little. "Always so ashamed to be noticed."

Jack's face colored. He glanced away, staring at the brick pathway.

"It's been a long time." Theo's voice was hollow but gentle.

"Yeah." Jack rubbed the back of his neck, tried to smile. "We're old men now."

"Not that old." A lifted eyebrow.

"God." Jack felt the burden of too many years, so many joys and too many stupid decisions. "I feel old."

They both paused, silent. Jack felt the distance between them as if it were a physical thing, a solid thing, and he wanted to reach out, smell that place where Theo's shoulder met his neck—and he remembered those few months, the stone wall next to the River Lee, Cork at sunrise, cigarettes laced with hash, and the most beautiful and fucked-up time in his entire life.

And he thought about his three children, whom he loved more than anything. Meg, the girl who'd cared for him, and their family, and their failed marriage. And the rumor he'd heard, back in January, about Theo's divorce.

The moment he realized he couldn't lie anymore.

"Yes, well…" Theo breathed out, shaky, and ran a hand through his still-perfect hair. "Right, so this has been… awful, yeah. Absolutely terrible." A shrug. "Good luck with the jacket, Gardner."

"Theo, I—"

But he was already walking away.

Jack had watched him go so many times.

Above him, hopping from branch to branch in the pear

blossom tree, a blue jay yelled out its sharp call, and a damp breeze ruffled its feathers, and Jack remembered the apartment above, filled with exotic birds, and the skipping of old records, and the way the air felt at two o'clock in the morning when they'd had too much to drink and the rain came down, mizzling, and lamplight refracted in the spider silk strands of Theo's hair.

Something twisted inside him and he made a sound like spitting up concrete.

He gripped the jacket, too tight, in his left hand.

Fuck.

Chapter Two

Theo told himself he never doubted that this was where he was meant to be, even though he could remember a time when all he wanted was to be anywhere but here.

That little boy who had wanted—

He shrugged. He was too old for dreams.

Father had gone to Gwynns and started dating Mother here, and all of his childhood friends were going—of course they were. And it was just the way it was, for his circle and his parents', old families which grew up together and lived well together and ruled the city together, and there was no question of the money.

Theo never thought about money at all.

Unless he was noticing who didn't have any.

And then he was merciless.

First day in the dorms, and Theo was fully arranged, with the best of everything, and he was going door to door as the unofficial welcome and fuck-you committee. The building smelled like fresh pencil shavings and lined paper and too many clashing perfumes; it was a heady smell, the beginning of things. Fourteen years old, away from home, a monitored independence.

Tom followed him with his significant bulk the way he had since they were children, and his other childhood friends were comfortable in their rooms. Genni had waved him off, perfecting her eyeliner and gossiping with her roommate, and Phillippe was already dug in to one of their textbooks, classical music playing on his stereo, the geek. But Theo—he was unsettled. Restless.

Theo wasn't nervous—not exactly—but he wanted everyone to know who he was and that he would always be at the top of the pile. Most of the other students saw, immediately, that it was Theo they'd need to compete with—and that they would never really measure up.

There were certain…expectations which came with being a Beaumont. His father made that clear in the car on their way to Gwynns, and he had made it clear his whole life. And his mother's entire elegant existence was the manifestation of these expectations; she played her role as a Beaumont perfectly. She could charm an entire ballroom with a glance and she was beautifully, stunningly silent when his father…

Well. Theo knew he needed to be like them, to earn the best grades and make lucrative connections; he was valuable as long as he proved—

He thought that, if he were enough like his father, powerful and respected and a tiny bit feared, his mother might take more notice of him. And his father might leave him al—

Might be proud enough to let him breathe.

He leaned against a door frame, his long, lithe body artfully arranged, and he looked into the last room in the Humperdink— God, what a dreadful name for an equally dull family—memorial dormitory building. Two twin beds were opposite each other in the small room, a window on the wall between; this was one of the less expensive rooms. Theo sniffed, his face cold and slyly scornful.

A skinny boy with messy hair was setting up his side of the room. His skin was a warm gold, his hands thin, bones showing, but they seemed strong, forceful. He had one (small and shabby) bag, a set of worn sheets, and he looked vaguely familiar despite being totally...unnoticeable.

An easy target. Hardly worth his time.

Theo felt that practiced Beaumont smile spread over his face with a little warm glow of malice.

He cleared his throat, and the boy looked up—and he had the bluest eyes, and rough, striking features, and Theo was shocked silent for just a moment, feeling something squirm low in his gut.

The boy returned to unpacking without speaking, as if Theo weren't there.

Theo had always drawn attention, at least from his peers. This dismissal was not acceptable.

"Welcome to Gwynns." His voice was perfectly pitched to sound polite—and entirely inauthentic.

Just a glance in response. No other acknowledgment.

"I'm Beaumont, Theodore—you know the Beaumonts, of course." He was sure that this...person didn't. Best to make him uncomfortable right away. Make him aware of how much of an outsider he already was—no family, no money, no name.

He clearly did not belong.

"Friends call me Theo." He watched the other boy's shoulders as they tensed, and he grit his teeth, again unaccustomed to being ignored. "You should call me Beau."

The other boy paused over his bag, facing away. "I don't think I'll need to be speaking to you at all, actually."

Of all the—"No?"

He turned to Theo, face set in mulish anger, glaring up from a three-inch height difference. How crude. And foolish, to show so eagerly how he felt already. "No."

"It would be better for you if you do." Theo smirked. "Not that I expect you to have anything interesting to say, of course."

The boy laughed, head thrown back, as if Theo were the person being ridiculous in this conversation. His teeth were shiny white and slightly crooked; Theo watched his neck as he laughed and was very aware of the frayed collar of his T-shirt against his collarbone, and that the shirt against his tanned skin was an emerald green.

Theo felt, in his cashmere sweater and perfectly hemmed trousers, unexpectedly very small. He had an uncomfortable flash of—

It wasn't as if he'd needed his parents to stay. Other mothers and fathers did—did coddle their children, setting them up in their rooms, giving hugs and fond kisses, but—

He hadn't needed that. After those few stern words from Father, they'd dropped him off with his luggage at the gate, porters lifting his bags onto a cart and rolling it away, and that was totally fine, and he wasn't about to be dressed down by this stupid, scrawny child when he could handle perfectly well his parents'...remove. When everyone else bowed down to him, rightly, even if his own mother and father—even if it seemed like he could never be what they wanted him to be.

He glared at the other boy, his ugly clothes and his gravelly laugh. Theo felt stripped of power—the power which he was owed as a Beaumont, the power he gathered up to shield him from... And it was Theo who belonged here, and to hell with him.

He stood up straight in the doorway, pushing his chest out and shoulders back. "Fine. Come on, Tom. There's nothing of interest here, clearly."

Tom shrugged, his faithful shadow, and Theo started to turn away, and then—

"I see right through you, you know."

He stared. A jolt of—no. He wouldn't let himself be—

"I don't care about your family name, your..." He looked

at Theo from his head to his toes, his glare as piercing as a needle, "Nice clothes, your money, nothing. I'm here to work hard, that's all. You're nothing to me."

Nothing. That word echoed in him. Familiar. Father's voice…nothing. Nothing.

"What is your name?" A low tone, almost a growl, between clenched teeth.

"Jack. Gardner." Oh, how common, but there was nothing common in his burning gaze, bright blue eyes which made him feel—feel something unsettled, lost. "Feel free to remember it. I don't care. 'Cause as soon as you walk out of that door, I will be forgetting you."

"I promise you." His voice was acidic, deadly. "You will not."

The other boy—Gardner—just shrugged and returned to unpacking.

Ignoring Theo entirely.

He felt like the help after being dismissed. He remembered his mother's cool smile as she stayed in their car and didn't watch him go.

Walking down the hall back to his own room, people nearly leaped out of his way, sensing the tension in his silence, in his long strides. All of these people he had intimidated and made small—everyone else had done what he wanted. What his father demanded. He couldn't—he didn't want one stupid boy to wreck that, take it away from him. His footfalls in the corridor were hard and violent.

And as soon as he closed his room's door behind him—almost slamming it in Tom's square face, though he probably wouldn't mind, used to Theo's moods by now—he hit the wall with a closed fist. His anger and fear and want and smallness in the delicate bones on his knuckles.

His parents had ensured, with all of their fabulous and meaningless money, that he had a private room all his own.

So no one minded that he left a smear of blood on the wall.

What an idiot. What a fucking tool.

Theo stood in the doorway to Jasper's dormitory room. A light sweat had broken out along his hairline, and his breath was shallow in his chest, and he tried to push it all aside—the way Jack still looked a little scruffy, despite his change in fortune, and his atrocious rats-nest hair, and his shocking blue eyes. Good-looking. Reviled. He had prayed that he wouldn't have to see him again. He tried to calm his breath, deepening it, slowing down and letting Jack fade.

Theo was here for his son, and who gave a damn that Jack Gardner had been here, that his own son was in Jasper's class?

What difference did it make, seeing him and remembering—

"All right, Dad?"

He focused on Jasper, who was watching him with a frown over his open suitcase.

"Yeah." He shook his head. "Sorry. You have everything?"

"I think so." Jasper looked into his case, serious and pondering. His son was—he was a little more sensitive. Theo's parenting had nurtured him, allowed him to be gentle and kind, in a way he had never been.

Jasper was the one thing in his life he had done right.

He regarded the other half of the dormitory room, mostly unpacked, the child probably downstairs, checking over the last details with the welcoming staff. Theo had wanted to give Jasper a better experience, a roommate to share school with, companionship, good years without isolation. The built-in bookshelves were crammed with tatty old paperbacks—he was doubtful that they could bear the weight—and a few posters were tacked to the wall, and a set of blue sheets with a hand-knitted afghan were set up on the bed. He wondered what this other child would be like, if he'd be nice or snobbish or—it kind of looked like—a total nerd.

It would be good for Jasper, maybe making a friend. Theo had ruled over his single room like a king but had known, deep down, how alone he was.

He watched Jasper setting up his side of the room, and yes, maybe he'd spoiled him a bit—his portion was stuffed with top-of-the-line lacrosse equipment, and autographed posters of musicians, and far too many iterations of the school uniform— but Jasper had never taken any of it for granted the way he had. He'd get along with his roommate, whoever he was; he had never been unkind. Walking into the building, Jasper had given a smile to everyone he'd seen.

He was a good kid. Lexi would be proud.

Though she wasn't here, of course.

He looked at his child—the child who looked so much like him—and saw Lexi's features in his face, too; he had her perfectly arched brows in a dark golden blond, and fuller lips, and a slightly upturned nose. Qualities that Theo had admired in her, spotting her at a cocktail party that year after he came home, thinking that—that he probably should get married, after all, even though…

Even though.

The divorce had been friendly as well as businesslike, the perhaps inevitable conclusion to a marriage which was more a transaction than a love affair. They'd both wanted a child, and they had worked efficiently enough together to make one. Alexia was everything he could have wanted in a wife— graceful, elegant, refined, and wickedly funny—and they'd been good friends, and Jasper had had a loving childhood with two parents who truly liked each other. And she had offered a sort of arrangement, but he couldn't let himself—

She had been right, to ask for the divorce. To let Jasper grow up a little, but then to let him see two parents who were—

Happier.

Maybe.

So Lexi moved back to New York when the papers were signed, when Jasper got his welcome letter from Gwynns, and he went up for weekends of shopping and theatre, and he was okay with it all, a mom in a high-rise with a glamourous life and a dad in the family home with his grand-mère.

And now he was where he was meant to be, here at Gwynns, starting his own life.

Theo would try not to miss him.

"S'cuse me." A polite—if ill-spoken—voice behind him.

He turned.

Memories hit him right in the chest, numerous and nebulous and wretched. The room reeled—for a brief moment he was worried that he would fall over. He grasped at a desk chair, subtly, just in case.

A thin, black-haired boy stood in the hall. He had blue eyes, a smattering of freckles across his nose, and a stuffed duffel bag. His hair was more textured, his skin just a shade darker, but he looked almost exactly the same as—

Theo felt his thirty-seven years hanging around his neck like a noose.

Twenty of those years in particular.

"Hi!" This from Jasper, and Theo took a deep breath and shut his inappropriately gaping mouth.

"Hey." The other boy walked in, slung down his last duffel, and held out his hand.

Jasper took it with a broad smile.

Already friendly.

Oh, God.

They looked—they looked so young. He had never felt like that, and a part of him was still convinced that he had somehow been older, all those years ago, when he first came to Gwynns. Jasper was still so fresh, untested. And Theo—when he moved in, he had already felt weary, desperate to prove something that he probably never would.

And this black-haired boy, so achingly familiar, looked just as childish, just as unprepared for the world. Jack had seemed more worn, already beaten down but looking up with defiance.

Had either of them ever been children?

"I'm Will. Actually, it's Gwilim. Gwilim Linwood Alistair. Don't call me that."

Jasper laughed. "All right. Will. I'm Jasper."

They smiled at each other. Theo remembered white teeth and the cords of a tanned neck and an attraction which he couldn't name, then. Theo watched these two children, so comfortable and youthful and content, and he was five seconds from losing his mind when he realized that Will had started staring at him with an odd look on his face.

He supposed he had been silent for rather too long.

He cleared his throat. "I'm Jasper's father—"

Will's eyes were wide and guileless as he said, "I wouldn't have guessed."

The little pipsqueak.

He ignored the snark, nodded. "Theodore Beaumont."

"Okay." He shrugged, not rude but not terribly interested, so eager to start this new chapter of his life. "Nice to meet you." He smiled, a little crooked, then started unpacking his bag.

He had no idea who Theo was.

Fuck. That hurt. But it's not like he should have expected—

Why would Jack tell anyone—especially his children—anything?

He remembered that they had always been…unspoken. Unnamed. Something that existed outside of time, even though it was beautiful and crazy and felt so fucking huge, the two of them together, raging and fighting and dancing and—

They were something abnormal. That life, the two of them, had never been here, in Baltimore. Didn't belong here. Though he had wanted—

He blinked, put on a blank smile, and tried to remember that today, of all days, was not about him. "All set?"

Jasper looked over at him, and there was a little worry hidden in the dimple on his cheek, but not for himself. "Yeah, Dad." He walked over, wrapped his arms around Theo, looked up with his open and honest smile. "Love you."

He wished he could hold on to this child forever. The only child he would ever have, who was so much better than he had ever been.

"Love you too."

Jasper smirked, cheerful. "Now go away."

He did, trying not to notice the friendly conversation behind him—a shy voice, sensitive, and a voice with sarcastic cleverness. A conversation he wished he could have had; a path untrod.

Outside the dorms, Theo put his hands in his pockets and wandered back toward his car, kicking a few bits of gravel around and trying not to think too hard, and the world was exactly as it should be, with his son at school, making friends, and Theo's successful investments, and the shine back on the family name, and he felt—

Entirely out of place.

This was the life he was always meant to have.
He loved his son.
He hated everything else.

Chapter Three

Margaret Daugherty—Meg—was the youngest in her family, with two older brothers (one who went on to be a doctor, and the other an architect, because everyone in her family was successful) and a very loving mother and father. Her hair was a vibrant auburn, she had about a million freckles sprinkled over her silky skin, and her figure was lean and toned from field hockey, and Jack had loved her impossibly since he was seven years old.

They met at the pool in Bolton Hill, their neighborhood of Victorian row homes and a few shabby apartments, art students and old ladies with perfectly groomed poodles. Meg wore a sharp red swimsuit and drank chilled cans of grape soda, lips stained purple, and she caught him sneaking in through the chain link fence behind the playground on the hottest days of summer. Meg was—she was his first real friend, sort of, and her family had that quality that normal people had, maybe, which meant caring and feeding and supporting. Meg always had a packed lunch with a salted butter and strawberry jam sandwich. After she met Jack, she started bringing two.

It was Meg's mom—curvy, her brown skin lined from too many afternoons out on a boat at the Eastern shore, thick red-black hair—who told Jack about the scholarships available at Gwynns Academy. And it was her dad who helped him fill out forms. He rolled up his shirtsleeves, exposing his pale Irish skin, loosened his tie, and coached Jack through the essays, the interviews. He loved them both. It felt like they loved him back.

He spent so many summers there, with Meg, at the pool or at her house, and cool spring afternoons with juice boxes and crackers in front of her TV, and Christmas mornings at their kitchen table when the wind was just too damned cold and he had to be—he wanted to be with them. With all the Daughertys. Maybe as a Daugherty, for those few hours.

His mom cracked a joke once. "Seems like you like them better than you like me," and she must have thought that was funny, because she laughed, her crooked teeth glinting and a brown bottle in her hand.

And he laughed at the joke too, though it wasn't funny at all, and he pulled his coat on and walked over to their row house on Bolton Street and…played pretend, for a little while.

And that was okay, wasn't it?

Meg went to a private primary school while Jack went to the local public school, and she was always destined to be a Gwynns girl—she was fierce and smart and stubborn, and she played field hockey like somebody had talked bad about her mother. She was absolutely wonderful. When he was little he knew that, someday, she was going to rule the world.

And he had married her, even after—after he had realized—

She was his family. He couldn't live without them.

The cab dropped him off in front of their house, the modest detached home just a few doors down from her parents' row house where he had spent so much of his childhood. Two houses that didn't belong to him anymore—where he'd never really belonged.

He let himself in the front door, placing his keys in the hand-painted ceramic bowl that Amy had made in kindergarten. How many more times would he do that—come into this place, with the family pictures and the framed finger paintings and the warm throw blankets crocheted by Deb Daugherty, such a good mom, such an incredible grandma? The little side table, slightly crooked, that Jason had built at the beginning of his retirement when he didn't know what to do with himself—all of these things, the things that meant love and togetherness and, Jack had imagined, forever.

Meg was in the kitchen, keeping his dinner warm, and Amy was already in her pajamas, with strawberry jam smeared on her cheeks. He settled into the hard-backed chairs at the table— a table that had seen so many family dinners, three children, and that last, horrible conversation. Meg put a plate in front of him, loaded with her buttery Southern-meets-Irish cooking, and it must have been good.

It tasted like dust.

Amy kicked her feet under the table with the endless energy of a small child staving off her bedtime. "Daddy, will you read to me tonight?"

He smiled down at her. "Sure thing, Ames."

Jack had fucked up in many ways, but as he helped Amy brush her teeth and wipe the jam from her sticky cheeks, he thought, *Yeah, I haven't screwed up being a dad.* She picked out her favorite—and too-often read, for him, but that's what kids did—picture book, and he remembered—

When Meg first got pregnant, which they'd both wanted so desperately, he'd been gripped by terror at the reality of it. What if he was too…too broken, too filled with poison, too dead inside to properly love a child? What if he were like his father, running away before he could remember him? What if he would be like his mother, disinterested, callous, self-absorbed?

What if he would look at a child of his blood and resent them bitterly because they would never have to live the way that he had, hungry, cold, forgotten? It was a terrible thing to be so afraid of whatever monster might live in him—of the ways in which he had been harmed.

But from the moment Jonquil had been placed in his arms—all ten pounds and fourteen ounces of her, because she'd inherited some of the strapping Daugherty size, and God bless Meg for pushing her out—Jack felt something deep within him unclench. He had never known love like this.

And that happened again—Gwilim, born a little early and still small, and Amethyst, the perfect package, seven pounds and bright red fluff. He loved all three of his children so much that it filled the dead parts of him. They almost filled the portions of his heart that could never be satisfied with Meg.

But having kids wasn't enough. Not to save a marriage that, perhaps, never should have happened in the first place.

"Dad," Amy whined, tucked up under her covers, a few teeth still missing, and it shouldn't have been so cute. "Pay attention!"

He rolled his tense shoulders. *Get it together, Jack.*

"Sorry, Ames. Where was I?"

"You were about to sing the song!"

Oh, great. His favorite part. He tried to avoid singing as much as possible, from Christmas carols to happy birthdays, and from the look on Amy's face he was rather entertainingly bad at it. But he did it for her—of course he did. The curse of being a father: loving your kids and being the butt of every joke.

He didn't really mind.

No one had ever read to him like this.

He made his operatic face, mouth wide open and chin quivering, and sang until Amy was almost crying with laughter. "Good enough?"

"Yeah, Dad." Amy took a deep breath, then hiccupped and fell dramatically back onto the bed, the beads in her braided hair clacking. "Oh, no!"

Just like her mom. Jack remembered the first time he'd made her laugh so hard that she'd gotten the hiccups and kept hiccupping for hours.

It had been a very long time since that happened.

Jack held out the customary glass of water, placed on the nightstand for this specific purpose. "What am I going to do with you, Ames?"

She took a sip. "Love me forever, 'course."

A classic routine, the answers long ago memorized.

"Oh, yes." He pretended that he had forgotten, that her words were a revelation. "I suppose you must be right."

"Just like always."

"Just like always." Jack leaned over and kissed her velvety forehead and pulled the covers up to her chin. "Night, Amy."

Her eyes were already closing, interrupted only by a quiet hiccup or two. "Night-night, Daddy."

At the door, he turned around and looked at his beautiful daughter, pink duvet tucked around her, and thought, how could I ever have doubted?

Loving his kids was easy.

He heard the clinking of dishes being washed downstairs.

Loving his wife—the right way—had proved too hard.

His steps on the stairs were heavy, and his whole body was spent. Back in the kitchen, he slid down into his chair, entirely and undeniably exhausted.

"You took a while getting home. What happened?" Meg glanced over her shoulder, hands wet and soapy.

"Just…dropped off the jacket, saw a few people, hit typical traffic on the Jones Falls Expressway."

"Too bad."

"Yeah." He scratched at a few sticky crumbs on the table.

"Did you see who Will's rooming with?"

The nameplate hadn't been tacked on the door when they'd all been there together—move-in times were staggered, and there were a few high-end bags delivered and placed on the bed, but no kid yet—but as he had left, the dorm mother put the name in place.

He got out of there fast, not ready for another run-in with—

He tried not to think about it.

"He wasn't there."

"Ah." She wiped her hands on a dishcloth, turned, crossed her arms. "What aren't you telling me?"

She knew him too well. He'd never been able to hide anything from her.

Except, you know, the one thing he shouldn't have.

He sighed. "Looks like his roommate is Jasper. Beaumont."

Meg laughed. Looked down at the floor with a rueful smile. "Of course."

"Meg—"

She sat at the table, reached her hand over to still his and hold it. "It's all right, Jack. I've made my peace with it."

He gripped her damp fingers.

"Did you see—" Her voice was quiet and tender.

He flushed and looked down at the table.

"You did, then."

Silence. She was far nicer than she could have been. He struggled to change the topic, anything to avoid this exchange. "I did get to see Charlie for a minute."

"Oh?" She pulled her hand back, not unkindly, and blushed, skin warming. "Makes sense. I suppose he would be…around."

Jack studied her face, a face he truly loved, a face he had seen in happiness and in sorrow. More freckles, and the gentle lines of laughing, and that worry line, right between her eyebrows, which he thought was new.

"You should—you should call him."

"Yeah?" She met his eyes. "And are you supposed to be giving your soon-to-be ex-wife dating advice?"

He rubbed the back of his neck. God, this was all so awkward. Meg must have seen the tension, and her next comment was perhaps both friendly and a vicious barb.

"And will you be calling the man you—"

He looked up at her, fast. There was a little meanness around her eyes, but mostly he saw an undeserved affection.

Theo had never been kind to her. Jack couldn't pretend—Theo had been a bully, and he'd watched Meg and how she was so easily popular, and how she loved Jack, and he'd turned his vitriol on her. What they hadn't known—couldn't have known, then—was how that nastiness was borne out of jealousy. How deeply unhappy Theo had been.

They were kids. He'd just seemed cruel.

"Let's not pretend that you don't—"

She reached out her hand again, got his fingers to uncurl. "You pretended about a lot of things for too long."

They were quiet for a moment, the ticking of their kitchen clock the only sound in the unnatural stillness of the room. The air felt stagnant, the heat of drying dishes, the scent of soap and jam, all the things he should have said surrounding them, weighing them down.

"I'm sorry." He felt a pressure behind his eyes. "I wish—I wish I were different."

Her voice was calm, removed, detached. "Jack. Will you contact him, or—"

"Do you really want to know?"

She just stared at him, placid. Waiting.

"I'm not sure. I don't know if it would do any good, now."

"Jack." She started picking at a spot on the table with her glossy manicured thumbnail. "Even after—even though we didn't work out—I do want you to be happy. If not with me, then…"

"That's the thing, Meg," and that pressure pushed harder, like every part of him was about to break, "I don't know if I know how."

"You really are an idiot." Her voice was fond, and what on earth did he do to deserve her kindness?

"No argument from me." He smiled across the table at her, and she smiled back. Sad, but genuine.

"Well…" She stood up. "I'm going to bed. You all right on the couch?"

He wished he could hold on to her, on to this dream of what his life should have been. What it was supposed to be. He wished he still wanted to grow old with her.

And maybe, for the first time, in that secret part of him finally revealed, he didn't.

Their children were so damned wonderful. So was she, but—

"Yeah."

She left the kitchen, returning the kiss he had given her that morning, the imprint of her lips on his forehead burning like a benediction.

As he unfolded his blankets that night and stretched out on the couch—squished and prodded and jumped on by every Gardner-Daugherty—he thought about wishing, and regretting, and he thought that he should be…something else. More sad. More angry, at least at himself. And he did feel sadness, and he felt so much shame, but…

He also felt…hope.

He pulled the crocheted afghan tightly around him, and he closed his eyes, and all he could think about was ice, and juniper, and an unbuttoned collar revealing the hollow of a pale throat, long frost-pale hair and the smell of smoke.

Whiskey, cigarettes, records skipping as they reached their end. A wild-eyed boy.

Everybody called the hill at the entrance to campus "the beach," and they treated it accordingly.

It was the day after all their final exams had finished, and the weather was Baltimore at its finest, the hot kiss of sunshine and a cool breeze like laughter running through them, ruffling his hair, caressing Meg's coppery skin as she lay out on a picnic blanket. Most of the students were down here, uniforms rumpled or totally abandoned, and there was a sense of freedom like a leash that had been loosened, at least for the moment.

Meg was in an embroidered crop top, loose jeans, and her abdomen was tight and toned; he'd stripped off his shirt, too hot in the sun, maybe enjoying, a little, the muscle he'd put on through hard work and good meals. As the wind blew, he smelled her—that Meg smell, the smell that meant home.

He had brought out one of his favorite novels, a book which had kept him company since he was nine years old, already reading far beyond grade level, the spine cracked in multiple places and a few pages coming unglued. As a little boy he had lost himself in fantasy—dragons and swords and magic, a life he wished he could have—and this book had been dropped in the bath and rained on and spilled on, and it smelled like aged paper, coffee, a world he yearned to leave behind. But today—the day was too good, even for this book. He couldn't get into it; he suddenly felt like his life, maybe, surpassed that childish longing he had felt for years.

There was a deep relief and disbelief in him that he had gotten this far, the end of freshman year, and he'd made it, and the exams he'd feared went so easily after all that studying, and he was at the top of the class.

It seemed unreal. Like it couldn't be happening to him. Like even though he worked so hard, he didn't deserve it. Meg beside him, so pretty in the sun, and her smile and laugh and the little sounds she made, settling into the grass.

Next to them, on his own blanket, Darius sat sketching with charcoal, and he'd brought out a boom box and was playing some Cuban jazz tape that his abuela had sent with him to Gwynns. Other kids were dancing farther down the hill, music traveling in the fractious air. It all seemed so—it was a dream. Dare's thick brown hair, nearly black, fluffed up in the wind, releasing his scent, incense and sugar and roses.

Jack felt young, finally allowed a few seconds to be a child, and he felt so old, because this moment was temporary, and he knew that real life wasn't really like this. It was just another kind of fantasy.

He was in between.

And not everything was perfect. Maybe twenty feet from them, from this peaceful illusion he'd have to lock away before returning home for the summer, were Theo Beaumont and Genni Jones. He'd been trying not to look at them—Jones in a skimpy bikini (because that girl had no shame) and Beau's shirt unbuttoned, pale skin turning pink.

He wondered if they were together.

He wondered if he and Meg were together.

"You have that face." Meg's umber eyes were open, watching him.

"What face?"

"The thinking-too-hard face."

"I'm not trying to. It's just my face. I have very little control over it."

Dare laughed into his sketchbook. "That's true."

Jack then made his disgruntled face, and Meg stuck out her tongue at him and smiled.

"We just finished exams." She sat up, so close. "So stop thinking."

"I—"

She was getting closer, leaning in, and he was frozen like a small thing being hunted, and he didn't know what was happening, and for some reason there was a—a splintering, where he thought yes and no at the same time, and she kissed him.

And he saw spring sunlight in the fur of her eyelashes.

He had forgotten to close his own eyes, so he did that, because that was what he was supposed to do, right?

Her lips were soft but a little chapped—she always chewed her bottom lip when she studied—and he put his hand on her shoulder. And he loved her in the way he thought love must feel, and somewhere in there, between feeling her collarbone and smelling her lotion and listening to the ascending piano part of the jazz on Dare's stereo, he realized that this was his first kiss.

It was—it was nice. Not exactly what he had expected, maybe, but it was Meg kissing him, so it must have been good.

"I think I may be sick."

His eyes snapped open, and he pulled away fast, blushing, and wiped his lip with the back of his hand.

Beau was glaring over at them, looking completely disgusted, and Jones was sniggering into his shoulder. He was flat on the ground, head in Jones's lap where she'd been running her fingers through his hair. He'd turned his face toward them; Jack wondered how long he had been watching, and then wondered why he cared. Beau made a dramatic grimace at Jones, and then he smirked with that typical Beau nastiness, rolled over onto his side in the grass, head in his left hand. The long line of his body stretched out, and his shirt gaped open, revealing so much sun-warmed pink skin, and Jack thought that he had never hated anything in his whole life as much as he hated Beau.

He was suddenly very aware of the fact that he was shirtless.

"Fuck off, Beau," Meg tossed over her shoulder.

"You fuck off." A snappish and thoroughly uncreative retort from Jones.

Dare slanted his eyes over at them and spoke quietly, exasperated. "Oh my God, seriously. The drama."

"Come on, Theo." Genni put her hand in his hair again, then pulled at the cuff of his sleeve when he shrugged her off. "They're not worth it. Not like he," she gestured at Jack, "Even matters."

His face was like a stone. "You're right, of course."

They stood, Jones in her bikini, those long legs oiled and tanned and lustrous, and Beau buttoned up his shirt, slow and precise, and they walked past, and—

For a moment it seemed like Beau—he towered over them, all of that height like something divine and unapproachable— and it felt like he was going to do something. Something violent, and wrong, and his face twitched, and Jack thought, *Oh God, I'll fight if I have to, but I really don't want him to touch me. Not—not right now.*

He felt the spring wind on his naked chest. And another splintering, yes and no and not knowing, really, what was happening.

Theo lifted his foot, almost as if to break Jack's nose, there in the grass, the skin of his ankle so fine and fair, and then he smiled, wicked, as Jack's breath caught. Jack's mouth opened— to yell or to breathe, to say stop. Theo blinked, looking down at Jack's lips, something twisting on his face. Like he didn't want to touch him, either.

And they were gone, strolling away cool and composed, and Meg shrugged, muttered, "Assholes," and leaned in and smiled at him, and she kissed him, lingering, and he remembered that girl he'd met so long ago in the red swimsuit, jam and Christmases and her parents and the kind of man he wanted to be.

He loved her. Of course he did. She pulled away, pushed him down into the earth, traced the frown on his face until he was wiped smooth, and rested her head on his bare chest. He loved her.

Everything else was just something he could lock away.

Chapter Four

The family home seemed even more cavernous without Jasper.

The Beaumonts, after their emigration from Quebec, had lived, currently lived, and would probably always live in a mansion just north of the city. It had extensive gardens and a tiled terrace and a kitchen he'd spent far too much money upgrading and it still felt, no matter what he did, anonymous. As if he, Theo, didn't live there. As if he were just the next unnamed Beaumont heir.

Lexi's things were long since moved out, and it felt like there were holes everywhere—her natural warmth was gone, and all that was left was antique furniture and portraits of deceased relatives and his cold childhood, echoing.

And Jasper's rooms, which Theo had painted every color that Jasper had ever asked in an attempt to leave a mark for his only child, were shut up until June.

Now, without his son, without his wife, it was just Theo and his mother and the cleaning service that came in twice a week.

And the portraits—his father's portrait. Which he had always thought was ugly and gauche, but he couldn't bring himself to take it down.

He himself would not be getting a portrait done. Let that tradition die with him.

He had retired to his father's—Theo's, for these eighteen

years—study. When he came back from his manic year in Cork, he'd put black curtains around the painting, hiding him, so he couldn't see those diamond-cold eyes looking down from the beyond. Or up from hell, more likely.

He needed a drink. His crystal snifter was waiting to be filled from a decanter of brandy. But somehow, that wasn't what he was in the mood for tonight.

Hidden behind a leather-bound set of W. B. Yeats's collected poems, on the bottom ledge of a built-in bookshelf, was a bottle of Black Bushmills. He moved the book, took up the bottle, and assessed the two inches remaining.

Almost finished, then. The fire, which he lit religiously every evening after supper, snapped and popped behind him as he tried to pour a measure in his snifter—and then he dumped out the whole thing.

Life is fucking short, he thought. *Or too long. Either one, really.*

That bottle had been there, waiting for him, a talisman, since he proposed marriage to Alexia. The paperwork finalized—a prenuptial agreement, a date set for the wedding, and an amicable verbal contract for having a child—he had snuck out of the house and visited the liquor store, alone.

He stared at rows of bottles, shining in the light—clear, claret, amber, dusty green—and realized he had tried almost every liquor in the place. He was struck by an almost physical ennui. He was so bored, tired of everything, his life settled now and his fate sealed. He had chosen this; he couldn't go back. And when he saw this bottle of whiskey, he remembered the first night that he and Jack had danced until sunrise.

He bought it.

And at every milestone he'd downed a glass. That night, the betrothal. The wedding ceremony and reception, elegant and sophisticated and passionless, all of the right people invited, their approval returned. An extra shot before he made love to her, and another glass when she got pregnant.

A double measure, when Jack was married, and another when Theo saw the first birth announcement in the paper.

The flavor—peat, smoke, herbs—was full of intensity, all those years ago, because as he sipped it his mind was taken over by that night. Jack's smell, Jack's taste. Records playing. A soft rain. But as the years progressed, the whiskey started to taste like his life, now, with all the bitterness and numbness. He measured out his life in glasses of whiskey, and Jack's life, too, and by now the flavor was dry as ash.

He picked up the glass, settled into a wingback chair in front of the fire.

To Jasper, he thought, warmth blooming in his chest. The best thing he'd ever done.

He took another swallow.

To Jack Gardner. And his small copy, forgotten jacket and all. And to Margaret, whom he had always loathed, and her cheerful family, of whom he was so horribly, sourly jealous.

He had learned not to be nasty, at least out loud. But here in his home, with his father hidden away behind black curtains, he felt an agonizing wrenching in his stomach, and he hated them all.

"Theo." His mother stood in the door, all soft fabric and sharp angles and silver-blond hair. She could still walk into a room and make the world stop breathing, her beauty as cold as steel.

"Mother." He put down the glass, moving to stand in front of the empty bottle like a little boy with a secret.

"Sit down and don't bother." She perched on the chair opposite, her affect so perfect that he could almost forget it was practiced over a lifetime of silence. "I've known about that whiskey for quite some time."

Disappointed. He felt that she was always so disappointed in him.

"Yes, well," he settled into his chair, took another swallow, "We all have our vices, don't we?"

"Indeed." Her voice sounded careless. Her pleasantries meaningless.

How did his mother still make him feel so small?

"I know you're not happy with me, Mother."

She pleated the edges of her tunic top, an old nervous habit she hadn't been able to correct, keeping herself busy in tense moments. Even now, a grandmother who had read storybooks to Jasper on the hearth of this fireplace, ash on her clothes and a crooked smile no one had ever seen, she retained her precision of movement, her crisp beauty. "Oh?"

He nearly groaned in frustration, setting his glass down on a side table. He inspected his nails, busying himself just the same and avoiding her judgment. "Beaumonts don't divorce."

He heard an odd choking sound, maybe a laugh, and his eyes shot up from his lap to her face.

"Oh Theo." She shook her head. "Perhaps we should have. Yes." She paused and pursed her lips. "I should have."

They both looked up to the veiled portrait, eyes drawn to the face they had hidden as if the black brocade could blow open and unleash...

"Mother..."

"It's past time I said it, Theo. Our lives would have been— well, quite different, if I had made different choices."

He tried to imagine a life without Alexander Beaumont. Without his firm hand and the punishments that came with it. Locked in the black wine cellar for talking back. Kept up all night for a week to complete homework, over and over, when he was caught with a book of fairy tales. Every word he spoke criticized and every action corrected.

He thought of a life without the thefts, the fictional charities and the long cons, the shady deals with Genni's father, the secret bank accounts and the investors who would never get their money back. A life without his classmates at Gwynns hating him because his father tricked their parents out of their college funds, promising miraculous returns as they handed over their cash. Without the bad press and humiliating trials. A life where he'd been able to be a child, if only for a few moments longer.

A life where his mother had chosen him. His safety. His happiness.

Where she had protected him.

It seemed entirely absurd. And beautiful in a way which hurt.

"Doesn't do a lot of good, now." He picked up his glass again, slumping back into the tufted leather of his chair. "I always—" His voice was halting as she stared into the fire, and he tried to reach her with his words like a small child grabbing for his mom's hand. "I thought you were disappointed in me. For the divorce."

"Theo." Her eyes were soft around the edges, the shadows of wrinkles lending depth to expressions which had always seemed hollow. "You gave me a grandchild. You've raised him very well—so much better than I did you. Alexia as your wife or not, you've made this family proud. You made a family where there wasn't a real family at all."

"Oh."

She tucked a strand of hair behind her ear. "But I do find myself—"

He fiddled with the short stem of his glass, knowing that something unpleasant was coming, as it usually did.

"Theo." He looked up, hearing an unusual grief in her

voice. "I am not disappointed in you, not ever. But I am sad, for your sake."

"Really." His teenage drawl spilled out.

"Theo," a bit of reproval, "Not because of the end of your marriage. But because you felt you had to enter into it at all."

A swift jab of shock and humiliation in his stomach. He nearly dropped the glass, a bit of whiskey sloshing over the edge.

"I should have known, as your mother, though I know I—I wasn't good at it." She laughed, a little bitter. "We never spoke of our...our inner workings. Or anything, really. That was my fault."

"I..."

She shook her head, fine silvery hair brushing her shoulders, not letting him interrupt. "I trusted that you could choose the right path. And I did not question, out of my own cowardice, maybe my selfishness, why you came back. We just didn't talk about it."

"Mother—"

"And you don't need to talk about it. You are a grown man now, not a little boy. And we can't change the past. I cannot change all the things I should have—and I just hope I am a better grandmother than I was a—"

Almost a grimace. Almost a full confession of guilt.

"But Theo..." She leaned forward in her chair, composure regained. He did, too, their faces so close. "You've been so terribly unhappy."

He took a deep breath. Smelled her lilac perfume. "You know I love my son. I would never change that. Not even—"

"I do know. He's a wonderful child, and I—" And then she shifted, eyes sharpening, and he saw in her the mother he should have had. He pitied her and loved her and he was still so, so alone. "But now, now that you are no longer married, now that Jasper is in school—I'll finally open my mouth, and…"

He nearly whispered, "What, Mom?"

"Be happy. Just be happy. Whatever that means."

He felt a tear gather in the corner of his eye. As it fell, she brushed it away with the tissue-paper tenderness of her lined fingers.

"Make me proud—no. You already do. You always have, even though I neglected to say it."

He felt a tremor in his heart, in that old wound.

"Theo, you should finally do what you want to do."

"Father wouldn't—" Another habit, remembering him. Heeding him.

"Fuck your father." Her voice was acidic and full of rage, and he gasped, choking on air. "I'm sorry to be so crude. But fuck him right down into his grave." She clasped Theo's shaking hands. "I should have been braver, Theo. I should have left him. I should have given you a better life. You will have to do better than I did."

"I don't think I have ever been brave, Mom. Not really."

"Well, then." She laughed a little and gave his hands a final squeeze. "Now is the perfect time to start."

He felt as if the world were ending—he was old enough to realize it was just his little corner of the world that was burning down, but young enough to feel like he'd never recover.

Prom night, Genni on his arm, Phillippe with a flask of absinthe, Tom stress-eating at the buffet, and he was riding high on the knowledge that this night would never happen again—and that everything his father had done would wreck every future night he thought he would ever have.

His father was a criminal. Genni's and Tom's fathers were complicit.

And their parents had fucked them over.

Other kids—whose families had been so thoroughly swindled—cursed at them in the halls.

Theo wished that, if his father had really needed to be a felonious megalomaniac, he'd done it someplace else.

They had already had so much money. Why had his father needed more?

Prom, and the absinthe, was thrumming in his veins, and he felt like Rimbaud and Verlaine and Oscar Wilde, sharply dressed and stunning and reviled. Genni on his arm in vintage Dior, tottering (mostly gracefully) in five-inch spikes, black hair sleek and shining.

They may have been universally hated, but they looked damned good doing it.

"Come on!" Genni pulled him up the stairs to the bell tower. Downstairs, balloons and gauze and fairy lights cocooned the dance hall in a soft purple glow. Theo climbed the stairs, melting into the shadows, and his patent leather opera pumps reflected snatches of light.

They hadn't bought new clothes. So much of the money was frozen, accounts put on hold, and they had ended up digging through all the closets in their houses to find something that didn't make them look—

Look like the peers they had mocked for so long.

So they were like Louise Brooks and Rudolph Valentino and it was good, and dazzling, and no one needed to know. His hair was perfectly styled, and Genni's skin was slick with sweat and body oil, and they sparkled. It was an act, but it was a good one.

"Hell yes." Genni grinned as she saw the bell tower was empty. They were alone.

The tower was lined with clear glass windows, and they could see out over campus, and the lights from downtown shone in the distance. They were far enough out of the city that they got a smattering of starlight, and it seemed like an in-between time—this night in May, with summer coming, with court dates and jail sentences waiting, and them in the middle between the earth and the sky.

"Come 'ere." Genni pulled him close, his back against cool glass. She pressed her delicately curved body against him and kissed his mouth. She tasted like licorice and Chanel lipstick.

It wasn't the first time they'd kissed, but it felt the same— he loved her, so much, and he wanted her forever, and he was entirely unmoved.

But what difference did it make, really? He curled his body down around her, meeting her lips, trying to push his affection for her, his admiration of her wickedness and hidden fragility, into their connection—hoping to make up for what he lacked.

Back in sophomore year they'd kissed for the first time, and he had held her hips, newly full and luscious, and he breathed in her sugared scent. He knew he was the luckiest man in Baltimore, to have her in his arms, but it—it felt like—

Maybe this was all he was allowed to have. It wouldn't be the worst way to live, maybe, because he did care for her, as much as he was capable of caring for anyone. And maybe the love he had imagined was entirely fictional, just another fairy tale. He loved her as much as he could and kissed her with that intention, here in the dark at the end of the world.

A sound from the staircase.

He opened his eyes. Genni kept kissing him, unaware; he kept kissing her, automatic.

Jack Gardner stumbled in, holding hands with Margaret Daugherty.

Theo felt a bit sick.

The perfect couple.

Jack, who had always rejected him. Jack, who, despite his

obvious poverty, managed to get the attention of all of the teachers, the coaches, the girls, leaving Theo in the dust. Jack, class valedictorian, and lacrosse captain, and everything Theo was supposed to be—everything his father had demanded of him. And Margaret, who was—he had to admit it—quite good-looking, with toasted skin and all that auburn hair, but who'd never had time for him, content with her stupid happy family and the certainty that they loved her.

They were laughing, maybe a little tipsy on cheap coconut rum, and he shouldn't have felt like this—he wasn't supposed to. Jack was in some ill-fitting rented tuxedo, and Margaret's dress was rough tulle, and they shouldn't have looked—he'd had everything. They were nothing.

Weren't they?

Margaret pushed Jack against the opposite wall, mirroring Genni, and began to nibble at Jack's neck. His head was thrown back, eyes half-lidded, and his hair was messy and untamed, and he was—

It was stupid. They were all so stupid.

Theo hated them all.

He tried not to remember that they had hated him first. That he'd scared almost everyone off with his natural, ingrained cruelty. Cruelty he'd learned from his father.

What a waste of a life, trying to be like him.

He was still kissing Genni. He wrapped one arm low around her waist, brought the other hand up to cradle her jaw, but kept his eyes open—and Margaret must have bitten down a little harder on Jack's neck, because he gasped and opened his own eyes wide.

And Jack saw him.

Theo held on to Genni, tried to focus on her, but he watched Jack, their eyes linked, and the kiss started to feel—he felt something more, listening to Jack's hard breathing,

watching him as he rested his hands on Margaret's tight behind. Genni moaned into the kiss, laughed a little, rubbing
against him and feeling—

Jack's mouth parted, and he was staring with unwavering
focus, and the look on his face—

Theo felt something building in him, and he was hot, the
cold glass against his back, Jack's blue eyes and the way he
wasn't kissing Margaret but was looking right at him, defiant and angry and something else, something he didn't want
to see, because—

Fuck. It was true.

Had always been true.

He didn't want this.

Genni thrust up against him, her pert breasts pushed onto
his chest, and she grabbed him, rubbing, and he was turned
on, tuned out like static on a television, and he thought, *Maybe,
if I can just hold on to this, the image, this horrible secret confrontation, I can love Genni properly.*

He could just—pretend.

Like he was doing with everything else.

He kissed her more firmly and let Jack's face burn itself into
him, and he held on to those perfectly proportioned hips, and
it felt so good, so right, and yes, it wasn't good or right, he had
no fucking conscience, but it was—it was better than nothing.

Jack made a sound, and Margaret laughed her unrestrained
and inelegant laugh, and Genni pulled away, distracted. She
looked at them and made an ugly face.

And then she turned back. Looked at Theo, her eyes trailing down, and she saw—and he could see the moment when
she realized that he had never, until tonight, responded like—

"Oh." Her voice was small, and her eyes were hurt. "Not her."

He grabbed her hand, pulling her back into his body, and

he put his lips right next to her ear. "No. Not...her," and he dropped his forehead on her shoulder, and said, "Don't—"

"Ah." She tucked a loose lock of hair behind his ear, "Fuck."

"Genni..."

"Goddamnit, Beaumont." She laughed out the words, but her eyes were wet, and she hit him with her half-clenched fist. He pressed his face against hers; he wanted to keep her close and he wanted to keep her quiet.

"I'm sorry. I'm so—"

"I guess I should have—" Her voice wobbled, just one more time, then strengthened. She sighed, and in that exhalation he heard her heart break, and he heard her accept him. "It's all right, hon."

She gave him one more kiss, sweet, and it felt like forgiveness and the end of things, "Come on. Dance with me."

They had to pass Jack and Margaret on their way to the stairs, and Jack made some kind of primal animal sound behind him, and Theo's heart stuttered. His body responded. He wondered, detached and shocked, if he was going to cry.

In some ways his world did end, that night, in the in-between space of the bell tower.

Genni never kissed him again.

Chapter Five

Jack woke up with his hand reaching out.

Something he would never tell anyone—something Meg could never find out—was that as soon as Jack heard about Theo's divorce, he started waking himself in the early hours of the morning by reaching out one hand. It was jarring, uncomfortable, because his hand never seemed to find what it was looking for, and so it was an absence which startled him out of sleep. It was an odd feeling to be awoken by nothingness.

Meg slept on his left side. She never noticed this new habit, not in those months before he told her the whole truth, when he sat on his need for the end of their marriage. It was Theo who had slept on his right side, Theo who curled up with him in a too-small bed. He and Meg slept in a practical manner; once their nighttime snuggle and quiet chat was done, they occupied their own personal space on their pillow-topped king mattress.

Tonight, Jack woke himself on their couch, his hand knocking over an empty water glass. He closed his eyes again, gritted his teeth, and tried to force himself back into sleep. But there was a light on, somewhere, a soft glow permeating the dark, and he heard the fridge open, a drawer being shut.

No chance of sleeping now, he thought, as he rubbed his eyes and hauled himself up. His back twinged and he wondered when his body had started to feel so old.

Just a few steps down the hall, and he knocked lightly on the doorway to the kitchen.

Meg looked up, a jar of chunky peanut butter on the table in front of her, and a spoon, mounded high, halfway to her mouth. Her mouth was hanging open, actually, and in that moment she looked so much like the little girl he had fallen in love with that he could cry.

"Don't judge," she muttered, and shoved the spoon between her full lips.

"Never." He went to the silverware drawer, took out his own spoon, and sat. "Share?"

Her mouth was thick with peanut butter as she mumbled, "'Course."

They both chewed. It was awkward and yet so familiar.

"Can't sleep?" He wiped his lips with the back of his hand.

"No," she sighed, "not tonight. I keep thinking, and it's keeping me up."

"What's that?" Jack pointed to a pad of paper with scratched out sentences and jumbled words in her curvy handwriting. "Working on a new story?"

He moved to pull the pad toward him, and she quickly pulled it back.

"No." She closed her eyes, pursed her lips, and then dropped her shoulders, pushing the pad back. "Go on and look."

"You sure?"

"Yes, yes. It's fine."

He picked up the pad. It was a list, and at the top it said, *Things to Do Without Jack Fucking Gardner.*

"Oh, wow."

"I'm sorry." She looked pained and a bit angry.

"No, it's…" He didn't quite know what to say. "It makes sense. It's very you."

"Oh yeah?" She laughed, just a little.

"Yeah." He smiled, a quirk of his lips, and he dug his spoon back into the peanut butter jar. "Determined. Defiant. Anal-retentive."

Her mouth dropped open again. "Thanks. I think."

"Is this list in order of importance or anything? Just so I know what I'm looking at."

She rolled her eyes. "Okay, give it back now."

"No, maybe this is stuff I need to know. Stuff I can help you—"

She was laughing, and he realized with some surprise that he was, too.

"Give it back, you jerk." She pulled the list out of his hands. "Honestly."

A pause, then. And the shattering feeling of loss, the brutal nature of his dishonesty, crowded the silence of the kitchen.

"You're my best friend, you know?"

His eyes burned at the smallness of her voice.

"Yeah." He cleared his throat, still thick with peanut butter. "Me, too. I mean, you're mine."

"I'm not really sure what to do now. So I thought…"

"A list."

"Yeah." She shook her head, thick braid rustling against her bathrobe. "And all I've got to show for it is stupid stuff like, *watch my favorite movies*, and *take hour-long baths without interruption*, and *eat caviar*."

"Ugh." He pulled a face. "Fish eggs."

"Delicious fish eggs."

"If you say so."

"I do."

Those words echoed and mocked them both.

"Hand it over."

She pushed the pad toward him, and he grabbed a pen from

the old jam jar which held pens and pencils, scissors, odds and ends, a catch-all trinket that had sat on that table for years.

"What are you writing?" A tone of alarm as he scribbled something down.

"Hold on." He finished, handed back the paper.

"*Write to Charlie.*" She blushed and looked exasperated. "Thanks. You seem to be very determined on this point."

"You should do it."

"Maybe I will, then. Fine. Give me your hand."

"What?"

"Just…" She grabbed his arm. "Hold still."

The pen tickled and dug in. "Ouch!"

"Oh, calm down, you big baby. There." She dropped the pen, face smug.

He held his hand up, and there, in her sweet feminine handwriting with a little heart at the end, was *Find Theodore Beaumont.*

"Meg." His stomach dropped.

"I know we talked about it earlier. And I want you to do it. That's what's on your list."

"My list?"

"The *what to finally fucking do* list."

His hand was sweating, his whole body anxious, and he tried not to think about Meg writing on the hand which had been reaching out for almost a year. "I'm sorry."

"I know you are. I'm sorry too. For not noticing."

"I can't live without you, Meg." He meant it, and he also meant that he couldn't live with her, couldn't live as her husband, couldn't bear the thought of having sex with someone he was incapable of loving the right way. Not anymore.

"And you won't. We have three pretty big reasons why. I'm not going anywhere." She picked up the peanut butter jar, inspecting it, trying to hide the fact that she was crying. "But maybe we should start living the way we should have lived—childhood friends. Family. Family we chose."

"Yeah." He rubbed his face, so tired, and then realized he had smudged ink all over himself.

"You *are* my best friend. You're my brother, really. That's what it should have been."

"Okay." He felt empty inside, and then a spark of something—something childlike and fresh like summer days and grape soda—made him say, "Write to Charlie. Do it."

"Yes, yes." She made a face at him, stuck out her tongue, then grinned, eyes wet. "Go get Theo. You better do it. Or else."

"Or else, huh?" He smiled. "Yeah."

Another pause. Safer, now. Less painful.

"And now, go the fuck to bed, for both of us."

He snorted, stood up, stretched. Shuffled back to the couch. Listened to her footsteps on the stairs. And then he pulled out his phone. Stared at it. Put it down. Picked it up. He thought about how brave his wife—his truest friend—was, trying to figure out a new life which might thrive in the absence of all the things they had built. And he knew he couldn't live as such a damned coward anymore.

He wrote the most clumsy, useless, two-in-the-morning email to the other person he had realized he could not live without.

He woke again, two hours later, with that hand reaching.

"What the fuck was that?"

Jack's hands damn near vibrated with anger. He wanted to use them.

He threw down his battered lacrosse pads, walking with violent purpose across the locker room. Theo sat on a bench, shoulders slumped, and the room was full of steam, the smell of grass and dirt, the departing laughter of other boys. He was stripped down to his shorts, pads and jersey in a heap next to him, and his cleats were thick with mud.

Jack wiped his face, sweat dripping from his messy black hair. Blood trailed down his leg from a long scrape—Theo had nearly knocked his knees out from under him, the head of his stick slicing against Jack's shin.

"Go away, Gardner." His voice was dull as it echoed against cold tile.

"Fuck off."

Theo laughed, a little, but not like anything was funny. "Yes, that. Do that."

"What the hell were you trying to do out there?"

Theo closed his eyes, leaned back against the cinderblock wall. "Play lacrosse, Gardner. Surely you're not too stupid to figure that out." At Jack's disgusted noise, he smiled, nasty. "But I could be wrong about that."

Jack moved in front of him, standing barely a foot away, crowding into his space. Everything was hot around them, and charged like lightning, and he had never wanted to hurt someone as much as he did in this moment, because—

It wasn't just that he played dirty, too rough. Theo was such a bastard about everything, so good-looking and cultured and—and God, Jack hated him so much, and his life was so perfect and spotless and easy, and Jack had to fight for every damn thing. And lacrosse was something he was good at, or supposed to be, and it just wasn't fucking fair that Theo had to be better at that, too.

He wasn't better. He was just cruel.

Jack's mind flashed back to the look on Theo's face in the bell tower, and he had not been cruel in that moment, no, but there was something...something too horribly dangerous in those silent seconds, and Jack hated himself too, his fear, his sudden awareness that—

"Stand up." His voice low and rough like gravel.

"Gardner." Theo opened his eyes, the silver irises cold. "Leave me alone."

"Stand. Up."

"And if I won't?"

"Then you'll prove that you're nothing more than Daddy's little—"

Theo rose up off the bench like a serpent striking, tightly coiled to fast and deadly, and he made a sound like coughing up glass, and he pinned Jack to the lockers with a painful clang. His bare chest was pressed up against Jack's, arms holding him entirely still, and he brought one hand up to put pressure on his neck.

"Fuck you," his lean features as sharp as a blade, "I should—"

Jack struggled to escape—to breathe. "What, Beau? You should what?"

Theo trailed his eyes over his face, down his wiry frame, and looked back up, holding him hostage and clearly loving it. "I should teach you a lesson."

And then his hand pressed down farther. Jack's vision grayed out around the edges. Theo slumped against him, breathing heavy, his lips snarling and close to his ear, and Jack realized with some panic that Theo was crying onto his neck, wet and warm and it felt—and Christ, that was too close, and Jack strained against him, pushed him away.

And he hit Theo's face with enough force to split the knuckles of his hand.

Theo fell back onto the bench and his head slammed into the wall. His lip had torn. Jack looked down at his right hand, bleeding heavily, and Theo's face, also bleeding, and he was filled with a cold horror.

In him was that ugliness, the ugliness that his father must have had, and his mom… It had always been there. He felt terrified of what he had done, his neck prickling with shame, and at the same time he felt—victorious, and god-touched, and so fucking turned on, and it was the most exhilarating combination; Theo was maybe unconscious, face damp and pinched with pain, and he thought that this was what it must feel like to be gloriously drunk.

And they would absolutely kick him out for this.

He listened to make sure Theo was breathing. Because if he wasn't—if Jack had—he knew he'd never—

Theo's chest rose and fell, a steady rhythm.

And then Jack ran.

He spent the entire night and next day in terror, waiting for the dean of students or head of school to show up at his dorm room and tell him to leave. Maybe for security to escort him out like some kind of criminal. He even packed a bag, looking at each item—the uniform, his textbooks, the newer fantasy novels he'd borrowed from Dare—and imagined where he'd hide them in his room back home. He barely slept.

No one came.

He saw Theo in class on Monday, his lip patched up. Theo didn't look over at him at all—not to insult, or blame, or tell a teacher what had happened...nothing.

It was a few days later—after he'd nearly killed Theo, and Theo had tried to kill him—that Jack finally heard all of what had happened...about Theo's dad going to jail.

He wondered, in a dark, bitter moment, if there were such a big difference between a mother who didn't feed you and a father who abandoned you for money.

He unpacked his suitcase. He thought about apologizing, about making some kind of amends, about finding commonality, maybe, with the boy he had always hated and always—

But Theo wouldn't look at him, in class or in the hall or on the lacrosse field, and Jack—

He realized he was too much of a coward to try.

So he watched Theo's lip heal, and he picked the scabs off his hand, and he kept his mouth shut.

Chapter Six

"That's it." Tom pushed a check across the table.

"You don't have to."

"But I can. I can do it now."

Theo looked at his oldest friend, his familiar face and his open, satisfied expression. He felt that twinge of guilt, but he also felt overwhelming pride.

They sat on low couches, glass-paned walls around them revealing all of Baltimore, hundreds of feet below. The bar wasn't full, not yet, but the servers were busy around them, whispering and preparing for a crowded, hectic night. Tom had picked up a menu and spent some time dissecting it— *Occupational hazard*, he had said—before he pulled out his checkbook and signed with a cheerful flourish.

It was a perfect September afternoon, blindingly beautiful here in the sky, and Theo itched to jump out and fly. He thought about how badly he had wanted freedom back when they were both so painfully young. Freedom that Tom now had.

The money on the table wasn't much, but it was the last of the investment Theo had made in Tom's first restaurant in New Orleans, and Tom seemed a little giddy to give it back. Theo hadn't asked for it—had not expected any of it returned—but as he watched his friend's face, he thought about what it must feel like to be entirely unburdened by debt. Theo had invested because he wanted to, but he could admit to himself that he also invested out of…out of some desire to apologize.

I'm sorry, he had thought, all those years ago as he passed over a check, *I'm sorry for my father. I'm sorry for what my family did to yours.*

Tom must have understood that irrational guilt, and as he handed over his own check today, it felt a lot like forgiveness. Like forgiveness was never necessary at all.

"I knew you could do it. I knew it."

Tom nodded, looked out over the city, took a sip of his ginger beer. "Yeah. Turns out I could."

"I'm…" Theo cleared his throat, a little tight. "I am glad you came up. Glad Gabbi's at Gwynns. She can look out for Jasper."

"Don't count on it. She's got a hell of a temper, just like Josie." Tom rolled his eyes, his frustration exaggerated and feigned. So pleased with his partner, their child.

"How is Josephine? I was sorry not to see her."

"Couldn't leave the restaurant. Thinks the whole place would burn down without her."

Theo laughed. "She's a strong woman."

"Damn right." Tom smiled, and it was just as tender and wondering as the first day he realized he loved her. Then— "Sorry about Alexia."

It was Theo's turn to look away, letting his eyes wander over the city.

"Yes, well. She said something that—well, she told me it was about time. Time for me to…" He felt an awful twinge of sorrow and guilt-ridden relief.

Tom's face was unusually shrewd. "You did love her."

"I do." Theo nodded, sure of his answer. "Just not the way a husband should love his wife. Not like you and Josephine."

Tom shook his head. "Still can't get that woman to marry me. We own a whole-ass restaurant together and she still says she needs her independence."

"Even so. You both…"

"Yeah. We belong to each other."

God, how that hurt.

A moment of silence then, which had always been comfortable between them. That quiet was welcome, a reminder of a friendship which had endured so much pain, so many challenges. Theo settled into the couch, and Tom watched him, thoughtful, until he spoke again.

"You talk to Gardner?"

Theo felt his face freeze, his body tense. "I'm not sure what you mean."

"I may not be a genius." Tom shrugged. "But I'm not stupid."

"I know." Theo sighed. "Sorry. No, I didn't. I don't know if I want to. Ever."

"Look." Tom took a particularly determined swallow of his drink and set the glass down with an audible clink. "I know I'm better in the kitchen than anywhere else. Hell, I didn't even know I loved Josie until she practically hit me in the head with a frying pan. But if you think I never noticed how you felt, you're not giving me enough credit. I've known you since we were in diapers."

Theo felt like an idiot, an entire fool in this thin blue air over Baltimore. That was one of the longest speeches he'd ever heard come out of Tom's mouth, and yes, he had not considered that perhaps Tom was so silent because he noticed quite a lot and didn't feel the need to say it.

"I don't know everything that went on." Tom looked down as he spoke, maybe unaccustomed to talking so much. "We both ran away, we were both pretty lost. But I know he was over there with you. I know you were happy, and I know that something happened, and then you weren't."

"No." Theo thought about the long years, the marriage, trying again and again to be someone he could never, ever be. "I was not."

"I'm not going to tell you what to do. But maybe you need a frying pan to the head, you know?"

"Ouch."

"Yeah. Sorry. I told you, I'm better in the kitchen."

"You're doing remarkably well, then." Theo breathed out, ran a hand through his hair, then asked, almost timid, "How did you know you loved Josephine?"

Tom took a moment, frowned. "I think… I thought I didn't know how to love. And then suddenly I did. And I didn't want to live a single day without her."

Theo remembered how he felt in those mad months, so perfectly imperfect, and the cold years since then. "I have lived so many days without Jack Gardner. I should be fine."

"That's the thing, though. Did you want to?" And then Tom lowered his voice, more gentle than Theo had ever heard him be. "Are you fine?"

Theo thought about every glass of whiskey and every time he played pretend and every choice he made to please other people. Every night he went to bed and hoped he would wake up with someone else.

"We ran away because we needed to. I found a home. I found Josie. You came back, but you weren't free, you know? You didn't let yourself be free."

"I thought it was what I had to do."

"Yeah. I don't have an answer for that." Tom drained the last drops of his ginger beer and picked up the menu again, studying it with a chef's trained eye. "You don't have to anymore, though."

"No." Theo looked out into the flawless sunshine and wished so badly to fly away and leave his heavy past behind. "Maybe...maybe not anymore."

"Good." Tom smiled, his rough face showing an ease, a new life without this last debt. "Now. Let's order."

By the time Theo got home, stuffed full of too-rich food and hand still tingling from Tom's enthusiastic final handshake, he could almost imagine a life where he had chosen to be free. To be himself. To be happy.

Almost.

He chose this pain, and God, did it hurt.

Face down in the tattoo chair, Theo listened as the needle buzzed, a thousand tiny pinpoints of ink drilling into his back. Tom sat next to him, not holding his hand, exactly, but lending the quiet strength he'd always dedicated to his oldest friends.

The tattoo artist had checked his driving license—twice, just in case—and wished him a happy eighteenth birthday before sketching out the delicate, intricate design. Theo's back was outlined from the nape of his neck to the soft hollows at the base of his spine. Black linework and gray shading, highlights whiter than his pale skin, the curve and fine strokes of feathered wings.

"Quite a choice for your first tattoo." The artist spoke with disbelief and a hint of challenge.

Theo stood up straighter and tried to summon the confidence he was supposed to have as a Beaumont—the confidence his father had demanded his whole life and shattered irreparably as he was handcuffed and dragged away in shame. "I can handle it, thank you."

Halfway through the tattoo, he wasn't as sure.

He remembered too many bad things and wanted to put them into every line scored on his back like the slicing of a dull knife. Theo had carried pain for years—the pain of a family which didn't know how to love him, and the pain of his father's backhand when he wasn't good enough, the pain of a secret inside of him which he hated. The pain of a mother who looked away too many times.

He winced as the needle pricked his too-bony ribs.

"Wish I could do this for you."

Theo turned his head, just enough to see Tom's anxious eyes, and smiled reassuringly…as much as he was able. Tom had always protected him. His face, normally rough-cast and immobile, showed deep frown lines and a quiet unhappiness at seeing Theo hurt.

"Thanks." Theo pressed his face into the cushioned chair. "But this is…this is something I need to do."

"Why?" Tom burst out. "It looks good, but…why? You've already—"

Theo understood what was unspoken. He had already been through too much.

But here he was, newly eighteen and manic with it, and he had lived every single day as someone else. He had been trapped, caged. He had been given the best of things, all of his family's money propping him up with clothes and lacrosse gear and fine dining and anything, everything they thought would make them look good. He had defined himself by that money, and the money made him seem—it made him cruel. It gave him permission to look down on everyone else, because he couldn't admit for so long that he was so unbearably unhappy.

That obsession with money and all the trappings of luxury was what finally brought his father down. Greed, the desire for more, always; tricking Baltimore's elite into investments which yielded nothing but a realization that they had been conned. Money destroyed his father, and it would have been funny, an amusing cosmic justice, if his father's schemes hadn't wrecked Theo's life.

Today he had handed over hundreds of dollars for a freedom which could never be removed, and he should have saved it, kept it in the trust fund that his father had nearly drained dry, but this…this was his choice. Pain.

A good pain.

The tattoo artist was in a near trance, all focus on his work, a sterile cloth in his hand to wipe away the blood. The room smelled like rubbing alcohol and Theo's sweat. And Theo's mind spiraled into that pain, and he breathed out, letting it go. Letting it all go.

His upper lip hurt.

"Fuck."

"You okay? Wanna stop?" Tom leaned forward, his voice a little panicked.

"No." Theo licked his lip. "I'm fine."

He wasn't. Of course he wasn't.

His mother had been so angry when he came home from this last year at Gwynns. The anger had shocked him until he remembered that she had always been protective of his face. The line on his lip, still a little pink from the long process of healing, was a blemish on the perfect aristocrat she expected him to be. He wanted to think that her anger was a sign that she loved him, but he had so little evidence of that type of emotion from his distant, cultured mother.

He licked that line on his face, the roughness on the inside of his mouth, and the clawing agony of the needle seemed to fade. This pain was nothing, nothing compared to that moment when he had Gardner pinned against the lockers, so fucking angry, so bitter, so boiling hot under his skin. And when the anger turned into something else—something he had tried to strangle, tried to deny—he almost welcomed the blow which split his lip and sent him careening into the wall.

Over and over, he worried the tear in his mouth. The artist hummed a little, tuneless, as he marked Theo's back with an indelible black scar.

"I don't know what I'm going to do." Tom's voice was low, quiet. They hadn't really talked about it. About the future.

A knife twisted in Theo's heart. "I'm sorry. I'm so—I'm so sorry."

The worst con his father had played was involving his friends' parents in his vile criminality. Theo felt such enormous guilt, and he wondered, even as his friends stuck by him, if he was to blame. If just by being their friend—linking their families closer over every year of their childhoods—Theo had ruined them.

"Nah." Tom shook his head. "Not your fault."

Theo laughed, but it was gritty and sour. He didn't think he would ever stop feeling responsible. "What do you want to do?"

Tom crossed his arms, thought for a moment. "I want to run."

"Yeah." Theo felt the needle digging into his spine and grimaced. "I want to fly, I guess."

He thought about fairy tales, those foolish things he had read, hiding in his closet and escaping his father's attention, his father's anger. He wanted to hide again, to live the stories, to rise far above the clouds until there was nothing left of his life here but the faint line on his lip and the relief of leaving it all behind.

"Where do you wanna go?" Tom leaned forward, hoping, maybe, for inspiration. For Theo to give him the answers the way he had in algebra and Latin and chemistry classes.

Theo felt the myths of his childhood pull at him. Standing

stones, fertile green fields, poetry and song. But he couldn't quite say it, not yet. It felt foolish, too much like a dream. In a quiet corner of his mind, he calculated the pitiful money he had left. Enough for a plane ticket, maybe. Enough for the fantasy his father had denied him. Enough to get the fuck away.

And enough to forget Jack Gardner.

"Anywhere." The needle dug in, and he yielded to it. "Anywhere but here."

Chapter Seven

Jack stood at the red door with white framing, the lintel an abstract arrangement of glass mosaic, and wiped his sweating hands on his jeans.

God, he was still so nervous.

Meg's closest friend from middle school was Darius Smith, and Jack might have been jealous, at first, because she wouldn't stop talking about him. And they had dated for a few weeks, that summer before freshman year, but as soon as he met Darius at Gwynns and Dare opened his mouth and began describing in exquisite detail the paintings he was working on in his advanced art classes, Jack couldn't help but love him, too. He loved him at his senior art show, and he loved him at his first gallery opening, and he loved him—even as a part of him was terrified, like a bug under a magnifying glass, tortured by an exposing light—when they went to his first drag show.

And he was proud, so proud, when Dare got married to Quinn as soon as it was legal. He'd cried when they exchanged vows on the steps of the courthouse—Meg handed him a tissue, rolled her eyes, grinned at him—and he tried not to think about the fact that he was so fucking sad.

Quinn—always studious, never without a big word or three, absolutely crazy about ethical philosophy—stumbled over his vows, and everyone laughed a little at how unusual that was, and Jack knew, God, how he knew, what it felt like to not be able to speak.

Quinn, his roommate for four years, had done so much for him, taking him in when he left his mother's apartment for good, and Jack couldn't imagine what his life would have been like without him, and without Dare's kind smile, his eyes older than the rest of him.

And he had broken their best friend's heart.

He rang the doorbell.

He heard a voice shouting, "Come on in!"

Dare and Quinn's was exactly as he would have imagined if he had tried to picture it when they left school. Organized, beautiful, comfortable, and warm. A bit madcap, smelling like incense and candle wax.

And packed with books, with art on every wall.

Jack wiped his hands on his pants again as he stepped through the door. Long, meticulously organized bookshelves lined the hall, and on the opposite wall were family portraits and candid snapshots: Daisy, his goddaughter, when they first brought her home after the adoption came through, and then Julian, carried by Quinn's sister, with Dare's dark skin and Quinn's unruly curled hair. Pictures of family by blood and family of choice: Meg and Darius as kids, grinning into the camera; Jack and Quinn caught reading—Quinn actually studying their coursework, and Jack lost in one of his dog-eared fantasy novels—side by side when they roomed together.

"Back here!" Dare called from the kitchen. They'd invited him over, texting after he'd dropped the kids off, knowing that he would be nervous to leave Will in particular. He'd agreed, missing them terribly, but then…

He kept waiting for Dare to hate him.

Dare had been brave, and Jack had been a coward.

Jules was more than big enough, now, to sit without a high

chair. He had paper and crayons in front of him, and an almost empty plate of cookies. Jack grabbed the half that Jules was about to drop on the floor, just for something to do, and then stood there, awkwardly, before he shoved it in his mouth. That parental habit of clearing every plate; the habit of not wanting to waste any food.

The cookie was wet. How nice.

Dare was bustling at the stove, adding finishing touches to what was sure to be a complicated dinner.

"Go ahead." He gestured with one slender and delicate hand at the table.

Jack sat.

There were a few moments of silence.

He stuffed his mouth with another cookie.

Oh God.

It wasn't as if they hadn't spent any time together since he and Meg had decided to divorce. Of course, Dare and Quinn had been told right away. And they were good to him, even though—even though they knew the reasons why. But Jack felt a tightness in his stomach, here in this warm place where he and Meg and the kids had shared meals so many times, pots of sweet Café Cubano over long conversation, and he hardly knew what to do with himself.

He was broken.

He was a fucking idiot.

"Glad you could come, hon."

His eyes widened, "Thanks. Um, me too."

Silence. Dare stirred a pot.

And then he heard the front door opening again, thank God. Quinn swept in from the front hall, tidy but a bit harried from teaching his college courses at Loyola and fighting city traffic, neatly arranging his jacket on a kitchen chair. Jack heard stomping on the staircase as Daisy—in her clunky combat boots, most likely—went straight to her room after a full day of classes at the Baltimore School for the Arts. Jules lifted his arms for a hug, and Quinn started to hug him back—and then saw powdered sugar all over his face.

"Oh Christ, Dare, what have you let him eat?"

"Hello to you too." Quinn glared at him. Dare shrugged, elegant, with an innocent smile. "Just a couple of cookies."

"A couple! I had two dozen here." He frowned. "They were for my book club."

"Jack had some." Dare kept smiling his serene smile, but with a bit of a twinkle in his eyes.

"Yeah." Jack coughed. The one. And a half. A soggy half.

"Ugh, well, if Julian wakes up in the night, he's all yours, Darius."

"Yes, my love."

Quinn crossed to the stove and peered at him, trying to guess how many cookies his husband—who was getting a bit soft around the middle—had eaten himself. "And if you wake up with a sore stomach in the night, you'd better leave me out of that, too."

"I wouldn't dream of disturbing you."

Quinn looked rather fierce for a moment, and Dare put on a look like a dressed-down schoolgirl. And then Quinn cracked, laughing, and kissed him on his sugary mouth.

They were perfect together.

"God, I want that." Jack hadn't intended to speak, but the words came out, and he couldn't get them back in.

Quinn wiped his lips. "Hmm?"

Dare lowered the flame on the stove, turned around, sat, and waited. Jack shrugged and looked away. "I'm sorry, I just—"

"It's all right, Jack. We did ask you over. And we know what's going on." Dare's face was honest and open in that disconcerting way, just as it always was.

Jack took a breath and kept going. "The way—the way you
are together. That thing you have, where you love each other
even when you annoy the sh—" He looked down at Jules,
wide green eyes staring back. "When you argue. It's always
been—you're meant to be. And I wanted that."

"Thought you could have it with Meg, you mean."

He looked up at Dare, still tall and elegant and striking,
even sitting at the table. There was a roughness to his voice,
but also an understanding. And it was difficult, jumping right
into this conversation, but they had been friends for so long
that it flowed out of him.

And there were some things he hadn't wanted to—didn't
want to talk about in front of Meg. Things she couldn't understand, even though she tried so hard.

"Yeah. Because—Dare, I did love her. I do, I swear. I
thought—we got through school, and my internship, and—
and she'd been waiting, and I wanted..."

Quinn's voice was quiet. "You wanted a home."

Jack picked up one of Jules's crayons—blue, with paper
peeling away—and clutched it in his fingers.

"You know." Dare leaned back, crossing his legs, turned
toward Quinn. "There are different kinds of meant to be, I
think. Different perspectives."

The corner of Quinn's mouth curled up, the way it always
did when Dare started in on his unique combination of philosophy and artistic intuition, which he had given up trying
to critique long ago.

"Quinn and I—we didn't always get along, you know."

"Well." Raised eyebrows. "We were friends, Darius."

"Yeah, but you were also perpetually annoyed with me."

"Admittedly true." They smiled at each other, still charmed
by their eccentricities.

"But you saw it, Jack, even before we did, that we were meant to—to end up here.

"You saw it from the outside. And that's a good story, a wonderful and romantic story—that kind of meant to be, but that's not what it feels like from the inside."

Jack frowned. "What do you mean?"

"There were days when I absolutely hated him."

That was Quinn, interrupted by an injured, "Oh, how kind," from Dare.

"Oh, yes, it wasn't real hate, but I…wanted him and wanted that feeling to stop and—look, as much as the world had already changed, it wasn't exactly easy, you know, being gay at Gwynns."

Dare picked up the last cookie, and in between neat bites, he said, "That's what I mean, then. So much getting in the way and, my darling husband," Quinn blushed, "You weren't always so pleasant yourself. So superior. So we were—"

"You were a mess," Jack interrupted, and he realized it was true.

For those four years, with his odd little group, his best friends, he watched them snipe, debate—be silently jealous, be possessive—reject each other, need each other. Admitting nothing. All of them were busy trying to get through school, get good grades, be noticed, but not too much and not for the wrong things.

It was difficult, he knew, being…different. Having feelings that—

It probably felt awful, especially for them, never truly passing, wanting what every young person wanted—just someone to hold—and feeling unable to have it. Being angry at each other for that desire; resenting the person you loved. Trying to hide it. And yet it was so obvious, from the outside, that they were meant to be together.

A dim and long-buried truth began to emerge before him.

He thought about bruised knuckles and gray eyes and a sneer which always made him so unreasonably angry.

Did other people—could they tell that—

"See, he's getting it now," Dare whispered in his dreamy tone, a bit of friendly mockery.

"Oh my God." Jack ran his hands through his hair.

"I think you're right, Dare."

"It happens every once in a while, you know." Jack heard the sound of a weak thwap of Quinn's hand on Dare's fluffy stomach. And then an "oof!" as all those cookies were probably unsettled.

"So you—you're trying to tell me—" He could barely put the words together. How—"Have you known all this time? How long—"

They shared one of those looks that only longtime partners can share. Dare tilted his head, light catching the warm tones in his hair, and Quinn spoke first. "About you? I guessed in sophomore year."

"What?" Jack didn't think of himself as much of a squawker, but that was absolutely a squawk, entirely undignified. Jules giggled.

"Oh, yes." Quinn passed Jules another sheet of Dare's handmade paper for doodling. "And I knew about *him*..."

God, they were really talking about this.

"I mean, you really did go around spitting at each other like territorial cats about to—" He caught Jack's shocked face. "Well. I knew about him in freshman year. It wasn't terribly difficult to figure out."

"Did you..." Jack spread out his hands. "I don't know, think about telling me?"

Quinn rolled his eyes. "What, like a teenage queer heart-to-heart? Honestly, what good would it have done?"

Rather a lot, he imagined.

"Yeah, it wasn't really our place to—" Great, Dare, too. "It took longer for me to really think about it—not like it was a big surprise, but my head is always in other things—but I thought…"

Oh Jesus, his friends were killing him.

"You thought I'd be all right stumbling along? Marrying Meg? Having three children? When I could have…" He trailed off, shoulders tense.

"You said it yourself, hon." Dare shrugged again, frowned. "I know you really do love her. And family—making our own families—is such a blessing. Goodness knows you're a great dad. I didn't think I had a right to say anything, and—you two were always so good together. And I thought it would be enough, even if…"

"Yeah." Jack slumped. "Even if."

Jack couldn't really be angry. Not at them, at least. He'd fooled them all, and himself. And it was just a stupid thing about adulthood that he should've figured out earlier.

You can't make someone into your happily-ever-after. Even if you love them—simply, quietly, completely. A part of you will always know.

Some part of you—the jagged parts—

A memory blossomed, unbidden, behind his closed eyelids. One thirty in the morning, when he and Theo had stepped out of their favorite club in Cork into the alley. Theo had convinced his boss to set up fairy lights and a few tables, but this night—a Saturday in July—the entire walkway was crammed with people, and the music flowing out of the club was blasting at maximum volume, and the whole place smelled of apples and malt and tar and hash. They'd been trying to find a space to talk, but a crowd of drunk university kids pushed Theo right up against Jack, Jack right up against the wall.

Bowie's "Rock 'n' Roll with Me" came on. One more shove from behind, and Theo's thigh was between Jack's legs, and Jack's head fell back against the brick, and somehow all of that emptiness, all of the rivalry, all of the burdens, all of the things they'd carried as unloved children—they were nothing. It was just a fine mist and a golden light and the muscle of Theo's thigh and the realization that yes, this. This man. This place.

They moved against each other, trying not to draw attention, trying desperately not to laugh, and Jack came so hard that his vision blacked out around the edges.

He had never been happier.

And he had never, not for one moment—not when she kissed him the first time on the blue-check blanket in the spring sunshine, not when they placed Johnny in her bassinet, not when they celebrated Christmas with all the Daughertys, not even when he watched her play field hockey with ferocity, her red hair burning up the blue sky—felt that way about Meg.

"Well…" Quinn interrupted his internal monologue, and thank God; Jack was dangerously close to crying. "I think it's about time to put this little one to bed."

He picked up Jules, tucking a few curls behind his ears, and then leaned over to pat Jack's cheek. "You're going to be all right, Jack. So is Meg." Jules squirmed, and Quinn looked like he might turn away, but then he placed a firm hand on Jack's shoulder. "You did the right thing, after all."

And then he winked, threw one last comment over his shoulder.

"Welcome to the team."

Jack laughed, thick, "Thanks, Quinn."

He blinked and cleared his throat. Dare let him compose himself, getting up and pouring them glasses of merlot.

"Have a drink." He placed a hand-blown glass in front of Jack.

He did, the wine acidic in his mouth. "Fuck, Dare. I've been so stupid."

"It's all right." He took a big sip of merlot and licked his lips. "I think we all have a right to be stupid, every once in a while."

Jack laughed again, a little bitter this time. "Yeah?"

"We know where you came from, hon."

He still felt shame, so unjustified because it wasn't his fault, thinking about—about his childhood.

They did know. Not all of it, but—

Enough.

When he left his closest friends' warm home that night, he was tipsy, wrung out, and lighter than he had been in years.

One horrible conversation done with, he thought.

Now on to the next.

It was Dare's idea, of course, going to Pride, that June after they graduated, and once it had been suggested, Meg begged Jack to come along.

He found himself at loose ends, here after school finished, before his internship started, and he was itching under his skin, like all of him was tight and tensed. He was hungry through every nerve—but he couldn't figure out why, what was wrong, what he longed for. His four-year struggle through Gwynns had ended with such normalcy—it felt mundane where it should have felt extraordinary.

And since graduating he just felt like he was…missing something.

So—Baltimore Pride, June in the city, the sunshine already turning his skin a warm golden brown and Meg's a caramel pink—speakers blaring out onto Charles Street from the event stage, and the smell of bodies and cologne, and liquor pouring out from every bar. It was frenzied and sparkling and crude and so unbelievably beautiful. And there was something in his chest, like a monster gnawing at him, and Dare coated him in a fine sheen of shimmer.

He'd looked at himself in the mirror before they walked down into the city. His muscles were well defined from years of lacrosse, body bulkier after three solid meals a day, his hair a mess of black strands and scented gel, his face made strange with glitter and kohl. He'd never—he never minded about what he looked like, before; he wasn't particularly handsome, he thought, but today he felt—he looked—

"God, you're hot." Meg grinned from behind him in the mirror, and he rolled his eyes.

"You have to think that."

"I do not. I would tell you if you were ugly."

"That I believe."

Meg kissed his shoulder. "Now, don't go getting picked up by some handsome stranger." She winked.

He rubbed the back of his neck and kind of grimaced. "Ha, right."

"You really don't know how gorgeous you—" She paused, then reached up to cup his face, tender and questioning, like she couldn't figure him out. Then she patted his cheek, just shy of a slap. "Come on, sexy. Let's move."

As they walked the mile down to Mount Vernon, Jack observed the streets through the corners of his eyes, alert and nervous. He didn't want—he didn't want anyone to see—

"Holy shit."

The crowd was thick and pulsing on Eager Street next to the Hippo, one of the historic gay clubs, and shirtless men and women with cropped hair were everywhere, and someone was carrying trays of gelatinous purple shots for a quarter a piece. Meg quickly handed over a dollar and got shots for all of them, Dare squeezing it out of the cup with delicate precision, Quinn regarding it dubiously before sucking it out, Meg knocking it back and digging in her pocket for more money.

Jack looked around him at all of these people—happy people, defiant people, people fighting against a world that hated them—and took three shots in quick succession. The grain alcohol rushed through him like a kiss.

They wound their way through the crowd, getting as close as they could to the parade route, and they caught beads and candy and condoms, tossed from the floats, and it was messy and hot and insane, and Jack thought that he maybe should have had some water before this. Because he felt wonderful, and that was a dangerous feeling.

After the parade had finished, they grabbed food from vendors, Meg ravenous as she always was, and they acquired more shots, the sun wheeling in the sky into the purple starless glimmer of light pollution, nighttime in the city. Music pounded around them; Meg wound her arms around his neck, and she was pretty and sweet like the first snowballs of summer. Quinn and Dare had found their way to an unoccupied corner and were doing their usual, quiet, intense debating—art or reason, feeling or logic—the throngs of people passing them by unnoticed. Two people in love but not ready to say it yet.

Meg's body was firm and still so soft against him, the smell of cocoa butter and wind, and he did love her, he did, of course he did, and—

A flash of light. Platinum hair. Holographic glitter, and a laugh that had always sounded so nasty, but which now sounded—

Free.

Genni Jones's blue-black hair in its signature flapper's bob swung loose and shiny in the gloaming, her thin arms resting on Theo's shoulders as they danced. She was wearing—of course—an utterly scandalous sequin halter top, jeans slung so low on her hips that he could see the edges of her hip bones as she twirled.

Behind Theo, Phillippe's dark skin shone with oil. He danced close and filthy, hands on Theo's hips, his chin resting on Theo's shoulder but rich brown eyes staring with unaccustomed tenderness at Genni.

And Theo—

He clearly didn't eat enough. If Jack had been at all sober he would have been puzzled—if not entirely put off—by his odd thoughts, but he stared at Theo's ribs, visible under his fine white skin, and thought, somebody should feed him. But his chest was muscled from lacrosse, his hair such a blinding blond, eyes darkened with liner, and as he turned, Jack spotted—oh, God—a massive tattoo climbing his well-defined back.

Wings.

It must have taken hours and hours.

Jack wondered if he would be able to withstand the pain.

Theo practically glowed in the streetlights, in this odd moment, set aside in time, when they existed outside of school and rivalry and hatred and blows. His face was relaxed, and Jack realized that he had never seen him that way, like he was finished with hiding. Like he had been hiding his whole life and had just now discovered this other option—the end of lies.

Meg leaned her cheek on his chest. He kissed her thick auburn hair. She smelled like chocolate and marshmallow and sweat and grass.

And Theo's gray eyes looked up, drawn to Jack's like two atoms which had been violently split and longed to be reunited.

And he smiled. A sordid smile—a dirty smile.

He wrapped his hand back, around Phillippe's neck, fingers winding through coiled hair—dropped his head onto his shoulder, eyes half-lidded but still staring at Jack. He ground his hips, a slow and sinuous circle, and his mouth opened, the inside of his lips a black cherry–red. Jack couldn't hear anything over the thumping bass of electronic music, but he knew down to his toes that Theo was making obscene little noises, sounds that he was communicating to him across the divide of flesh.

Jack couldn't look away. He couldn't.

He was going to be sick.

The purple shots—and he was up to five now—roiled in his stomach. He started breathing heavy, his mouth watering, and his vision blurred, a kaleidoscope of Theo, his hair, his skin, his shocking sounds, splitting and swirling in him, and he pushed Meg away and ran into an alley and vomited up magenta gelatin and bile.

"Party foul!" a striking man in dangerously high heels shouted drunkenly.

Jack turned away from the mess he had made, wiped his mouth, slid to the ground with his back against brick.

He hadn't felt—he hadn't been missing something. Not for those horrible moments when he saw—

No, no—not this. Not now.

Not again.

His stomach was empty. He chewed a stick of mint gum. He went back for another shot, and Theo and Genni and Phillippe had gone. Meg frowned at him, worried, and he shrugged, grabbed her—but not too rough—and danced against her back.

Later, back in his childhood bedroom with the window stuck open and the oppressive Baltimore heat flowing in, he closed his eyes against his dizziness and dry mouth, and blond hair flashed behind his eyelids like the afterimages of a full moon.

When he woke up, his sheets were covered in glitter.

He hated himself and he hated this place, this apartment where he had felt so small, and he realized that he had always felt: unimportant, and hidden, and unloved, and so fucking hungry, and he couldn't stay here for one more moment.

He caught his reflection in the mirror, eyes smudged, cheeks flushed, looking so tired. He had a moment of—of dissociation, maybe, where he couldn't tell if he were young or old or real or fake, if he were the boy who loved Meg like crazy or the man who—

Theo had seemed so free.

He turned away. He didn't want to be this Jack, anymore.

He packed his bag with his few items of clothing, and his worn-out suitcase with his hoarded collection of fantasy novels, all their bindings cracked—called Quinn, asked if he could stay at his house in Guilford. Passed his mother in the hall, who looked at him, still sweaty and sparkling, and let him go.

He would never see her again.

Out in the fresh air of that June morning, all of his belongings stuffed into a battered backpack and heavy suitcase, Jack Gardner started laughing and couldn't stop until he cried.

Chapter Eight

Dad—
Just wanted to check in and see how you're doing. Miss me already?

School's fine so far. Classes are going well, though there is more homework than I had expected (even though you warned me ahead of time, sorry for not listening). I've talked with the lacrosse coach and it looks like I'll be starting practice soon in the reserves. Thanks again for all the lessons and the gear—really excited for the spring.

The dorms are really nice. Hyacinthe's on the girls' floor of course but she's come over a few times to study (also known as bitching, just like Big G) but she won't let me into her room. I'm guessing it's a total mess...whoever said girls are tidy had never met actual girls, I think.

I didn't realize that Will's dad is Jack Gardner—did you know him? His picture's up on the fourth floor with all the scholarship kids, guess he's done a lot for the school. Anyway, Will looks just like him and is basically embarrassed about it all the time.

I get along with Will pretty well. Actually, he's a great roommate. We spend most of our time studying, I guess. It's nice to have a real friend here already (other than Hya).

Anyway, everything is going just fine. I do miss you, of

course, but I'm sure you're just as excited to have some space as I am...ha.

I love you and give Grandmere a hug for me.

Jasper

P.S. If I know you as well as I definitely do, you haven't actually left the house since I got here. Go out and have fun, Dad. Don't be a total loser now that I have my own life...

His kid was such a little shit.

God, Theo missed him.

And apparently Jasper was able to do what his father never had—have a Gardner's friendship without even trying. Just by being himself. Those few moments he had seen them together—it wouldn't take long for them to be friends, naturally. Like that friendship was meant to be.

Theo had ruined any possibility of that for himself by being, in general, a huge asshole.

He sat at the desk in his suite of rooms, checking his private emails as he always did before he started his day. He took these extra moments to lounge around in his favorite French terry dressing gown, the smell of verbena and juniper bubbles flowing in from the en-suite bath, a cup of espresso steaming within reach.

Yes, he had lived a rough life for several years. Yes, he could do it, and he did it well.

Yes, those were some of his sweetest, most delicious memories.

But great God above, now that he could live a life of opulence, he would do it to the hilt. It was a payoff, the prize at the end of the puzzle of practical adulthood. Feel like shit about yourself, take a luxurious bath with two-hundred-dollar per-fumed oil.

He closed the email from Jasper, opening a few others—a quick note from Genni (he really should get Jasper to stop calling her Big G, which annoyed her to no end, but it was just too wonderful), excited about Hyacinthe's acceptance on the field hockey team. A missive from Josephine, partially in Creole French, asking him to please send down Tom as soon as possible, *the kitchen needs him, merci.*

And there, nearly lost in his inbox, an email with a terri-bly familiar name.

Theo's hands shook, just a little, as he opened it.

Theo—
Hi
God. I don't know how to start.

It was nice running into you (literally, I suppose) yester-day, though it wasn't exactly something I'd planned out. I don't know if you heard, but some things have changed.

I don't want to say all this in an email. And I know I don't deserve any of your time, after...everything. But I'd really like to see you. Can I buy you a cup of coffee?

Say yes.

Jack

Oh, and I've gotten an email from Will about how much he's getting along with your kid. Who knew they'd be room-mates? You should probably get coffee with me if only to prepare for (possibly awkward) future social situations.

He closed the email, closed his laptop, and shot back his espresso.

Just like Gardner, he thought. Bumbling, inexpressive, and manipulative.

He had promised himself. When Jack left—and then when Father died, and when he decided to come back to Baltimore, start a family, live up to his mother's expectations—Theo had promised himself that he wouldn't let it hurt, anymore. He knew that he'd probably see Jack at Gwynns, or hear about his most recent charity work, and maybe he would remember a thing or two, but he wouldn't let it—

He was too damned old to feel like this. Like something in him was shattering. Like he couldn't breathe.

Theo stood, stripping off his robe and hanging it behind the bathroom door. He slid into the tub, built to be large enough for two, though he'd never shared it with anyone. Not even Lexi. Bubbles reached all the way to his chin. He closed his eyes.

He had to make the hurt go away.

So he imagined something else.

He moved his hand down his body, running over lithe muscle, over soft, fine hair. He felt himself grow hard. He tried to put together images, not a person: a mouth, open; unruly hair, pulled under his fingers; tanned skin, sweating; music, smoke, darkness; a choking sound, as he pushed too deep, over and over...

His hand sped up, and God, this was better than thinking about—

Toned muscles, and blue eyes like sunshine, and that mouth, the way it hated him sometimes, and the way he plowed into it—

Laughing at dawn and the too-small bed and birdsong—

Slow dancing, high as fuck, in that shitty apartment, cans of cider attracting flies—

Singing along with the trad band at The Thirsty and shots of Goldschläger and pulling down the back of his jeans and—

And that time they fucked in the hotel when Jack ordered champagne and—

Jack when he slid home for the first time and the way he looked—

Jack, fuck, and the sounds he made in the alley and—

Jack, when he said I love you and—and—

Theo came with a cry.

Empty. Hollow. Hating himself.

Fuck you, Gardner. He dunked his head under the water, and if there were any tears they washed away, down into the drain.

Cleaned, dried, groomed, and calmed, he sat at his desk. He opened his laptop. He typed out two words which he already regretted.

Gardner,
Fine.

It felt good, throwing things. He was considering getting fabulously drunk. Mother probably wouldn't like that. She hadn't liked the tattoo either, but he absolutely did not care.

The police had come yet again for more of his father's files. He couldn't imagine what was left, but they always seemed to find new documents and give him filthy looks with superior smiles, clearly enjoying his utter mortification.

Everybody loved to watch him fall.

A crystal wineglass smashed against the wall as if by magic. His movements were automatic, like violence preprogrammed. He wondered if this rage had always been in him, just waiting for its moment to emerge, fully grown.

He was still for a moment—debating what to pick up and

hurl next—and he heard voices in the hall. He went to stand by the door.

"Mr. Gardner."

Oh, shit. Perfect.

He was too tired for this.

"Mrs. Beaumont. Hi."

Their house—this beautiful place of antiques and rich fabrics and chilly distance—had been ransacked, both by the police and by Theo's anger. Theo knew that even the front hall looked ramshackle, undignified, and he imagined Gardner's face as he observed his family's…decay.

"How can we help you?" His mother's voice was still so cultured and precise. He wondered how she got up the nerve.

"I—I'm just here to check on—"

"Ah."

A silence so awkward that he could feel it from the other side of the door.

"He's in the study."

He heard a rustle of—most likely—scruffy sneakers.

"Mr. Gardner."

"Yeah?"

"You will not hurt him again."

Theo ran his tongue along the inside of his lip. The scar from where Gardner had hit him was still there, silvery, with a roughness in his mouth. His mother had hated to see his perfect face marred. He looked so much like her. When she had seen the scar, she'd seemed more disappointed in him than angry at Gardner, but now—

"I won't."

"Fine." Another rustle. "Do not make me regret giving you what little hospitality we have left to offer."

Theo snorted—his mother still pretending as if—as if there were anything good, here. He moved away from the door, picked up another wineglass, and aimed at the wall next to the door.

He let go when the door opened, glass shattering around Gardner.

"What the—" Gardner ducked, crystal splinters raining down around him. "Beau—"

"Gardner." He smiled his nastiest smile. "Nice to see you."

"Um." He looked at a loss for words, which wasn't entirely new for him. "Right."

Theo flushed. Gardner's eyes were blue, so blue, and he remembered looking into them too many times—to fight, to denigrate, to despise—after lacrosse practice, at prom, at Pride when he was so stupid, so fucking—

"What are you doing here?"

"I wanted to—I heard more about—"

"Ah." He picked up a paperweight, tossed it up and down in his left hand. "Come to gloat."

"No, I—" Gardner didn't seem capable of speech.

Theo wondered, despite himself, what he looked like. He slammed the paperweight on the desk. "It's what I would do. If this," he gestured at the room, the drawers of the desk pulled out, ruination everywhere, "Were happening to you."

"I know." Gardner's nostrils flared. "I'm not like that."

"No?" Theo licked his lips. "You sure?"

He stalked forward, stopping a foot away from Gardner, who was for some reason breathing heavily. His muscled chest rose and fell, and his skin was flushed.

"Isn't this just what you've always wanted? To see me—to see us brought low like this? After everything I've—"

Gardner started to lift a hand. Theo could smell his skin.

It seemed terribly important that he not touch him right now.

Theo leveled his best—okay, not his best, but he was trying—glare.

Gardner dropped his hand, started to cross his arms, thought better of it, and made fists at his sides. Giving no quarter. "I—no, Beau." His voice cracked, "Theo. I—I never wanted—"

Theo snorted, moved away. "I doubt that."

He leaned back against his father's massive desk, crossing his ankles and shoving his hands in his pockets. "Why are you here, Gardner?"

Gardner gritted his teeth. He looked angry, which was deeply insulting. Theo thought that if anyone should be angry, it should probably be him. "Oddly enough, I don't know why. I guess I wanted to see if you were all right."

"All right?" He laughed. "Yes, absolutely. Fantastically all right. Never been better."

"And I wanted to…"

"What?"

"Fuck, Beau. I wanted to apologize."

Silence. Jack looked pathetic, as if Theo had bullied an apology out of him, which he was sure he hadn't. Jack ground his toe into the carpet, angry and red-faced. Theo's lip tingled, not quite healed.

"Are you going to?" Theo tightened his fists in his pockets, fingernails digging into his skin.

"Theo—"

"Don't say my name." Theo felt his face thinning out the way it did when he was threatened and trying to scare people away. It was an uncontrollable reflex—he had been trained to be like this. "Don't bother apologizing, either. I don't have enough energy to care."

Gardner looked away, humiliated, then squared his shoulders and regarded Theo with his typical mulish stare, which Theo had once thought was a sign of stupidity but now realized, much to his shame, was a show of strength. Theo felt stripped down, naked, assessed for flaws. There was something about his eyes, the way they cut into him, which didn't feel—didn't feel bad.

Fuck, he hated him, and why had he ever found him—

"Fine. Beau. Whatever." He rubbed the back of his neck. "This was stupid."

"A new sensation for you, I'm sure."

Gardner slumped, defeated, and started to turn away.

Theo didn't want him to go. God, he wanted—

Something in him broke. Theo felt sick. And guilty, which was—irritating.

"Gardner—wait, I—"

Gardner was staring through the lead-paned windows onto the once perfectly maintained lawn.

"Look, I—"

"Don't strain yourself."

"Ugh," Theo scoffed. "Why are you so—even now—"

"I know you don't like me, all right? Never have. And I—" Gardner looked as if he wanted to say something, then changed his mind at the last moment. "I don't particularly like you. I just wanted to—"

"Thanks," Theo interrupted, fast, like he should get it over with and forget it as soon as possible. "For checking. And for the...apology. Whatever."

Gardner looked at him, surprised.

Took a step forward.

"I'm—not all right. But maybe I—"

"You will be." Gardner's face was so serious and unexpectedly understanding.

Theo had never missed an opportunity to mock him—his ugly clothes, his loser friends, his poor manners—but maybe he...maybe those all came from somewhere.

What had happened in Jack Gardner's life, to make him look at Theo like that, like he knew...there was some commonality, a knowledge that Theo had only recently attained, that it seemed like Jack had known for a long time. He thought about his cruelty.

It wasn't much fun for Theo to examine the ways in which he'd been a total bastard.

"Maybe."

"Yeah."

Gardner had been moving closer, lifting his rough hand again, and he almost put it on Theo's face. Theo's body thrummed with—with the way Gardner had looked at Pride, the glimmer of the night and his darkened eyes, and the intensity of his stare in the bell tower, and he wanted to be touched, now, more than anything he'd ever wanted. And he knew if Gardner touched him, put that hand on his face, he'd never be the same, and it would all be too real, and he just couldn't live with that, and he jerked his head away, and Gardner stepped back.

"Goodbye, Gardner."

He cleared his throat, a splotchy flush warming his face. "Bye, Beau."

Theo closed his eyes and did not watch Gardner go.

And his head dropped, and there was a scream inside of him. Like he had been denied something.

He picked up another glass.

The sound of it crashing against the wall was less satisfying now.

Now. He had to do it now.

He had to get out of here.

Chapter Nine

Jack hadn't realized that one chance meeting—in a closet, no less, and he'd laugh at that if he had the heart—when he was fourteen years old would change his destiny.

At Gwynns, they'd always trotted him out for fundraisers and alumni cocktail parties, and he had borne it, grateful to be there but itchy in borrowed clothes which didn't fit quite right, and maybe weren't meant to.

He knew that in some ways he was a charity case—though he did work hard, harder than most, and was athletic and intelligent and generally easy to like—so he put up with it, being a symbol, proof of Gwynns Academy's supposed generosity. He tried to use the good manners his mother had never taught him, and he tried to fit in, but donors liked to see his rough edges, the ways his clothes were a little too big; they took one look at him and pulled out their checkbooks.

He was the model of their philanthropy and an easy excuse for their tax deductions.

And that was all right. It was just one more price he had to pay.

So yeah, big parties, cocktails he wasn't supposed to drink, and at one of those first events a well-dressed woman put a hand on his arm, kind and impersonal, and he started breathing too hard, his tie choking him, and he went to hide in the coat closet.

Where he bumped right into a short, pudgy gentleman who was staring mournfully at his undone polka-dotted bow tie, lying limp in his hands. "Sorry, I—"

"It's all right," the man mumbled, but he didn't look up from his crumpled silk tie. "I'm lost."

"Um." Jack looked around the closet, wondering how one could get lost in this small space, and if he should indicate the way out.

"I hate these things." The man waved the bow tie around and sighed.

"Oh?" Jack had a terrible moment when he thought he might laugh, which seemed inappropriate. The poor guy really did look pathetic. "Would you like some, um, help?"

He nodded, and Jack carefully took up and knotted the silk tie, his fingers brushing a smooth-shaved neck.

"There. Um."

"Thank you kindly…"

"Jack."

"Jack." He smiled, dimples in his plump cheeks. "Franklin Smith." He held out his hand; they shook.

"Nice to meet you, Mr.—"

"Frank'll do."

Jack was unaccountably charmed, some anxiety within him easing. Frank was—different to all the others at this dull event. More real, somehow, in a suit which looked impeccably tailored and in which Frank looked deeply uncomfortable. There was something about him that was—that echoed in Jack, some sort of sameness, like two fish that had found themselves outside of their tank.

He smiled at Frank, Frank's eyes twinkling. Then he set his shoulders, realizing that he'd been in here quite long enough, and that it was time to return to stilted conversations and condescending smiles.

"I hate these things, too." Frank gave him a kind look, perceptive and speaking aloud Jack's thoughts. "Been coming for years, now, can't say no."

"Hmm." Jack put his hands in his pockets.

"They never leave you alone if they think you have something to give."

Jack thought about the next four years, being dressed and groomed like a prized pony, and maybe the years after that, carrying the weight of his history as an underprivileged child graced with the trappings of unimaginable wealth.

Begging for it.

He was still a kid. It felt like too much.

They did go back to the party, and it was dull, mini crab cakes, bland and unseasoned, and cheese trays which no one ate, and Jack kept seeing Frank at more parties over the years, and he was good to talk to as adults rarely were, and he—

Frank started buying his books. His uniforms. Jack wasn't supposed to know that—his bills were just magically paid, and only a gossiping secretary let Frank's name slip. He never fully figured out why he did it, not until Frank pulled him aside, after he was named valedictorian at his graduation, and offered him an internship. Casually mentioning, like it was nothing at all, that Frank had grown up homeless. How he'd never had real family.

How he now had a lot to give.

Here, in his office, Jack looked over the quarterly report—Frank's name still on every letterhead, despite his death fifteen years ago—and thought about that history, how he was indebted, and the wording of Frank's will: *To the son of my heart, Jack Gardner.*

All because of a bow tie.

Thank fuck he'd researched how to tie them.

He dropped the papers, missing Frank deeply, and stood, walking away from his desk.

Something that he could never tell anyone—one more secret for him to bury—was that he never saw Frank as a father. Frank was a dream, a wish...the true ticket out of poverty he imagined but never thought was real. Jack had loved Frank, of course, but he would never be able to separate the money from the man. It made him hate himself—one more bit of evidence that he was broken inside.

Years working here, the internship which turned into a career, skipping past college and careening right into wealth management, running a business that often ran itself, his bank account pretty damned significant—certainly considering where he'd started—and he was so grateful. He put money where it could do good; he paid for more scholarships at Gwynns, far more than they had ever offered before. He donated to various charities, lots of them, and he knew what it was like to go to formal galas and cocktail parties and be friendly to the kids like him who were still dressed up like evidence, like paper dolls. He was glad to be doing so many good things.

And he was also...quietly miserable.

When he was a kid, he thought he knew what it would mean to be wealthy. He would watch the rain sliding down his bedroom window, splatters of moisture leaking through, the lights of the city dazzling through the lens of thunderstorms, and he had imagined that having money was like that light and the way it shone through cold rain—something stunning and vivid and implausible. Thunder rattled the windows and he wanted to be like that thunder, powerful, something to be noticed, something which couldn't be denied.

He thought that money would make him happy.

But there was that feeling in him, the feeling he'd had for

practically his whole life, that he was incomplete. Money bought him food, and some decent clothes, and his kids got braces, and Meg could work in sports journalism, traveling and working her way up the ranks in a dying industry, and there were always presents under the tree, and he never got cold. Those were all blessings he had never had; to feel anything but gratitude was unfair, selfish. He could raise children who always had enough, and he always had enough, and—

That was happiness, wasn't it?

Jack closed his eyes and flashed on the stupid, incoherent email he had sent Theo.

He'd been happy, then. In the apartment in Ireland, with hardly anything, but with someone to—

And now he wanted to run away again—he felt trapped by all of the things that he had always coveted. His picture up at Gwynns, and a closet full of (still somehow ill-fitting) suits, polka-dotted ties, respect from dull and important people.

He stood at the double-glazed windows at the top of his office building, no heat or cold or rain coming through, and he felt entirely empty.

A sound from his computer—his email pinged. He crossed to his desk, settled into his chair again, and his heart beat twice in quick succession as he opened a two-word email.

Theo.

He wondered if Theo had learned how to be—he didn't sound happy either, but it was—

Maybe it was a start.

He had told everyone he was going on a European tour. And he had meant to, but he was…waylaid.

Jack had never been anywhere or done anything. His world was pretty much Baltimore—everyone he knew was from Baltimore, and he'd spent every day and night of his life in Baltimore, and it wasn't like his mother would have been able to send him someplace—study abroad, vacation, anything—so his experience, despite the four years at Gwynns, was limited.

About a month after he accepted Frank's invitation to work at his firm, he showed up to the office for his first day, butterflies in his stomach and a weight on his shoulders. Everything depended on his success. But Frank took one look at him and said, "Jack, you need to see more of the world." And he wrote him a check which was, to Jack, obscene, which Jack thought he couldn't possibly take—but Frank insisted, and he took it anyway.

It wasn't a bad thing, was it, to seize an opportunity?

So few adults had ever been kind to him.

So now, after graduation, after a month without school when he sat around in Quinn's spare room and felt confusingly lost, Jack thought—

I'm going to go somewhere. Where no one knows me. Where I can be a kid, for once in my miserable life.

Quinn helped him arrange the flights—his father was a board member of an airline and found the best deals, though the routes could be unusual—and he'd be stopping in Belfast first, and then on to London, then Paris, and end up in Rome. He thought about pints of Guinness, and seeing the London Eye—using some of the halting French he'd had to learn at Gwynns, eating al dente pasta and watching young women in flowered skirts on bicycles with baskets full of bread. He had no frame of reference, but he thought that the rest of the world must be beautiful in a way that Baltimore never could be.

And all of that had sounded really, really good.

"Still can't believe you're doing this." Dare hugged him, warm in the summer sunshine. "I'm so glad you are."

Dare and Quinn had, of course, showed up to see him off. Dare had actually packed his suitcase—with maybe a few creative pieces, but Jack hadn't had the heart to look too closely. Quinn, after setting up the flights, had given him some highly suspect tips on how to flirt with European women, despite never having any inclination to do so himself. And Meg had talked about coming for a last hug, but she was trying out for the field hockey team at Johns Hopkins University, and anyway, things hadn't been the same since—

Well, he had plenty of time to figure out what he wanted. After a bit of a world tour, and time on his own.

"Jack, you will be careful, won't you?" Quinn adjusted the collar of his shirt—newly bought through Frank's generosity and actually his size—without meeting his eyes.

"Give him some space, hon. Jack knows what he's doing."

"I think I should be safe, Quinn." He gave him a crooked grin. "I think Europe is probably a lot safer than Baltimore, if we're being honest."

"Yes." Quinn sniffed, and gave him a bit of a slap on his shoulder. "But you've never—"

"I know. But I—I think it's a good thing. For me to be alone for a while."

Dare put a hand on Quinn's arm—a new development, there, but entirely natural and long-awaited—and Quinn stiffened for a moment, and then he relaxed into it. "You're going to be all right," Quinn said, with a reasonable amount of conviction.

"Of course he will." Dare offered his hand for Jack to shake, laughed, then pulled him into another hug, pressing his soft, perfumed cheek to the side of Jack's head.

Quinn sniffed again, but wrapped Jack in a tight embrace, patting his back. "Okay, then. The first flight will take you—"

"I know, I'll be in Belfast for about five hours, then I'll get the flight to London."

"Since you'll be there…" Quinn pulled back with a bit of

a gleam in his eye, the one that always heralded *academic re-search*. "You might as well see some of the murals."

"Sure." Jack looked up at Dare, who was staring fondly at the back of Quinn's head. Then Dare rolled his eyes, not in a mean way.

"I heard that, Darius."

"You heard my eyes?"

"Haven't you figured out that he'll always know every-thing?" Jack grinned.

"So he says."

Quinn reached out and grabbed his hand, fast and tight. "Just. Be careful, Jack."

He was just worried about him. It was still—sometimes they felt so young.

How could he tell him that this was—that he itched to get as far away from all of them as possible? He loved them all, but... Quinn wanted to keep everyone right around him, not quite adjusted to this new life, no school, the future stretch-ing out, unknown. Quinn would be going to George Wash-ington University in the fall, out in DC and away from all of them, and he acted like he wanted to preserve this summer as if nothing could change. As if he could keep them all safe.

Jack knew there was no safe. For him, there never had been. So he'd find a new kind of danger, just in being by himself. No one to answer to. No closeness, no responsibilities. Noth-ing but this golden summer before his adult life started.

No chance of the kind of love that held you down.

He thought about Meg. About promises he'd been care-ful not to make.

It was time to go.

He took one last look at his best friends in the entire world, and maybe he should have felt a bit sad. But when he slung his bag over his shoulder, suitcase in hand, and walked away, he thought, *thank fuck*.

The flight—seven hours, a few movies, some subpar food— passed quickly, though he couldn't sleep; he greeted dawn over Ireland with desert-dry eyes but a kind of lightness, like up here in the plane he was made of air. Ireland stretched out, fresh, sparkling, so green.

It was shocking in its beauty.

Maybe it was the sleeplessness, maybe just the anxiety and relief in doing something new, but flying in over Ireland was— he was euphoric. He'd never seen anything like this place, and the grass and rocks and beaches breathed out with all of the possibilities of life—teeming and wild and unknown, mysteries to be unraveled but never fully understood. The plane tilted and circled, and he was drawn toward the earth like an arrow finding its target. As the wheels hit the tarmac, he felt something click in him, as if he'd been missing a piece of himself, as if he had just realized the absence of a limb as it regrew. His feet seemed to meld into the ground as he entered the airport and yet he was buoyant. He had a fire in his head.

He knew he could wait in the airport—read, or watch other travelers, or catch a bit of sleep—but he...

He felt like he needed to get out.

Like a part of him belonged here.

He walked out into cool air and ducked into a black taxi- cab that seemed to materialize before him.

"Where to?"

He had, despite his fey mood, no idea. And did he have—he felt in his pocket for the money clip Jason Daugherty had given him, stuffed with pounds and euros, and yes, of course, Quinn had snuck in a piece of notebook paper with a list of murals.

The nag.

"Um." He passed it up.

"Bit of a tour, then?"

"Yeah, thanks."

At least he'd have something useful to report to Quinn in his first letter back.

The driver kept up a running commentary in an almost impenetrable accent. Jack let his voice wash over him, staring out the window at a foreign city, eyes soaking up shades of gray as the shipyards went by. He remembered something from some history class—the shipyards had been bombed in the Second World War. Now they were complete, towering cranes fragmenting the blue sky, industrial and almost violent in their starkness like the areas of Baltimore he'd never explored.

He thought about the kind of people he hadn't met at Gwynns. Children of industries which functioned with calloused hands and strong backs. A legacy of hard work. Of a kind of struggle that he, despite his upbringing, had never had to face.

Staring up at mural after mural, reds and oranges and greens, Jack felt that burden of legacy continue. Lines drawn in the sand—separation, alienation; the evidence that people always found reasons for violence. They found ways to hate and hurt each other; they found in-groups and out-groups, gods and goddesses and politics and excuses. Concepts to blame.

Blood. Tradition. Faith.

He remembered bloody knuckles and a split lip and stupid, childish rivalry.

His life seemed very small.

Who was he, compared to this?

The cabbie interrupted his existential nonsense. "Where to next?"

Jack, standing in the shade-cooled street, ruffled his hair.

He felt so tired. "Not sure, I guess. I'm supposed to go back to the airport."

"On and up?"

"Something like that."

The driver leaned his iron-gray head out of the window and gave Jack a penetrating stare. "Or you could do something else."

He frowned. "Yeah?"

"Go on, my shift's about over. How'd you feel about a pint?"

Jack glanced at the wristwatch, nice but unostentatious, that Deb had given him as a graduation gift. He had some time before his next flight. Not much, but—

And he felt…maybe he could go off the plan, a bit.

"All right."

"Name's Aengus, by the way. And you?"

Jack realized that in this moment, he could be anybody.

He didn't know who else he could be.

"Jack." He stuck out his hand, and they shook.

"Get in, then."

They dodged through city traffic and pulled up in front of a cozy-looking pub. Aengus flipped his light off.

Inside the pub, Jack noticed a shift, something different from the few bars he and his friends had been able to bluff their way into back home. It felt—there was a warmth, maybe. It was almost the way he'd hoped that Gwynns would be, as if magic would tingle along his skin, welcoming—but this was just a normal pub, nothing particularly extraordinary. But he could hardly describe it, the place seemed…old. Like the earth was singing up to him. He was an alien here; he felt welcomed.

An Irish trad band in the corner was tuning up their instruments. Aengus ordered a couple of pints of Guinness, and Jack watched as the bartender poured them, slow and careful.

Creamy bubbles sifted up through dark beer, and he felt like that liquid, thick, carbonated, smoothed out.

He thought about his favorite fantasy novels, and he remembered the rule, never accept food from the fairy folk. He grinned a little to himself, feeling utterly ridiculous. The stout was slippery on his tongue as he took a defiant swallow, the music was lively as it surrounded them, and even if this tiny pub were a place of wildness and trickery and magic, he was content to take the chance.

"So tell us about yourself, Jack." Aengus licked foam from his lips, the hint of gray whiskers catching drops of beer.

"Um, well, I'm on a—" What had Frank called it? "Gap year, I guess."

"University next year?"

"Internship."

"Well done. But—I hope you don't mind me saying—you look like a man needs a new start in life. To do something a little unexpected."

Jack opened his mouth, and then—

"Oh sure, you're thinking, a year off, that'll do the job," and Aengus took a healthy swallow of stout, "But I'll bet you have a plan for this year. Everything decided. Your planes, your hostels, down to when you'll wash your pants, am I right?"

Jack thought about the carefully scheduled flights, the reserved bedsits, the folded new clothes in his case. Every stop along the way had been suggested to him, arranged for him, and Jack had just...agreed. He had figured that he didn't know enough about the world to make too many decisions by himself.

He frowned. Aengus waited, placid. A mature face; youthful eyes.

And then Jack had the oddest thought. About Genni Jones.

Jones, whom he'd spotted slumming at the college bar across

from Johns Hopkins after he and Meg had taken a tour; Jones, splitting pitchers of beer and flirting outrageously with Phillippe Dumont, and the few words he'd overheard between rounds of pool and kisses with Meg.

Theo. Ireland. Yes, Phil, really. Cork. Who the hell knows why. Ran away.

And then Jack was thinking about Theo, that last uncomfortable meeting at his house. His slate eyes, intense, and his filthy lips, and that feeling, the itching thing, the lack.

Theo, whom he couldn't call Beau anymore, not even in his head. He thought about all of that vibrating anger, the inexorable pull, the feeling he didn't want to understand, and he knew that the formality of last names was no longer adequate for a relationship which was…

Well, whatever it was.

"Oh, I know that look."

"What?" Jack blinked. Aengus laughed and tossed back half a pint at once. "Whoever she is, son, you'd better be after her."

Jack nearly choked on his own beer. "*What?*"

"Ah well, you don't need to play coy with me, but I'll leave you your secrets." And he winked. "But there's something in you, Jack, that's calling out—for your other half, or for adventure, a good long wander—or maybe just to forget."

Jack shrugged a bit, and looked down at his soggy beer mat.

"Sure." Aengus nodded, decisive. "You'll never find that with a plan. You just need to go."

Jack turned his wrist to look at his watch one more time. He was about ten minutes away from being too late for his flight.

"I'm off home now. My Caer is like to toss me out if I don't get there in time for my tea. Should I drop you at the airport?"

His suitcase, so carefully arranged, was at his side. His agenda was probably ruined, at least until he could arrange a new flight. He had stout in his belly, and he had money and the freedom which came with it. He had no one to answer to, and nowhere, really, to be.

And he had that overheard conversation. He told himself it was just—just natural curiosity. And maybe it would be good if he did something…different.

And he'd never been to Cork, after all.

He looked up at Aengus, and Aengus looked mildly back.

"Could you take me to a train station?"

Chapter Ten

They called them the "Gwynns Alumni Strip Poker Nights," but there were only the three of them, and they never played poker. Though Genni did sometimes take her top off, but that was just the way she was, and Theo hardly noticed it by now.

Genevieve Jones, resplendent in a French lace brassiere, was still a stone-cold bitch, and he still loved her to death. When he was younger and their mothers arranged playdates (while drinking prosecco and complaining about everything), he thought he'd be all right with marrying her someday.

That, obviously, did not happen—their disastrous prom night encounter made sure of it. And she deserved far more than the half-life he would have given her. But he still knew he would never be able to live without her.

She sat close to the fire, the tanned skin of her torso glowing in the light, body just a little gentler with motherhood and age. Her hair, still in the same flapper cut, was deep black, and fine particles of shimmer on her cheeks picked up the wavering firelight. She was the most beautiful woman he had ever known. She made a lot of really dreadful faces. She was wonderful.

"Pass me that, would you?"

She held out an imperious hand, and he refilled her glass and his own from the pitcher of Manhattans. The only sound out of Phil across from her was the turning of a page and a contented sigh. Phil's large frame, athletic despite his academic pursuits, fit snugly into his chair, and long fingers held a slim volume, and he had neatly removed his shoes, merino wool socks covering his shapely feet.

During college Genni had married Phillippe Dumont, who'd inherited quite a lot from his mother but was lucky enough not to inherit her tendency to choose rich older paramours to marry and then wait, with not a lot of patience, for them to die off. His father was the first of these, an Algerian-born Frenchman, and Phil had maybe always wondered what kind of man he had been. His mother had never allowed him to know.

When Genni and Phil married, they married for love—both children with complicated and generally disliked parents, they knew what it meant to need affection. To need someone to share affection with.

That wasn't, of course, the story they told. By now their extended circle (and maybe half of Baltimore) had heard about the "desperate one-night, three European countries affair, which they just had to keep going, darling." But Theo knew them best. They were starved for love, and they gave it to each other unreservedly. When they came home from that brief trip together, they were inseparable.

He had also needed—wanted desperately—that kind of affection, and he had thought he had it, but Jack—and then Lexi tried, but he couldn't—

"Don't you look an absolute misery." She was smirking at him, those thin red lips settling into their typical wry shape, but he saw some concern, there, too.

He did not want to talk about it. "Missing Jasper, I guess."

"Hmm." She stretched out, feet propped up on the Victorian footstool in front of the fire. "I don't know why. I'm relieved to have Hyacinthe out from underfoot."

Phil snorted, head still in a book of poetry. "Right. Must be why I found you cleaning out the linen cupboard."

"Hey, I clean!" She wrinkled her nose. "Sometimes."

"Darling." He looked over the pages, gold-rimmed glasses perched on his dark, patrician nose. "If you're cleaning, that means something must be desperately wrong."

She balled up the stem from her cocktail cherry and threw it at him. "All right, fine. I miss her."

He gave her a little smile, and she smiled back and winked.

They were too sweet, in their caustic way. It made Theo sad.

Lonely.

"Ugh," Genni muttered at Theo. "I can hardly bear to look at you. What on earth is wrong?"

He looked away, stared into the fire.

"Do you know who I spotted jogging around campus like a madman the other day?"

Theo's eyes snapped up at the sound of Phil's voice—always calm with an unnerving quality of silence, with something deadly running under the surface.

"Who, love?" Genni swirled her cocktail.

"Jack." Phil met Theo's gaze with a piercing intensity. "Gardner."

Genni's jaw dropped open, her pretty face looking bizarre with surprise. And then she turned to Theo. There was pity in her eyes. And a solid grudge. "Theo…"

"I have nothing to say on that subject."

"Funny." An angry tone, her face like a pit bull's. "I have rather a lot to say."

"Well…" He shifted, placed his glass down. "Don't."

She wouldn't let it go; he could tell already. "Is that why—"

"Genni—"

"Did you talk to him?"

He closed his eyes. Of course she knew, she always knew everything—she could probably see Jack Gardner's shadow cast over him like a shroud. "Yes."

"And?"

"And…" He thought about that email, and his response, and how idiotic he probably was to want and hope and— "Nothing."

"Sure looks like nothing."

"Gen—"

"I should have castrated that man when I had the chance."

"Look…" He leaned forward, elbows on his knees and head in his hands. "Just. I'm not—I won't do anything. But—Jasper's rooming with his kid, and—and we should probably—"

"What?"

He was staring at the floor, eyes blurry, his silky hair between his fingers. "I think we need to learn to get along."

"Get along." Genni's voice was low and condescending, and he felt immense gratitude that it wasn't him that she was really angry with. At least not anymore.

And he felt a hand on his hair, calming him, because no one could be as vitriolic and comforting at the same time as his childhood best friend.

The woman he thought he would marry.

"Theo," from Phillippe, "You need to be careful."

Theo felt tension in his neck as he ground out, "I know."

"Are you going to see him again?" Genni's hand tightened on his scalp.

"I—yeah. We're getting coffee."

He felt her shake a little, and he was worried she would explode. Genni's anger was legendary, and usually glorious to watch.

Then he realized she was laughing. "Oh my God, you are so stupid."

"I am aware, thank you."

She patted down his hair like he was a wild animal, and sometimes he felt like he was. He smiled in a way which was mostly a grimace. "That son of a bitch is never going to leave you alone, is he?"

He didn't have anything—he had been left alone, didn't she see, for so long, and there weren't any words, expressive or profound or even rude, which could answer her.

But Phil was there, and he didn't have to. "He doesn't want him to."

It was…almost nice, to hear it out loud. For someone else to say it.

He'd been carrying it for too long.

It also felt terribly pathetic.

Theo sat back up in his chair, picked up his glass and peered into it, wishing that the cocktail would make this all easier.

"Ugh." Genni took a sip from her glass and licked her red lips. "Jack Gardner. Ugh."

"I agree completely." She pursed her lips at him, and he rolled his eyes. "Well, most of me does. A lot of me."

"Not enough. Can't you just go find some boy toy and enjoy your new bachelor lifestyle like a normal person?"

He laughed, a little lightness in his chest for the first time in days.

"I mean I can get you a new apartment downtown, so you don't have to bring hookups to this drafty old—"

"Hey." He nudged her elbow on the side table. "Be nice."

"Darling, I do not know how."

Another snort from Phil's side of the room, and a muttered, "How true."

Theo rested his glass on his thigh, breathing out a long sigh. "I love you both, you know."

"Well," she leaned back, high heels glinting in firelight,

"We love you too, of course. Just—for fuck's sake—take care of yourself. You're the only Theodore Beaumont we have. We've gotten attached."

She waved a hand as if it were all distasteful, talking about feelings, but her face was soft.

"Yeah." He took another sip, thought about—about the coffee date, and about a marriage that didn't work, and holding on to him when he couldn't bear to get out of bed, quite yet, and the two crooked teeth behind his lower lip and the way he was so stunning in his artlessness. "I'll be careful."

The room was silent other than the snapping of logs in the fire, and they drank their Manhattans, and all three of them knew that he wouldn't be careful at all.

He lit the next cigarette with the burning butt of the last.

Six in the morning, and the sun was on its way to rising. Theo's head was still a bit thick from last night; a group of American girls had homed in on him as a fellow countryman and bought him a couple of shots of Jameson before they figured out that he would definitely not be going home with any of them.

"Sorry, you're not exactly my type," he'd shouted in an upturned ear.

She looked at him, perplexed. "Blonde?"

"That too," he laughed, "But no." He made an extravagant gesture in his chest region. And a bit of a disgusted face.

For a moment, he worried. And then the group of girls broke out into giggles, and the petite redhead yelled out, "You should meet my brother!" And all was well.

That was when they started drinking tequila.

"Oh God." He massaged his neck with his left hand, the muscles coiled up into knots.

Finishing his second cigarette, he wedged himself into the

closet-shaped shower, not waiting for the cold water to heat up. A quick scrub with Tesco-brand soap, a brush of his teeth, and he fluffed his hair with a threadbare towel before running a bit of pomade—his last luxury—through the asymmetrical strands.

It had taken him a while to get used to living without all the money he'd taken for granted his whole life. Oh, he could do it. He learned quickly what it was like to need basic priorities like food and shelter and care very little about the rest, and... He'd wanted to live a different sort of life. A simpler life. But it was new.

He wondered, if he had been born without all of that marvelous privilege...

Would he have been happier?

He pulled the lapels of his jacket up around his ears and began the walk down into the city center. His apartment was up the hill above the university, and it was a nice twenty minutes or so to his job.

Yeah, I have a job, he thought. He imagined his father's pinched face across the cold table of the prison's visitation room. *That's right, Dad. I'm a fucking cleaner.*

He'd been lucky, actually. In that first week—living off the small trust fund he'd managed to cash out before leaving Baltimore—he wasn't sure how he would survive. He'd had no plan; he'd just left. After—after the tattoo, and after that odd encounter with Gardner, after he had witnessed Theo wild and degraded and out of control, he knew he couldn't... Couldn't continue the life that his father had shaped for him. Destroyed for him. And—

There was maybe a part of him, an unspoken and reviled part, which needed something from Gardner which Gardner was incapable of giving. He remembered that hand, reaching out, the way his skin almost hummed with longing. He didn't want that; he wanted it too much. Four years of hating him and wanting him and lying to himself—he needed to forget that. He needed to pretend it wasn't real.

He thought about Genni, her face when he told her that he was leaving. She'd put her hand on his shoulder and it ached with the absence of attraction, of arousal. Her eyes were clouded, sad for him and angry; and she was panicking, her own father nearly as culpable as his. She'd asked him why he was leaving but she knew the answer—most of it. And then she'd pushed him away, fierce.

"Go on." She crossed her arms, looked down, glared up at him. "Run."

So he left a curt note for his mother. He didn't want to live through another moment when she barely acknowledged him, another confirmation of her well-mannered and long-standing apathy. And he did run, he kept running, taxi to airplane to glossy black cab, and then he was here, jobless, no idea of what he was doing, and he was filled with horror, and he was free.

He found an apartment, put down a deposit, counting his money and dreading whatever catastrophe which might come next. But he had still gone out dancing and drinking, night after night, raging against uncertainty, and he usually ended up at Danny's when the pubs closed and the nightclubs opened.

His first gay club. His own place.

He nearly laughed at himself, walking along, thinking about those first moments when he could just be. Be Theo, not a Beaumont, and gay as a fucking picnic basket. It was absolutely terrifying. He'd gone a bit mad with it.

On his fifth night, he'd actually fallen asleep in the toilets, which is where the day manager found him that morning. He'd shouted and cussed, Theo had screamed a bit, and then Colin looked at him—he was probably too thin, and worn out, and pitiful—and he said, "You'd might as well make yourself useful." And he handed him a trash bag.

Theo never knew he'd be so grateful for the opportunity to clean up other people's messes.

It wasn't great money, but for now it was enough. And Colin had recently started him on other tasks—just counting up the till, but with a few hints that he might be asked to do more—and most of all he felt useful, which was an entirely new sensation.

Theo stopped off for a coffee with too much cream—the only form of calories he could consume this early—and noticed a bit of movement behind him, the feeling of interested eyes on the back of his neck. He gave a flirtatious smile and a wink to his favorite barista and turned—Theo could probably flirt with a tree if he were so inclined—but he just saw the door to the café swing shut.

He had moments like this. When he felt like he was being followed. As if his past were a person, chasing him. He didn't know if it was anxiety, or guilt, or his former certainty that he was the center of the universe, a habit he was trying to break.

Usually, that feeling edged out of his consciousness as he went through his routine. He was here, in Cork, working hard, partying harder, getting the bare minimum of sleep necessary, consuming ridiculous amounts of caffeine and nicotine. No one really knew him here—at least the Theo from Baltimore. The Beaumont. Life in Cork was rough and dirty and really quite good, as long as he had accepted that it was bad, deliciously. That for the first time the only person he was harming was himself.

But today, as he made his way toward Danny's dim doorway, he felt that thing, following him. Something that should have been left behind in Baltimore along with his family's shame.

He turned, just once, as he went into the bar.

And Jack fucking Gardner ducked around the corner.

His heart seized up, his mouth watered, and he longed for a third cigarette.

He thought about a hand, reaching out for him.

Something he should have left behind, indeed.

Chapter Eleven

"Oh my God."

Jack stared at his reflection at the menswear shop, trying on new clothes, and he felt like a complete ass. The salespeople had given him a large private dressing room with far too many mirrors, and he comforted himself with the knowledge that at least no other customers would have to see…this.

Meg had started dropping hints—not entirely nicely—that if he were to start this new bachelor life, he had better update his wardrobe. He could admit that he'd never really gotten the hang of buying clothes that fit. He just felt silly trying, even though he could afford it, and who cared if everything was perfectly tailored? But he had this coffee…engagement…with Theo, the day after tomorrow, and he wanted to—

He thought it might be good. To look nice.

"You look fine, Jack."

Meg sat on the tufted bench in the dressing room. They were trying to do the "friend" thing, and when it didn't feel painfully awkward, it felt as natural as breathing. He'd taken her with him as moral support—she had almost insisted, laughing and informing him that he shouldn't be left alone to make fashion decisions—and she was taking great pleasure in approving or vetoing every item. It wasn't exactly how he had planned the day, but it saved him from having to think about it, really.

"I—"

Popular style had moved on a bit from when he was a teenager, and he was still unsure of skinny jeans, but that seemed to be all that was available. He wore a fitted shirt which showed off his broad shoulders, and maybe he did look good, but he was thirty-seven years old, for goodness' sake.

He felt like an idiot.

Not a new feeling.

"Is this really all right?"

Meg looked at him with her critical eye and a fair amount of exasperation at his insecurities. He remembered her appraising glances before they went to Pride, and how she always thought he was handsome, if a generally ridiculous human being. "I think he'll drool all over himself, to be honest."

"Uh—" An awkward stutter.

He hadn't actually mentioned what had inspired this shopping spree. But she knew him. She always had, even though there were some things about him she really didn't.

They had such a long history together, from those early summer days at the pool to the grueling nights with wailing infants. He thought back to some of their best times, moments which somehow seemed more perfect now, since he had made the decision to leave her. Those memories hurt in such a beautiful way, because he had tried to build a life around the simplicity of childlike affection. He looked at her reflection in the mirror behind him, and he felt the weight of each day he tried to make himself into the man who could love her. He remembered—

A Japanese maple grew near the stone gate to the school, and Jack had passed under it often, enjoying the shade and few moments of leafy calm, but he hadn't climbed it until that bright day in May, his sophomore year, when he hadn't completed his chemistry homework and he needed someplace to hide for an hour.

Skipping homework was incredibly stupid, and skipping class infinitely more so. Quinn would most definitely yell at him, but he'd probably help him finish it.

Maybe a part of him thought that, if he didn't complete his homework, they wouldn't let him go home.

It was the first of May, actually, just a few more weeks of school before he'd have to pack up and return to his mom's apartment for the summer, and he looked at the tree and thought, what the hell, why not? He launched himself up into the branches, hand scrabbling against smooth bark, and once he got up there he heard a familiar, comforting voice.

"Well hello there."

Meg smiled at him, eyes closed but knowing exactly who had joined her. She was already perched in the tree, her legs propped up on a higher branch, face tilted back to the sun. Everything about her appearance was golden and sweet, lit and shadowed by the rustling red leaves, and even though he knew her so well, she seemed almost unreal, something out of a storybook.

"Um, hi."

She opened one eye. "You've found my secret spot. I don't usually see other people up here."

"Why exactly are you? Up here, I mean."

"Why not?"

He straddled a branch, feet dangling, and frowned. He supposed it was a stupid question, really, but her presence was so unexpected that he couldn't figure out what to say.

"Come here often?" He nearly bit his tongue against his even more banal question.

She laughed at him, a little unkindly, as he blushed. She closed the one eye again and smiled up at the air. "Yep."

"Oh."

"Sometimes I just need to…get away."

He thought about her good grades, about how she was so well-liked, how she fit in perfectly here when he did not. He couldn't imagine what she would need to run away from.

"So you climb a tree."

"Not every tree. Just this one. My own private getaway."

He frowned again, embarrassed. "I'm sorry to interrupt, then."

"Jack." He could see her roll her eyes, even under her closed eyelids. "I never need to get away from *you.*"

"Oh." He looked down at the ground, uncomfortable.

"So are you going to come over here and kiss me, or what?"

He looked up, a little dizzy, and saw her warm eyes wide open and inviting. Something about her gaze made him feel that his world was unsteady, known and yet unknown in a mysterious way. He felt a light sweat break out along his hairline. He wanted to climb over and give her the kisses she was practically demanding, and yet…

"Uh…"

She snorted at him, misunderstanding. "Jack Gardner, are you afraid of heights?"

He supposed that was an easy way out, and he didn't want to think about why he needed it. "Maybe."

"Fine, fine. Stay over there, you big coward."

He wanted to argue back, but then he thought… *Yes. Yeah. A total coward.*

"Just stop thinking bad thoughts." Before he could interrupt, pretend he didn't know what she meant, she continued. "You're not allowed to think bad thoughts in my tree."

He suddenly remembered the pages of homework he hadn't completed and felt a stab of guilt and anxiety in his stomach.

"Stop it, Jack."   •

"Okay. All right." He leaned back onto a thick branch and propped his feet up, mirroring her position. "What should I think about?"

"Only beautiful things. Delicious things."

He glanced over at her, and she was truly beautiful, with her red-brown hair and her toasty skin and all the things he knew about her, all the things he still didn't know. And it was May, the real first breath of spring, Baltimore before it was stifling and humid, and yeah, he had homework to do, and he'd be going home soon, and something…something was dreadfully wrong with him that he didn't want to kiss her, but—

Beautiful things.

His mind flashed on different hair, blond, and pale skin, sea-gray eyes, refined features. And if he closed his own eyes and let the image float, incorporeal, a fantasy, he could almost pretend that what he was feeling wasn't wrong at all.

He allowed himself, in that moment, to imagine a different life.

For the next two years he spent Tuesday afternoons in the Japanese maple with Meg.

It became one of the best parts of his childhood. Their childhoods.

All these years later and she was still that girl to him, even though clinging to their youthful romance was one of the worst mistakes he had ever made, and in this sorrowful and necessary abandonment of their past, he wished that they could climb a tree again.

He watched her in the mirror, and he also wished that the image behind him was blond and pale and nasty and sarcastic and wild.

He had to move forward.

He wanted Theo so badly.

He had to let go.

"What do you want, Jack?"

His shoulders tensed up in the mirror, Meg's voice breaking through the constant surge of memory that had been plaguing him more and more as he got older. He never meant to hurt her.

And he missed Theo so much that he could hardly breathe.

Could he really say it?

"I want...him."

"Well." She cleared her throat, shook her head, and rolled her eyes. "Okay. I was talking about the clothes."

Oh no.

"Meg..."

"It's fine." She looked at him for a moment, studying his flushed face, and she murmured, "I think you always have. Wanted him."

He laughed, shamefaced, but it felt incredible to have that essential and painful truth spoken out loud.

He wished he had known, back then. Had let himself know.

Though he remembered what he was like as a teenager, and had he allowed himself to fully realize his desperate attraction to Theo Beaumont he probably would have sought out professional help.

"Yeah."

"I think you should be careful, though."

She was always so concerned for him. He smiled back at her.

"If I've got the story right... I think you may have hurt him. Badly."

Or not.

He slumped. "Yeah. I know."

"Oh, Jack." She stood from the bench, came up behind him, and put her steady hands on his shoulders, standing on tiptoe. "You're going to get it right, someday."

He laughed a little. "I hope that day is really soon."

"Well…" She brushed her hands down his shoulders, smoothing out a few wrinkles as she went. "You should get this outfit, for a start. Though I think you need a little—"

She grabbed a scarf—a purple paisley, great—and arranged it around his neck. "There."

"You must be joking."

"Maybe I am." She patted his chest. "Maybe it's a little revenge." Her eyes sparkled with mischief.

He watched himself in the mirror. He could almost see that sixteen-year-old boy who climbed his first tree hiding behind his eyes.

He bought everything Meg had picked out. Even the scarf.

He knew he would never wear it, but—

It was nice. To have people who cared for him.

He hoped he had the capacity to truly care back.

This was a terrible idea.

Truth be told, he had in his life possessed many terrible ideas. Sometimes he felt like going to Gwynns was his worst ever, even though it had led to so much good. He was still, even now, an alien in that world, and he wondered if he'd ever feel like he was—

And so much of the way he'd behaved was terrible, rejecting people—and going to Pride in June, and suggesting to Meg that they sneak up to the bell tower, and following Theo into the locker room when—

But this—his idea to follow Theo yet again, in a foreign country, no less—was completely, definitely, and staggeringly terrible.

Jack leaned up against the brick building around the corner from where he'd watched Theo duck into a closed club. His heart was racing and his hands were sweaty. He rubbed his dry eyes, still sandy from the few snatches of sleep he caught on the train.

It was a miracle that he'd found Theo at all.

He'd wandered for quite a while after stepping off the train, and found himself ducking into a small café, desperate for coffee. It never occurred to him that he'd be able to find Theo (even if he had fully admitted to himself that he was looking for him) on the first morning of the very first day—it was as if the universe decided to give him what he had wanted, but without any adequate preparation. He wondered if his life was just destined to be him, bumbling along, finding trouble at the most inopportune of moments.

God, his hair was probably a mess. Jack stood up straight and caught his reflection in a shop window. "Fuck."

He tried, without success, to flatten his hair.

He slumped. Oh well.

Why on earth had he decided to do this? He shook his head to clear it and decided that his little—this odd turn of events—was a problem for a different Jack. Some later version of himself who'd maybe gotten a few more hours of sleep. And breakfast.

It was still early, barely anyone passing him on the sidewalk. He stuck his left hand in his pocket and used the right to lift his suitcase again, and realized that if he didn't want to sleep on the street—in an unfamiliar city, no less—he'd have to find someplace to stay.

God bless that check from Franklin.

So he walked.

He'd noticed very little, stumbling to the café, and noticed nothing at all after seeing Theo's shining blond hair. But now he took stock of the city, just on the edge of wakefulness. The air was fresh, with a hint of damp, like a cool bath on a hot day. It felt like a city that came alive at night—he noticed pub crammed up next to pub, boxes of red flowers lining gold-painted windows. White and purple weeds bloomed between the gray stones of a low wall, a river running through, down past a hill and deeper into the city. And he still had that sense of something magical, something bigger than himself, a voice which whispered, *Yes.*

This is where you are supposed to be.

He crossed the river, took a turn—entirely on some unknown instinct—and found himself in front of a large Victorian building. The Metropole Hotel.

It looked cozy, though much, much nicer than he was used to, and he shrugged as if to say, *What the hell. I've got the money. And it's probably cheaper than London or Paris.* He checked in, heart skipping a beat as he heard the price, that old instinct of never spending anything because there was nothing to spend.

Once he'd gotten into his room, he fell immediately onto soft white linen and down-stuffed pillows.

I've come a long way from that damned filthy bedroom, he thought.

Before he sank into sleep, he remembered flashes of golden hair and pale skin, and he was too tired to question the soft smile that he pressed into the mattress.

He woke hours later, groggy but energized. He had slept through most of the day, and in an uncharacteristic surrender to luxury he called down for room service. A ridiculous amount of food, actually, all so fresh and wholesome, cream and butter and tender pastry. Fully fed and well rested, he opened his overstuffed case.

He remembered that he had let Dare pick out his new clothes.

He knew now that he was going to kill him.

Years of wearing hand-me-downs and secondhand uniforms left him…unaccustomed to clothes which fit properly. He picked out a few items, struggling to get them on. And maybe it was just him, but it seemed a bit unnecessary that his jeans hug his butt (and such) with this level of, um, snugness.

The shirt wasn't much better. He could see, as he stared in the bathroom mirror, the muscles he'd put on over four years of lacrosse and dining hall meals. He wasn't—it wasn't obscene or anything, but he was a lot more fit than he had been after fourteen years with his mom and the meager paychecks which fed her and never seemed to feed him.

He looked—well, he looked good.

He remembered an exotic combination of body glitter and eyeliner.

And he was uncomfortable.

But that wasn't exactly new.

And now he stood, regarding himself in his too-tight clothes, debating his next steps.

It wouldn't be weird, would it? He was eighteen, and he'd been pretty preoccupied with struggling and scraping by for basically his whole life, so it would make sense, wouldn't it, for him to go to a nightclub. And he did know where a nightclub was, after all—and the fact that he knew about that because he'd seen Theo go in was just a coincidence.

And if he saw Theo, that would be…good. He shook his head. Fine. It would be fine.

He had been right about Cork coming alive at night. Young people spilled out of every doorway, it seemed—university-aged men with cigarettes hanging at the corners of their mouths, the women with them in neon high heels and shockingly short skirts. It was loud and jarring and rich with scents, cologne, sweat, bright red geraniums, clove and hashish. And no one seemed to look at him, as he ducked through crowds and kept his eyes wide open. He was just another kid, out on a Saturday night, not wonderful, remarkable, cursed at, coveted.

Just him. Just Jack.

He took a deep breath before opening the door to the club. Theo's club.

I'm going to do this, he thought, and he set his shoulders. *For no particular reason.*

Music slammed into him like a punch to his gut. It was dark, that darkness pierced by flashes of colored lights reflecting on shimmering bodies coated in soft glitter. The dance floor was packed, people writhing against each other, and it was three deep at the bar.

And he needed a drink, he thought, suddenly, if he was going to get through this.

Fifteen minutes later and he'd acquired some sort of blue concoction which tasted like coconut and orange. He tried to take small sips, pacing himself, and then he noticed—

Oh. Most of the people on the dance floor were men.

Very attractive men.

He drank half his cocktail at once.

Hard, lean muscle skimmed and slipped, hands dipping into the backs of trousers. Tousled hair brushed against arched necks as bodies were embraced from behind. All that glitter—eyes lined with midnight blue shadow seemed to speak of promises, intent. Some of what he saw could be called dancing, and it was—it was almost carefully coordinated, like the ballet, like war, and it was filthy like fucking, and Jack cursed as his mouth remembered the taste of purple gelatin, and his jeans felt even tighter.

No, no. Please, he thought, *this was not—not what I was looking for.*

He finished his drink.

And then he saw him.

Theo was, of course, in the middle of the press of bodies, and he shone brighter than anyone there. If the other dancers were like ballet, he was like flying. The soft fall of his hair was disheveled—Jack had never seen it like this, because his hair had always been so meticulously styled—and brushing over his eyes. His long limbs wrapped around the neck of a shorter brunet in front of him; muscled arms twined around him, from behind, as another man grinded against his back. And he was breathing, heavy, the way Jack had started to breathe—Jack's exhale was Theo's inhale, and Jack wanted to feel that breath on the soft skin below his jaw, and exchange something with him, blows, barbs, something more, something he had never let himself think about.

Something he had felt when he had glared at Theo on the lacrosse field, or watched him twirling his pen between long fingers in class, or when staring through shadows at a pained and hungry face, and—

Something he had tried to lock in his bedroom as he left, those summers home from school when he couldn't sleep and he shoved his hand down and bit his left knuckles and—

Theo was turning toward him.

Jack ran.

He pushed through more muscled bodies and ran to the toilets, blessedly empty. He leaned over the sink and breathed, breathed, tried to screw up his eyes against what he had already seen.

Get it together, Jack. Stop. Just—

The door opened behind him. Jack kept his eyes closed. He heard the door swing shut again, and then he heard it lock.

"I suppose I should be gratified that it's you having a meltdown this time, Gardner."

Oh, fuck.

"Nothing to say?"

Jack turned around, fast enough to make him dizzy, and clenched his hands into fists.

"Hmm." Theo looked unimpressed. "Going to hit me again?"

Theo stood there, calm, leaning against the wall. Hands in his pockets. Unthreatening.

He was stunning.

"Leave me alone, Th—Beau."

He laughed, damn him. "I think I should be telling you to leave me alone. I don't remember inviting you here."

Jack's hands were beginning to shake, he was holding those fists so hard. "I didn't—"

Theo scoffed. "Did you really imagine that I didn't spot you this morning?"

Jack felt his face grow hot. Theo smirked. "Your appalling hair is really hard to miss, you know."

Jack flushed even more. "What are you doing here?"

Jack heard his own voice—too loud, rough. He meant—he didn't know what he meant. Here, in Cork? In what seemed to be a gay bar? In the toilets, with him?

"You—" Theo's eyes were wide. "What am I... Gardner, this is... Oh, honestly." Then he rolled his eyes. "Hit me or don't. Just—relax, for God's sake, and figure out what to do with your hands."

Jack had the sudden and utterly mortifying urge to laugh.

"Fine." Theo removed his hands from his pockets, standing up straight. "I'll make it easy for you."

"Wha—"

"Maybe you want to see it better, hmm? Where to aim."

It was like a dream—a nightmare.

Theo moved forward like something liquid and slippery, and he stopped just inches away from Jack—Jack could feel the heat of him, and his breath, and he clenched his fists again because he couldn't let himself—and Theo leaned in and said:

"Look, Gardner. Look at what you did."

Jack looked, really looked.

Theo's lip—how had he never noticed—he was horrified.

He wanted to touch him.

Chapter Twelve

It had been eighteen years since he'd been in a gay bar, and Theo thought that they must have been a lot more enjoyable when he was nineteen.

Genni had declared him "far too desperate, sweetheart" as poker night drew to a close, and Phil had offered to take him down to Grand Central in Mount Vernon. Genni had picked out his clothes—it certainly had been a long time since he'd dressed to pull—and he felt beautiful and fashionable and unaccountably shy. His shirt was unbuttoned just enough to show the top of his chest, the hollow of his throat, and he felt, for some reason, entirely naked.

Music pumped through the dark space, and Theo felt that some late-night element was missing until he realized there was no cigarette smoke clouding the dance floor. Times had moved forward, and so had he, and yet a part of him remained stuck, frozen in the past, a young man filled with panic and need and a longing for Jack's body pressed against his own.

"Here you are." Phil handed him his martini on the rocks, and he debated drinking it all in one great gulp; maybe drunkenness would make this easier. There was a clashing of things—cologne, and dim lights, and the music in this space pressed down, compacted by the music of the lesbian bar upstairs. He was surrounded by men, kids as young as he had been, and men his own age, every body type, and he got looks from everyone, assessing, and a part of him was aroused even as he was uncomfortable.

Maybe he should just—for so long he had denied himself this. Closeness. He hadn't wanted to let anyone near him; he didn't want to open that door.

Phil was cool, energy coiled in his muscles, as he drank his scotch, and his eyes flitted from man to man. His refined features garnered looks, too; some of the bar's patrons gazed at them both, wondering. Wondering if they were together; hoping they were a package deal. And he had thought about that once—Phil was so handsome, so striking, some deep pulsing of attraction for his friend within him, but he couldn't. Genni would kill them both, even though Theo knew full well that they sometimes brought…additional friends into their bedroom. There was too much between them all. And he imagined that kissing Phil, such a close companion, would be about as thrilling as kissing a potted plant.

"I don't know what I'm doing here." Theo turned toward the bar, his back to all the men dancing behind him. He was tense, quiet; Phil sat with him and put a hand on his arm.

"I know." He sipped his drink. "But we thought it might be good. To try."

Theo laughed a little into his gin, poked the sliced lime with his cocktail straw. "Try what?"

Phil gave him a long, incisive stare.

"I'm not some poor middle-aged man finding out about his sexuality too late. I already know—have known—"

"Of course." Phil swiveled on his barstool, and Theo followed, gazing into the crowd.

There was freedom, here, if he chose to grasp at it. So many attractive men, here in this conclave, and he thought about pulling someone into a dark corner, or taking someone home, shocking his mother and not caring, really, about the look on her face. And so much of him wanted—he wanted to be touched. He craved it, always had, this sense of closeness.

And it had been easy when he was younger, in the brief time before Jack came; he'd thrilled at the casual nature of anonymous sex. It rendered him nameless, just a body, just a mouth to fill. It had been hot and numbing and satisfying. An itch he had always needed to scratch. He was aroused by possibilities and disgusted by the reality, disgusted by himself. He'd lost the ability, the knack. He leaned back against the bar, hot eyes on all the things he wouldn't let himself have, and he prevaricated.

"Not like anyone here would want to go home with me." The gin and vermouth sweetened around the lie in his mouth.

"Oh, right." Phil rolled his eyes, managing to look even more handsome in the plebian gesture. "That must be why everyone in the place can't stop staring."

Theo knew that, and flushed. "That's just my body. Nothing to do with me."

"Your body needs things, too."

He shook the ice in his glass, looking down. He could feel Phil's stare on his cheek. "Yeah."

"Have you really never—"

"No. Not since—then."

"Hmm." Phil finished his drink, lifted his elegant fingers for another. "You're overdue."

"I'm not unfaithful." As if that had been the real reason why he hadn't—

"Right, you have all of these monogamy ideas." A false shudder.

Theo snorted. "It's not a dirty word, you know."

Phil picked up his new glass, clinked it with Theo's. "I suppose."

"Phil, I just can't—I couldn't—"

"But you can now, love. Maybe you should."

He felt the gin in him, and the Manhattans they'd shared back at his house, and there was a dizziness, not from the alcohol but from feeling he was up on a ledge, high, moments from flying. A vertigo of choices. Of a future laid out in front of him, uncharted, unplanned. He felt his pulse in his throat, exposed, beating at a different rate than the bass of the music, off-tempo and mad.

He missed Jack so much that he could slap someone. Slap himself.

"I just want you to see that there are more options, if you want them." Phil nodded at a young man, dark-haired with a crooked smile, who'd been darting his eyes over, hungry. "Don't you think you could want someone else? It would be simple. You wouldn't have any trouble finding—"

"Have you ever wanted anyone other than Genni?"

Phil lifted an eyebrow.

"For more than one night, I mean."

It was Phil's turn to stare into his drink, half a frown and then a warm, shy smile on his face. "No."

"It wouldn't be simple for me."

"It's not simple for me, either." Phil pursed his lips, "But I know that I'll always need—I've never had any shame about this."

"I wish that it were just shame." Theo shrugged, unhappy. "Shame I could deal with, or at least reconcile. But—"

"You still want him. He's the one."

He hated hearing it. The idea seemed so childish. "What did it feel like? Before you and Genni—"

"Mm." Phil aimed a lazy smile over at a rowdy group taking shots, inspiring a bit of a sputter from a man in a tight tank top. "You know. I wanted her, wanted to be hers. And I was willing to wait."

"Yeah."

"But I had hope, Theo. I'm not sure if you do."

Theo's heart kept beating, too hard, in the back of his throat. "Maybe I'm meant to be alone."

"No one should be alone."

He was suddenly angry. Why was Phil pushing this? It was too—it was unfair.

"Life isn't perfect for everyone, Phillippe. Not everyone gets their happy ending."

Phil was unmoved by his tone, implacable, like a stone wall holding back high tide. "You're right. I still think you deserve one, though."

Theo thought about the nasty person he had always been, and that feeling in him which meant hating everyone, and that desire to throw things and make a mess and ruin his life and be his own ruination. He'd tried, tried to be good, tried to be more; he feared himself. And maybe that was why Jack had—

That last fight, when he said those things, reverting to a self he thought he'd buried—

"God, do I?"

Phil swallowed the last of his scotch. "You do."

Theo laughed a little, bitter, finished his own drink.

"You're not going to pull tonight. Never intended to." Phil put his glass down, ice rattling.

"No." Quiet, guilty. "I'm sorry."

"Oh well." Phil's teeth shone against his lips as he smiled. "Worth a try. And I've gotten a good view of the merchandise."

"You're incorrigible."

Phil stood, tossed down a fifty-dollar bill, winked at the bartender. "I am what I am."

Theo was, too. All these years later—he was the same.

They wound their way through the crowd, and Theo felt

like the night was grabbing at him, all of these hands and hips and mouths, and each brush of someone else's body was like fire, like life, like dying, all at the same time.

It had been so long. His skin was ravenous.

He remembered another nightclub, and the cold concrete of the toilet floor, and looking up into blue eyes.

The foul-fresh air of Baltimore at nighttime jolted into him as they stepped out of the dark and into the glimmer of street-lights. Phil's dark skin was rich and flawless in the glow, his own pale and wan and aching. He went home, as always, alone.

God, how he wanted.

Gardner was half a breath away from his face.

He had seen his retreating back and had known that back as intimately as if he had clung to it before, and he watched him as he ran into the toilets, looking like he might be sick. It was familiar; he remembered those brittle and blinding moments at Pride, the opening of his mouth, the look on Gardner's face before he ran away then.

He had never considered the possibility that Gardner might want him back. And even if he did—even if he were reading him correctly, the tortured frame, the wide eyes—Gardner might be too scared to do anything about it. That golden image corrupted.

Theo had stopped being scared of so many things. He had chosen to fly and he had already fallen.

He was slid up between two bodies, had considered pulling one of them into the toilets, and he was nearly fully aroused, and he wanted neither of them. He knew, had known, what he wanted, and he thrilled with the possibility that he might—and that Gardner might—

And he wanted to follow him, and press him up against the

sinks, an echo of that day in the locker room, a heavy breathing and a hatred and a want. His lip burned.

Two selves struggled in him. The protective, the cautious and cruel, and the self which couldn't care at all, anymore, about his own safety. The self that flung him into a fire, disregarding the burn, heedless of the consequences of this mania, this need. He knew that if he followed Gardner into the toilets, he wouldn't come out the same person; he had never liked himself that much, anyway.

This was just one more way to burn.

He smiled, filthy, at the man in front of him, and reached back to run his fingers, final and regretful, through the other man's hair. He detached himself. His whole body was buzzing as if there were some electric connection through space, through bodies and colored light and the toilet door, between him and Gardner, that boy, that man.

He had stopped at the bar, savoring this moment before he would be so epically stupid, took a shot.

And now, in front of Gardner, the smell of citrus and coconut on his lips, and whiskey in his own mouth, he breathed out, daring him. Daring him to look. *This is what you did to me*, he thought.

This is what you do to me.

Gardner's pupils were fully blown, just a thin ring of sapphire around the deep black, and his chest was rising and falling like something snapped up in a trap. Theo had the power and the control for the first time, what he'd wanted ever since that first meeting in the dorms, and yet he felt hypnotized in this moment, some wild animal caught in a floodlight. He couldn't tell, really, who was on top—didn't know which one of them would win this silence, a long-overdue confrontation.

Heat poured off Gardner and he felt boiled, he felt nuclear, he wanted to lick it and eat it and warm himself, and those eyes were on his face, that place on his lip which he tongued, over and over, keeping a link to that violence, his weakness, a moment of unwilling submission.

How many nights had he lain in his bed in his private room at Gwynns, licking over his lip, remembering Gardner under his pressing hand, his flesh rising and responding and—

He had told himself he just got off on the power of that moment when he was holding someone down.

And the silent encounter in the bell tower, and Pride, and feeling beholden, and wanting to lie down with a heavy body resting on his.

His mouth was watering from the harshness of the whiskey and from thinking about—about other things, other bits and pieces he could pour into him, filling, mindless, a body. Skin, hardness in his throat. He kept Gardner there, Gardner's fists clenched, his mouth partly opened with his heavy breath. Gardner was holding himself back and leaning into him, his face drawing closer as he was pulled in by that scar.

He felt a tingling, his face down to his knees, like he knew what he wanted to do, falling, asking, opening. It had been this way, always, even when he didn't know, really, what this feeling was. He'd kept himself from touching Gardner as much as he possibly could, and his skin sang with these echoing seconds before he finally gave in.

It was sex and it was something else.

Here in his nightclub, the space he had claimed as his own, he knew he was creating a new kind of scar; he was slicing himself up on the honed edge of Gardner's eyes. It was a tragic mistake, it was so terribly stupid, and it felt absolutely wonderful, and he hated himself. And that was his life, wasn't it? That was how he was made, how he functioned. He could hardly bear himself; the urge was too strong.

God, his jeans were so tight, it was painful, and he reveled in it, and he leaned in farther, tilting his head down in those scant inches, and he waited. Watched Jack, watched him lick his own lips. Theo spoke nearly into his mouth.

"Like what you see?"

He felt a dark smile, an invitation, a plea.

"This is all you."

Chapter Thirteen

Jack was surrounded by music.

He and Meg had season tickets to the Baltimore Symphony Orchestra, and they had box seats hanging over the stage, and Meg was in a pretty dress, long lines and bare shoulders. He'd taken off the clothes he'd bought this afternoon and armed himself in one of his nondescript suits, the customary polka-dotted bow tie snug at his neck. He remembered a pale hand, collaring him.

As they dressed for the symphony, Meg still teased him about his clothes, and if there was a little sadness in the routine— a little heaviness between her eyebrows—it was just a part of this new life. Some necessary stage between the past and the future. An intermission.

Tonight was the Piano Concerto No. 5, E flat major, Beethoven. He could almost feel the pianist's fingers as they made precise love to the keys. The conductor was energetic, dynamic, and the violinists' arms were cutting through the air, tight, practiced. These seats invited them into the over-whelming frenzy, into the lulling sweetness, and he was a part of it, experiencing an auditory climax. He thought about the DJs at Danny's, the way they had woven in all of those electric sounds like some elaborate approximation of fucking.

Meg moved her hand on the chair to grasp his. She pulled it back, frowning. Set her shoulders, offered it again. He wrapped his large fingers around her own. It did feel like friendship, and nothing more.

How long had that been the case?

Forever, the music sang out. For all of time.

He couldn't help but lose himself and his control in the music, sucked into it and thrumming, and he imagined being here with Theo instead, his impeccable clothes, his soft hair. Sneaking over dirty looks. A life he'd been so scared of. Cocktails in the lounge, all of those experiences between them, taking their youth in the clubs forward into this, adulthood, music to enjoy which hurt in a new way.

Sliding a hand up his lithe leg. Wondering how much they could get away with, here, on display.

He felt a thin sweat on his hand now, and gave Meg a squeeze before he let go. She closed her eyes, surrendering. Such a world he had built.

He knew other people in other box seats, faces he'd smiled at, names he'd made himself remember, important people whose money he managed. He and Meg had dined with them, charity dinners, and danced; they were married within the scope of a society he didn't, after all, want to be in. They looked good. They loved each other.

Outside was a spitting autumn rain, ozone, that smell of concrete, and they were damp, but the music here was so scalding that he almost felt steam rising from him. That chilled place had begun to boil, at least for the moment. He was syrupy, occupying this space, sliding into hot water, piano and cello and upright bass.

He felt that warmth gather low in him. He couldn't stop; he was alive, awoken.

Soon he would see him.

He hadn't known that the absence of something could hurt like this, like a crucial part of a symphony unplayed.

Meg's eyes had opened, and she was watching him, and she saw it all on his too-naked face, and she pitied him. She didn't have it in her to be angry, not really, because he'd stuttered it all out, all of it, in that horrible conversation when he'd spilled himself to her. And she—she understood it all, even this lie he had told, because she did love him. But he had hurt her, and here they were, in a usual place, doing this usual thing, and all he could think about was Theo. And she knew.

Theo lived in his head—the Theo from the nightclub, and from their bed; the Theo who almost broke his nose, and the Theo who kissed him. But it was another Theo who was so dangerous, because it was a man he claimed as his own now, in this new life, a Theo who was a father, a Theo he could go to the symphony with. A Theo borne entirely of his imagination, a fantasy, a silvered scar faded with time. It was that Theo, a golem, who'd broken up his marriage.

He had no idea if that person existed at all.

Beethoven eased into him, as seductive as the heavy beat of the dance floor. He lost himself.

He dreamed.

Music blasted into the toilets, pounding into his chest.

Jack was still, trying not to reach out, trying not to touch that place—that imperfection—trying not to run his fingers over newly discovered roughness.

Theo was so close, smelling like alcohol and sweat and vanilla.

"Like what you see? This is all you."

Theo's face had always been perfect, but now—now there was a silvery scar bisecting his upper lip, and Jack remembered with a visceral pull that horrible fight, the most profound act of brutality he had ever committed.

And now, here in this shadowed bathroom, lights flickering, he saw the results of his anger—that silvery scar on Theo's lip, and he knew that he'd be wearing Jack's mark as long as he would bear the tattooed wings he'd spotted at Pride on his back. Jack's violence would always be a part of him.

Something in Jack's jeans twitched.

What the fuck.

Theo's eyes widened. "You do, don't you? Like what you see."

There was a cold sweat on the back of Jack's neck. "No, I— look, I'm sorry, I—"

"I don't think you are. I think you liked doing this to me, Gardner." Theo spat his name, backing away an inch, then smirked. "I think you want me on my knees for you."

The air was entirely still. A heavy bass thrummed around them. The lights flickered, graffiti shining on the walls.

And Theo Beaumont dropped to the floor.

Oh, Christ.

"You've always wanted this, haven't you, Gardner? Me, submitting to you. Begging. Groveling."

Theo moved forward until he was right there, below Jack. Jack stared down at his upturned face, his irises almost entirely black.

"Go on, Gardner. Here I am." He threw his arms out. "You going to hit me? Make me bleed for you?"

Theo leaned in, just those last few inches, and breathed hotly against Jack's jeans. He looked up at him, breathtaking, from under golden lashes.

"Or is there something else?"

Jack had stopped breathing, that must have been it—that was why he was so dizzy, and why he gasped out, "Fuck, Beau."

Theo laughed. And then rubbed his pale, smooth face against Jack's denim-encased prick—which was harder than it had ever been.

This was not how he expected this evening to go.

That's what he told himself.

"God, you just had to be hung, didn't you?" Theo muttered entirely to himself. "How the fuck are you fitting in those jeans?"

Jack was in extreme danger of falling over.

"Should I get you out of them?"

He couldn't remember, later, if he nodded, but he would always remember the whimper which was unmistakable for, "Yes, please, fuck."

Theo slid his hands up Jack's legs, slow, agonizing, and reached the button of his jeans.

And then he caught Jack's eyes, and grinned. "Well, I'm not going to."

He stood, too quick for Jack to catch the movement, and walked to unlock the door.

"I don't know why you followed me here, Gardner. Maybe you're having some sort of post-school crisis—frankly, I don't particularly care.

"But if you come back, it'll be you begging." The lock clicked, and Theo turned back and fucking winked. "And I won't stop."

The door to the toilets slammed closed.

The walk back to Jack's hotel went very quickly and took far too long.

He nearly fell on his face trying to pull down the too-tight jeans, but when he wrapped his hand around his swollen, neglected prick, it took two swift pulls before he came, shuddering, imagining Theo's filthy red mouth.

Chapter Fourteen

Dear God, Genni was right: he *was* stupid. Why was he here?

Theo sat on a bench in the park next to the Washington Monument on Charles Street. He'd sat down because he'd been pacing for far too long, and he needed something else to do with himself before people started to give him funny looks.

He walked past the coffee shop first, of course, fifteen minutes early, and then realized that Jack was sitting there, back to the window, and even his back was familiar—those clean, broad lines—and he thought he might be sick.

Thirty-seven seemed too old to feel like a schoolboy with a crush. But he apparently had no control over—

A couple walked by, holding hands, a poodle leashed to one of their wrists. They were maybe in their sixties, a little chubby with it, and worn rings glinted on their fourth fingers. He wondered how long they had been together before they got married—if they had called themselves husbands even when they weren't seen by the rest of the world. The shorter man laughed, and the taller stooped down to kiss him, and their dog made a canine huffing noise like happiness.

Theo felt like hitting something.

Fuck Jack Gardner.

He hadn't thought that the world could change. He hadn't thought that he could change. His youth was so truncated by his own choices, and he could hardly remember why—why he

had felt such an urgent need to marry, to reproduce, to assim-
ilate. In Ireland he had been so free, so defiant, and it wasn't
easy there, but it was so good. But the Theo who came home
let go of those things. Buried them without giving himself
the grace to mourn. He had blamed his mother, but looking
back at that young man, looking at all the years since then,
he felt exhausted by what was very likely his own cowardice.
Maybe his greed—maybe the family money changed him.
Maybe he was, after all, his father's son.

And Jack—he had really thought that Jack had cared for
him. That he could be loved for the person he truly was.
Finding out that that inexplicable happiness was a lie was—

He really wanted a cigarette right now, even though he
hadn't smoked in almost seventeen years.

Kids from the art school around the corner huddled on another bench, flirting and cursing and being young, and he
could hear the traffic all around him, smell city smells like
smoke and urine and stone and plants, and the early-October
air was still warm like the end of summer screaming out against
the oncoming chill. Theo pulled his jacket tighter around him
despite the warmth, the collar up against his neck, and he ran
his tongue along the inside of his mouth in that habit he had
since he was eighteen.

Baltimore was all around him, in that fecund and foul in-
terplay of life and decay, and he thought about Cork and the
way it had seemed so alive—even at two in the morning, all
the kids lined up to get fast food, eating fried chicken sand-
wiches and letting the grease soak up the booze. Everything
seemed so bright there, and it was just as blinding here, sometimes, but he missed it, oh God, he longed for the life he had
before real life reasserted itself.

Before he started hiding. Before he came home. Before
Jack left.

It seemed almost like a dream. Like he hadn't done any of those things. He'd signed his soul away—for the Beaumont family, for a wife, to have a child, to fix everything, to deny himself because it was just so much easier—and maybe that Theo who lived in Cork with Jack Gardner in his bed had never really existed at all.

But Jack was waiting for him in the coffee shop, his shoulders strong, his hair going just a little bit gray. Jack was evidence—Jack was proof.

Theo closed his eyes. How much was he willing to fuck his life up, now?

He remembered when Jack had asked him the question—the question that many newly out or not quite out yet people probably asked—when did you know?

"When was the first time you—when did you realize you were…different?"

They were sitting on the stoop outside his apartment building, smoking and drinking from bottles of pear cider, five in the afternoon and pregaming for a night out.

"You're just digging for compliments, aren't you?"

Jack rolled his eyes, shook his head.

"I could blather on about a certain oddly attractive black-haired asshole. I'm not naming any names." Jack laughed. "But I think I always knew."

"I always thought—you and Genni—"

"Yeah." He took a drag from his cigarette. "I thought me and Genni, too. She certainly thought it. But there was always something—"

"Missing," Jack spoke, looking somewhere in the distance.

"Yeah." Theo scowled, still feeling bad about leading his best friend on. "I thought I could make that work."

"But?"

"But."

"Mm."

"You?"

Jack frowned, looked down at his lap. "I guess—I—I never got the chance to think about it. And there was always—"

There were things he wasn't saying, and he didn't say her name, some sort of mutual agreement to make them both comfortable.

"I'm not very good at the whole feelings thing." Jack said it lightly, self-mockery covering discomfort. Insecurity.

"I wouldn't have known."

"Nice."

"I guess it doesn't really matter, in the end."

Jack looked at him, questioning.

"What difference does it make? We know now, right? And we can—" Theo gestured with his cigarette. "Live."

"Yeah." Jack smiled, slow, but there was something reserved about it, like he didn't know if he could believe it, yet.

And it turned out, of course, that he didn't believe it. He'd lied.

Theo pushed himself back against the bench, feet planted, and he held on to that disappointment, and the feeling of being young and ripped apart, and tried not to think about how wonderful it had felt, then, to live.

Maybe he shouldn't have put all of that away. Maybe he should have tried with someone else. Maybe he should have taken someone home, that last night with Phillippe.

Maybe he should have forgotten Jack Gardner and his stupid hair and his utter selfishness and the way he loved—

"Ugh." Theo's voice was too loud, and an older woman walking her Yorkie jumped. How embarrassing.

He stood up, lifted his head, relaxed his shoulders back. Held himself tall.

He walked across the street, put his hand on the door to

the coffee shop, and put on the blank face that had kept him
sane and made him despise himself for almost twenty years.

His eyes found Jack immediately. Jack didn't see him—he
was talking to the barista, an awkward smile and a flush as
they spoke, those blue eyes wide and shy and so beloved.

He wondered if Jack had ever—if he had let someone else,
someone like the barista or a friend or a stranger in a nightclub—
if it had really been just sex, all that time.

He heard the barista's flirting, and saw Jack's clumsy smile,
and Theo's heart shattered into a million pieces.

"Again, please."

Nine thirty and the sun was just beginning to set. The
Thirsty was packed with American exchange students, and
Theo was going shot for shot with a short, curvaceous girl
with a Long Island accent. She was covered with tattoos, and
he'd pulled off his own shirt to show her the wings he'd gotten as soon as he turned eighteen.

All healed now, the tattoo was still his gift to himself. God
knew his parents had nothing to give him. And he had wanted
to—to rebel, and say fuck you, and the girl here in the bar ran
her fingers over his back and he thought, *Yeah, this is me.* Damaged, marked. What a relief to have the inside on the outside.

Gwilim at the bar was making some layered concoction
of grenadine, blue curaçao, and Goldschläger. Theo could
feel the alcohol starting to course through him, and he felt at
his back pocket for his crumpled pack of menthol cigarettes.
Wednesday night, trad about to start, and he hoped he'd be
just drunk enough to shake off the memories of last night.

He licked his lips, feeling gold leaf under his tongue, and he
thought about tight jeans and a thick cock and the look on his
face, pained and desperate and hungry, and the way his own

mouth watered, and the brief moment when he'd considered unzipping those trousers, and—

It felt like he'd always wanted Jack Gardner.

And he didn't know when wanting him bruised and bloody and shamed, on the floor or in the locker room or in the class-room, changed into—into the other thing, the hidden thing, the thing that kept him up at night. Maybe it really was prom, maybe it was earlier—but it seemed like it happened all at once, naturally, like water breaking through a dam to revert to its natural course. And then he couldn't think of Gardner without imagining what it would feel like to have him under him and in him, to hold his hands down, to pull him into dark corners, to have him whisper, *Please.*

The curvaceous girl, Annie, held up another red, white, and blue shot. They cheered—a muddled "Slainte!"—and tossed them back. Gwilim rolled his eyes and set up the next round.

Theo had needed a few hours away from the club—he hoped that Danny's wouldn't now remind him of looking up at Gardner from the cold concrete of the toilet floors. So he came here, to The Thirsty, Wednesday night with the band and the kids who seemed so much younger than he felt. A palate cleanser, like parsley sorbet between rich courses of duck fat and cream.

He looked over at the guitar player, who flushed under his hot gaze, and he let himself remember the night when he first discovered this bar—another Wednesday—and the way those steel-string calloused fingers scraped the soft skin of his hips, the way his hot mouth opened and enveloped Theo, the way his voice was roughened as he sang "Fisherman's Blues."

Another relief, to have it fully confirmed, proven, that this was who he was, and this was what he needed.

Maybe tonight, when the bar closed down at midnight, maybe he'd take that nameless guitarist and—

Theo pulled back. As delightful as that sounded, it suddenly didn't seem like it was enough.

Fuck Gardner, he thought. *Fuck.*

"Come on, can't quit now!"

Shot number four. Annie gasped at the toxic combination, then reached up and pulled him into a sloppy kiss.

Laughing, he pulled away, leaning down to whisper, "I don't like girls, sorry."

"I don't like boys, darlin', but you just looked so sad."

He looked down at her, surprised. She shrugged, and then he shrugged back.

The band started up in earnest, and by now all the students had memorized the set, all the words of the oft-repeated songs, and the room was filled with the not altogether in tune shout-singing of drunken voices. Annie started in on a bottle of Bulmers pear cider, and Theo leaned back against the bar and just—watched.

They all seemed so painfully young.

He had no legitimate right to think that, but as he observed clumsy flirtation and excessive drinking and a bit of groping in dark corners, he wondered if any of these kids knew, had even the slightest perception of how their worlds could end so easily. The way his had. He figured that they all had their own stories—heartbreak, boyfriends and girlfriends back home that they pretended they weren't cheating on, parents who maybe didn't love them enough (but did, really), papers to write and promises to keep.

But he—his life had been destroyed by the person he had been taught to worship without question, his father, the criminal, violent and hated and feared and idolized, and it seemed like too much to bear. Were they raging against that kind of pain, too?

Had they been so deeply hurt for so much longer than they wanted to admit?

And how many of them knew, intimately, what it felt like to stare up at a stupid, poverty-stricken boy with slightly crooked teeth and a huge fucking prick, it turned out, and realize that—that they were never going to be who they were supposed to be?

All of those dreams broken.

He was sickened by his own self-pity. He couldn't stop himself.

He looked at Annie's sweet, round face, and imagined turning his adolescent cruelty on her, the genetic code of denigration and spite that he'd inherited, the weakness in him that was self-hatred turned outward.

In many ways, he had been a monster.

The grenadine grew sickly sweet in his mouth. He ordered a shot of Jameson and loved the burn, like punishment, like cauterization, like a flaming brand of his sins and the way to forget them.

He couldn't stay here.

He wanted to sweat it all out, all the alcohol and all the pain, and then he wanted to drink it up again and vomit it up at sunrise.

Danny's was busy for a Wednesday. He wasted no time getting to the center of the dance floor, and he let his body move, almost mindlessly, to the bass which seemed to echo in his chest. He felt eyes on him from every direction, and he let himself experience fear and rage against it, reveling in the danger of possibilities. A pain he could control. Another pain he inflicted on himself.

Some of the eyes were more intense than others. The closely cropped hair on the back of his neck prickled, and he licked his lips, and he knew without needing to look that Jack Gardner had come back.

But he did look.

And there he was, in another tight T-shirt—blue this time to match his eyes, Jesus fuck, so gorgeous like every secret fantasy Theo'd ever had—and a pair of dark wash jeans that did absolutely nothing to hide—

Fuck fuck fuck, how he wanted. And it looked like Gardner wanted, too. It was too much, and he had to have it.

Their eyes were locked. Gardner tilted his head, a gesture, *come here.* Theo smirked, performing, trying to regain some sense of control, and shook his head, and crooked one finger.

You come, he thought. *Give the fuck in.*

And then he thought he might choke on the off-time thumping of his heart as Gardner did.

Gardner was none too gentle getting through the crowd. He shoved aside the man—entirely forgotten—in front of Theo, getting a bitchy look and then a hasty retreat in response. And Theo couldn't blame the man. Gardner looked, for once in his life, a solid, confident threat. He was thick with muscle and taller than Theo remembered him, and there was something dark behind his eyes.

Something that screamed.

And then Gardner stopped, stood still, and those cobalt eyes flashed, once, and then shied away.

Ha, Theo thought. *Not as tough as you pretend.*

This was his world.

He was in control here.

He thought that, defiant, and ignored the voice which mocked him—a voice that sounded too much like his father— saying that he was weak, that he would never be normal, that he could never resist Jack Gardner. *So the fuck what,* he nearly shouted back, *just let me, let me—*

He reached out, one hand on the back of Gardner's neck, one hand low around his hip.

Let me have him.

Gardner shook, a fine trembling, and Theo lined them up, hips and chests locked, and started to move, taking Gardner with him. Dancing in a club was altogether different from the dancing they'd done at school affairs, room between bodies and adult eyes watching for anything untoward, because nothing was like this, nothing was like this vertical sex, the hysteria, the need. Nothing was like fucking with your clothes on in front of a hundred other people.

Gardner exhaled. It sounded—agonized, and so fucking good, and Theo laughed low in his ear, and Gardner dropped his head to the crook of Theo's neck, wild hair along the side of his face.

He wondered if they'd get to the begging.

"Fuck, Theo." Gardner grabbed him, thrusting slow and strong. "Just—please."

So that was a yes on the begging.

"You ever done this before?" His breath was soft on Gardner's ear, and he was jealous and possessive thinking of him with anyone else—thinking about him wrapped up and sweating with Margaret, maybe—and then he bit the tender skin of his earlobe and sucked.

Gardner's voice was almost too quiet to hear over the pulsing music of the club. "I've never done anything."

A hot thrill ran through Theo, like victory, like a final confirmation of superiority, like ownership, and then a low, sweet bloom of something he didn't want to call tenderness.

Responsibility.

"Come on." He grabbed Gardner's hand and pulled him out the front door, through a knot of smokers, and across the street, up the stairs of the rain-washed courthouse. They ducked behind a stone pillar, and he pushed Gardner right up against it.

He took a breath.

Gardner looked—he looked almost as if he were drugged, or drunk as fuck, because he was breathing hard and his eyes were hazy, and it seemed like he could pass out at any moment.

Theo frowned. "You all right, Gardner? Did you drink too much, take something?"

Gardner shook his head, eyes sharpening. "One drink."

Could he really—was he acting like this just because of one dance?

Because of Theo?

"What do you want, Gardner?"

Jack clenched his hands, his teeth, leaned his head back against the pillar.

Fighting himself—and losing.

"You know what I want."

Theo laughed, bitter. "I know what parts of you want," and he reached forward as if to run his hand along Gardner's length, stopping less than an inch away. "I'm not so sure about the rest of you."

Gardner opened his eyes, head still against stone, looking at him under his thick black lashes. "Please, Theo."

God, his name on those lips—

He stepped a little closer, put his hands on either side of Gardner, leaning in without touching. The stone was cold and rough, but the heat coming off Gardner was scorching.

"Please what, Jack?" He said his name like broken glass.

"Just fucking touch me."

"Prove it." He growled low in his throat. "Prove that you want it."

Theo closed his eyes against—against Gardner, and his heat, and everything he'd ever wanted. And then he felt strong

hands on his hips, and they pulled him tight against that unbelievably hard cock.

"Touch me, Theo." His voice was too tender. Theo hated it.

So he leaned forward and bit Gardner's hot neck, hard, the
way he had wanted to since seeing him in the bell tower, and
Gardner groaned, some animalistic thing he'd never imagined he would provoke but suddenly couldn't live without,
and Gardner was unzipping Theo's jeans, and he quickly un-
zipped Gardner's, and they were both bare in the damp-cool
night, and Theo took them both in one hand—

"Little help here, Gardner."

And he did, he wrapped his firm fingers around them,
clasping his hand with Theo's—

"Fuck, you're thick." The words spilled out of Theo's panting mouth.

Gardner dropped his head down to Theo's shoulder, his response muffled—"And you're fucking gorgeous."

He nearly came from Gardner's coarse voice, and that
wouldn't do, so he bit him again, and spoke in low tones—

"I can't wait to have you in me, splitting me open, fuck,
I'm going to ride you until you can't remember your name,
'til the only thing you can remember is—"

"Oh my fucking God." Gardner froze, then shook out a
desperate, *"Theo."*

Watching Gardner as he came was like hearing a symphony,
all these little parts, little painful broken things, coalescing
until he was too beautiful, too suspended in time, and the
wetness on their fingers as they nearly held hands was like a
benediction, and when Theo came like he'd never come before he thought, *Jesus Mary and Joseph, I could love this man.*

"God, that was incredible." Gardner looked so well-fucked
and attractively stunned that Theo wondered just how quickly

he could get hard again—and wondered what he'd look like when—if—

And yet Gardner had made no move to kiss him.

Theo longed for that, another dam breaking.

He started, painstakingly, to rebuild his walls.

Just sex, then.

"You get what you were looking for?" Theo pulled away, wiping his hand on Gardner's shirt, zipping himself back up. He pulled out his pack of cigarettes and tried not to notice his hand shaking as he lit one.

"I—" Fuck, Gardner looked shattered.

He had no right. Not when it was Theo who was—

"It's been fun, Gardner."

Turning his back was too hard, almost impossible, but it had to be done before Jack could see how much he hurt. He started to walk down the stairs, back to the club, back to find a stranger who didn't—who didn't make him feel—

"Did you mean it?"

Gardner stepped out from behind the column. Theo turned—oh Christ, Gardner was struggling to zip his jeans, and he was covered in come, and yet he looked so earnest, so innocent and unpracticed, how did he manage?

"Mean what, Gardner?"

"What you—" He blushed. "What you said. About..."

Ah. "You fucking me? Putting your cock up my—"

Gardner rubbed the back of his neck, and why he thought that was hot, he did not know. "Yeah. That."

"You sure you want that?"

He was silent. Theo took one last drag of his cigarette, then dropped it and ground it out with his boot. "I'll tell you what. You think about that. What you want."

Gardner looked up, hope and fear battling on his face. Theo took a few steps closer to him.

"Go back to your—wherever you're staying. Take your come-soaked clothes off." Gardner blushed again. "Or leave them on, stay nice and wet. Get in bed. Wrap your hand around yourself."

Theo ran his eyes down Gardner's body, lingering on his already nearly full cock. God, he wanted more of that. He looked into his eyes and gave him his best smirk. "And then think of me."

He turned to walk away again, then shouted back over his shoulder, "I'll be at the university quad at six tomorrow morning. Bring coffee. If you're brave enough."

As he crossed the street and ducked back into the club, he thought about that image—Gardner, biting his lips to keep quiet, his pulsing prick in hand, wet from both of them, his head thrown back—and didn't know if he hoped he'd show up tomorrow or prayed that he wouldn't.

But at least he'd had this. This one night. The culmination.

Maybe, if he was lucky, it hadn't been the biggest mistake of his life. Maybe he'd get to keep the memory.

Maybe then he could move on.

Chapter Fifteen

The barista was pretty cute.

Jack sat at the coffee bar next to the picture window at the front of the café. He had a huge mug of coffee—a latte with too much milk and too much caramel sauce, which made it perfect—and he'd just ordered a double espresso with a small pitcher of cream. The barista set it out in front of him, and he moved it over, claiming the next barstool.

The clothes he had picked out weren't that uncomfortable—he'd pulled on the loosest pair of jeans, a soft T-shirt, a blue wool sweater—and he shouldn't have felt like this, all tied up and bound and entirely bizarre like a child who'd never dressed himself before. But he sat there, in that crowded café, and he wondered if Theo would be able to tell that he was still just a kid playing grown-ups.

He sat, drinking coffee. And he waited.

He was fifteen minutes early, which was unusual for him, but he had been nervous and jittery since last night and couldn't stop himself from rushing to get here. The coffee probably wouldn't help his nerves, but it was an effective prop—see, nothing to watch here, nothing out of the ordinary, just a guy nearing forty in the midst of a sexuality crisis (for the second time), quietly drinking coffee and pretending he's not about to—

The barista looked over at him and gave him a smoldering look and a flirty wink.

Really. Jack was almost twice his age.

And Jack felt—he felt nothing. As far as he could tell, the young man was absolutely his type—tall, slender, messy blond hair, a tattoo peeking out from under his collar. One hundred percent the kind of guy that he thought he should go for, age aside. But all of those features, the things that were nice to look at, lacked the spark, the crucial element, the piece that he'd been missing for so long.

He'd done all the things you're supposed to do, you know, when you're facing down a lack of passion with your wife and considering that you might really, truly, after all that bother, be attracted to men. He knew he had enjoyed the hell out of every fucking second with…

He tried for so long to put that away. Pack it down somewhere. Under his business suits—in a filthy apartment he'd never see again.

So he read some erotica, and watched some porn—and dear Lord, the variety and amount on the internet was staggering—and it was arousing in a general way (unfortunately more arousing than intimacy with Meg, damn it) but again, there was this—this gap. And for so long he thought he could live with it.

Until he heard the news: Theo's divorce. January, and the beginning of this disaster, and he couldn't stop thinking about it.

And he was rock fucking hard.

He couldn't live with it anymore.

So, yeah, thirty-seven years old, three children, an almost ex-wife, about to be homeless—because he didn't want to keep imposing on Meg, who was already too good to him—and he could just give himself a smack because it wasn't men he wanted, not men he was leaving Meg—the girl he'd always loved—for. Not the cute barista, who practically screamed power bottom; not Justin at work, who'd flirted and slipped over a hotel key on a business trip and kindly laughed off Jack's stuttering rebuff; not any of the fantastically attractive athletes he'd met through Meg's job. No.

It wasn't a sexuality crisis.

It was a Theo crisis.

Jack glanced at his watch. Just a few minutes more. He tensed his shoulders and shook his head and then thumped it down onto the granite bar.

He kept it there for some time.

"You okay, lover?"

It was the barista, of course. He'd come around the bar and was leaning one hip against the wall, zipper at Jack's eye level. Jack picked his head up fast and stared up at him—a cheeky grin at the corner of his thin lips, all his body language saying, *Take me home, will you?*

A flash of movement behind him.

"Gardner." The voice was arctic. "Why, exactly, is this… child…calling you 'lover'?"

Oh, fuck.

"Theo, hi, I, um." He tried to stand up but was penned in.

"And who are you?" A snippy interruption from said child.

Theo raised his left eyebrow and looked down—the barista was maybe three inches shorter—and said, very quietly, "I'm you in about twenty years. A little advice." He sat, picked up the espresso with his long, nimble fingers. "Don't bite off more than you can chew. This one," he nodded to Jack, "Is hard to swallow."

"I don't think I would have any problems with that," and the barista threw in another wink. He really was relentless.

Jack barked a laugh at the sheer nerve, then covered his mouth in embarrassment.

Theo looked up to the ceiling, then sighed. "I'm sure you would do your best. But trust me." He met the barista's eyes, "He's not worth it."

Silence.

The barista slinked away, outclassed. Sounds in the café started to filter back in—spoons clinking, laughter, steaming milk, all normal everyday sounds which seemed jarring; Theo was with him, and today was not a normal day.

"Thanks for that," Jack said, half sarcastic and half truly grateful to be rescued. "I sort of expected you to eviscerate him."

Theo sipped at his coffee, then stirred in a little cream. Less, now, than he used to. "I was young, once. Prone to throwing myself at handsome strangers. And you've always been—"

He shut his mouth and looked a bit like he'd swallowed a frog. It was a terrible face, and it made something in Jack's chest melt.

Theo was so beautiful when he was accidentally unattractive.

"Hi." Jack's voice was soft, and he desperately hoped they could start again—at least, start today again.

"Hello, Gardner." Theo looked down at the cup in his hands, as if only now noticing it, and frowned. "Please tell me I'm not drinking someone else's espresso."

Jack laughed a little, awkward. "No, I, um. I ordered it. For you."

"Oh." Theo pinked up around the edges. "Thanks."

"So I—"

"Would you—"

They spoke at the same time, then fell silent. Jack gestured at Theo—*you first*.

"Yes, well... Your email was—unexpected." He took another sip, then set the cup down, "And pretty much incomprehensible, by the way."

"Yeah."

Jack rubbed the back of his neck, an old habit. He heard Theo's breath catch and saw him clench his jaw and look away.

"Is there—do you have some explanation as to why you wanted to, to talk, after…" Theo trailed off, and behind his still-perfect pale skin and his shining fall of hair and his undoubtedly expensive suit, he looked deeply unhappy.

"I do, yeah." Jack cleared his throat, about to explain, when Theo interrupted.

"It does seem that our children…get along."

Jack smiled, and he saw a hint of laughter in Theo's gray eyes. "Get along, yeah—I've gotten a lot of emails along the theme of 'Jazz Beaumont is our lord and king.'"

Theo looked pleased but shuddered dramatically. "Horrid nickname, I don't know why—"

"Well, with a name like Jasper—"

"Oh, right, and Gwilim Linwood Alistair is such a winner—"

"Hey, I—" Jack stopped and wrinkled his nose, "Yeah, okay, that's on me."

Theo almost smiled, brows lifting, "Did you really name him after the bartender at The Thirsty?"

Oh my God, Jack thought—"Um, I guess I did."

Theo looked like he might laugh now, sharing in the memory. And then his gaze frosted over. "You didn't let Margaret pick his name?"

Jack froze, too. He thought back—back to when they started talking about baby names. He'd cared too much—he maybe always felt that Jack was a stupid name, too plain, just not something that made sense for the kind of life he had now, the life he wanted to give his children. So he picked more complicated names, Jonquil and Gwilim and Amethyst, and

Meg was fine with it, though she did laugh at him. She liked to see him smile.

She just wanted a family with Jack. And he wanted one with her.

He'd got it, and he was still miserable.

"How—how is Margaret?" Theo's voice was stilted, uncomfortable, but still practiced and mannered despite the insincerity. Jack knew that voice and squinted at him.

"Are you trying to be nice?"

Theo scoffed, then rolled his eyes. "Yes. God knows why. Do you think this afternoon will go better if I start throwing things?"

Jack breathed out a bit of a laugh, then wrapped his fingers around his mug. He stared into the milky-sweet brew, not really knowing what to say—even though he felt he had so much to say, had been holding on to it for years.

Maybe he was worried that if he opened his mouth, it would all—it would be real. He'd start talking and tell Theo everything—from how badly he wanted him, right now against the glass window, to what he'd had for breakfast that morning; from the way he'd looked at Meg and wished she were sharp and blond and mean to what he'd been imagining when he wrapped a hand around himself in the shower last night, clenching his mouth shut so he wouldn't make a sound. Everything.

How he still dreamed of lazy mornings, drinking the dregs of canned cider, burying his face in the soft hair along Theo's neck, kissing him between cigarettes. Fighting with him and fixing it. Planning a life, a little bit.

How he'd woken up, every morning for almost twenty years, expecting to see Theo. Putting a record on. Mixing up instant coffee. Dancing naked in front of the mirror.

Loving him in that way he told himself is only possible

when you're young. When your heart is still fresh enough to break.

"Meg and I are getting a divorce."

The reaction was fast and unmistakable. Theo's face went white, and his hands clutched his cup. He didn't move.

And his voice was cool and so fucking calm when he said, "Oh?"

"Yeah."

Theo cleared his throat a bit. "I'm not sorry." A shred of a sneer.

"Me neither. I mean, I wasn't when I heard that you and Alexia—"

"Why are you getting a divorce?" Theo shot back, fast. A little too loud. And he made the frog face again.

"Why did you?" Jack's voice was suddenly just as hard, like ice. He had to know if there was any—

Theo leaned back, body relaxed now, but vicious, snakelike, with a promise of violence. He smiled a creamy smile. "Alexia was a wonderful wife. She has been a good mother to Jasper. She's beautiful, entertaining, and my mother cares for her."

Jack felt a hot flash of—yeah, it was jealousy. And anger that someone else, some woman, had touched him. It wasn't fair for him to feel this way, not when he had—but he felt it just the same.

"So?" It was almost a growl.

Get a grip, Jack.

"If Alexia has one flaw, at least from my perspective, it is that she is a woman."

Jack blinked. Theo's mouth tilted up.

"So definitely still super gay, then?"

Theo finally laughed, a real one, though understated. "As you have cause to know."

He looked up through the blonde fringe of his eyelashes,

then tossed back his platinum hair. Jack flushed. "Well, um. Yeah. So—"

"Might I assume that a similar issue is the cause of your impending divorce?"

He said it in such a disinterested tone, as if nothing could have mattered less. But Jack knew him—knew the tells, the tiny movements, and Theo had always lied in the same way— with a twitch at the corner of his right eye.

He cared, Jack realized, and he started—just a little—to hope.

"More or less."

"Mm."

"Actually, I..." Jack trailed off.

There was a bit of space between them, here at the bar, under the window, and Jack didn't know what to do with his words, because that bit of space was nineteen years' worth of regrets. Good things, too, like kids, and hard work, and family, but...

Jack started to move his hand forward. Just a little, just to see if—

"Have you found a place to live, Gardner?"

He jumped back at Theo's clinical tone. "Um, what?"

"I assume you're letting Margaret keep the house. You'll need a new one." Theo was suddenly all business, as if this were a lunch with clients, and not drinking cold coffee with the walking human disaster he used to fuck in dark alleys.

"Yeah, no, I don't have anything lined up yet."

"Mm."

Theo pulled his cuff back, glancing at his watch—which gave Jack an opportunity to run his eyes over the sharply tailored suit one more time, over his slim wrists, and Jesus fuck he just wanted to rip all those layers off and lick every inch— and frowning. "I've got a meeting, need to run. But I have a good friend who's the best real estate agent in Baltimore. Discreet. Email me if you want her to set something up."

Theo stood, all elegance and remove. It was happening too fast.

Jack felt like he nearly shouted, his voice was so rough. "I'll email you?"

Theo paused, buttoning his slimming coat. "Yes. You will email me."

He looked down at Jack, and for just a moment the facade cracked, and Jack could see the long shadows of his truest, worst mistake.

Theo's voice was low, dangerous, and deadly serious. "I will never chase after you. I will never seek you out. If you want my time, you will work for it."

Jack's mouth was dry.

"Yeah, I." He swallowed. "Of course."

He watched Theo's back, the slender lines of the coat, the perfectly hemmed trousers, the impeccable posture, the long fall of shining hair.

That didn't go at all as he'd expected.

Jack was always letting Theo walk away. Making him walk away.

He didn't want to do that anymore.

When his alarm went off, Jack burrowed his head farther into the down pillows and groaned. Why was he waking up this early?

He rolled over and stretched, lazy, down to his toes. Tired or not, he felt unusually fantastic. His whole body was relaxed like a spiral of honey off the comb, the bed so soft, his muscles slack. He had never felt like this.

Eyes still closed, he recalled flashes of abstract details from last night—the club, the courthouse, the grit of the stone behind him, and Theo's hand. Theo's mouth as it bit him and as his whole body released, as if he had been waiting his whole life for that sharp pain.

His eyes snapped open. Shame came in the wake of re-membered pleasure.

He had really done that. After four years of struggling and hating and wanting, hungering, more than anything, and tell-ing himself that it wasn't true, it couldn't be, and he had—

He thought about home, Dare and Quinn and, oh God, Meg—what would they think if they knew that the most plea-surable moment of his eighteen years was clutching at Theo in the dark, giving in? He and Meg, they weren't—they were together, but not together, no real commitments, not sure where the next year would lead them, but—

What would they all think if they knew he—

A part of him that he had thought he had amputated won-dered, what would his mother say?

He tried to think back to kissing Meg, winding his fingers through her dark red hair. He felt an echo of his lingering childhood love, like a sepia-toned photograph. Something pre-cious but aged, like a snapshot in a family scrapbook.

But Theo—

Theo was that moment in *The Wizard of Oz*, you know, when she steps out into a new world of too-saturated pig-ments, the miasma of flowers and red glitter and golden bricks. When Jack had watched a wibbly copy of that film on their fuzzy television, he'd almost been sick from the transition—black-and-white was so much closer to his life, the way it had always been, and little Jack had wondered in that moment if he would ever truly see in color.

And now he had.

And it was five in the morning, and he'd only gotten four hours of sleep, and he was full of disgust at this fully realized truth, and even so he was going to get two cups of coffee and meet Theo in the silvery light of sunrise.

And it felt so good. Dangerously good.

He pulled on a pair of jeans, a fresh shirt, a hooded jacket, and stopped by the café he'd seen on his first morning here. He wandered up the hill to the University College Cork campus, smelling the river, watching blackbirds take flight.

In his whole life he had taken so few moments to notice beauty. His childhood was bereft of beauty. Everything here was still, crystallized in the hour before waking. The grass of the quad was perfectly manicured, soft and trimmed and so green. He watched the shimmer of the rising sun and the breeze caressing blossoming trees and he felt a part of it all, as if he could fragment and become an essential element of this place, removed from the rest of his world.

It felt so much like a dream—this hour, this day, this place— and he wasn't sure if he ever wanted to wake up.

Theo, waiting for him—God, Jack could get used to that, being wanted—was washed out, almost white in the faint strains of sunlight, and yet another beautiful thing he thought he'd never get to see. Get to have.

"Gardner." Theo held out his hand for a paper cup, eyes still clouded with sleep.

"Beau." He imitated the regal—if exhausted—tone and passed him his coffee.

Theo rolled his eyes. "Do shut up." He took a sip, looked away. "It was—perfectly acceptable when you used my given name." Theo waved his hand. "Feel free to do so."

Jack felt a smile pull at his face. He'd never realized how totally awkward Theo was. "Oh, right. Theo."

The name tasted good as he spoke it. His voice was softer than he intended, with an undercurrent of—something. Something too nice for the guy he'd pulled off the night before.

A history unspooling from his tongue of two people who'd always, it seemed, known each other in the deepest places.

Theo blushed, just a pale tint of color.

"You should call me Jack." He sat on the bench, the hood of his jacket warm around the dark bruise on his neck that he hoped, for some reason, wouldn't heal too quickly.

Theo pulled out his pack of cigarettes, offering one to Jack, flipping open his lighter. He debated—"What the hell?"—and had Theo light both. They were quiet for a moment—Theo as he took a long, practiced drag, and Jack as he puffed lightly and tried not to choke.

He was not successful.

Theo gave him a little pat on the back, just shy of too rough. "Fuck, Jack." His voice broke a bit on the name. "Not a smoker, then?"

"Not really." But even as he said it, he felt the first hit of nicotine to his system. Another thing he could get used to, and fast.

"So, you're what?"

"Making up for my uneventful teen years, I guess."

Theo raised his eyebrows straight to his hairline. "Uneventful? Captain of the lacrosse team, class valedictorian—this is you we're talking about, right?"

Jack took another drag, shrugged. "Well. Rebellion-free."

"You did toe the line, I suppose."

"Yeah." He breathed out, smoke curling through the air. "Yeah. Never had much choice. No time for anything...out of the ordinary."

Jack shot him a shy grin. Theo crinkled up his lips and sipped at his coffee.

"I suppose I'm making up for lost time, myself." A wry smile. "As you might have noticed."

Jack leaned back against the bench, some of that morning

lassitude still flowing through him. He relaxed into it, letting his legs fall open, and the side of his thigh lined up perfectly with the side of Theo's. It burned like an electrical shock.

"Hmm." Theo startled, turned his eyes away, but left his leg where it was. "This coffee is shit, Gardner."

Jack's mouth dropped open. Still a bit of a spoiled brat, obviously. "Feel free to get it yourself." He frowned, looking down into his cup, "What's wrong with it?"

"Sugar does not belong in coffee." Despite the complaints, he drained his drink. "I take two shots of espresso, Gardner—" He grimaced and corrected himself as Jack nudged his leg with a smooth slide of their jeans. "Jack. With cream. Get it right tomorrow."

Theo took on that pink tinge again. It looked odd on his face—it was naked. Vulnerable.

Tomorrow. He was offering—Jack didn't really know. He didn't know what to hope for. Except he'd never felt like this, like everything inside of him was balanced on the edge of a cliff, like he was in that farmhouse, careening in a tornado toward unknown ground. He had been carrying too many things that had damaged him as a little boy, and he had fulfilled the expectations of the people he wanted so badly to love him, and it felt like each choice he made was no choice at all, but a mindless submission to a world that didn't care about him, really, at all. And he'd done what he was supposed to do, subverting the expectations of his poverty, putting up with the abuse, earning his place in the world, and he was glad of it, but this—

This was entirely his choice.

He would be doing this for himself.

Black-and-white—morality, duty, sporting events with clear rules, things he should and shouldn't do.

Or full fucking color.

He jumped—he chose—he fell.

He brought Theo coffee every morning for a week and a day.

And on that next Friday night, when he danced with this man—so stunning, so damaged, just as hungry and broken as he was—Theo leaned over and said:

"Save yourself a walk tomorrow."

He pulled Jack close and bit his neck and held him as he nearly fell apart.

"Come home with me."

It was an easy decision, despite this betrayal of Meg and home and everything he was supposed to be, and he finally got to see, got to feel—

Theo in the glow of streetlights as they stumbled up the hill—Theo, as he pushed him against a stone wall and thrust their hips together—Theo, and the way he took off his clothes, practiced and perfect and unaccountably nervous—

The chirping of birds and the way he rolled his eyes and muttered, "Fucking Cathal."

The sound of the record player, skipping, and an old LP, David Bowie's *Low*.

A spliff and its thick smoke, the way the night blurred around the edges, the way it was impossibly searing when he wrapped his lips around Theo for the first time, and how Theo gently fucked his face and he choked and it was exactly right, exactly what he—

And lubing up his fingers, pushing them into impossibly tight heat, watching Theo throw his head back onto his lumpy pillows, finding that spot that made him shiver and cry out and clutch at his hand and demand in that cultured but newly shattered Beaumont tone, "Get in me, Jesus fuck, Jack, just—"

Pouring himself into that heat, every inch of him, and how was it possible with that slender body with the silvery scar on his lip and the blackened tattoo and God, no one told him it could feel like this—

Theo holding his face, whispering, "You're so fucking beautiful," and Jack knowing, for once, that it was true—

Theo as he clenched, sucking him in farther, giving a broken cry, his whole body jerking as he came between them, and holy fuck, it was so hot, Theo's come wet on their stomachs, and the tender fucked and fucked-up gaze, and Jack coming with such excruciating pleasure that it was exquisitely painful.

Like his whole heart shot forth from him, unbound. Like he'd stay there, in him, forever, if asked.

After, Theo looked—he looked like he couldn't believe this had happened, that Jack had wanted to be with him, as if he were unaccustomed to being touched and terribly surprised that it was Jack, someone made precious in this still morning light, who had touched him. His face was pink and open and shy and wondering.

It made something in Jack's chest hurt. It was familiar. He closed his eyes against it and buried his head in the delicate arch of Theo's neck.

"You're still getting the coffee," Theo mumbled as he drifted off toward sleep.

Jack held him and kissed his shoulder and yawned. "'Course."

The sun rose. The first sunrise they shared.

Not the last.

Chapter Sixteen

Theo had not expected to feel like such an idiot for so much of his life.

He'd made a lot of personal progress. He was a better person now.

It seemed really unfair.

Jack had, in fact, emailed him. Asking for help finding an apartment. And now he was stuck, because he was too fucking weak to shut Jack down and bury him for good. Just a few words, and Theo was his.

He was a fool.

But he texted Genni, asking—without naming Jack—if she had any good properties with a lot of room (presumably, he'd want bedrooms for the children) and she'd written back right away, because of course she had.

Which led him to today, standing here in front of one of the more modern developments at Harbor East, waiting, as always, for Jack.

The scent of the water was familiar, something a little bitter and rotting and salty, and Theo could see a glimmer of light in the slow undulations of the Inner Harbor. Fall was here, trees clinging to brown and ochre leaves, and a few seagulls cried out. This was the shiny part of the city, constantly redeveloped, the place that politicians wanted tourists to see, and it seemed just as false as it was beautiful. So many secrets hidden, a constant decay, reinvention hiding something darker. And yet the ground beneath him vibrated with a sort of history, and the water whispered of times long past, and he felt lulled into this, Baltimore, a story, a song.

Genni was inside the penthouse apartment in the new development, "setting the mood," as she called it—usually lighting some candles and baking cookies so the cinnamon sugar smell filled the space, inspecting the cleaning job of the corporate service she always hired.

If she'd known who was coming, she probably wouldn't have bothered. Or she would have poisoned the cookies. Which didn't sound like the worst course of action, at the moment.

Theo stared out over the water. Jack was late.

He began to pace in front of the gate. The building had elaborate security measures and glass and steel polished to a silver gleam. It rose high above him, so unlike the historical row houses that had been torn down in preparation for new development, and yet it maintained a certain charm, the wrought iron gate, the interior walls of exposed brick. He had no idea if Jack would like it, and a little mean part of him felt pretty damned good about possibly wasting his time.

And another part of him, which he was resolutely ignoring, wondered if he wasn't just excited to spend any time with Jack at all.

He gritted his teeth. Fuck that.

He heard footsteps behind him, and the strong bay breeze carried a familiar scent—bergamot, oakmoss, labdanum. Fresh and earthy and distinctly Gardner, like wind over a lacrosse field, sweet vermouth, and the rot-rich floor of the woods and creek behind Gwynns.

He took a moment, just three seconds with his eyes closed, to revel in the scent, and remember.

"Hey." Jack's voice, soft and tentative. "This the place?"

He turned, and Jack gestured up at the impressive building. He was unusually well-dressed, an emerald green sweater and charcoal trousers, that black hair with silver highlights ruffling in the breeze. Theo wondered how he was able to look so handsome, even after twenty years of separation, of aging. His heart clenched; he smoothed out his face.

"Mm. The agent's inside."

"Please tell me it's not the whole building." He looked up, intimidated.

"No, Gardner. I doubt even you have that much money." He jerked his head. "It's upstairs."

"Oh, okay." Jack opened the gate, gave a little bow, smiled crookedly. It should not have been cute. What a dork. "After you."

Theo entered a code on a keypad next to the front door, a buzzing sound indicating it was correct—Genni had given him access for the day—and he turned toward the camera above them, showing his face. Jack looked surprised.

"Neat."

"Impressed?"

"Definitely."

The door slid open, and they walked through a lobby with marble floors, a large floral arrangement sitting on a cherrywood table, an elaborate but modern chandelier, two elevators hidden in a warmly lit niche. Everything was hushed; everything felt like discretion and money. It smelled of white gardenias and green tea, a hint of smoke, a whisper of imported scotch.

"Isn't this kind of—"

Theo looked over at Jack, who seemed uncomfortable, biting his lip as he trailed off.

"I know it's maybe nicer than what you're used to, Gardner. But it's one of the safest buildings in Baltimore, which I figured you'd like for when the kids are here."

"True."

They stepped into the elevator, and Theo entered in a second code, a light popping on for the top floor. Jack looked tense. Anxious and out of place. "It's just—it's so nice."

"And you don't deserve nice, hmm?"

The elevator didn't seem to move at all, totally smooth and soundless. Theo leaned against one wall, while Jack propped himself against the wall opposite.

Jack shoved his hands in his pockets. "I didn't think that you would think so. After everything I…"

"Well," Theo looked down at the glossy elevator floor as he spoke, "What I think—" He paused, just a moment too long.

The doors opened.

"Holy shit."

Theo didn't look into the apartment at first, but watched the shock and wonder cross Jack's face. He had forgotten—in all the publicity for his charity works, in Jack's financial success, in his perfect family and picture up at Gwynns and all of that fabulous nonsense, it was easy to ignore the facts of Jack's childhood. The ways he was already screwed up, long before—

He remembered the night they'd both struggled to close his window all the way. It was usually nice to keep the window open, the temperate Irish air blowing in over their skin, cooling their sweat, but that night it was a little colder after a day of steady rain. Theo tried to slide the window down, and then Jack attempted to put all those muscles to good use, but they couldn't do it, and—

Jack was breathing too hard, showing the whites of his eyes like a spooked horse, freezing cold and sweating buckets. Theo panicked at the look on his face, wrapped him up in blankets,

holding him, as Jack started to speak in a toneless voice as if
he couldn't stop himself.

The apartment in Bolton Hill. His bedroom window, stuck
open, and how he slept in his coat during the winter, and that
time when he was thirteen and he tried to insulate it with
duct tape and a ragged old blanket, and how his mom walked
in, probably drunk, and watched him cry and walked away
again, expressionless.

The moldy ends of loaves of bread that his mother left open
on the counter, and that he ate after she went to bed. The mag-
gots growing in boxes of cereal that he stuffed in his mouth
before noticing—

The way she didn't hit him—not really, Jack said, not after
the time she grabbed him in anger when he was three and dislocated his arm—so it couldn't have been that bad, and why
was he upset, now, when he'd never have to go back, when so
many other people had it so much worse? He hadn't starved,
Jack insisted, he'd just—been hungry. And that bedroom was—
he'd always had a place to live, after all—and his mother wasn't
to blame, really, she was probably doing her best, and—

They just didn't ever have enough money, and that was the
problem, obviously—it was the money, always the money, and
not that she spent what little she made on herself—

How she called him right before he left the country to talk
about—about needing help from him, now that he had made
good—and he'd hung up, finally grown and strong and inde-
pendent, and wasn't it hilarious that he'd felt a little sick just
hearing her voice?

Jack had laughed, Theo remembered that so clearly. Like
it was all so funny. Neglect and abuse and the little ways that
he coped, laughing, rubbing at his nose, shivering in his arms,
and then Jack kissed him with such fierce, violent intensity

that Theo hadn't been able to blurt out, *My father locked me in our cellar, sometimes, and the back of his hand was so strong, and—*

And Theo was so angry. He took Jack into him, both of them still cold, and it was rough and desperate and so, so good.

"Jesus, Theo, look at this place."

He shook his head, eyes clearing, finally wrenching his gaze away and toward the apartment. And it was stunning. Perfect. He could kiss Genni, if he didn't know by now that she'd slap him.

Theo glanced back at Jack's face, comically blank with surprise, mouth hanging open, and felt a wild giggle climbing up his throat. Swallowing the undignified noise, he watched Jack enter what must have been the nicest apartment in the entire city.

He wished it were his. He drank down that bitterness, composure regained.

Dark—nearly black—hardwood floors stretched out in a large room that was floor to ceiling windows, looking out over the Baltimore skyline, the red Domino Sugar sign and the glimmer of light on the water. The space was completely open, with a large kitchen in a minimalist style taking up the left side. An island, ice-white marble with sleek black cabinets, had room for four barstools.

It should have been cold, new and unlived in, but it was fully furnished with thick rugs and plush couches, a real fireplace, open bookshelves with recessed lighting, everything seeming soft and cozy and perfect for long afternoons with endless hot cups of coffee.

It was romantic. He tried not to imagine himself spread out on the soft velvet of the couch, firelight warming his naked skin, and failed.

Across from the elevator, on the other side of the open room, was a wrought iron spiral staircase that reminded him of the metalwork in New Orleans, old and whimsical and darkly magical. Jack walked over to run his hand along the cool marble of the island, and Theo heard a very distinctive sound—

The stiletto-sharp clack of Genni's high heels. He saw her coming down the staircase, regal as ever, fine features and a flawless tan, and he saw the look on her face when she realized who the mysterious client Theo had begged her to take really was.

"You must be joking."

Jack's head lifted, some tension released—it was like he was mesmerized, God, this place was perfect—until he spotted Genni. "Um, Jones?"

"Dumont, for some time now, Gardner." She gestured in what was supposed to be a casual way, clearly showing off the massive diamond on her ring finger. The stone—three carats, if Theo recalled correctly—glimmered with iridescent fire.

"Congratulations. Um, I guess."

She rolled her eyes in that very distinctive Genni moue of distaste and then continued in her descent down the staircase.

The timer on the oven dinged. Jack jumped.

"Get those, would you?" she said, over her shoulder, as she came to embrace Theo.

Jack, bless him, grabbed a linen dishtowel and actually took the cookies out of the oven. Genni hugged Theo very tightly indeed, and whispered a simple but eloquent, "What the fuck?"

"Just do it for me, please, Genni."

She backed up and held him by the shoulders, looking torn between hugging him again or shaking the hell out of him. Both of which he needed, it felt like. She straightened, cleared her throat, and pasted on the smile that had made her one of the most successful real estate agents in Baltimore. "So, Gardner. What do you think?"

He looked very uncertain as to his welcome—which he should have—and placed the cookie tray on the range. "Um, well, it's…very nice."

"Very nice." Her voice deadly as she crossed her arms, manicured nails tapping against her elbows.

"It's great!"

"That's what I thought."

He made a show of looking around the room. "Are there, uh, bedrooms?"

Genni turned to look at him with a face that said, *Is this fucker for real?* Theo shrugged and fought the urge to laugh. He could admit to himself that even now, making Jack uncomfortable was too fun to resist.

"Come with me." Her tone was brusque, heels clicking back toward the staircase.

Theo did his best not to watch Jack's muscles move as he followed him up.

There were, of course, bedrooms, and four of them as Theo had requested. Three rooms for the children, which shared a hall bath, and—

"Oh, wow."

And a primary suite, also fully furnished, with a huge fourposter bed and blue-and-gold linens.

Jack squinted at Genni. "Gwynns colors, huh?"

"I thought it was actually for Theo," she mumbled. "Finally getting him out of that drafty old—"

"Let's look at the bathroom," Theo interrupted, elbowing her none too gently on his way across the room. Hell, she could be a bitch.

But as he took in the huge walk-in closet, stocked with velvet hangers and elegant shelving, he remembered why she was such a good friend.

This was definitely the right place for him. Too bad it was for—

"I don't have this many clothes." Jack looked around, gormless again.

"I am utterly shocked to hear that." The Genni snark in full effect.

Theo felt that laugh bubbling up, watching Jack look around like a freshman at Gwynns, and Genni glaring at him like she was five seconds from throttling him and hiding the evidence.

And he didn't really—he didn't want to look at why, but having these two particular people in the same room was—

He was happy. Just, quietly, a little warmth in his chest. It was a new experience, them together, and for a brief moment he let himself think about this merging of two worlds, something unusual and comforting, something that felt like home. But watching Jack and feeling this way wasn't new at all.

Oh Christ, he was screwed.

Through the closet and into the bathroom, they admired the deep soaking tub, the frankly obscenely massive shower, the double sink, the black-and-white tile, the gold fixtures. It was absolutely perfect.

Jack still looked…uncomfortable. He leaned over to Theo, his back to Genni, and muttered, "I don't need all this."

Theo didn't look at him, just kept his eyes staring at the bottom of the tub, and his voice was quiet but firm. "Jack."

Jack's breath stuttered.

"You don't have to lock yourself in that horrible apartment for the rest of your life."

He felt Jack's shoulders shake, once, like the beginning of a sob.

"Or the closet, for that matter." His voice was sly and mocking, which seemed to do the trick as Jack choked out a surprised laugh.

"Gardner," Genni barked out. "Let's talk price. Leave Theo up here to drool over the walk-in."

"Nice, Genni."

"Like you didn't want to."

Jack trailed after Genni like a duckling imprinted on an un-willing mother, and Theo heard that intimidating clacking as they went down the stairs. He ran his fingers along the dou-ble sink—she really had picked the perfect place for him, and he hoped that Jack would take it—and stared into the mirror.

Too many years ago now, he and Jack had crowded around his tiny sink, brushing their teeth, worn out but keyed up as eighteen-year-old kids usually are. They'd been out all night, and Theo was about five minutes away from being late to work, and he'd nudged Jack with little energy and said, "Why the fuck are you still up? You've got nowhere to be, go the fuck back to sleep."

Jack had grinned at him, mouth full of toothpaste, and spat—lovely—before he said, "I just like brushing my teeth with you."

His heart had pounded too hard. "You are really weird, Gardner."

Jack had wrapped his arms around him from behind and kissed his neck, sleepy. "Maybe so. I don't think you mind." He slapped his ass. "Now get to work."

He looked at himself in the mirror, large and sparkling. Catalogued every fine line, the few hairs turning silver, signs of maturity hard won since that summer in Cork.

He'd been lonely for so much of his life.

Making his way toward the staircase, he heard Genni's voice—the dangerous voice. He froze. "What do you think you're doing, Gardner?"

"Well, I'm trying to buy an apartment..."

She laughed, derisive. "And you will, I'm getting you a good deal, by the way. But you know exactly what I mean."

Theo held his breath.

Jack's voice was quiet. "I do."

He wished he could see Jack's face.

"Do you know what it was like, back then?"

"What—"

She kept talking, fast. "He came back strong, you know. He took control of his home, the rest of the family fortune that his asshole father hadn't...and he helped us, all of our group at Gwynns, who I'm sure you wouldn't spit on if we were on fire..."

"Hey, that's not—"

"Shut up. He's fucking tough, you know? But if you think you didn't," her voice broke, "Didn't hurt him, you're an idiot."

Silence. Theo was trembling—from anger, from shame, from gratitude to his best friend for caring so much.

"I have no intention of hurting him again. Ever again."

He heard Genni take a deep breath. "From the look on your face, I almost believe you. But know," the heel-clack noise, firmer this time, "If you do, I will come back here. And I will have no problem, whatsoever, ripping off your fucking testicles. Got it?"

"Yes." Jack sounded legitimately scared, which was smart of him, then resolute. "I won't hurt him, Genni. I—I—"

"Don't say it, not until you... I'm not sure you even know how to—" She paused, and he could almost hear her silently pull herself back together, gathering her professionalism around her like a cloak. "You know what, fine. Now," he *could* hear the predatory smile, God he loved her, "Let's talk."

Jack bought the apartment—and all the furniture in it, even, it turned out, the blue-and-gold linens—because how could he not?

And if Theo went back to his house, alone, and imagined all of his clothes lined up next to Jack's, their books on the same open shelves, their toothbrushes aligned, his on the right, Jack's on the left...

Nobody needed to know.

★ ★ ★

The first time they kissed was on a bench, next to the river, hidden under a copse of oak trees, right at the edge of the university campus, and he hadn't meant to do it, swore to himself that he never would, but he did it anyway.

It was Lughnasa.

When Theo was small, hiding from his father with a thick stack of books in the closet of his bedroom, he spent hours researching different locations that he might run to, and there was something about Ireland—the land, the history, the mythology—which spoke to him. Most people wouldn't have known this truth about Theo, that he longed for something deeper, that he desired more than anything a connection to something bigger than himself. He'd never felt entirely comfortable where he was, even though he pretended; Baltimore was his father's place.

So he fell in love with warriors and kings, goddesses and gods and lovers, Cuchulainn and Emer and Oisin and Aengus, and he lost himself in this, this place he hungered to see, and the old stories were a part of him.

And he left behind the false surety that his father had forced on him as a Beaumont in Baltimore, and today—today was Lughnasa, that first of August, and he had Jack Gardner with him, and he was exactly where he had always wanted to be.

He should have known that he couldn't stay here—he should have known better than to think he could keep this.

And he should have known better than to kiss Jack after nearly a month of fucking and drinking and laughing and—kissing made it real. And on Lughnasa, when marriages were once made, a year and a day to see if it would work, if love could grow, if passion might stay.

It was by its very nature a magical time, one of those in-between times, the wheel of the year turning, the first harvest, the invitation. And he'd been sitting there, smoking as usual, with Jack there next to him, and the river running, and he'd been thinking about the stories he had told himself, and Jack put his arm around him, a little.

"What are you thinking about?"

Theo leaned back into Jack's muscled arm, flicked his cigarette into the water. He put his hand on Jack's thigh. "I'm thinking about fucking you right here on this bench."

Jack laughed, and he blushed, shaking his head. "No, you're not."

Theo ran his hand along the firm curve of Jack's leg. "What do you know?"

"You have a tell. You know, when you're lying."

He pretended offence, scoffing, "I do not."

Jack leaned in, nose nuzzling his hair and mouth close to his ear, whispering, "I know every fucking thing about you, Beau."

His heart seemed to stop, and he growled, "You think so?"

Jack moved closer, ground out in the scalding tone of their former rivalry, "Scared, Theo?"

And he sucked at that spot on Theo's neck, right over his pulse point.

He was.

"Fuck you, Gardner."

He swung himself up and over, straddling Jack, thighs holding him tight; Jack's hands slid up his legs, cupping his ass and pulling him closer, letting one hand wander to the center of his back.

He was breathing hard, and his vision was red around the edges, afternoon light flaring in the corners of his eyes, and Jack's cock was thick under him, and he was smiling and smiling, two crooked teeth visible and beloved, and Theo hated him, he hated him so much, had hated him practically forever, and he grabbed Jack's horrible hair in two fists and touched their lips together, finally, and devoured him. And Jack made this small sound.

There was this feeling that he would get in his chest, sometimes, that he thought he must have been born with—some sort of inherent flaw, a curse, like a faltering heart. It was the feeling of Father putting down one of the hunting dogs, just a puppy, for being born too small—the feeling when he'd had a nightmare when he was five and wet the bed, and his mother told him he was too old to be comforted and shamed him. A wrenching, like when Jack had first rejected him, like when Genni had kissed him in sophomore year, and he'd felt nothing, and that nothing ached with the life he thought he should have and now knew he never would.

That was the sound Jack made. The heartbreak sound—the voice of everything shattered. And the sound echoed in his chest, two pains perfectly in tune, this moment on the bench, on Lughnasa, the first harvest before the end of summer.

It was golden like cider, and bitter like anise, and he kept kissing Jack, pulling out these little ugly sounds—and it was so fucking incredible, and he wondered, deliriously, why he hadn't been doing this his whole damned life.

Jack, under him, thrust up, and Theo ground down, and they moved together there in the daylight. One of Jack's hands came around and rubbed up against his prick; he pushed into it, chasing that moment, biting and sucking and worshipping that mouth.

"Jesus fuck." Jack pulled away for a breath, panting.

"Shut up, Jack."

But he couldn't, he was noisy, he'd break from the kiss to beg him to touch him, for fuck's sake, and Theo whispered in his ear, "No, you fucker, you're going to come like this, right here, where anybody could see, and I'm not going to do anything but ride you and kiss your stupid mouth and tell you what a filthy bastard you are, how much you want it, how much you're gagging for it—"

Jack latched on to his collarbone and groaned and shook, and Theo followed him over, pushing into that rough hand twice more before he came. They were damp and hot and breathing hard, and Theo dropped his head to that honeyed place at the juncture of Jack's neck.

Jack started to laugh. "I guess you did fuck me on the bench."

He leaned his head back, and Theo looked down at him, both of them wet and messy, and he kissed him then, one more time, and it was sweet.

And then—it was like they'd been waiting to do this all along, maybe even before they had ever met, because wherever they went—the club, or The Thirsty, out for a quick dinner, any available alley, or on one memorable and mortifying occasion, the butcher counter at the local market—Jack would grab him, touch-starved, and kiss him until he could barely breathe.

And sometimes—sometimes Theo would push him away, just for a moment, because he had so much more practice being cruel and removed than being intimate. Sometimes Jack would kiss him and then pull back, scared. Disgusted with himself, maybe, just for a second, before he relaxed and kissed Theo again.

But they always ended up here, faces pressed together, and he didn't know if, now that he had Jack's lips and tongue and little hurtful noises, he could survive without them.

Now, in the dazzling sunshine, he just breathed in Jack's smell and Jack's smile and Jack's taste, and it was as fresh and ripe as golden apples from the tree.

A year and a day later, Theo packed his suitcase, turned off the lights in his apartment, left the keys with Cathal.

It had been eleven months since he'd last kissed Jack.

He wouldn't do it again for almost twenty years.

Chapter Seventeen

Jack stood in the middle of his new apartment, paperwork signed, a last ugly but victorious look from Genni Dumont, and Theo was—somewhere else. He hadn't come back to watch the sale go through. Why would he? They had exchanged phone numbers, Theo's face blank and tight, just—just because they might need to talk about the kids. But Jack hadn't had the courage to call.

Dumont had smiled a vicious smile as she finalized the purchase. He had a sense that she enjoyed taking some of—a lot of—his money, and he knew that behind that smile was something that hated him. And he couldn't blame her, not after—

She had left with one last comment, almost too brief to be noticed, like a warning she didn't really want to give: "Don't fuck this up." He thought that she had been talking about more than real estate; he wondered if it was, maybe, her version of giving her blessing. Like a threat that had kindness underneath.

He looked over the apartment, this shining and echoing space, and he felt those words in him, around him. *Don't fuck up, Jack. Not again.*

Jack felt like he was starting over. He felt like he had no idea what he was doing.

He had never let himself notice, digging himself out from under his childhood, how little forward progress he had really made. He stayed in Bolton Hill, with his childhood best friend, with the family that had adopted him in everything but name, and he worked at—now owned—the same company as he had right out of school, that one meeting with Franklin when he was fourteen controlling every year to come. He was bored at work, exhausted by his influential clients and their finances, but blessed by it, going in every day, still trying to prove something. He was grateful for so many of those things—could never negate how necessary and important all of those people and places were to him—but he had never...

He had never changed. He had never lived up to the person inside of him whom no one else had seen.

No one but Theo. Theo had known everything about him.

How could he manage to feel so successful on the outside and like he had wasted his whole life on the inside?

Jack walked over to the windows. The sun was just beginning to set, darkness creeping in earlier, now, and the red light of the Domino Sugar sign was glowing out over the water. He saw the angles and glass of the National Aquarium across the harbor, the smokestacks of the old Pratt Street Power Plant, new builds, old bones. All of it was a part of his story; up here in the penthouse apartment he could see the evidence of a life he had lived, this life in Baltimore, moving neither forward nor backward. A quiet life of big things. A life of monuments and monumental actions—marriage and children and financial success and a lie he had kept on telling. The lie that kept him frozen.

He loved Baltimore the way he loved Meg; Baltimore was home. Looking out over the city he felt such a surge of rightness, of belonging—and this new apartment, so modern and unfamiliar, was an extension of that belonging, like a new chapter in an often reread book. He hadn't been sure that he could find a home now where he felt welcome, because he'd never had to do that on his own. But he liked this place, and he liked himself in it. He liked the story as if it were something he could tell someone else: Jack Gardner, multimillionaire, in this penthouse apartment with a view over his whole world. A castle, a kingdom, a myth.

But maybe all of that was a myth, something which held very little truth. Because up here, so close to the sky, he had no idea who he really was. Who he was without the story.

And it had been that way for quite some time.

Right after Amethyst was born, and he and Meg had decided they were finished with having children—three was enough, if not more than enough—Jack had been haunted by a small voice, the voice of himself as a child, asking, *Is this all there is?* And he shook his head against it, trying to clear his mind, but it echoed all around him. He moved through his days, his nights curled up with Meg, reading to the kids, walking through the city with strollers and ice creams, and everything almost seemed to mock him, murmuring.

You know, Jack, that voice had said. *You know this isn't what you want. What you've always wanted.*

But you chose this.

He tried—he'd known that there was a moment, different moments on different days but on every day nonetheless, when he thought about a time when he had been happier. When he had been—been honest. Those were the thoughts with blond hair and gray eyes and a deep arousal which had seemed, now, so far out of reach. He didn't know how to reconcile the Jack from Ireland with the Jack who loved his family, and so he put it away as much as he possibly could. He was split, two selves diverging and neither content, but he didn't know what else to do. He thought he could just—just keep going. Maybe if he pretended long enough it wouldn't feel so bad. So he built his story, his path, brick by red brick.

He walled himself off, as he had done since he was a child.

And he loved his children. Jonquil, always moody and unpredictable, and Will, quiet and intuitive and dreaming, and Amy, very like her mom, always ready to laugh until she dissolved into hiccups. His children kept him there, married to his first love, the woman who felt more like a sister than a wife; they were an easy excuse, the reason he lied for so long.

But that was a lie, too. He used them. His three kids were just one more story he told himself of why he couldn't be who he wanted to be. Who he was scared to be. That wasn't their fault; they were a gift.

But this apartment—his apartment—was proof that pretending would never be good enough. And he was alone with a self he had never accepted.

He turned back toward the open space, looking at the sparkling kitchen, the cozy set of couches by the fire, and his feet echoed on the wood floors, the world talking back at him again.

He had asked for the divorce. He had finally chosen. He accepted that there was more in life he wanted, he needed. And now he was alone, and he had to face it. All the ways in which he had let his fear control him.

He remembered one day so clearly, a day when he had made this decision which haunted him—a day at Gwynns when he locked himself away—

There had been scabs on his knuckles; he tried not to pick at them.

Another bright day on the beach, that steep hill, and he'd come out here unaccompanied, sinking into grass which hadn't been mowed. He tried to lose himself in this, the earth, prickling greenery. Meg had offered to join him. He'd asked for a few moments alone. Didn't want to look at her face.

He didn't know how he had become this thing—this violent thing—and he was almost sure he had always been this way. Maybe it had started when his father left; maybe it began when his mother dislocated his arm, an event he could barely remember and desperately tried not to. But Jack studied the back of his right hand, the grooves in his flesh that he made, cuts from the friction against Theo's face, and he thought, *God, this is who I am. This is what I was made.*

It was hot, an early-summer heat which promised more, and there on the hill Jack wanted to rip it all up, somehow, this world, the things he was, the things he was supposed to be. He itched from the grass and from a hunger which clawed at him no matter how much he ate. He closed his eyes; there was a red glow under his eyelids. He pressed his knuckles against cheek—it hurt.

He remembered that first day, out here, at the end of freshman year, and the bottom of Theo's bare foot, so white and fine, as it hovered over his face. He wished that Theo had done it—had broken his nose, maybe. Then it would—it would be fair. Justified.

He thought about Theo's foot, and Theo's bare chest, and his blood. He was so hot. He peeled off his shirt and balled it up under his head and let the air melt into his skin.

There was a pain in his stomach and he—it felt like an illness and it felt like that moment he never experienced with Meg, his body operating, biology mocking him.

He couldn't be like this.

There were things in his past which he had chosen to forget, as if they had never happened. If he tried, he could dredge them up, heart pounding, but he knew that those memories were locked away for a reason. He didn't need them, couldn't focus on them. Those things were in his way. He protected himself.

And so this—the way he felt about Theo—would have to

be another thing which he partitioned off. A splitting. Another thing he would have to live with, which he would silence.

Sometimes, here at school, when he was working hard and struggling for the best grades and kissing Meg, he would shove every bad thing into the cold bedroom where he'd grown up, a corner of his mind he could ignore. The bad things were there, waiting for him, but for nine months he put them away. He needed to put—put Theo and his tears on his neck into that cold and forgotten room. A place he never wanted to go.

Soft footfalls, a gentle rustling, to his right. He kept his eyes closed. He smelled the wind.

He turned his head in the grass.

He was dazzled.

Theo stood thirty feet away, maybe, and his eyes scanned the horizon. There was still the shadow of a bandage on his lip, his face like an ancient statue worn harsh by time. His hair reflected the afternoon light like silver needles, glinting. All of that pale skin shone, polished white granite with flecks of some reflective mineral. He looked like he could unwind, unspool, fly away.

He looked so terribly lonely.

Jack didn't know—couldn't tell if Theo had seen him. The grass was long, his body cocooned in blue-green. He wanted to look away, to close his eyes, to hide further. But he was drawn to this moment of Theo in isolation, unaware. Maybe thinking that he was unwatched.

Bury it. Bury it, Jack.

But he couldn't. He felt that native thing low in him. The hunger. He didn't know who he could be without that hunger. Without hating Theo. Without wanting—

Here, watching him, Jack could almost feel that wiry body against his chest, the hand on his throat, the wetness. Theo fell into the grass, so graceful even as he was damaged, sat with his head in his hands. His hair a curtain across that honed face.

Jack wanted to hollow himself out, carve away those bad things in the bedroom, and he wanted to wedge Theo inside of him like a thing he couldn't keep. He wanted him against his bruised knuckles, he wanted him under his tongue, he wanted to kiss him and hit him and ask, why, why?

He imagined getting up, bare-chested, walking over, sitting next to him, knees against knees; he imagined ripping off the bandage, regarding what he did, trying to see if it would scar. Holding him down; being held.

He thought about Meg. How much he loved her. But he couldn't look away—couldn't see anything but grass and sky and Theo, that boy, that person, an avatar of the things in that room, deadly, desired, despised for the way he made him weak.

He wanted him more than he wanted food.

He wanted him, in that moment, more than he wanted family.

He did close his eyes then, against that shocking pain. The person he couldn't let himself be.

In that dark corner of his mind, he opened the door of his bedroom.

Theo made a sound. Jack chose not to notice the quality of that sound.

The early-summer wind smelled like vanilla and gin, botanical and sweet.

Jack was hungry.

He locked it away.

And even though he did get to have Theo—even though they'd had those months together, even though he did love him, had always—

He had still been that boy, so scared, so hungry, even as he'd sworn that he was Theo's, and Theo's alone.

And now he had this apartment and he had been so wrong for so long. He had built his life on that wrongness. He had thought he could be happy in this lie.

He wasn't ready to move in yet, delaying. He wanted more time before everything was irrevocably changed, and he and Meg hadn't—

A jolt of anxiety. There was a lot that he and Meg still needed to work out.

A lot that he still needed to do.

He pulled his phone from his back pocket, a tighter fit in these new snug jeans, and cradled it in his hand. Knowing what he wanted to do; scared to do it. He scrolled through his contacts, fingers hovering over a name he'd breathed into his pillow every night for over half of his life.

He didn't know what to say.

He typed out, **Hey**, and hit send with a jolt of apprehension and desire. Stuffed his phone back into his pocket, because he knew that if he didn't, he would stare at the phone with too much anxiety, waiting and hoping and longing. He felt like a teenager. Maybe, in trying so hard to grow up in an acceptable way, he never grew up at all.

He took one last look around the apartment, his back pocket ticking like a bomb, and he thought about this new story which might end up being more than a lie.

He went back home—to Meg's home—and smiled and kissed Amy's cheek and let himself tell a lie for just a little while longer. And he waited for his phone to ring.

Kissing was—it was intimate.

For that first month, Jack hadn't really noticed that they didn't kiss. Kissing Meg had been—it was warm, comfortable, a natural extension of their friendship, and he had never been really bothered about it. It hadn't been underwhelming, exactly, but it also hadn't seemed too terribly important. Meg liked kissing, and so he kissed her. He wanted to make her happy, after everything she had done for him.

But with Theo—he knew Theo's mouth, he knew the foul words he'd always aimed in Jack's direction, he knew the smirks, the bitterness. Theo's mouth felt like an extension of his own, all of his ugliness reflected back at him. Thin lips which had been unkind as often as they were soft with pleasure; a tongue which cut. And he had never felt anything else like this, as if he were completed in his brokenness. Kissing Theo was like fighting; kissing Theo was like a prayer.

That first kiss on their bench by the river opened something within him, like a door which had been barred, sealed, a bifurcation of his mind. He suddenly knew what everyone had been talking about; it was a revelation which he came to too late. And he couldn't help himself now—he watched Theo's mouth and he wanted it all the time.

And maybe—maybe he had done too good a job, back in school, cutting off and burying what he really wanted. Maybe he should have stopped being so surprised by this consummation and the way he craved it.

Tonight, they'd been out until the clubs closed, and they were leaning up against the wall of their preferred chip shop. All around them were other kids, lined up and waiting for their food, or huddling over a paper bag of chips, and he could smell sweat and salt and vinegar. There was a mingled sense of fatigue and mania and heartbreak and sex, something which couldn't be captured or recorded. A slice of time which remained timeless.

Theo, in unaccustomed grubbiness, had salt crystals scattered across his lips—he was licking his fingers, savoring malt vinegar, and his hair was such a mess. It was a moment unplanned, something he had never had the capacity to imagine. Something he could never have counted on.

He almost—there was a part of him which ached for the Theo he had known before, the coiffed Theo and the unkind, the aristocrat, the aloof. The archetype which he hated and envied. He had never understood how much of that was a mask. He wanted to own that Theo just as much as he wanted to make love to this one—to destroy him, remake him, worship at shined calf-leather shoes.

"What?" Theo wiped his hand across his lips. "Do I have something on my face?"

Jack had been staring, captivated. He reached out his left hand, wrapped it around Theo's trim waist, pulled him in.

"Yeah. Let me—" He drew himself up, stretching just a bit to make up those two inches, and kissed Theo's salty mouth. Theo struggled for a moment, and Jack could tell that even now, some part of both of them fought against what they shared. But he kissed Theo, again and again, hands tight on Theo's biceps, trapping him.

It felt like digging fingers into a bruise.

Maybe it was the acid of the vinegar finding every raw place in his mouth, every bit of friction from when he chewed the inside of his cheek or brushed his teeth too hard. It was imperfect. But the pain of that kiss, here under vague starlight, the smell of the deep fat fryer, cigarettes, the ketchup that other American kids asked for and Theo wouldn't lower himself to eat—it was a part of Jack. Had always been a part of him. And kissing Meg had never felt like this.

Theo wound a hand through Jack's hair, scratching lightly at his scalp, and Jack wondered how Theo, still at war with himself, had learned to be so affectionate. Like it was easy. He could feel himself beginning to be aroused—not that desire for Theo was ever too far out of reach—and Theo pushed into his body, and his heart beat like a bodhran in his ears, the endless pulsing flow of the River Lee.

Kissing Theo was unstoppable.

And it was terrifying, because he knew, he finally knew that yes, there was a love beyond comfort, beyond deep friendship, beyond Meg's soft skin. It was a love he had craved without knowing its name, a love he didn't think could possibly exist. That had never seemed accessible to him.

A love for a perfect boy made imperfect. A fallen prince; an idol destroyed.

Theo pushed him away then, and he had that surprised look on his face, the vulnerable look. Theo seemed just as—just as unbalanced, like the world wasn't what he expected it to be. As if Jack wanting to kiss him were a terrible and wonderful gift, and he was unworthy. And there was something lingering behind his eyes, gray as gravel, words that neither of them had been taught how to say.

Theo looked away, uncomfortable but obviously pleased, and picked at the chips they had crushed between their chests, something to do to keep from reaching out and grabbing Jack again. He blushed. "You are so embarrassing, oh my God."

"Can't help it." Jack leaned back against the wall, elbow brushing against Theo's arm. "I'm not really good at the self-control thing."

"Tell me something I don't know." Theo smiled at him, eyes still shying away.

"Home?" That word was just as intimate as kissing. Jack wondered when Theo's shabby little apartment had become his, too—his place. Where he lived and where he was—where he was fully himself.

"Home."

The last few chips were tossed in a trash can; Theo rubbed his greasy fingers on Jack's T-shirt. Jack had learned that Theo liked to see him messy. Liked his unkempt edges. Liked him. Liked the scruffy boy just as much as Jack liked Theo's flawlessness. "Oh, thanks."

"Any time."

Back in their apartment—home—they wedged themselves into the small bed, their positions familiar and intertwined. Another unexpected thing, wanting to touch, even when they weren't having sex. Cool night air flowed through the window and Jack pulled their blanket up, a cocoon of them, together, huddling for warmth and for—

Jack tried to imagine a future of this. Them. In those last few breaths, evening out before they fell asleep, it seemed almost possible. His sharp and caustic man, brought low and more beautiful for it, a fallen angel. And him, a boy still defined by the past, by what everyone thought he should be, but finally choosing something else.

And he wanted it. He buried his nose in the back of Theo's neck, right against the shorn strands of blond hair, and he wanted him with a gaping maw of hunger and deprivation and need. And he whispered words against Theo's skin, Theo fast asleep and unknowing, and he poured out a lifetime of that need, words broken and halting until his low voice was scratchy and unpleasant in his throat.

He slept.

He dreamed of returning home.

When he woke, panicked, guilty, Theo turned to him, gray eyes open and a bit wild and his. Belonging to him. And he knew he could never want anything as much as he wanted this.

Chapter Eighteen

Theo often ate in the kitchen.

He couldn't stand, sometimes, eating alone or with his mother in the dining room, the long ebony table that had once been ruled over by his father, the uncomfortable chairs, the silence. He felt so isolated by the bareness of those moments, nothing in the room with him but the life he wished he had had. And sometimes Mother, whom he—he couldn't help but resent, even though she had softened with time. She hadn't seemed all that interested in him to begin with, so why dissemble now?

Despite her recent tenderness, he held in him the knowledge that any affection she felt was limited. Couldn't be real. And sometimes he wanted to scream at her, unhinged, even though his choices weren't her fault. *Look at what I gave up for you!*

So he was here, in the beautifully remodeled kitchen, a book open in front of him on the butcher block island, a bowl of soup and a crusty roll. He fed himself mechanically, feeling no pleasure in taking sustenance. He just knew he had to do this, had to eat, even though he—

His phone pinged. He opened his text messages. His heart stuttered as he read one stupid, useless word.

Was that supposed to tempt him?

What did Jack want him to say?

He wished he had never given him his number.

He still felt sick, a disturbed wincing in his stomach from the time spent with Jack in his new apartment. Talking to him again—Theo had never wanted to need something like that. When he got married to Alexia he relearned affection, relearned how to laugh—she really was a wonderful woman, and he took real pleasure in their occasional phone calls and letters—but that other thing, the raw thing, was buried. No one had access to it. It was his pain and his alone. He pushed his cell phone away.

Even Genni—he didn't want her to see this. The loneliness. The wanting. She'd known he was hurt, but the full truth of it was—it wasn't for her to know.

Sometimes he caught Phil looking at him, that quiet and invasive stare, and he thought that maybe he knew. He remembered the way that Phil used to gaze at Genni, before they were together; he thought about a small boy's longing for stories of his father; and Theo thought, yes, maybe Phil did understand. Maybe he sees right through me. And Tom—Tom had learned how to love, almost accidentally, and Theo tried not to be bitterly jealous that his childhood friend had gotten it so right, so soon.

But still he kept it unspoken. It didn't need to be laid out for anyone, a history of his utter foolishness. And by keeping it silent he hid it from himself. Not completely, but enough.

He ate. He drank too much coffee. He worked hard, he donated, he raised an incredible child. He did his best.

He thought of Jack, the burdens that he had always carried and his weakness. His cowardice which was borne out of the sins of the people who should have cared for him. Theo hated feeling this pity, this compassion, for the man who'd hurt him so completely. He wished that he could just be angry.

How could one inelegant message send him spiraling like this, imagining—

Jack. His shoulders, so strong, and the way he rubbed his neck. The scent of him that was integral to the attraction, somehow smelling like home and magic and mystery and the sacred. The look on his face when he saw the apartment, and the image that had struck Theo of his own pale skin against the charcoal velvet of the couch, Jack there, maybe kneeling between his legs, all of his tanned flesh exposed.

Theo tore off a piece of his roll. Dipped it in the soup. Chewed.

Waking up with Jack in that huge bed, a sumptuous experience they'd never be able to share. Would they keep to their own sides, needing space in the night, turning their backs out of practicality—or would they curl up in the way they always had, fully intertwined, needing that contact, needing reassurance that they both were there? Eyes opening at first light, meeting, grumpy and disheveled, whispering, *Good morning.*

New habits to get used to, things they'd developed in their time apart. Little things they didn't know about each other. Jobs to balance, and taking care of the kids, and returning to that bed at the end of the day and laughing and kissing and sliding together and coming like—

He turned a page in his book. Half reading the words. Ignoring his phone.

The images sped through his mind, unstoppable. A fire in the fireplace, a home which never got cold. A kitchen island with their kids gathered around, no long table or silence or distance. Getting out of this damned mansion, away from his mother—moving in his clothes.

And Jack, there with him always, making the coffee, bringing it up the spiral staircase and spilling some along the way, and Theo giving him shit for his clumsiness. Nakedness and caffeine and all of those little things.

For so long he'd thought—told himself—that what he

missed was the sex. He could, for the most part, get through what he'd needed to do with Alexia, closing his eyes or looking over her shoulder, and it was—it was all right. But he did long for it, a broader body, muscle and sinew and stubble on cheeks, heat pooling in his gut as he imagined taking a man into him again. He had thought so many times—despite his recent refusal to act on those thoughts—about going out and finding someone else, if only for a night. And Lexi had even, after one miserable attempt to conceive when he couldn't pretend for one more moment, told him that she would be fine with that, that she would still care for him, but…

It wasn't the sex. Sex was just sex.

He missed being in love. He wished he had never learned how.

So it got pushed down and locked up and bound with silken rope and he never, ever wanted to look at it again.

And then he saw Jack. And he knew those feelings had never gone away.

He pushed away his dinner, barely touched. And who the hell cared if he ate enough?

Nothing would ever be enough. Not food, not money, not booze. Nothing would fill him. Why bother?

He put his head in his hands, fingers digging into his scalp, and tried to put it all away. He should have known how to do this by now. He'd been doing it for almost twenty years.

He let himself regard one last image, like limoncello crème brûlée after an exquisite meal—firelight on Jack's golden skin, glinting in the silver threads in his hair, as he lowered himself and lined them up and kissed him as if they had been doing it their whole lives.

He couldn't respond to Jack's text, he couldn't, because—all he could think about was the way it should have been, snapshots of a life, Jack kissing the back of his neck, laughing, teasing, and Theo telling him to shut up in the way that meant *I love you*. So many images he held up in his mind like gold-leaf iconography. His mouth watered at the picture of them, two fragmented people, made whole, and he let that picture burn through him like a bonfire in his head.

And then he let the image go.

At least for now. Until he couldn't stop the conflagration of what he wanted from destroying him again.

"If you put more chocolate Hobnobs in that basket, I will, in fact, murder you."

Jack laughed at him, hand halfway in the basket. He dropped them in with a grin. "Will you?"

"Well," Theo tossed back a bit of his fringe that was hanging in front of his eyes, "Maybe not murder. Maybe just withhold sex."

Jack lifted an eyebrow, a habit he'd picked up from Theo. He tried not to think that Jack was better at it than he was. "Somehow I really doubt that."

"You never know. Maybe I've grown tired of you."

"Oh yeah?"

Jack crowded him against the shelves of the shop, tucked away in the back corner with rows of biscuits. The air smelled sweet and dry like oats. Theo blushed and looked down. Considered saying a few nasty words to get Jack away, just for a few moments, so he could catch his breath.

There was something domestic about this part of their lives, something that seemed adult, or like they were playing at being adults. An old married couple, out to do the shopping, occasionally holding hands in the dairy section. It was—it wasn't something that Theo had anticipated when he came here. He'd assumed a lot of things, even if he hadn't formed a real plan of what the hell to do with himself. He had imagined a fair bit of casual sex, quite a lot of drinking, and very little sleep. And that had been relatively accurate, at least until Jack Gardner reemerged, interrupting this newly invented life. He had never considered whatever this was—building a sort of routine. Little things and cozy things and things which made him sugary inside.

"You never know, I might have reached my Gardner limit." Snide insincerity in his voice.

"I don't think so." Jack leaned in farther, hooked a finger through Theo's belt loop. "Come on. Tell me."

"Tell you what?" Theo shot back with some irritation. He knew what—this wasn't the first time they'd had this conversation.

Jack kept that eyebrow lifted with a little wobble in his dirty smile. Trying to lighten this dark thing he was hungry for. "You know."

"Oh, honestly." Theo looked into the basket, then met Jack's eyes. "You can't possibly need—"

"I do."

"Fine," he muttered as if he were unwilling to say any of this. "I like you, all right? All hail Jack fucking Gardner, not nearly as boring or stupid as he looks, acceptable to spend time with." And then he shot him his own filthy smile. "And let me tell you, his cock—"

"Okay." Jack laughed, pulled away, red-faced. "I think we can stop there."

Theo pushed him back a little farther, the basket between them. "You sure? You don't want me to tell the whole grocery store," he gestured to an elderly woman with her own basket, eavesdropping shamelessly, and lowered his voice, "How much I love having you stretching me and filling me until I can't fucking bear it because you are so thick that I—"

"Jesus." Jack's pupils were dilated, eyes almost black. "Be

quiet, all right?" He seemed suddenly embarrassed, ashamed of his attraction, even though he had started this. "You're obscene."

"True." Theo felt oddly hurt from this small rejection, and his mouth sharpened with cold superiority, protecting himself. But then he grinned, unguarded, looking over Jack's tense body, and melted a little. "But honestly, I—you're all right. I think I can put up with you."

"Oh." Jack softened, put one finger through that loop again, leaned over their basket, and kissed him. "Ditto."

If Theo had known—well, no, he knew himself pretty well, and if he had known how badly Jack needed reassurance and praise, he would have tried to wreck him even more. And the temptation was always there, a leftover shard of their animosity. Jack had always seemed so proud, preening in the affection of his friends and teachers and coaches, and Theo had tried to find every gap in that armor to rip him apart. He hadn't been able to stand the way the world seemed to bend around him. It was easy to belittle him for his lack of money, his worn clothes, because those were the only flaws he could access. He hadn't understood, during their years at Gwynns, that Jack's poverty was the smallest part of what had damaged him.

And he had loved to mock Jack's relationship with Margaret because it did look so flawless and because—because he wanted it. He understood that better now, the bitter envy. Jack had seemed so content with her.

But this Jack, the Jack he knew so intimately—he blossomed with every kind word. He kept checking in, demanding affirmations, hoping that it was all true. That anyone could really care for him, for who he really was.

Theo—he wasn't sure that he liked the fact that he did care so much.

He had fallen in too deep.

He cleared his throat. "Why do you keep putting in all these digestives, anyway?"

And now Jack blushed again. "You need to eat more," he mumbled.

"I—"

"I think you'd forget to eat if I weren't here."

Theo's mouth opened, as if he could respond and deny it, but he didn't know what to say. It was true—before Jack had been here, he'd eaten only when he was so hungry that he was dizzy, and the world took on a gray tinge. It just—food didn't seem that important until his body demanded it. What he craved wasn't food.

He tried for a light tone. "You have some sort of feeding kink?"

Jack frowned at him, maybe a little angry. "Look, I—" He let go of Theo, took another step back. "I just know what it's like to be—to not eat enough. I don't like it when you do that, not when you have the option to eat properly."

"Oh." He felt a little warmth in his stomach and put his hand on Jack's neck. Pressed their foreheads together. "All right."

Jack relaxed into the contact. Theo heaved a false sigh.

"Put in the biscuits, then."

Their basket heavy with the essentials as well as too many chocolate biscuits—and Jack tossed in more sweets, he was insatiable—they took it up to the till and paid, doing that weird little shuffle of whose turn it was this time. Theo didn't enjoy, not really, being treated as if he needed help—but Jack enjoyed having the money to do what he wanted for the first time in his life, so Theo mostly humored him and let him hand over the cash.

It felt—sometimes it felt transactional.

"Am I the woman in this relationship? The little wife with her weekly allowance?"

Jack pursed his lips, half-amused. "You're the one with the job. I'm the one you come home—" His voice broke and he cleared his throat. "Come home to."

"True." Theo nudged him. "Lazy. Anyway, being gay— we're kind of both men, by definition."

Jack eased a hand into his pocket, the other gripping onto the grocery bag. "Right."

He didn't sound happy. The lightness of their banter gone.

He got like this, sometimes: a little prickly. Theo was never sure when this mood would arise, and too often it led to arguments which echoed their time at Gwynns. He knew that Jack wasn't all the way ready to—to say the words. For Theo, this life was his new normal, a normal he embraced; more than normal, it was thrilling. This was what he'd been waiting for so long to say out loud, to accept about himself. Somehow, despite the fact that Jack needed and soaked up that reassurance and affection and praise from Theo—despite all the incredible and entirely filthy sex they were having—he wasn't comfortable yet.

That was okay. It was clear that he still—

They had this time. Them. The possibilities.

They had the clubs and the bars and the music, but they also had the grocers, and the cups of coffee, and washing their laundry in the sink, hanging it on a line. Holding hands just to touch. Fights which led to the deliciousness of making up. And that was new and strange but it was so perfect, maybe, because it stretched out, jet beads on a string, as if it could be like this all the time. For the rest of time.

Maybe this awkward adjustment period was just a necessary step on the way toward—what might come next. It was just the first bit, the stuff that came before the rest.

They walked up the hill toward their apartment with the tiny refrigerator and the cupboards hanging precariously from the plaster walls, and there was something in Theo which was scared, which still hated Jack for making him feel this way, which wasn't ready to know what it felt like to need someone. And if Jack wasn't ready to speak about this part of himself, maybe Theo was—at risk. But it was too late, he knew it was—somewhere between dancing and fucking and picking up milk and having someone feed him, Theo had built a life with Jack in it.

He didn't want to find out what his life would feel like without him.

He was glad, in a way, that Jack didn't know how to say the words. It kept him safer; he could pretend that he had the power to refuse him.

He wished he could push him away.

Chapter Nineteen

"Ugh." Jack fumbled for his phone, tucked next to his pillow and vibrating, and hit a button, hoping it would shut the hell up.

He had given up waiting for a message from Theo. He never wanted to look at his phone again.

He rolled over on the lumpy couch. He had decided to wait, just a few more weeks, before moving into the new apartment, holding off on…what was coming. It was maybe seven in the morning, and he'd felt the fatigue of too many heavy days, so he'd tucked himself in as soon as Amy's light had gone off last night.

Meg had gone away on assignment, somewhere—writing an article on the new experimental training routine of some college north of here—and she'd booked a hotel and taken the weekend to herself. It seemed totally fair; they both needed some space. He'd been a house dad for the weekend, which was fine by him, more time to spend with Ames before…

Fuck. He punched the cushion under him, not really awake yet but still worrying.

He couldn't move out yet.

They hadn't told their children.

It was stupid and wrong and truly poor planning, especially since he had actually bought the new apartment and everything would have to change. But to them, from the inside, it just felt like—

They hadn't been close—the way a married couple was supposed to be—for a long time. They lived their lives in parallel,
each going to work, caring for the kids, doing their assigned
tasks, and it was almost as if their lives were totally unaltered
by this massive shift between them. They had love for each
other, lots of love, just—they were already separate. They were
childhood friends; they felt like roommates, the shift happening almost entirely naturally, even as they both wondered, in
the back of their minds, what was missing.

But it was going to change, of course it was, because he
wouldn't always be here to read Amy her favorite story and
sing atrociously, and Meg wouldn't be at the new apartment
to make sure Will and Johnny combed their hair.

And he wouldn't have anyone to kiss in the mornings, or
laugh at the newspaper comics with before bed, or hug a little and pretend—

"Jack? Jack, come on…"

He twitched under the duvet, his mind half in sleep and half
in all the things he'd been turning over like a stone, rubbing
and rubbing 'til all the rough edges were worn smooth. The
realities of what was to come. Would Amy want to live here
full-time, closer to her school, or would she want to live with
him, deeper into the city? And Johnny—her moods could be
unpredictable, a surly teenager all the way, and Will always
looked at him with an odd combination of fondness for his old
dad and exasperation that he just wasn't quite bright enough.
Which Jack absolutely agreed with, these days.

Sometimes it felt like all he had were these worries, the
ways in which he might disappoint people.

"Oh my God, Jack…"

He squeezed his eyes shut, stretched out and breathed in
and let himself drift—

Long, silken hair, silvery against navy sheets. The face he

always made, right before he opened his eyes, like he could murder Jack for waking him up. The stretch of pale skin, and the obscene sounds he made as he smelled that first cup of coffee. All of those familiar things altered by adulthood—no more late nights, and calm mornings, starting in on the cross-word, maybe, and tossing it aside and reaching down, down, under the covers, and wrapping his hand around—

"Jack Gardner, if you don't get your ass up in five seconds..."

His phone was shouting at him.

He rolled off the couch in shock and hit the floor with his face. And, um, other things.

Exactly how he liked to wake up. Christ.

And yes, that was Meg snickering through the video screen of his phone, also fallen to the ground next to him, which he had clearly answered rather than turning the hell off.

"Oh, Jack." She tried to cover her eyes, but kept gawking at him. She was laughing pretty hard now.

"I'm up, I'm up," he mumbled into the floor, not actually getting up.

"Do you need help or something? Do I need to call the fire department?"

"No," he sighed, pulled himself into a sitting position. "What's going on?"

She giggled a bit more, but then her face turned serious, and she looked down. "Jack, I have to tell you—"

He yawned. "What, hon?"

"Look." She stared up at him, suddenly fierce and a bit de-fensive. "I know I said I'd be at Towson University—" Oh yeah, that was it. "With their field hockey team, and, well, I was, but I ended up finishing early, and, uh." It came out in a rush. "I actually slept over with Charlie and..."

His sleepy brain paused, processed, caught up. And he laughed. "Are you trying to confess or something?"

"What? Jack…" He could practically hear her eyes as they rolled up to the ceiling. "No, though you could be a little… something."

"I'm happy for you." He gave her a soft smile. "Really."

"Well then. Not like I did it for you, but…" She gave him a dirty look, and then a fond one. "Anyway. That's not why I called." And then she mumbled, "None of your business anyway."

He felt that heaviness settle back onto him, "True. Why did you call?"

He scratched at the back of his head, trying not to feel awkward. He wondered where this conversation was going and how soon he'd be able to switch on the coffee maker and get the hell away from his ongoing guilt.

"Will spotted me." She crossed her arms, then in a mumble, "Kissing Charlie."

"What? You—what? How—" And then oh, right. "Charlie. The headmaster at Gwynns. Of course."

"Yeah."

"Fuck."

"I think it's time to tell the kids. Obviously."

"Right." He stood up. "Right."

He sat back down on the couch. Thought about what Amy might say, asking too many questions, wondering if they still loved her. He stood up again in a panic. Thought about Will looking disappointed in him (which was not altogether unusual, God, he was so outstripped by his youngest son). Fell back onto the couch with a thump.

"Jack, are you, right this moment, totally losing it?" Meg was still staring up from his phone, cripes, sounding rather too amused.

"No, I mean, maybe," he mumbled, rubbing his face. "But aren't you—aren't you even a little bit worried?"

Her jaw dropped and she shot him an incredulous look. "Worried? Jack, I've been out of my mind with worry. Not," he must have made a horrible grimace, "Because of us, but yeah, because of the kids. But...you should have seen Will, last night. He was—"

"Inscrutable?"

She laughed. "No, actually. Not this time. He was open and just—he was just calm."

"Oh."

"Yeah." She took a deep breath, squared her shoulders. "Bring Amy for brunch, all right? And we'll—we'll just do it."

"Okay." He put his head in his hands, then looked over at her. "I love you, you know."

"And I love you, you queer lunatic." She sniffled, then shot out, "Now fuck off, it's early and I want to get laid at least one more time."

He heard a familiar, deep voice behind her, shout, "Meg!" with an uncharacteristic squeak, and then Meg laughing, full-throated in a way he hadn't heard in too long as she ended the call. He shook his head and let himself fall back onto the couch one more time.

He didn't deserve her.

Amy had needed no convincing to visit her siblings at Gwynns.

She was still annoyed that it wasn't her turn yet, after all, eager to grow up the way children always are, and any chance to sneak into the Academy was much appreciated. As Jack watched her—taking in all the details, memorizing the stone and brick and the smell of cut grass—he felt the shadow of his first moments, here. Gwynns was his first real home.

It did feel different now. He knew the campus in such an intimate way, the trees and the creek and the tower, but all of his memories were colored by an adult perception, the years changing his childhood, the knowledge of himself that he didn't have, back then.

The whole place felt like his mistakes.

The air smelled like Theo.

He missed him. He would give anything just to have him here and love him properly the way he should have done, immediately and without reservations.

Okay, Jack. He shook himself. *Get a grip.*

Charlie had set up a private room in the dorm building—not, Jack was relieved to find, his personal quarters as headmaster—with a light brunch and a view over the big hill at the entrance to campus. Meg was already there, of course, and Jack gave her shoulder a little squeeze as they sat on squashy chairs by a marble fireplace. "All right?"

She nodded and held out her arms for an exuberant hug from Amy. "Mom, can you believe we're at Gwynns?"

"We are?" Meg looked around, pretending shock.

"Mom..."

They laughed, so alike in the way they sounded, the way they looked. Textured auburn hair and freckles and too much fun like the bubbles in champagne.

The door opened. Johnny wandered in, eyes on her phone, clunky headphones over her ears. She was banging her head and totally ignoring everything around her. She threw herself down, legs splayed over an armrest and back crammed into the opposite corner of the chair, and kept rocking out.

"Teenagers are lovely, aren't they?" Meg's voice was as dry as the Antarctic. Jack laughed through his nose, and Amy giggled.

He heard quiet voices in the hall. He tilted his head at Meg, who shrugged, and he walked over toward the door. And there was Will, also listening to music—one earbud in and the other trailing off...

And attached to Jasper Beaumont. Okay then.

They looked so young. So very serious, a blond head leaning over his son's black hair.

It ached.

He cleared his throat—Jasper blinked up at him, and Will just glanced over as if he'd known Jack was there all along.

"Hi, Jasper."

"Hello, Mr. Gardner." He held out his hand, earbud still in. "How do you do?"

He tried not to laugh at the stilted manners, more authentic but equally as practiced as his father's. He took Jasper's hand. Shook firmly.

"Very well, thanks." He coughed a little and blushed, because somehow he still felt outclassed by miniature Beaumonts. He dropped his hand and gestured at Will's phone. "What're you listening to?"

Will spoke up. "David Bowie, 'Ziggy Stardust.' You heard of him? Jazz loves him."

A dizzying flash, a lithe body dancing, the smell of smoke, a sordid smile and a sharp mouth. He guessed it made sense that Theo would want to share his music with his kid.

Jack didn't know if he wanted to laugh or cry, and he nodded and did some weird combination of both, which earned him a very strange look from Jasper. Not dissimilar from his father's frog look—but more like it had been Jack eating the frog, and Jazz was just too polite to mention it.

It was very much time to move on.

"Will, we've got brunch going in here—"

"Yeah, Dad." He and his blond shadow finally detached, and Will smiled at Jazz, shy. "See you later."

Jack nodded his goodbye, watching Jasper walk away with a bag full of books and a head full of music, and he thought about another boy, and what his life should have been, and wouldn't it have been better, that first day in the dorms, if he'd shaken his stupid hand.

Things could have been so different.

He turned away, and then just kind of…stopped.

The day was too much.

"Jazz's dad is divorced, you know." Will said it almost to the empty hallway, not looking at his dad, who was maybe quietly falling apart. "He says that it's better for everyone, because now everyone can try to be happy. All the way happy, you know?"

He wrapped his hand around Jack's elbow, holding it the way he'd done as a little boy, and Jack could feel how his kid was growing up but that he would always, still, be his. Be Will, his child, his heart on the outside of his body.

"Come on, Dad." He pulled him around, so gentle. "Time for brunch."

Brunch was a selection of fruit, pastries, and the thick black coffee that the students weren't supposed to drink but Johnny guzzled anyway, which was somewhat worrying.

Bruch was also extraordinarily uneventful.

Jack watched his kids' faces as he mumbled and stuttered, as Meg put a hand on his arm and explained in a calm voice what was going to happen. She was so strong and so unmoved, here with their children, telling them about this massive—his biggest fuckup. And the kids watched them, and they just—

Amy, upon hearing the news, got stuck on one crucial detail—"So what you're saying is that I'm going to have two bedrooms, right?"—and kept quietly whispering to herself, "Two rooms. Two whole rooms…"

Johnny, forced to turn her music off at the beginning of the conversation—New Orleans jazz, which Jack had never seen anyone rock out to before, but Johnny gave it her all—and actually listen, gave an epic shrug which seemed to indicate *Nothing to do with me* and *Is there a reason you're interrupting my day with this?*

And Will—he kind of glowed. He looked proud of them.

After, when the kids took Ames down to wander around campus, he and Meg sat there, shell-shocked at their children's nonchalance.

"I guess—" She looked sad, just a little, and then relieved, like everything finally clicked into place. "I guess we haven't really been married for a long time."

"I am sorry." He could hardly bear to look at her.

"You know what? I'm not."

"No?"

"I have three beautiful, brilliant, crazy children with my best friend in the whole world." She wiped one eye, mostly dry, and smiled. "And holy mother of God, Charlie is a rock star in the sack."

"Oh my God."

She laughed. "Oh, get over it. You can't tell me that you're not looking forward to climbing a certain blond bastard like a tree as soon as possible."

Well, she was right about that.

"This is a weird conversation to have with the woman who bore your children."

"Jack." She leaned forward in her chair, grabbed his hands. "We still have...we have time, you know? We have the years to fix our mistakes."

She ran a hand through his hair, gentle, and then ruffled it up.

"And hell, as a woman I am in my sexual prime, so...you've set me free, in a way. There are a hell of a lot of things I'd like to do. Maybe some things about me you didn't know, either."

She gave his wild hair one last pat. "Don't be such a sad sack. You'll never get anyone to fuck you that way." He choked out a laugh. "But I think." She took a deep breath. "I think you should see if you can move out sooner rather than later."

He felt this moment—another ending. Maybe the real end, finally.

Back home, he sent off a text to Genni Dumont, and he started packing a suitcase. Amy insisted on supervising, which resulted in her rejecting every article of clothing that he had bought before that shopping trip with Meg—great, more women ruling his fashion choices—and he resigned himself to spending a few more hours updating his wardrobe.

Though he wouldn't be filling the whole damn closet at the new apartment, that was for sure.

"I really will get two rooms, right?" Amy looked up at him from her perch on the end of the bed, braids tight to her scalp, dark-lashed eyes wide. He had a feeling that the question wasn't exactly what—she wanted to ask something else.

"That's right." He plopped down, sitting on the suitcase and hopping a bit to make it close, feeling a little spark in his chest when Amy giggled. "And you can come stay whenever you like, you know? You can even live with me sometimes, if you want. It'll be your house, just like this one."

"Really?"

"Really really." He put his arm around her and squeezed. "You'll always be my little girl, and I'll always be your dad."

"Dad," she whined at his tight hug, elbowing him. "Ugh, don't be sappy."

He laughed and let go—her elbows were actually quite sharp—holding his hands up in a gesture of defeat. "What am I going to do with you, Ames?"

She looked up at him, narrowed her chocolate-brown eyes. "Love me forever, 'course."

The words held more—more conversations they'd need

to have, more years to come but in a different pattern, more truths she wasn't old enough for yet.

But, for now, he knew what to say.

"Oh, yes." He kissed the top of her head. "I suppose you must be right."

She leaned on him, her small body tucked perfectly under his chin. "Just like always."

"Just like always."

"You know." Jack was running his fingers over the light down of Theo's arm. "I still technically have a hotel room."

"Mm?" Theo hummed, eyes closed.

"I mean, you know I go there while you're at work to get my clothes and stuff."

"Mmm." Theo was often incoherent after his morning shift, and they usually spent afternoons lazing about in bed, drifting in and out of sleep.

"Even though a bunch of stuff is here now."

"Gardner," he muttered, still not opening his eyes. "Why are you talking?"

Jack laughed quietly, trying not to disturb him further. "Sorry." He kissed the top of Theo's head. "Just thinking."

"Well, stop."

"All right, all right." He paused, then couldn't stop himself from mumbling, "I just thought…"

"Argghh," Theo grumbled. "Okay, tell me what it is, then shut your fucking mouth."

"Never mind, then." Frustrated silence.

"Dammit." Theo opened his eyes. "Don't be like that. What is it?"

"Just… I was thinking it would be nice if we, you know, stayed over at the hotel. Got room service. Had a bath."

"A bath." Theo picked his head up and raised his eyebrows. "Are you trying to tell me something?"

Jack slapped his arm. "I'm telling you... I want to do something nice. For you."

"Oh." Theo turned pink, then made a haughty face. "As you should."

"So, tonight? We can stay in?"

"Yes, yes, all right, very nice, shut up."

Jack chuckled, kissing him again, "You're so charming, Theodore Beaumont. That must be why I—"

Theo snored.

Jack's heart beat hard and fast.

He'd never really said those words before, not even when he whispered against Theo's skin in the night, and he probably shouldn't—

It was probably for the best that he'd fallen back asleep.

"Are you fucking kidding me?"

Jack had just unlocked the door to his hotel room. Theo stepped in, took one look around, and whirled on Jack.

The drama queen.

"You've had this room the whole time?"

He shrugged, embarrassed. "I know, it's too nice, I didn't really need to—"

"You are the biggest idiot in the world." Theo looked pretty offended, then froze. "I'm going to look in the bathroom!"

Jack stood, still half in the door, wondering just how badly he'd messed up.

Theo's excited voice called out, "Oh my God, this tub would fit both of us..."

Jack laughed, shut the door behind him, listening to Theo's muttering.

"Could anybody really be this stupid, living in my awful

apartment for… God, the towels are so soft… I think I am going to kill him…"

"Everything all right in there?" Jack sat on the edge of the bed.

"Everything all right, sure, now he asks…" Theo kept mumbling as he came back into the room and put his hands on his hips. "Well."

"So it passes Beaumont inspection, hmm?" Jack leaned back onto his elbows, toeing off his shoes. Theo flopped down next to him and sighed, then waggled his hand around.

"I suppose it is sufficient."

Jack reached over, grabbed the waggling hand, held it.

"It would be better, of course, with champagne."

"Oh, right. I'll, um." Jack knew he had the number for the front desk somewhere. "I can just call down—"

"You will not. I give great phone." Theo leered.

"You just want to order people around."

Theo looked over at him, very serious, then his mouth twitched, and he started to laugh. "Yeah, I really do."

Champagne ordered and delivered—and Theo did give great phone, which turned him on more than he thought was necessary—Jack ran a steaming hot bath.

"Let me." He grabbed Theo, motions a little too rough from never learning how to be tender, and he ran his hands under his shirt, along the taut muscles of his abdomen.

He undressed Theo slowly, raising goose bumps on every inch of skin he touched.

Theo's face was pink. "What are you doing, Gardner?"

It was—it was so intimate. Jack wanted to have this—these things, these feelings of knowing someone down to their bones. Being able to touch. "Taking my time."

He knelt, unbuttoning Theo's jeans, inching the zipper down, dragging his fingers over his wiry thighs. He rubbed his face along Theo's prick—already very interested, fuck yes—and breathed in his scent. "God, I could do this forever."

Theo wound his hands through Jack's hair and pulled, tilting his face up. "Gardner." His voice was hushed and still, like the near-scalding surface of the bathwater. "Don't make promises you can't keep. All right?"

Jack nuzzled his face into Theo's hand, nodding and closing his eyes, and he slid his pants to the floor. He licked Theo, root to tip, and Theo groaned, pushing his prick into Jack's watering mouth.

Jack moaned around him. God, he loved doing this. Theo laughed, rich and thick like maple syrup, and shoved him away. "Take your own clothes off, will you?"

Jack smiled up from the tile floor. "Eager for the bath, hmm?"

"Do shut up, Jack." Theo stepped into the tub, pure, milky skin sliding under the water. "And come here."

He didn't need to be told twice.

He did wonder, as he ripped off his clothes and gasped his way into the hot water, why he felt the way he did, all light and fluttery, when the guy he was so busy fucking told him to shut up.

Because it's Theo, a hidden part of him whispered. *It's always been like this.*

And maybe—maybe nice wasn't what he'd ever wanted.

Jack nestled himself between Theo's legs, Theo's firm cock pressed up against his ass.

"Fuck, this is good." He relaxed back onto silken skin, made slippery with bath oil.

"See, a little luxury never hurt anyone."

"I think you may have convinced me." He moved back, rubbing himself over Theo's prick, feeling it catch between his cheeks.

"Oh, fuck." Theo shifted behind him, trying to regain some control and picking up the glasses of chilled champagne he'd placed on the sink. "Drink up."

It was almost—it was stupid, because here in the hotel was nothing like real life, nothing like the way he'd lived as a kid, but it was homey; the two of them were natural and comfortable together, even when they yelled, even when Theo threw things at him and all Jack could do was duck...and it was too soon and too fast, but it seemed like a universal truth, like there was nothing other than this, this fact, the way they felt about each other.

Just six weeks, he thought, of going out and partying and cooking instant noodles and splitting the grocery bills—but this, them, it wasn't just six weeks. It was four years. It felt like their whole lives.

Jack sipped cold champagne, nose tickling from the bubbles, and he clenched. "Fuck."

He turned, setting down his glass again, and climbed on top of Theo, water sloshing over to the floor. He ran his hand over Theo's neck, over the firm planes of his chest, his tight pink nipples, down over his stomach, gripping onto his cock.

Jack stroked, slowly, pressure just a hair too light, and watched the mingled frustration and pleasure shifting on Theo's face. "I want to do something."

Theo rolled his eyes back. "Well, you should damn well do it."

He laughed, then bent over and kissed that spot under Theo's ear. "I want you to fuck me."

While he spoke, he pulled, firmer, and Theo tensed, gasped, and came.

"Uh." Theo blushed a little and thunked his head back on the edge of the tub. "I think we're going to need to wait a minute."

Jack dropped his head to Theo's neck. Tried not to laugh. Started smiling against his skin.

And giggled.

"Are you laughing at me, Gardner?"

"No." He tried to hold on to himself. "Not at all, never."

"I'll have you know that you had nothing to do with that." Theo twitched, lifting his head and grumbling.

Jack kept his face where it was, grinning. "No?"

"It was the bath, obviously."

"You get turned on by baths?"

"Well," still prickly, but running his hands gently over Jack's ass, "What else do you do in a bath? It's just a...common association."

Jack picked his head up and kissed Theo, right at the corner of his mouth where he kept his secret smiles. "Makes sense."

"Of course. Now get off me, I'm boiling."

They dried off, thoroughly taking advantage of the fluffy towels, and fell back onto the bed. Theo reached for Jack's— achingly hard—cock, but he slapped the hand away.

"Just—let me." Jack got up onto his knees, sat back on his heels.

Theo's eyes were so soft, the gray as misty and ephemeral as Irish rain. "You planning on putting on a show?"

He gestured toward Jack's prick, practically dripping with arousal, and Jack shook his head, shy. But then he felt a sense of resolve—

He wanted everything. Every stupid, sexy, dirty thing— he wanted it all.

Jack lifted one of Theo's legs, planting his foot on the mattress, then the other.

"What are you doing?"

"Shut up, Theo."

"Well, fuck y—" His voice came to an abrupt stop as Jack mouthed at the tender skin of his inner thighs.

He wanted—he wanted to memorize all of him, all of this skin like new ivory, all his little sounds and sighs. Letting himself possess what he had always coveted. He licked the juncture between his legs, sucking on the soft skin, the very tops of his thighs; he swallowed around his prick, rapidly filling, taking him in as far as he could. Weeks and weeks of this—he knew Theo's body, knew that he could fit him down the back of his throat, nose pressed into curled golden hair.

He wanted to kiss secrets into his skin.

Pulling off, Theo whimpered—and Jack moved his mouth, down, and lifted Theo's legs over his shoulders.

"What are you—"

"Guess."

"Jack—"

"Shh."

Theo was sweet and smooth from oil, and Jack pressed the flat of his tongue against his entrance, then kissed him there, filthy, the way he kissed his mouth.

"Ohhh—" Theo's legs clenched and released and kicked at his back.

"Ow, you fucker," Jack muttered, then licked around Theo's rim in a spiraling curl.

"You—sweet holy fuck—you try staying still, when—"

Jack sucked hard—Theo smelled so good, how was he always so perfect—then laved him with gentle swipes of his tongue when Theo dug his heels under his shoulder blades. "Jesus, why are you so rough..."

Theo moaned, high and long, and breathed out, shaking. "You know you love it."

A feeling like something trapped inside of him.

"I do." Jack wrapped a hand around Theo's cock—hard and

hot and fuck, so ready—and pushed two fingers into him, curling up. Theo raised his chest, head thrown back, stomach concave—and he was like a fucking sculpture, right here in this moment, in marble, glittering, something fit for a museum, something to worship.

"If you still want me to—ah, please, right there—to fuck you…"

Jack pressed, once more, against that bundle of nerves—left his fingers there, still and firm, while he leaned over Theo and kissed his mouth. Theo wiggled and he pulled his fingers away.

"Jack, have you…" He was quiet, and blushed a light pink. "Have you really never done that before?"

"I told you." Jack dropped his body, his cock brushing up against Theo's, and they both moaned. "I've never done anything."

Theo chuckled low and dirty. "Well, you are a fucking natural."

Jack thrust down, breathless. "Have you ever—has anyone else—with their mouth, I mean—"

He pulled back to catch Theo's eyes, which were clear and entirely guileless as he shook his head. "Only you."

"God, I love that." Jack reached down and wrapped his hand around the base of his cock, fuck, what Theo's voice did to him, "I wanna be the first and the la—"

Theo made a sound, an angry and feral sound, and flipped them over. Not letting him talk. He sat back and pulled at Jack's hips—Jack felt his softened skin rasp against the cotton sheets, his ass nearly in Theo's lap. Theo growled again, rushed out of bed—

"What—"

And pulled a bottle out of their overnight bag.

He poured lube on his fingers, a whole mess of it, and wrapped both hands around Jack's nearly painfully hard cock.

Three quick pulls, and then he stopped, running his left hand down, one finger resting against him.

"Do you trust me?"

Jack lifted his own hand, twined it with Theo's right, slick with lube and precome, and he was deadly serious. "Theo, I do."

"Thank fuck," and Theo slid a finger in.

It was new, and it was strange, and it was perfect. Theo was gentle with him—not tentative, no, but almost reverent. Shocked into a kind of revelation that he was doing this, that Jack was letting him. That he wanted him to. Jack felt him slip in another finger, and the stretch was so good, because it was Theo stretching him, Theo's long fingers, his smell everywhere, his face so serene and predatory and that twitch in his eye that showed he was nervous. He looked dangerous, like something untamed, and he held Jack in his hand like a bird he could crush, and when he found Jack's prostate it was like coming home.

"Please, Theo—"

"What do you want?"

"Please, I—"

"Tell me, come on."

"Theo," he nearly cried out, but maybe it was more like a whimper. "Please, fuck me."

He pulled Jack's hips up farther, leaned forward, pressed in, slow and careful. Wonder on his face. And it hurt, God how it hurt, but it wasn't merely a physical pain; it seemed like the real hurt was somewhere else, because after about five seconds he felt full and fantastic and fucking cared for and cradled and—and—

"God, you look—"

"Kiss me."

Theo leaned forward, Jack curled around him, holding on

too tightly, both leaving bruises. Jack's prick was swollen, rubbing against Theo's stomach, and Theo was just thrusting home, over and over, not too rough but just hard enough, and he kissed Jack like it was air and they were drowning, and—

"Fuck, I love you—"

And it was Jack who said it, who finally broke, God, after all of that denying and hiding and lying he'd been doing for years, and Theo growled again like a bear in a trap, bit that place on Jack's neck which never had time, now, to heal, and Jack pulsed and poured out what felt like his entire life, everything, all of the truths in him, holding on to Theo like a vise.

"You bastard, you fucking—" Theo's movements stuttered, shuddering, and he came with this sound like—like—

He fell onto Jack, smearing come over both of them.

"I told you. I told you, not to make promises you can't keep."

Theo was shaking. Jack held him and kissed his ear and he might have been sorry for making such an awful mess of things but fuck, that had been absolutely incredible, and it was true that for those few blinding seconds he'd never loved anything the way he loved Theo.

And that was just the way it was.

That was maybe the way it had always been.

"So what'd you think?" Theo's voice was calm, almost bored, as he rolled off and stared at the ceiling, still panting. "Is the great Jack Gardner a bottom after all?"

He turned his head, looked at Jack, mouth mocking but eyes soft.

"Oh, I dunno." He nudged Theo's shoulder. "I may need to try it a few more times. Just to be sure."

Theo wrinkled his nose, one of those hidden smiles at the corner of his mouth. And he closed his eyes and sighed. "I'll have to check my schedule."

"Oh, nice."

"Now be a love," his voice caught, "And bring me my fucking champagne."

In the morning—after three more rounds, and he'd had to tap out after the second, sore and stretched and dripping but fucking reborn—they checked out of the hotel with all of Jack's belongings.

"You sure?" Jack walked close to Theo on the sidewalk, stumbling only a little but relishing in it.

"Yeah." Theo lit up a cigarette, shoulders tight. "I just don't want to get used to it."

He passed a cigarette over to Jack—who nearly missed him, in the click and whoosh of the lighter—saying, "And I love you too, you horrible motherfucker."

Chapter Twenty

Theo'd never expected to be in the headmaster's office again.

Though knowing the wild streak of impulsiveness in his son, he probably should have.

Charles Humperdink was burdened with a terrible name, a persistent clumsiness, and horrible anxiety. He was a legacy—his family had practically founded the school, hence the buildings bearing his surname—but he earned every good grade, working silently where others complained and bragged, and it was no surprise at all, really, when he was named the youngest headmaster in Gwynns's history.

He may have wobbled a bit on the way to the podium as his posting was announced. But he was smarter than most of their classmates, and worked harder, and was kind to all of the students where former headmasters had been cold. Gwynns was changing under his guidance; it was a more nurturing place. And Charles was nurturing by nature—even when they were children and Theo was at his nastiest, Charles had offered compassion.

Theo remembered all the times he'd been unnecessarily cruel to him. How he had taken it, stoically. As if that were just the price of admission—to bear the teasing, the bullying, and quietly prove his worth. To make his world a better place.

And he had. Theo shifted in his leather wingback chair, carrying a load of guilt for who he had been.

And his son sat across from him, not looking guilty in the least, though he was.

Charles had called him around ten that night. Theo'd been going over his investment portfolio—his friends didn't need his money anymore, but he kept an eye on their success, Genni with her real estate business, and Phil running his tech company, and Tom with his restaurant in New Orleans—and he had just changed into his dressing gown. Hoping to get a good night's sleep; praying that he wouldn't dream about—

But there was Charles's voice on the phone, still sounding nervous but, he had to admit it, with a much more commanding and confident presence than he had remembered.

Now, in this office filled with leather-bound books, formal but comfortable chairs, and a collection of rare orchids, Theo wanted to look at anything other than Jasper's defiant pose. His son's eyes darted between Theo and Charles, and he arranged his face in an expression of remorse.

Like that was going to work. Theo had practically invented that particular pout.

Charles looked at them both, eyes flitting back and forth, placid but with a hint of nervous energy. Occasionally he'd look away, gaze darting toward a closet—Theo thought that maybe Charles was still afraid of him, and he felt terrible.

He sighed heavily and turned back to his only child. "Jasper Diarmuid Beaumont. Would you care to tell me why I've been called here at ten at night?"

Jasper fiddled with the sleeves of his pajamas sticking out from under his jacket. He muttered something inaudible.

"Go on, Jazz." This from Charles, who sounded altogether too forgiving.

"I—I—" He managed the well-bred Beaumont tone, but his face shifted: stubborn, mutinous, with a hint of self-righteousness.

It was actually a bit funny. Also quite irritating.

It sounded suspiciously like a Gardner.

"You what?"

"I just had to get out of the dorms, Dad."

Oh sure, in that case...

"This is something you had to do now, when you should have been in bed?"

"Well..." He lingered on the word, drawing it out. "It's my campus. I live here. I just wanted to go for a walk."

Theo had a visceral flash of a long-blurred memory—nights that he, himself, had snuck out, he and his friends wandering along the creek, Phil reciting poetry or some nonsense and Tom snacking on food he'd stolen from the kitchens. Genni's lipstick nearly black in the dark. Feeling like they owned the world. He would be a hypocrite to be upset with Jasper for doing the same, but—

It was his child. Jasper was just a boy.

Theo knew his parents had never worried like this, but he was, despite the agony of it, glad that he did.

His voice was calm but cold. "Did you think that going into the woods might be dangerous? And that it is, for that reason, not permitted after curfew?"

"Well, we didn't go really far."

His mind snagged on something. "And the 'we' means you and Will, I'm assuming."

"Um, yes."

"And where is he now? Did he manage not to get caught?"

Heaven help him, Jasper looked more ashamed to have been discovered than to have been wandering around the woods at night.

Theo may have needed to face the fact that Jasper was, in almost every way, his kid.

Silence. Charles's eyes flicked away again toward the wall,

and then Theo heard a noise outside the door. Jasper looked toward the hallway, just moving his eyes.

Theo should have known. Will could have probably gotten away with this, but he and Jasper were inseparable. It was ridiculous.

He sort of wanted to laugh. Oh, well. He closed his eyes, hoped for patience, and called out, "Will, why don't you join us?"

A head with messy black hair appeared—setting off too many flashbacks to count—and he saw glittering blue eyes which did not, at all, convey remorse. He walked in, very calmly, and wedged himself on the seat next to Jasper.

"And what was your role in this?" Charles seemed comfortable letting him take the lead, at least for the moment.

"It...may have been my idea to sneak out. And how to do it. Sir."

Ah.

It was a very sad day indeed when a Gardner was the brains of the operation. Theo sighed, rubbed his eyes, longing fervently for a glass of brandy and his bed. "I don't even want to ask how you got past security... Headmaster, I hope you're going to call Will's father, also."

Charles nodded in a stilted way, looking at the wall, and Will interrupted—"I mean, he can, Mr. Beaumont, but I don't think he needs to. My mom is probably here." He gestured toward Charles, who'd started blushing and didn't look like he would ever stop. "In the headmaster's quarters."

An embarrassed twitch and widened eyes from Charles. Interesting.

"Ah." Pushing that very firmly to the side, at least for the moment, Theo leaned forward. "Fine. That's—fine. Do you two understand why you're in trouble?"

"'Cause we got caught?" A mumble from Jasper. He was technically correct, of course. Not that Theo would admit that.

"No, Jasper. Will. It's because going out into the woods after curfew is dangerous." He ran his hand through his hair, considering pulling it out. "You can't just leave the dorms at night, expecting to emerge perfectly safely. Your teachers didn't even know where you were! What if—"

"But Dad, you did whatever you wanted when you were at Gwynns! And Mr. Gardner—"

"Yes, we were young and stupid. Do you think we want you to be the same?" he almost yelled, which was very unlike him, but he'd felt like he was stretched too thin recently, right up on the edge of things he simply couldn't handle.

"Boys." Charles's reproof was quiet. "We want you to do better, be better than we were. That's our job as adults. To help you. Keep you safe."

"Oh." Will looked down, frowning. "Yeah."

Both boys did look chastened, but Theo had a sense that this wouldn't be the last late-night phone call he'd be getting from Gwynns.

He sighed. "All right. Headmaster, what consequences do you recommend?"

"Three weeks' detention."

Jasper gasped.

"Charlie—"

Theo blinked in surprise as Will used Charles's first name, totally inappropriately. Perhaps there was a lot he didn't know about what was going on in the Gardner-Daugherty family.

"Do you think you don't deserve it?" Charles could actually sound quite stern.

Theo was gratified to see Jasper nudge Will, who slumped and muttered, "No, Headmaster."

At least his son was a good influence.

A pause—Charles really was skilled at this authority thing, letting the silence stretch ominously. "Now go on to bed, boys."

They nodded, stood, heads bowed.

"Jasper," Theo called him over, took him by the shoulders, and wrapped him in a firm embrace, which he bore stiffly. "Just be safe, all right?"

Jasper hugged him back, softening. "Yeah, Dad. Love you."

"Love you too."

He watched the boys as they walked toward the door, and if he noticed the sly smiles they sent each other—already planning something else, no doubt—he let himself ignore it. He had far more complex things to worry about, honestly. He leaned back in his chair and threw a glance at Charles under half-lidded eyes. "So. Margaret, hmm?"

Charles colored again, and his eyes flicked toward the closet. Utter silence in the room, other than the ticking of a mantel clock and the sound of a fine mist falling over the purple orchids.

And then that damn closet door creaking open as the woman in question stepped out—in a rather too clingy nightdress—from what was apparently not a closet but the hallway to Charles's quarters. Theo's heart thumped, missing a beat.

Charles was going to have an aneurism from blushing so much.

"You handled that well, Beau." She plopped herself down in the chair across from him. "Thanks. I knew Will was probably involved, but I didn't want to come out, given..." She gestured at her lack of appropriate attire. He remembered that she had always been a bit...gregarious, but this seemed to be going too far.

"No." He felt a hysterical laugh at the back of his throat, totally undignified. "I don't suppose you would have."

"Our kids are such a mess, aren't they?" She shook her head, then grinned. "Nothing like we were, of course."

"Of course." He felt a bit faint.

He became aware of the fact that at some point, his mouth had dropped open in response to Margaret's sudden appearance, her negligee, and her total comfort in parading around in far too few clothes in front of him, her high school bully. He was sure he looked desperately gormless. He closed his mouth with an audible clack of his teeth.

"I think perhaps I should…go." He stood quickly, needing to be anywhere but here, with Charles—who truly appeared like he might pass out at any second—and his ex-lover's ex-wife in her scandalous bedwear. Who was being rather too friendly with him, considering—

"Didn't take you for a prude, Beau," she teased.

He ground his teeth and considered telling her where, exactly, her so-called straight husband had on many memorable occasions put his mouth.

Prude, ha.

"I'm sorry, Beau—Theo—" Margaret reached out and caught his wrist. "Look…"

He looked down at her hand, which she then took back, grimacing.

"I just wanted to say… I don't want you to think I hate you, or anything." Her plump lips puckered like she was sucking a lemon.

"No?" He looked away, slumping, "You have—there are reasons why you might."

Her eyes thawed. "Yeah. But," she sat up straight, firm, "What happened when we were kids—all of that—I know you, you were raised in a particular way, not a very nice way, and we were still young, and—"

He felt his shoulders tense up around his ears, and his whole body seemed to burn, and he felt a stinging on his lip. "I still behaved the way I did," a deep breath, "And with Jack—"

"I have no illusions that Jack wasn't the asshole in that situation."

His head shot up, and she continued.

"My hus—" She rolled her eyes. "Jack Gardner is many wonderful things. A great dad, philanthropist, all that. But I know, better than most, that he can be a selfish prick."

"Oh." Theo felt very small. And kind of vindicated, a gift he didn't expect to receive from Meg Daugherty.

"And he's also very easy to love." It came out in a rush. "I understand—"

"Margaret..."

She stood, facing him, the strap of her nightgown sliding down one shoulder, and with uncharacteristic tenderness she took his face in her hands. "I'm not angry at you, all right? I know that you—you and he—" She blew out a breath. His cheeks tingled where she touched them. "Just. Thank you."

She was thanking him, and for what?

He remembered staring at her picture in the paper—beautiful and ethereal in the engagement photo, in a canary-yellow sundress, Jack holding her, and Theo had hated her with such bitterness that he thought he'd never recover, and he'd smoked a whole pack of cigarettes and ashed all over her perfect fucking face.

He laughed, still bitter in the deepest parts of him. "Why? Why thank you?"

Her eyes were kind, meeting his, like she knew exactly how he felt. "For letting me borrow him for a while."

He couldn't say anything, words and doubts and shame stuck in his chest. She patted his cheek and let him go. Charles sat there, apparently having decided to politely ignore the uncomfortable exchange, but as Theo left, he shot him a gentle smile.

Theo thought he might be all right, someday, with calling him Charlie.

He was back in his house by eleven thirty, undressed and under the covers by eleven thirty-five, and he still felt Meg's hands on his face. He spread out, naked skin delighting in cerulean silk sheets, nestling himself in the middle of his down mattress. Trying to enjoy his luxurious life.

He couldn't sleep.

At midnight, he got up, grabbed his phone, and typed out a text in his usual curt tone before he could stop himself. Just four words, and maybe—maybe he could have—

They really were—the marriage was clearly over. He didn't want to hope, didn't want to unlock the thing in him that he'd hidden for so long, but—

He read it over, once more, and sent it off. As he lay in bed, the words echoed, over and over, so endless that he heard them in his sleep—

Jack, we should talk.

"Should we get a cat, do you think?"

Theo was in their tiny kitchenette, fully nude, staring at the remains of Jack's box of sugar—because he sweetened even his instant coffee, the heathen—holes chewed straight through, and granules loose on the counter.

When Theo had decided to run the hell away from everything—from the stupid things he'd done, from his mother who always judged him despite her own unforgivable mistakes, from the burden and deep shame of visiting Father in prison, the horrible wrecked home and all the angry people that he and his family had hurt—he hadn't realized that his new life would involve...vermin.

Jack had maybe laughed at him and called him a princess

when he leaped onto the bed the first time he saw a mouse, but really, why should he have been expected to deal with rodents?

"Mm."

"Helpful." He looked over at Jack, who was still in bed, the layabout. "Jack."

He didn't move.

Theo walked over to the bed and kneeled on the edge, swinging one leg over to straddle him. He grabbed both of his hands and pinned them over his head, then twisted his hips, grinding down.

"Jack Gardner." Theo gripped his wrists, leaned down to place lingering kisses on the stretch of neck he always kept bruised and that Jack never complained about. "Are you listening to me?"

Jack struggled under him and thrust up, not trying to get away but ready to fight, that friction between them always. "I am now." Theo sucked on an earlobe. "You kinky bastard."

"Good." He sat back, straightened his hair, put his hands on his hips, and grinned. "So?"

Jack grabbed his hips and flipped them over, shoving Theo's knees up, pushing against him. "So what?"

"Do you—ah—think we should—Christ, all right, find the lube—get a cat?"

Jack wet his fingers and shoved in two, then three, in quick succession, Theo still slippery and loose from their first fuck once he got home from going over the club's books with Colin. "A—your ass, so perfect, Theo, I swear to God—cat?"

"Yeah." His voice was high, too loud, and Jack thrust in with one smooth slide. "Oh, please—"

Jack set a punishing pace, tilting his hips up and stroking incessantly against Theo's prostate, grabbing his cock with his come-and-lube-drenched fingers, jerking him fast and rough.

"Oh holy fuck, Jack—"

There was little tenderness here—and that was okay, sometimes they needed this; sometimes one or both of them needed something harder, more painful, to fuck away the bad stuff. Memories. Ghosts. Sins.

Secrets.

And if it seemed rougher today—if something felt off, a little wrong—it was just a part of them, their life together. The bad days when they couldn't forget their pasts. When they couldn't overcome their hatred of each other, even as Theo loved Jack with every part of his desolate soul.

Theo's eyes rolled back in his head, breath heavy, and he clawed at Jack's arms, almost drawing blood. His whole body tensed up, and Jack pulled out and wrapped his hand around both of them and fuck, he'd never get over the feeling of coming with him at the same time.

After, Jack was solicitous, kissing over his stomach, smoothing his tongue against his roughened entrance, wiping him clean. Almost apologizing.

"Not that I'm complaining." Theo ran his fingers through Jack's hair, a disaster as always. "But what was that?"

"Mm." Jack propped his chin on Theo's chest but looked away. "Just...in the mood, I guess. For that."

"All right." Theo ruffled his hair. "So. Cat, or no cat?"

Jack rolled over, staring at the ceiling. He didn't reach over and take Theo's hand. "I have no opinion on cat."

"So." Theo nudged him with his elbow. "Cat."

"Sure, Theo." Jack closed his eyes, smiling halfway but looking somehow defeated. "You can get a cat."

August was nearing its end.

Many of the summer exchange students had already gone home—back to their boyfriends and girlfriends, their normal lives, where they'd give smiling kisses and laugh a little and lie a little and never really tell the truth about what they'd done. The city wasn't empty, but there was a feeling of waiting. An idleness.

Even so, Friday night and the club was full up, shots being poured at the bar, and Jack was drinking one of those fruity turquoise things that smelled like tanning lotion. It was his third—and Theo'd been keeping up, shots of whiskey, and the night was hot and sweltering, and they grabbed ice cubes from behind the bar and ran them over each other's necks while they danced. Licking up the water, the hint of shimmer he'd finally convinced Jack to wear for the first time since Pride, a little over two months ago.

They were perfectly in tune, knowing each movement of their bodies, knowing the ways they fit. He held on to the thick muscles of Jack's backside—fuck, he was hot—and rubbed his full cock along Jack's, just cheap fabric and sweat between them.

Jack had a fourth drink. Theo took another shot.

Midnight in Cork, in the summertime, getting down to the last three cigarettes in the pack, good craic with the DJ between sets, passing a joint around, and if Jack seemed—if he felt just slightly different—they were just drunk and high and dehydrated and—

"Come on." Theo took Jack's wrist, pulling him off the dance floor, shoving him into the toilets.

"What're you—"

"I've been wanting to do this for months." He pressed Jack back, up against the sinks, "Years, probably," and he remembered that he hadn't locked the door, but he was in too much of a hurry to care. He felt the smooth surface of Jack's abdomen, the dark buds of his nipples, as he ran his hands under his thin shirt and kissed him, feasting at his mouth.

Jack kissed back like he always did—brutal but tender, and breaking. "That first night—"

"Yeah." Theo smirked down at him from his not quite two-inch advantage. "I owe you one."

He dropped to his knees. Music pumped, rhythmic and toneless, and the graffiti glittered on the walls, and he rubbed his face against the twitching mass of Jack's prick.

And he paused.

"I do, you know." He started speaking to Jack's zipper, but looked up and met his too-blue eyes. "Owe you. I'm—I'm grateful."

He lowered the zipper, pushed the jeans down, glad he'd adequately conveyed to Jack that boxers were a waste of time. He smelled so good, like dancing, like flying, like something both ancient and brand-new.

Like freedom.

Theo opened his mouth, licked delicately around the head, sucked, just a little, and pulled off. "Thank you." Jack's face looking down at him was so lovely, so serious... "Thank you for being here. With me."

"Theo, I—" Jack wove his fingers through Theo's golden hair, shaking.

"I thought—I thought I would always be alone, that no one could... Thank you for the gift of this life." He tongued at the slit, held the base of Jack's cock in a firm grip, and winked. "Now pull my hair and fuck my face, will you?"

Jack laughed, and maybe he was also crying a little, and he did pull his hair, and Theo took him down all the way, until Jack gave a choked moan and pushed him back—

"Fuck me."

And Theo bent him over the sink, their flushed, damp faces panting in the mirror, Jack's hair as black as soot, Theo's silvery scar flushed and visible as he held himself against the wall, a permanent sign that Jack Gardner would always own him.

And when Theo came, he watched his own face as he whimpered out, still almost against his will, "God, I love you."

Jack reached behind him, kept Theo buried deep, cried, came, and whispered back, flat, "Love you too, you asshole."

Back at the apartment—as they cleaned themselves up, went back for drinks, for more dancing—a mouse skittered over paper, crumpled up and shoved under the bed. A bit of writing flashed in the shift of light. *Dear Jack*, it said, and there might have been other words, letters like D, maybe, or M— but the rest was hidden in shadow and ash.

Chapter Twenty-One

The long-awaited text had arrived first thing, Jack barely out of bed, still in soft flannel pajama bottoms and a threadbare T-shirt, items which had escaped the purging of his closet. Four words from Theo—and they sounded anything but cheerful, but Jack let himself, in this sleepy first hour of waking, imagine his smile.

He wrote back immediately, his answer guaranteed before he'd placed his fingers on the touch screen. **Come over.**

It was late autumn, the sun still misty over the rooftops below his apartment, brief fragments of light refracted by the large, shining windows, giving his living space a rainbow sheen. Jack stumbled down the stairs, turned on the fireplace; even though the apartment was temperature-controlled and well-insulated, there was a part of Jack—some secret sliver in him—that was always cold. Now, with the luxury of a fire, he soaked up warmth like something cold-blooded. He didn't see why he should deny himself, as an adult, the cozy atmosphere he'd never had before.

It was his apartment, after all—his own space, this first home that was truly his and his alone.

He tried not to feel like it was empty.

He'd dropped Amy off with Deb and Jason last night—her grandparents were always so pleased to take her, and despite recent events, Deb had gathered him up in a big hug. Maybe she saw on his face the deep discomfort that he felt, there in the house where they had always welcomed him—he didn't understand how she could still, somehow, care for him.

"We wish you had felt like you could tell us," Jason had said, clutching a cup of coffee, his shoulders heavy but his voice so kind, as Jack and Meg had gone over to tell them the news, what was happening and why. "We wouldn't have loved you any less."

Jack still found that hard to believe, even though he needed that love so desperately.

And now he had his own home, and life was moving forward, and he imagined Deb and Jason in this space, the first people who fed him, still the first adults who cared. The grandparents of his children. His family.

He looked around his apartment, everything so sumptuous and clean. With all of the furnishings in place, he hadn't needed to make a lot of purchases, but the first—and most expensive—houseware he'd bought was a top-of-the-line espresso machine. As he handed over his platinum credit card, he'd ignored the fact that he, himself, wasn't that invested in high-quality espresso. It just—

It made sense, right? To have it. For guests, and such.

Creamy, too-sweet coffee in hand, he fell back into the deep plush of the velvet couch. He propped his feet up, right over the left, and looked out over Baltimore. He thought about light and thunderstorms and what he had imagined and what it was really like.

Luxury really was—it just wasn't what he'd been used to. When he'd first realized how much money Frank had left him—first known how drastically everything in his life would change—he'd felt...not excited, not really. It had almost felt like shame. How could he justify it, being wealthy, when he'd survived perfectly well on table scraps, on a lumpy mattress in a cold bedroom? He wanted more than that, had always dreamed of it, of course, but this kind of wealth… Especially since Frank had seen him so like a son, and he hadn't been able to reciprocate those feelings… He didn't feel like he deserved it.

But here, in front of a glowing fire, nestled into deep cushions, a view over the city, croissants in the pantry and warm drinks whenever he wanted them—

It was nice.

He thought Theo would be comfortable here.

The panel next to the elevator, with a security camera feed showing any guests at the door, chimed.

"Gardner." A chilled and familiar voice.

"Um." He walked to the panel, pushed what he hoped was the right button. "Hi."

A long pause, in which he could practically taste Theo's customary morning irritation, and Theo didn't show his face to the camera. "Are you going to let me up?"

"Just put the code in, I left it in case—" He trailed off.

In case he came back.

"Oh," then silence. Another chime, and a light flashing above the elevator.

Jack didn't know what to do with himself, palms sweating, feet icy. He started preparing a second cup of espresso. Because, well, it seemed like a better idea than staring at the elevator like a crazy person.

Though the security measures were pretty neat. He had a view right into the elevator, and he knew he'd be able to watch Theo as he came up—he imagined him running his fingers through windswept hair, maybe a little unsettled, but then smoothing out his face in that remote Beaumont stare, all traces of nervousness gone.

He had always been so beautiful. Untouchable, until he wasn't.

Jack missed, fiercely, the days when he could have all of Theo, when he didn't put on his masks. His perfection all mussed up; his heart open and raw. But losing that closeness, that vulnerability, was his own damned fault.

He'd been so fucking stupid.

He quickly looked away, down at the coffee, as the elevator doors slid open.

"Your child is a menace."

Theo certainly knew how to make an entrance.

Jack set down the espresso and looked up. Theo did look annoyed in that exhausted morning way, all white and gray, impeccably dressed and every hair in place. Jack felt very scruffy in his threadbare pajamas. Too late to change, now.

"Which one?" At Theo's confused look, he clarified, "Johnny is a menace to your face. Will's a menace behind your back."

"While I do not doubt that all of your family is as much of a disaster as you are," Theo came over, pulled out a barstool, perched on it ram-rod straight, "I am referring, of course, to your middle child, Jasper's roommate."

"Ah." Theo held out his hand, waving it a bit, and Jack handed over the coffee before realizing what he was doing and that, yeah, that was why he'd made it. "Will. Okay. What did he do?"

"He..." Theo took a sip, moaned obscenely. "Christ, this is good. He convinced my son to go wandering the woods, at night. Figured out how to sneak out of the dorms."

Jack's mouth dropped open. "No."

"Yes. Almost impressive given the enhanced security since we were there." Theo looked down his nose at him, somehow, from the stool. "Seems like your son is a great influence—"

"Like you never left the dorms after curfew—"

"And is indeed a fourteen-year-old menace, just like his parents were. And let me tell you, his parents…"

"Hey!" Jack walked around him to the couch, and Theo swiveled on his barstool. "What about his parents?"

"Do you know what I discovered when I was dragged to the headmaster's office at ten last night?" Theo smiled like a shark, all sharp angles and teeth. Like he was about to go for the jugular and enjoy the hell out of it.

Jack fell back, picked up his coffee. He had a feeling that he knew what was coming—especially considering the reason why he'd dropped off Amy with her grandparents.

"Your wife—"

"Ex-wife—"

"In lingerie." Theo looked both disgusted and delighted at what he felt was scandalous gossip.

Jack laughed. "Surely she wasn't in lingerie in front of Will and Jazz."

"No." Theo frowned. "She was hiding in a closet. So that's another family characteristic, I suppose."

"A closet?" Jack tried to imagine Meg crammed into a supplies cupboard and couldn't.

"I thought it was a closet. Turns out it was the hall to Charles's rooms. Gave me quite a shock."

Jack snorted and patted the seat next to him. "Come 'ere."

Theo rolled his eyes, put-upon, a little anxiety in the fine lines between his eyes. "If I must."

Clutching his mug, he came over and sat primly on the far end of the couch—as far from Jack as he could get. Jack sighed and rubbed his neck. "I knew about Meg and Charlie."

"Did you."

"Yeah." He shrugged. "I'm happy for them."

"Margaret." Theo slanted his eyes over and smiled, faking his old nastiness. "Quite the minx."

Jack spread out, legs open, nudging his knee against Theo's foot. "That's my ex-wife you're talking about."

"And now I've seen more of her than I ever desired. Ugh." Theo wrinkled his nose, took a sip of coffee. "Let's move on, shall we?"

They sat quietly, the fire warming the room, and it should have been uncomfortable, all the history between them, but it just felt so good—at least to Jack. Here, with Theo, in his new apartment, the smell of coffee and Theo's cologne, and he was exactly where he wanted to be for the first time in twenty years. Low sunshine on the horizon made everything gold and orange, and he felt like he was on the inside of some sort of dreamscape. A place that couldn't possibly exist.

"I'm glad you took this place," Theo murmured.

"Me too." Jack put his arm along the back cushions, hand just two inches from Theo's neck. "Thanks again for the help."

Theo colored, looked at his lap. "Yes, well… I don't think Genni was too happy with me."

"Thanks even more, then." Jack looked around, still delighting in all the details of his new home. "It suits you more than it does me, really. But I like it." And then quietly, his heart in his throat, "Just the way I like y—"

"Gardner." Theo's eyes meeting his were storm-gray, angry, scared. "What—please don't start something—"

"But I want to, Theo." Jack placed his cup down, pulse racing, and turned, tucking one leg under the other, staring, probably making another damned mess. "I want you, God, how I—"

"Shut up." Theo's face was tight. "Just—" He breathed in deep, closed his eyes, ground out, "Walk away from me. Now. To the windows."

It sounded as if he were being dismissed, sent away, but there was something in Theo's voice like a promise.

Another choice, another cliff, another house plummeting to the ground.

Jack had never been so certain and so terrified at the same time.

He went to the windows, staring out over Baltimore, and hoped. It was so quiet. Then a low voice, closer than he expected, almost in his ear. "Put your hands on the glass."

He felt the autumn chill against his palms.

"I'm—I'm going to talk, a little, and if I say anything you don't like, tell me to stop."

"I won't."

"Fine. Know that you have the option."

He felt Theo's hand, running down his rib cage, over the side of his abdomen, over his hip. The hand exerted delicate force, tilting his hips up and back. His skin prickled into goose bumps, hot and freezing at the same time.

"Spread your legs." Jack complied quickly. "Well done."

How could he have forgotten, for even one second, what that voice could do to him? He felt his cock filling, thick and heavy against his pajamas.

Theo dropped his forehead to the back of Jack's neck and breathed, frustrated, pained. "Why do I let you—"

His breath was so warm, and Jack leaned into it before Theo could pull away. "You can do anything you want, Theo. Anything."

A bitter laugh. Theo moved back, voice turning impersonal, detached.

"Take one hand off the glass. Pull your pants down." Jack moved at once. "Slowly, Gardner. Take your time."

The flannel was buttery soft, sliding down over his skin, catching on his damp prick. Sweat beaded between his shoulder blades. He felt slender fingers and sharp nails against his skin, spreading him.

"Have you let anyone else fuck you?" Theo's voice was dispassionate, but there was something, some insecurity he couldn't hide.

"No." Jack shook. "Never."

"Good."

"Have you—"

"You don't get to know that, Gardner." His chest pressed against Jack's back, arm coming around, hand cradling his cock, firm and inexorable. "I don't belong to you, not anymore. You're going to stand there and wonder and doubt and think about all the other men who might have—" His hand was speeding up.

"Fuck, Theo—"

"Lube?"

"Yes—just—side table—"

"Keeping lube in the living room?" Theo almost sounded entertained, like something could be funny in this intense moment, but then—

Jack heard a drawer open then slam shut, and then those fingers returned.

"Still gagging for it, aren't you, Gardner? Didn't even move." Theo slicked his fingers, ran them down the tender skin, held them, still, over his rim. "Tell me, how often did you close your eyes, fucking your perfect wife, and think of me?"

Jack clenched, relaxed. "Theo—"

"Think of the way you shoved into me, splitting me open with your massive cock, making me beg?"

Jack shivered, whimpered, "Almost every—"

Theo breached him, skilled, and found his prostate with a quick twist, rubbing with no mercy.

"More."

"You're in no position to make demands, and I was trying to be careful with you." His voice was mocking and bleak. "Not that you deserve it. But fine. If you want more…" Theo shoved in another finger, stretching him, making Jack cry out.

The glass was so cold against his forehead, Theo's fingers hot, in him, around him.

"Your turn to beg, Gardner."

The words burst forth. These words were so easy. He'd been holding on for so long. "Please, Theo, I'll do anything, whatever you want, God, I've missed you, fuck—"

Theo slipped in a third finger, pressing down, and circled the base of Jack's cock and held tight. Denying him the chance to come; controlling him.

"Ah! Christ, I want you in me, please…" He felt wetness on his cheeks.

"Why do you think you deserve me?"

Jack closed his eyes against the bitterness of Theo's voice. Pressed his forehead harder against the glass. "I don't."

Theo was still, and Jack could feel that coiled, violent intent, and he craved it.

"Fine." He heard the rustling of fabric, the sound of a zipper, and Theo entered him with a heartbroken noise, like he was dying.

Oh God, it had been so long, and it was painful with such limited prep and it felt just right, just exactly what he wanted.

Jack took his hand off the glass so he could reach down and—

"Oh no you fucking don't." Theo slammed his hand back over Jack's, pressing him back against the window. "You're going to come like this, untouched, just a hole for me to—"

"Theo—"

Theo fucked into him hard, breath on his neck, one hand

holding him down and the other gripping his hip, pulling him back, leaving marks that Jack already knew he'd wear and cherish until they faded away. The pressure built in him, overwhelming, boiling like bathwater, sweet and cloying like too much rum, smelling and tasting like Theo, Theo by the water, and in the alleys, and dancing in fey dawn light—

And the way they'd done the grocery shopping together, arguing over what cookies to buy—

Walking Theo back from work in the afternoon sunshine, when he got promoted and grinned to split his face—

Meeting all his friends, these new people who knew nothing about his past, who adored him—

Holding him after he threw things and cried and raged against himself—

Loving him in the little, quiet ways, in the ways that should have meant forever, that meant growing old, getting a cat, brewing the coffee, the things he hungered for and ran from and Theo, Theo, this man—

Theo pulled his hip, tilting it with unerring precision, still knowing all the secrets spots, and Jack did take his hand off the window and held him, wrapped his arm back, fingers scraping the back of Theo's scalp, and he came in such agony all over the window, and Theo cried, brokenly, "Jack!"

Pulsed in him. Gave himself over. Gripped him in a just-fucked embrace.

Held him.

Pulled out and let him go.

Zipped up. Wiped his hands clean on the back of Jack's shirt. Ran fingers, once, through his long hair.

Jack turned against the glass, breathless, helpless.

Theo appeared unmoved—clothes perfect and the Beaumont mask in place. "Thanks for the fuck."

"Theo, I—"

"I will email you if I have any further concerns regarding the children."

Jack pulled up his pajamas, shaking, then reached out. "Theo, please—"

Theo stepped away, economical and meticulous in all of his movements. "Goodbye, Gardner."

Jack had to reach him, had to stop him this time, and he grabbed his arm—

"Let go, Gardner." Irate, immovable, his flesh like a stone, and then the cold veneer splintered and Theo closed his eyes. "Please, Jack."

He sounded fractured. Jack dropped his hand.

Theo crossed the room, stepped into the elevator. Jack watched him go. Stood there, for a full minute, longing—

And then he winced as he flopped back onto the sofa, legs shaking, shell-shocked and freezing cold. His heart was still pounding, his breath labored, and he felt unbelievably good, sexually fulfilled for the first time in almost twenty years, and horribly ashamed of himself.

He wished, God, he wished that Theo had stayed.

He wished that he didn't feel like he'd broken his heart all over again. Because he knew that voice, the tones of saying please—it was Theo, entirely wrecked. And he had asked him to—had wanted—

He picked up Theo's coffee, tried to leech off any lingering warmth, the imprint of his lips. His mind was jumbled, sex and love and resentments and all of that culpability, that ugly thing still in him.

He hurt, but he deserved it—hurting people was all he seemed capable of doing. He hurt Theo when he was in school, splitting his lip, and then again so pathetically in Cork—and he hurt other people, Meg, his first love, whom he wasn't capable of loving in the right way. He really had stumbled along leaving disasters behind him, and—

He gulped down the cooling coffee, jittery. He thought about what Theo had said, about Meg and Charlie, and he hoped, for a moment, that the end result of his lifetime of incompetence would be happiness. If not for him, then for his best friend in the whole world. Charlie could be good for her; Charlie was—

Maybe he could give his kindness to Meg. His compassion. His clear care for children. She deserved all of those, and more.

And Theo deserved—

Here, propped up on the couches in his new apartment, body sore and spent and languid, with the windows clear and open to the skyline of the Inner Harbor—he missed Theo, the boy he had been, the man he was now, and he didn't want to—he couldn't let this happen, let him go. He couldn't leave him hurting.

He got dressed, sore, terrified.

He had to find Theo.

He had to move forward.

He had to fix this.

Jack had to go. That was what he told himself, anyway.

Theo was due back from work any second; Jack was staring at his packed suitcase.

The letter from Meg was still crumpled up under their bed, less than a week after he'd gotten it, but Jack didn't need to read it again to remember.

He'd written a quick note at the beginning of the summer, obviously, just to let everyone know that his plans had changed, that he was exploring Ireland after all, but that he'd be back. He'd come home, after—

It was a normal sort of letter, that was the funny thing.

Nothing big, or earth shattering, just bits of news. Meg had made the Hopkins field hockey team, and one of her brothers had just gotten engaged, and they were all getting ready for college in a few weeks, and—

Dare was already working hard at the Maryland Institute College of Art, and he was doing more amateur drag nights, and Quinn was plucking up his courage to ask him out—which Dare knew, because of course he did, but he was keeping that to himself like a sparkling secret because he wanted to let Quinn have the experience, Meg said, of asking for love and getting a resounding and unreserved yes.

Something about that twisted in Jack. It hurt.

Every time he said it to Theo, those words which terrified him, there was a part of him which didn't want to admit it. It was true, so true, and yet it was…impossible. Unacceptable.

Meg's letter had been running through his mind, incessant, and he had memorized every detail. She wrote that she had run into Frank at a cocktail party at Gwynns, and he'd talked about how proud he was of Jack, how excited he was to have him as a part of his firm, and there was no rush, she wrote, for him to come back, but he should know that they were all looking forward to—

A bit of complaining, then, about Deb, who in the wake of her oldest son's engagement started talking about grandchildren, that motherly twinkle in her eye: how many, how soon, and Jack had laughed at that bit, and started thinking—

And a quick line of denial from Deb herself, who wrote that she would never rush anything, of course not, not for any of her children, and that he had better be taking care of himself—

A sentence or two from Jason, fatherly advice that he had always craved, an admittance that he was looking forward to retirement…and maybe being a grandpa wouldn't be the worst thing in the world. Jack read those sentences with shame, and pain, and a deep longing—

He was too young, far too young, they weren't even talking about him, but—

And a last few lines, nothing too emotional or romantic but still sweet and fresh and soft, about how she hoped he was having a good time, and that she missed him.

Signed, *Meg D*, with a messy sketch of a heart.

It was simple, and easy, and familiar.

He had to go.

Jack stared at his case and remembered Meg, her fierce smile on the field, the way he'd kissed her, her smell of cocoa butter and cream and turf, the way she looked like her mom.

Deb's big hugs, and Jason tinkering, forgetting that Jack wasn't one of their children, not really. Frank, patting him on the back with pride, and Quinn, studying and planning and working so hard against his own fear, because he knew down to his socks that he loved Dare and didn't want to wait one more moment.

The life he'd always wanted. The success and the affection. The family that, no matter how hard he tried, wasn't really his. Not yet.

And it was too early, and he was too young, but he thought—he thought it would be nice, someday, to have kids who looked like Meg, who maybe looked a little like him. Kids who'd never grow up the way he—

He couldn't have that here.

He looked around the apartment, taking in all the details: the patch of damp plaster in the corner that never seemed to dry, the pokey little bathroom with the cracked mirror, the kitchenette stocked with his favorite cookies. The record player, the stack of LPs. The blue cotton sheets, serviceable, almost soft enough. The little tin of pomade, down to the last few drops.

The sound of feathers rustling, the lingering smell of hash.

Looking at it now, it almost reminded him of—

It wasn't anything like the life he'd imagined for himself. This little apartment was just too close to the way he—the place he—

And so what, if he really wanted—if he wanted to have—

He thought back to a night in early July, when they'd danced straight through to sunrise, talking utter nonsense, laughing, sitting on the front stoop and chain smoking. It had been a beautiful night, and he'd felt purged, like every drop of sweat was an asperges, the salt-slick wiping away his sins. They'd talked about a lot of things, and without really thinking about it, Jack had slurred out, "Do you wanna have kids, d'you think?"

Theo laughed. "Fuck no." He leaned back against the stoop, looking up at the fading darkness. "What would I have to pass on? No."

He stubbed out his cigarette, waited five seconds, lit another. "Let the line die with me. Here lies Theodore Alexander Beaumont." He gestured broadly. "Good fucking riddance."

It had made sense, at the time. Maybe—maybe they were both too broken.

He thought of Theo, his tousled hair, his smooth skin, his nasty looks, the way he smelled—the fine trembling in him, his legs and hands, and the way he kissed. The way he loved him, maybe, but it wasn't—it wouldn't be—

Was it really enough? Enough to make a life out of?

His whole body was screaming at him, saying yes, yes—

But that was just his body, just a mechanical thing, and it didn't necessarily mean—

And deep in him was an ugly thing, a petrified thing, a mewling—he had never intended to fall in love with a man. He couldn't be—even though Dare and Quinn were, he couldn't—couldn't tell his friends that he was—

And it wasn't...all right to feel this way.

As far as he knew it, love was supposed to feel comfortable, and cozy, and kind: a mom, a dad, brothers, sisters, soft kisses, and the feeling of things made by hand, skill and focus and sweet intentions. Loving Theo wasn't any of those things.

Loving Theo hurt, it ate at him, it was an impossibility. Even in the quiet moments it was burning up and wanting to die and hoping to live forever, as long as he could have this, his arms, his bones, his sharp smiles, the ways in which he was irrevocably broken. Sometimes he looked at Theo, dancing, buzzing with caffeine, slow and sticky with booze, and he felt something ripping in him, like he'd never be the same. Like he'd never been a normal person, and that was all right, because the person he loved wasn't normal, either.

And that was—

Maybe he could tell himself that it was never love at all.

Theo opened the door.

He was energetic, cheerful. Now that Colin had him doing more work around the club, bookkeeping and advertising and any odds and ends he was up for, he'd started coming home with a little more excitement. He liked his work, and he was good at it, and he was getting recognized, which Jack had realized, at some point, was new for him.

He tossed his keys down, pulled off his shirt, exposing his tattoo, his nakedness. His vulnerability, which was for Jack, and Jack alone.

"Hi." Theo brushed a kiss on Jack's cheek, which burned like a brand. "How was your—"

He froze. Stared.

"Are you going somewhere?" His voice was chilly, but his chest and face turned a splotchy pink.

Jack wished he had hidden his suitcase. He almost wished he had already left. "I—"

A pause.

"Theo, I'm—I'm going home."

"Are you?" His words as violent as the crack of a bullwhip, and then fragile. "Will you be coming back?"

Jack felt sweat gather, prickling all over his body. He couldn't bring himself to answer.

"Ah. Of course not."

He mumbled, staring at the floor, "I was thinking—I wanted to—"

"You wanted to what?"

And that was the goddamned question wasn't it, and there wasn't really a good answer, and he started to feel angry.

Angry was good. He understood anger; anger at Beau was an old friend.

Anger had run under the surface of even their happiest moments, here in this fantasy, this life they tried to assemble out of their jagged parts.

Theo was so handsome, a little more solid now, and his face was closer to a smile than a smirk after these months, and Jack—he hated Theo, he must, because when he looked at him he felt smashed up inside.

Jack's voice came out ugly. "This wasn't supposed to be forever, you know."

"Oh really?" Theo laughed, mean. "That's funny, considering that you've told me that you—"

"Yeah, well." Jack cut him off. "I've got things—my internship and stuff."

"Right. Stuff."

"And I—Theo, this was just supposed to be—I was always supposed to go home."

Theo sat on their one chair across from the bed, his whole body still but tense. Anticipatory. "Why now?"

"What?"

"Why now, Jack?" He pulled out his pack and lit a cigarette. Didn't offer one.

"Look, it doesn't matter—"

"It matters," he exhaled, smoke spiraling, "To me."

Jack sat back onto the bed, looked at his hands. "I just—I got a letter, and it made me—I feel a bit homesick, and—"

"Who sent the letter?" Theo knew, somehow. But he wanted Jack to say it, wanted him to confess.

They'd never talked about her.

"Meg!" Jack shouted, then more quietly but still fucking angry, "It was from Meg, all right?"

Theo's voice, very still, as sharp and deadly as a scalpel—"Can't bear to be queer, can you?"

The air in the flat was thick with smoke and sweat and buried rage. Theo stood, went to the window, opened it all the way.

"You know what, Gardner? I always thought that between the two of us, I was the coward. Guess I was wrong."

"Excuse me—" Jack nearly spat.

"This ridiculous charade…these months, every fuck, every pitiful…" Theo slammed a fist against the wall. "You wanted me to feel something for you, compassion and gratitude and—"

"Theo—"

"After all that, I… You made me…" He laughed like choking. "After all that you're going home. To Margaret. Who is, I think you may remember, a woman."

Jack flushed, scalding and sick.

"This summer… I've figured you out, Gardner. Why you've

always been like this, so fucking selfish." Theo leaned his head against the peeling paint of the window. "You've talked a lot of shit about the kind of person that everybody else wanted you to be. About the way Gwynns treated you like some fucking example, about—

"But that's stupid. It's so stupid. Because you see yourself as the center of the fucking universe." Theo laughed with the jarring friction of broken glass. "You can't imagine a life where it's not all about you. Where you're not that example.

"You were *poor*." Theo spat the word, laughed. "That's what you always say. That there wasn't enough money, and that's why you had to be the—the poster boy for overcoming bullshit. But that's just another excuse."

His words were honed blades, well-trained, practiced. He dragged on his cigarette, breathed out the smoke, readied himself.

"You were abused, Jack. Your mom hurt you. Every day she didn't feed you, she hurt you. And if you're expecting pity from me, you'd better look somewhere else. Because...you were abused as a kid? So what?" Theo's shoulders tensed, and he spoke quietly. "So was I, you asshole. But you're supposed to—I want to move forward, and you—"

Theo took another drag from his cigarette, maybe to stop himself talking. Jack wanted to hit him, and wanted to crowd up behind him, press against his naked back, say *no*, and *fuck you*, and *please*.

Theo whirled, and his voice was so familiar—it was the voice he'd used to torment, to bully. "Yeah, you got fucked up by your mom. She taught you how to be afraid, all the time. How to hate yourself. And that hate is eating you up. But you fucking let it. You lie to yourself, blame the poverty, and you don't accept the simple truth that your mother was a monster. So you need to be the shining example, the captain, get the highest grades, land the internship—you need people to worship you, so that—"

He dropped the cigarette and ground it into ash on the scarred carpet. And then he met Jack's eyes—and his gray irises, dark as slate, were colder than they had ever been. "You want people to worship you so they don't see who you really are. You're just a poor kid who scammed his way up. And I'm not going to be a part of that, not anymore. You can fuck right off for all I care."

He took a step toward Jack, bristling, and the apartment felt like that moment before a lightning strike, ozone and electricity.

His face was vicious. Fuck, this hurt.

"Go, do your internship, whatever. Marry Margaret, stick your prick in her, fake being... Have her pop out a brood of redheaded brats. Make the perfect family you need to prop up your ego. Just know that this time, the only person who's forcing you into that filthy apartment is you. And that you're locking everyone else in there with you."

Theo crossed his arms over his chest, holding himself back. Hiding his ribs, his shoulders, making himself small. Jack clenched his fists, teeth nearly cracking as he ground them with the pressure of his tight jaw.

"It's almost funny, your selfishness, but it's mostly pathetic. You're willing to hurt other people, you know? Even Margaret—you think she's going to appreciate a lifetime of your lies?" Theo snorted, derisive. "All because poor little Gardner never got a real hug."

Jack was hot, through every cell, and his nails were cutting into his palms, and the anger let him pretend that his heart wasn't breaking.

Like this wasn't his fault.

"You need to shut up, about me and about my—my family. You said it yourself, your family definitely fucked you up, so how dare—"

He wanted to hurt Theo right back, slicing him open. Theo just laughed.

"That's how I know what I'm talking about. I never got a real hug, either." He met Jack's eyes, and Jack could tell that it was probably the last time he'd see him so raw, so open.

So breakable.

"But I was willing to try. With you. I thought—"

"What?" Jack's voice cracked, almost desperate.

"You said you loved me, you son of a bitch, and I fucking believed you." Theo was all white now, ghostly. "And I had never—not to anyone—" He shook his head, yelled, "Fuck! You're just like everybody else. A user. Just like my fa—"

His voice broke with grief. He stopped himself, closed his eyes, and opened them with a sneer fixed firmly on his face.

"So go on, use Margaret and her family up until they hate you, just like your fucking mother did. Just don't ever, ever come crawling back to me to make you feel better about your miserable life."

Theo turned, staring back out into the street. And then without deigning to look over his shoulder, he spoke, quietly, the last words that Jack would get from him for nineteen years.

"I'm not your whore anymore. Get the fuck out of my apartment, Gardner."

Jack stood, picked up his suitcase, crossed to the door, and closed his eyes in shame when he heard a broken voice behind him.

"You've taken everything I had to give."

Chapter Twenty-Two

"Fuck!"

That was a Ming vase he'd just shattered against the wood-paneled wall of his study. Quite a lot of money to throw away, but at the moment, he could not have cared less.

Once he'd walked out of Jack's building, he'd found the nearest corner shop and bought a pack of menthol cigarettes. Then, after a fast and angry internal debate, he'd gone into a liquor store and bought a bottle of whiskey, and then he'd come home, and he'd started throwing things.

He was too old for this.

It felt fantastic.

He wanted to die.

"Theo—what—" Mother entered the study, looking at the destruction with wide eyes. He wondered if she cared more about him or about the things he had bought for her.

It wasn't fair. He knew she cared now, but he had a whole lifetime of carrying her apathy, and right now that bitter burden was a comfort.

He lit up a cigarette, took a shot straight from the bottle. "I'm not in the mood for company, Mother."

"Given the state of this room," she walked farther in, hitching up her slacks to avoid shards of pottery, "I think you need it, even if you don't want it."

"Mom." He slumped, covered his eyes, tried not to cry. "I just need to be angry, all right?"

"Theo, what—"

"Just get out."

She gave him a long, considering look, and then left. Even though he'd sent her away, he felt that old pain. No one ever fucking stayed.

He picked up a glass paperweight, red and orange swirling through it like fire. It seemed fitting—he drew it back and hurled it at the wall, leaving a dent in the paneling.

If only he could be destroyed so easily. But he just kept on fucking living.

It was cold in the house, too cold, and he remembered what it was like, back then, when the police were trampling through, dismantling his life—and before that, with his father still here, the sapphire-and-diamond Gwynns class ring leaving an imprint on Theo's cheek, before his mother said, "Not his face, Alex—please." His closet and all of those books full of fairy tales and the constant, unending fear permeating the air like a foul perfume.

Maybe he'd never left there. Maybe he carried that putrid decay in him. Maybe it came from him, rot arising from his very flesh.

"Fuck, fucking Gardner." He picked up something else—a sterling silver candlestick—and threw it, relishing the clang. "Why did I—how could he—fuck!"

He took a drag from his cigarette, whirled drunkenly, glared with swollen eyes at his father's curtained portrait. "You were right after all, Father. So fucking weak."

The air seemed to vibrate with his anger, and that was a familiar feeling, so like the first time that Jack left, when every second was full of this, the disappointment and the hatred of everything he had ever been. He stared up at the painting, eyes wide.

He was raving.

"How did you know? How could you tell that your precious, pathetic, only child would be," he gestured wildly at himself, "Like this? Useless, idiotic—never good enough—a fucking catamite to Jack fucking Gardner—"

"Theo!" A strident, terrified voice from behind him. He turned, saw Genni's face, and all of that energy in the air pulsed and then burst like rotten fruit as he fell to the ground.

"Gen…"

He was suddenly, blissfully numb.

He folded in on himself, knees propped up, head dropped, the bottle dangling from his hand. "What are you doing here?"

She tiptoed her way into the room on scandalously high heels and stared down at him, stern but not cruel. "Oddly enough, I'm here for poker night, which we planned a week ago. I heard ranting and your mother—looking supremely shaken, by the way—sent me in."

He laughed. "Of course. Didn't want to deal with me herself."

"Hmm. Yes, I am sure you were very receptive to any offer of help." She sat down on the ground next to him, arranging her tight skirt, taking off her tailored blazer. He didn't know what to say to her. He never wanted her to see him like this. "You going to share, or what?"

He handed over the bottle of whiskey.

"Ugh." She swallowed, disgusted. "I don't know how you drink this stuff."

"I like it."

"Yes, well," she leaned her shoulder against his, "You always did have terrible taste."

He snorted. "God knows that's true."

She studied the chaos in the room, all the fractured heirlooms now worthless. "I'm assuming this is a Gardner-shaped breakdown."

"Fuck, Genni…"

"I would be more than delighted to kill him for you." She did not sound like she was joking. "And I represent some great properties, you know—places to hide the body."

He laughed soundlessly, shaking. "God, I love you, Genni. Tell me again why I didn't marry you?"

She reached for his pack of cigarettes, tapped one out and lit it, blowing coils of smoke. A breath. "Probably because I am such an unremitting cunt."

"Have a cunt, more like."

"That too."

He held out his right hand. "Light another, will you?"

"What am I, your servant?"

"I'm having a meltdown." He wiggled his hand. "Help."

She snorted, very unappealingly, and lit his cigarette. They smoked for a while, silent.

"I fucked him."

She looked around at the mess again. "You shock me." Stretching her long legs in front of her—and flashing the lacy tops of her stockings, the vixen—she sighed. "How exactly did that happen?"

"You curious about the mechanics, or—" He could practically hear her roll her eyes. "Sorry." He tensed up, then tried to relax. "There was a problem at the school, so I contacted him to discuss it, and—"

"Not so much with the talking?"

"Ha." He took a swallow of whiskey. "Not so much."

She stared at him, sighed again—much more heavily—and looked away. "God, this has been a long time coming."

He couldn't say anything. He still carried—he wished for a different life.

Genni scowled into her lap. "You should know, I'm saying this entirely against my better judgment." Turning his head to look at her, he watched her face. She looked conflicted and not a little pissed off. "I think you didn't notice, when we were looking at the apartment, the way Gardner looked at you."

A pain in his chest. She ground out her cigarette on the carpet. He frowned. "Nice, Gen."

"Yes, you so obviously care about the rug." She lifted an eyebrow, gesturing to the destruction around them.

He laughed, shrugged. "All right. So…"

A growl at the back of her throat, "Jack Gardner. He is the stupidest person I have ever met. He is an utter disgrace to any sense of style, gentility, or culture. Sometimes I think I hate him more than I hated my useless criminal father."

"Tell us how you really feel."

She thwapped his knee with the back of her hand, her diamond ring digging into him. "And he is very clearly, in his idiotic, artless, common way, madly in love with you."

"I don't think—"

"Well, that's obvious."

"You always make me feel so much better about myself."

"Yes, well." She took a big gulp of the whiskey, then stuck her tongue out and coughed. "Nasty. Look. As much as I don't want a permanent Gardner accessory in our glorious Gwynns family…" Theo laughed. "When he looks at you… It's all on his face, all right? Everything. So damned uncouth."

"Genni…"

"He loves you. He watches you like he's never seen anything more—" She shrugged, uncomfortable. "Anything more beautiful. Precious. And you are, Theo." He looked at his lap, avoiding her kindness. "Don't forget that, please.

"Theo, he left his wife. And if he's finally admitted—far too late, the idiot, but still—that he wants to make his life with you in it, and you…" She trailed off, put a hand over his. "Do you love him?"

"God." He put his legs down, interlaced his fingers with hers, closed his eyes. "I wish I didn't."

"Do you want to be with anyone else?"

She knew the answer. Had known since that night in the bell tower.

He shook his head.

"Mmhmm." Then he heard a smirk in her voice. "He a good fuck?"

"Genni!"

She blinked her eyes at him, playing the coquette as always, and then she leered.

"Ugh, all right," he mumbled under his breath. "The fucking best. Christ, his cock—"

"Let's stop there, shall we?" She shivered in disgust. "I am already struggling to keep this appalling whiskey down. But Theo, darling—maybe you can—oh, I don't believe I'm saying this—but maybe you can be happy. With him. Really, truly happy. And the world—it's better than it was, you know, back then. It would be…easier."

His voice was small. "I'm scared, Gen."

"I know."

"What if—"

"Fuck the what-if. You've been what-iffing for too long. Just—do the thing, all right, because you deserve—"

A knock at the door. He looked up, a little fuzzy, hot tears in his eyes, and—

Of course. Who better to see him breaking down in his study. Again.

"Gardner."

Jack stood in the doorway, absolutely awkward and out of place, but he—he didn't notice the mess, any of it, and didn't even glance at Genni or her French lace stockings with frilly garters. He was just staring at Theo with such naked intensity that—fuck, maybe she was right.

Theo felt Genni tense next to him. She glared at Jack, then kissed Theo on the head as she picked up her jacket, stood, and muttered, "Do you want me to stay?"

He shook his head, reluctant but certain. He guessed this confrontation was inevitable, like they'd been hurtling toward it for twenty years. Hopefully he could get it over with fast and then get so damned drunk that he forgot his name.

Or maybe—he looked at Jack's face—maybe there was something—

"All right." Genni kissed him again, and in a whisper, "Just try, would you?" She crossed to Jack, the heel-clacking noise angry and brutal. "You!" she barked, and jabbed at his chest. "Testicles!"

"Understood."

As she left—muttering with artistic profanity all the things she wanted to do with his intimate parts—Jack kept looking at him, and looking, and Theo—he was a mess, the burning butt of a cigarette in hand, and whiskey in his bloodstream, and he loved him, painfully, without doubt, and it was the absolute fucking worst, and—

"What are you doing here?"

"I'm here," and he dropped to his knees like a dramatic madman, the remains of the Ming vase cutting into his skin, "To beg."

Jack was gone. An irrefutable fact. A truth.

Who cares, he thought, *and who the hell needed him in the first place?*
Theo stalked through the club, right to the middle of the

dance floor, and wedged himself between two hard bodies, desperate for the cleansing fire of someone else's touch. His muscles were sore from crying and trying not to cry, and he felt, for the first time since he'd gotten to Cork, entirely unclean.

He smelled something rotting. The scar on his lip almost burned.

"Hi, gorgeous." A voice from behind him. Theo reached his arm back and wound his fingers through coarse hair. He felt solid, warm, good to lean on, but his scent wasn't quite right.

And the man in front of him was attractive enough, but he couldn't help compare—his hair was too tidy, his leer too obvious, and whatever he was grinding up against Theo's leg was…unsatisfactory.

Please, please, Theo. Just forget about him. Forget.

He felt a stiffness against his ass—a promise of a fairly respectable size, there—and he arched back, turning his head and shout-whispering, "You wanna get out of here?"

"Fuck yes."

Theo turned and dragged his eyes over his form. Well-built, dark hair, that blue-cream Irish skin. He looked like—

No, no, don't do this, you stupid fuck, it'll only—

It would have to be good enough.

"Name's Finn." He grinned. He was rather handsome, more handsome than Jack, if Theo thought about it. He could not care less.

"Hey, Finn." Theo smiled without warmth. "Mine?"

"Sure." Finn reached into his pocket and pulled out a small plastic bag. "You want?"

Adderall, the poor college student's cocaine.

Oh, well, it would keep him awake through his shift in the morning.

They did lines in the toilets. Finn rubbed up against him. "I could have you right now. God, you're beautiful."

Theo caught his reflection in the mirror, with the blurred images of dark hair behind him, and he thought, *Fuck, I had Jack Gardner, here against the sinks, and he had me on my knees for him, and he went home to Margaret and respectability and he was so far away—away from—*

He couldn't stay in here.

"Come on." He pushed Finn off. "I want you to fuck me in an actual bed."

The walk to Theo's flat went quickly, the Addy coursing through his system like lightning. Finn was not rough, exactly, but careless. Sloppy. He tried to be sweet, maybe, but it came out as clumsy and childish. He'd pinned Theo to the door of his apartment, and Theo let him—he wanted to give in, to yield up the parts of him that had awakened when he'd lived with and loved Jack fucking Gardner. That died when he left.

If he let his vision relax—if he let himself see details like abstract snatches of bad dreams, he could almost pretend that the dark hair under his fingers was blacker, messier, softer. He pulled on Finn's scalp when he got too close.

"Come on, wanna come when you're in me."

Finn looked all too delighted. "No objections from me."

It all went too fast and not fast enough. Finn used a lot of lube, and he slipped in and out of Theo's body, and he kept trying to cradle Theo's face in some misplaced nod to tenderness. Theo shoved his hand in the direction of his cock, and he gripped it softly.

"Harder, fuck."

With the movement over him, in him, and the hollow physical pleasure, and the smell of Finn's cheap cologne, Theo let his mind wander. Float. He let himself be lost in this, another man's body, the mechanics of fucking, a numbness.

He came. It was—acceptable. He kicked Finn out with a perfunctory, "Thanks." He forgot his name five minutes later.

He stayed up all night, playing records, lying in bed, sleepless. Dirty.

The next day, he enrolled in business classes at the university.

He worked harder than he ever had at Gwynns, and he liked it, back in the grind, working at the club all day, classes in the evenings, studying, drinking coffee, weaning himself off the cigarettes, and if he couldn't stop himself from exploding every once and a while, and he cried and raged it was just—just a part of the experience. College stress, and running the books for Colin, and forgetting to eat, now that Jack wasn't there to—

He tried, peering into the cracked mirror, to apply concealer over the scar on his lip. It didn't work. He cried, briefly, and decided he didn't need to look at himself that much, anyway.

He started writing to Genni again, and Phillippe, and Tom. Genni was always complaining about Phil; Phil was always raving, in his mannered and loquacious way, about Genni. It came as no surprise, whatsoever, to get a gushing—and far too detailed—review of Phil's performance in bed. Apparently they'd spent a "truly magical" weekend romping around Europe, and that was that.

He knew that they would last. It was guaranteed—that they would be able to have—

And Tom—Tom's dad had been just as guilty as his own, but was stupider, and got caught for far more, and wasn't as nice when he was screwing people over. So Tom was miserable, that first year after school. Everyone they knew hated him.

He'd always protected Tom, sort of. Tom was smart about simple things—which were, in many ways, more complex—like having friendships and loyalty and affection; but he wasn't particularly smart when it came to school. He was a fantastic

lineman—no one could dare to get through his solid bulk—
and he was brilliant with a packet of instant noodles and pil-
fered spices from the school kitchen. So Theo had looked out
for him with homework and tests and extra lessons, and Tom
cared for him in turn. They were friends, true friends.

That—real friendship—had always been hard for Theo.

Theo had nearly forgotten to think about Tom when he ran
away, and he carried guilt for that; he'd abdicated his responsibility. So he wrote to him, and encouraged him, and Tom did
run away. He moved to New Orleans—away from Baltimore,
from the social circle of people their dads had fleeced, from
dirty looks and drinks spat in—and Theo kept writing from
Cork, helped him manage the money he had left, looked out
for him again. Tom went to culinary school, and he promised
to send back pastries with buttery dough and dark chocolate
and orange liqueurs.

He was learning how to be happy. Theo hoped he was able
to do the same.

And Tom met a French-speaking Creole woman in his
cookery classes. He wrote to tell Theo, stunned, that he
thought he loved her.

And that was good. More than good.

Theo was maybe a little lonely, but he didn't bring people
home anymore.

Genni sent him the *Baltimore Sun*, sometimes, for the financial section. He started thinking about the money that
hadn't been touched by his father's crimes, and how he wanted
to help his friends, maybe fund some of their business ven-
tures. Ways to invest, improve. A better way to be wealthy
than what his father had done. He studied every bit of news
in those papers, feeling Baltimore echoing—thinking about
the person he had been.

He didn't want to be that person. He wanted to do something else. He tried to bury the bitterness, the sense of how nothing was fair and never would be, but sometimes—

He saw an engagement announcement in the paper. A picture, blue eyes, a yellow dress.

He smoked his last pack of cigarettes, ashing right over the grinning faces of people he didn't, it turned out, know very well at all.

And then, at the end of that next July, Father died.

Killed himself in prison. Too cowardly to live with the consequences of what he had done.

Theo was relieved. He grieved against his will. He was, almost immediately, very wealthy indeed.

So he came home. Back to the mansion, which he had renovated and repaired. Back to bitching with Genni over cocktails, and glasses of absinthe with Phil, and Tom sending him recipes, trying to remind Theo to eat. Investing in his friends, his Gwynns family whom everyone still hated. Making more money, silently donating, not to Gwynns, but to the public schools. Grinding, even now.

He made something of himself, not as a Beaumont, but as him—Theo. He caught, every once in a while, a strange, solemn look on Mother's face, and he figured he had better start planning for a child of his own. Maybe everything would be a little easier if he just did what was expected of him.

Alexia was a lovely woman, with a truly stunning laugh like sex on concrete, and she and Mother spent hours together, very happily, and it wasn't her fault, not really, that he couldn't—

And Jasper was pink and blond and chubby and so fucking cheerful and oh, how Theo loved him—

And Jack was a father, three times over, when Theo couldn't bear to try again, another fault, another failure—

And he let Jasper play with the hunting dogs and nurse the runt of the litter by hand—

Tom had a little girl with toasted brown skin, Gabrielle, and he was so delighted, his doughy face beautiful as he held her in his arms, and he sent her up to Gwynns, made sure they all looked out for her, didn't let the stain of his past touch her—

And little Hya Dumont dug in the gardens with Jasper, getting dirty and laughing and trailing mud all through the house—

And Theo read them stories, so many stories, because he wanted to teach them to dream—

And Alexia, so much stronger than he was, sat him down and said, firmly, lovingly, "It's time."

And on many of those days, he didn't think about Jack, really.

It was a lie, but a necessary one.

He didn't know that on all of those days, Jack was thinking about him.

Chapter Twenty-Three

Jack Gardner had always wanted Theodore Beaumont.

And, as much as he hid from it, raged against it silently, locked it up in a dark bedroom with the cold and the spitting rain and the moldy crumbs—he knew exactly when wanting Theo shamed and bloody and broken had revealed itself as wanting to hold him and never let go.

Because Theo had been shamed, bloody, broken, lip split and barely breathing, and all Jack had thought was no, no, please—

I can't live without him.

He had left him in that locker room—ran away, panicked, terrified of his own capacity for violence and the sudden knowledge, the true root of him, the explanation, the reason he kept going, day after day, Theo, hated, beloved, beautiful as he was baptized by his own blood. It was a hideous kind of love, nothing warm or soft about it. It wasn't like the love he had for Meg, who was sweet and kind and a little acerbic and a lot stubborn, a girl who loved him back, who made him feel good about himself, and who felt like family already.

Jack felt a shard of something digging into his knee, probably cutting him. He stayed still, hardly breathing.

He couldn't help but remember that boy in the locker room now. Theo sat, hunched over himself with his elbows on his knees, those long legs folded up, and he held the still-burning butt of a cigarette. A bottle of Bushmills sat next to him, not quite half gone. And he looked the same to him—all the years were meaningless, the laugh lines, the hair lightened by age— he was his Theo, the person he knew, down in his soul, he needed more than he needed air.

The person he'd injured, terribly. More than once.

The person he'd always, his whole life, woken up wanting to see, and the person he'd cleave to until he closed his eyes for the last time.

"You what?" Theo's voice was like gravel. He stubbed out the cigarette. Cleared his throat.

"Beg. I'm here to—"

"Fuck off."

"No."

Theo stared, running his eyes from the top of his head to his knees. "You're bleeding, Gardner."

Jack looked down. The blue-and-white china had indeed cut him, and he was bleeding—maybe more than a little. "That would explain the pain, then."

He stayed kneeling.

"Oh for fuck's sake." Theo took a swallow of whiskey. "Get up."

Jack's knees creaked as he stood—he may have felt like a teenager, inside, but his body was one hundred percent thirty-seven years old, and it hated him.

"Come here." Theo jerked his head.

Jack walked over, dripping, and when he stood next to Theo, Theo used the edge of his sleeve to wipe at the cut. Jack hissed.

"It's just a scratch, Gardner. Don't be so dramatic." Theo squinted up at him, his refined features going all pointy, like they had been when he was a boy. "So?"

Jack frowned.

"Beg!" Theo lit another cigarette—God, how could he still smoke like this—and offered one to Jack. "Sweet mother of God, what the fuck."

Jack sat down next to him—moving, just in time, a razor-sharp piece of splintered glass stuck in the carpet (which he thought that maybe Genni had left there, just for him)—and fiddled with the cigarette. He opened his mouth, and nothing came out. He coughed, tried again.

Theo snorted. "Why did I ever bother with you?"

"I'm sorry, I... Oh, what the hell." He lit the cigarette, breathed in, got instantly buzzed, "I'd forgotten how disgusting and wonderful these things are. Let's not tell our children about this, all right?"

Theo got very still. "Yes. You always preferred to keep me your dirty little secret."

A dizzy flash of shame, remorse, and Jack crushed the cigarette. "That's not what I meant, Theo."

"No?" Theo started laughing, acidic, eating away at the unnaturally stagnant air of the study.

Jack sat, mute.

"You can't do it, can you? Telling me you're here to beg—to beg me to—" Theo's voice broke off, thick. "And you can't. Just another fucking lie." He threw his cigarette across the room.

It was Jack's turn to curl up on himself, forearms on knees. He felt the space between them, the space where Theo wasn't touching him, like an endless chasm. He remembered the green hill, a bandaged lip, his hunger.

"I realized, in the end," Theo's voice was casual, relaxed, like they were discussing the weather, "That you didn't mean it."

"What—"

"We were young, I know that now, though it didn't feel

like it at the time. Maybe—maybe you thought that telling me that you—that you—ugh."

Theo picked up the bottle, drank for three precise seconds, and offered it to Jack, who shook his head. He wiped his lips with the back of his hand, marked with Jack's blood.

"Maybe you lied like that to make me feel better, I don't know, or because you felt sorry for me. But," his voice was so small, "It was a really fucking shitty thing to do."

"I didn't lie."

Theo sneered. "Of course you did. You left."

"I was wrong." Jack let his legs widen, his knee just an inch closer, and felt Theo radiating heat, anger, betrayal—and deep hurt. Hurt that he had caused. "I was so wrong, to leave you."

He looked at the carpet, glass and burn marks, and he thought about how he had been so scared, back in the coffee shop, to open his mouth. How he hadn't, then. He remembered watching Theo's back as he walked away, and the sound of his strangled voice, that last day in the apartment in Cork. He breathed in—

"And I was stupid to believe you could have ever loved me. After all—look at—" Theo gestured around the room. "This is what I do. This is what I am. After everything, I'm still... I've worked so fucking hard to be better. To be a—a good person. But look at this, I'm still such a goddamned mess, still so—Jack Gardner," he shut his eyes, and laughed, once, "Could never love me."

Jack's heart twisted in him.

He finally spoke. "Oh you are stupid."

That was...not how he intended to start. Theo's mouth gaped open. "Thanks."

Jack relaxed his legs further, pressing up against Theo—and Theo's breath caught, but he didn't pull away. "Have you really been thinking that I didn't love you, you monumental jackass?"

Theo's profile looked uncertain—angry, and flushing pink, and maybe really rather offended.

This was not going as well as he had planned in his head.

"You're doing a brilliant job of convincing me at the moment."

"Theo, I was a coward, and I did run away, and it—" Just touching him like this, just being close, was so beautiful, like everything he'd ever wanted and everything he'd ever lost, and he hoped he could stop his idiotic mouth and make it say the right things.

"I was so scared. I was stupid, and I... And then I had what I had thought would be the perfect life." He took Theo's left hand, held it, and God, his skin was still so soft. "The life that I'd imagined since I was a kid. That I thought I was supposed to have. And you were right, in so many ways, because it wasn't—I was trying to make myself—"

"You were hiding." Theo's hand tightened.

"Yeah. Hiding from a lot. Hiding from—"

"Your mom."

"Fuck." Theo looked over at him, questioning. "I'm sorry, it just...still hurts to hear it. To say it."

"I know." He squeezed Jack's hand, just for a second. "Me too."

Jack took in a shaky breath, and continued. "Anyway, I hid. And because of that, I have three amazing children. And you have Jazz—Jasper." Theo nodded, with a fleeting smile. "So I can't regret that, even though—"

"What, Gardner?" He almost sounded...hopeful. But still so fragile.

"Even though, in every other way, I wish I had stayed. Because Theo, God, I love you."

Wetness gathered in his eyes, his nose stuffed up, and maybe this was what he'd been scared of, in the coffee shop, and in his new apartment, and each day that he'd made himself survive, numb, without Theo.

He'd never learned, in that horrible apartment in Bolton Hill, in the freezing cold bedroom with the mice and the cockroaches, what it meant to love someone. To really love them—not for what they made you feel, but for who they were.

What it meant to hold your heart out, beating and bloody, when as a starving child no one had ever loved you back.

Jack looked at him, his face and his wrists and the blood on his sleeves, and it wasn't anything soft or easy, and his lip would always have that scar, and Jack would always be that little kid who didn't quite know how to love, and it—it was difficult.

But Theo was essential. Theo was necessary; he was inevitable.

Jack couldn't spend his life without him. Not anymore.

The words seemed to settle into him, a solid mass of self-hatred and longing and fear. But he had to try—he kept talking. "I loved you from the first time I saw you at that nightclub. I loved you suddenly, and I loved you bit by bit.

"I loved you when you stalked around the school trying to act like—like you had it all together, like you were in charge of everything, and I loved you when I saw you throwing stuff and yelling and—

"I loved you on the lacrosse field, and in the classroom, and every time you were a horrible bastard; I loved you in that bathroom in Ireland when you forced me to look at your scar, the scar I made, and I loved you when I made it.

"I loved you when our lives together were jealous and bitter and violent, and I loved you when they were beautiful and messy and wild. And God, I'm so proud of you for the life you've made now.

"You think I couldn't love you?" Jack's breath shook out, nose running, and he smiled a watery smile that probably looked like agony. "How could I not? Theo, I—I've spent twenty years trying to do without you, trying to pretend, and when I look at the rest of my life I—I see the years stretching out and I can't lie anymore, I won't, and—

"I love you because we don't fit. I love you because we are both such a mess, such a fucking disaster—I love you because we—I mean, we have kids and lives and jobs and all I can think about doing for the rest of my life is sharing those things with you and trying not to mess them up and fucking you on every available surface, by the way. I love you because I left; I love you because I should have stayed. I love you with every fucking part of me.

"And you—I don't know if you feel the same way, and I know I don't deserve it, but I just wanted you to know that I—You're everything I was too stupid to admit I needed. Whatever you choose, now, I just need you to know—Theo fucking Beaumont." He paused—Theo had almost laughed. "I have loved you every single day of my life. I will go on loving you until I have no more life left.

"And I will love you if you love me back or if you walk away."

Jack was scraped clean, hollowed out, and maybe he hadn't breathed enough during all that, because he felt dizzy and sick. He'd never been able to talk like that—hadn't been capable of feeling like that. But while he was making an utter embarrassing ass of himself, Theo had turned, wound his fingers through Jack's hair, met his wet eyes with gray irises like a storm, clearing.

"Jack." His breath shook. "I can't live through you leaving again. I can't do it."

"I won't. Ever."

"We have children."

"They'll sort themselves out." Jack sniffled, not particularly attractively.

Theo did laugh, and he looked so—"I think your ex-wife is secretly a nymphomaniac."

"I'm openly a nymphomaniac. For you."

Theo's eyes clouded, just for a moment. "We should probably be reasonable."

"I am so fucking done with being reasonable."

He snorted, and ran his hand down Jack's neck, and—"Genni hates you, you know."

"I had noticed that. But I—don't repeat this—I think I love her, for how much she loves you. She is kind of scary, though."

And Theo gracefully ignored that last bit, and he was leaning closer, face so tender and warm and scared—"You owe me. A lot."

"I'll pay you back. Whatever—however long—do you want a vacation? Expensive gifts? Sexual slavery? The entire walk-in closet? Or I can get you that cat—lots of cats—any number of—"

"Jack." Theo was smiling and smiling.

"What?"

"Shut up."

When Theo kissed him, they clicked right into place— Theo's smirking lips tilting, covering his, and it was like dancing, and running over the green field, and laughing in lamplight, and drinking hot cinnamon liqueur; it was bath oil and champagne; it was being so terribly young, and growing so beautifully old.

Jack Gardner had always wanted Theo Beaumont.

This time he intended to keep him.

Chapter Twenty-Four

There in the study, with Jack finally kissing him, this older man he had loved so fully and so foolishly when they both were young, Theo closed his eyes, and he was finally warm. His body was here, and yet he was eighteen, free, back in Cork, and he was so full of memory, the way Jack tasted, his scent, the small sounds of their paired brokenness, and the years meant nothing.

He was home.

Warmth glowed under Theo's skin.

His body was long, muscles singing after his shift at work, everything stretched out from lifting and scrubbing, his mind buzzing with his new assignments, and Theo felt the quiet pleasure of working hard and being noticed. He fit here; he existed in a new way.

September was just a few days away. He had a sense of forward momentum which he, for the first time, participated in—controlled. No one dictated his path; even as he obeyed whatever demands Colin made of him, he knew that he did it for himself. For his own happiness and for his own survival.

And he had Jack.

Theo had fought against himself for so long.

This walk back to his apartment had become one of the best parts of his day. Cork was so temperate, a hint of heat and a breath of cool air, and he felt at home—if it rained his body sang a song of poignant melancholy, and if the sun shone to burn the sky he felt wild and loose like each cell could split, his body and soul breaking into a million small parts and flinging those parts into the universe. And if he let his awareness float, eyes unfocused, he could settle into a dream state which felt more real than he had ever anticipated. A dream of the man waiting for him.

He felt like one of those stories he had read to himself as a child. A lover; a god. An epic poem. A play.

Sometimes Jack would walk into the city, meet him at the door of the club, but—Theo liked this. The loneliness which came with the knowledge that the loneliness was temporary.

When he'd arrived, he'd lived with a sort of promise of his life ending. When he drank, he drank to unmake himself; the cigarettes were a promise he swore, an oath, die fast, die painfully, die soon. Death in life—he'd operated with this assumption that all parts of him were destined to decay. And he wanted that, had wanted it so fiercely. He was tired of his name, his past, all of the things in him which he hated, all of those items of personal proof that he was worthless. And it had felt good to give in to that, to demand finality. A frenzied farewell.

And now—now he had Jack, up the hill, up the narrow stairs, tucked away in a shitty apartment with the crumbling plaster, the tiny shower, the cracked mirror like the fragmented pieces of their selves. The records they listened to together, and the sugar on the counter. And he didn't want to follow up on that promise of death anymore; he figured he had something to live for.

In this half-awake moment, his muscles sore and languid, his mind taxed, nicotine, caffeine, he let himself ease into thoughts of Jack like slipping into the sea. Waves pulling him, taking him out, pushing him back to shore, back into his shell which had begun to splinter. Those thoughts carried him through the day like a secret in the back of his mind, a fire which he fueled with desire and his longtime longings met. Fulfilled.

Sometimes the days were hard, the nights confusing, Jack holding parts of himself back. They argued sometimes, screamed; Theo threw things and Jack stared at him with irate stubbornness. Theo knew that that might always be true— if they ever returned to Baltimore together, it might still be hard. It might take Jack some time to tell everyone, to let their childhood world in on this new thing, them, two pieces of one whole. To invite his friends and adoptive family into the new normal. Theo—he wasn't sure what his own welcome would be, and his mother might be disappointed or angry or—and Jack's friends, Margaret and Darius and Quinn, they might still resent him for the bastard he'd been.

But he would do it. He would apologize, he would humble himself, he would show that he had changed, he would stand in front of his mother and say, *Yes, this is who I am, love me, or don't.* Because he had Jack. And everything else was just a step on their unified path.

His legs pumped, the long walk up the hill adding tension to his slow-moving flesh. He didn't walk quickly; he delighted in this feeling, like being drunk, high, like waking up with the fatigue of too many manic days. Energy thrummed in him; he kept it collared.

Everything he wanted was up at the top of this hill. He savored the moments before he reached him like an aperitif. Jack was the feast, the fullness, the satiation. Here in this quiet space, just Theo inside his own mind, he reveled in anticipation.

When he'd left Jack this morning, Jack had barely woken to receive a last kiss, eyes tightening against the light. Theo kissed his lips, and his closed eyes, and that place on his neck, and he mumbled words across the tanned skin, endearments, teasing, sharpness, tenderness. Words like "love." He'd never called anyone that before. It tasted good.

He had—he'd denied it, pushed it away, wanted to hold himself back, but it was true, so true, the way he felt, and the way Jack must feel about him, because he said so. And he thought Jack might be ready; he thought about all of those affirmations which Jack needed, and he realized he would give those affirmations, joyfully, for the rest of his life.

Halfway up the hill, and his lower body ached, that place where he and Jack joined. The place that he had claimed. Last night, coming home, Jack had pulled him down to the bed, gently guided his legs over his shoulders, pushed in with a fragile desperation, kissed him in that wrecked way. He was so beautiful, that look on his face, dark hair falling into his blue eyes, and Theo hadn't known that he could love anything this much. He carried the evidence in his body. It almost felt like his genetic code was irrevocably altered, mutated. Nothing but this.

He felt a smile bloom over his face, unrestrained. He felt so good, so wonderful. The sun, the pale mist, the greenery of the college campus; the gray stone, and the pavement, and these few breaths, waiting.

He reached his building, the three-story house, birdcages in the windows above his own apartment. His window, which they'd struggled to close, that day when he cradled Jack. He saw no movement in his apartment; Jack was probably still asleep, or maybe lazing about with one of his much-loved novels. Theo was filled with an incredible vulnerability.

He belonged to Jack; Jack belonged to him.

Just a few days left of summer, of this August which had brought him so much—kisses, a hot bath, doing the shopping; falling in love with the man he had probably loved for his whole life, and saying it out loud.

He took his time, again, walking up the stairs. Savoring.

He thought about forever.

He opened the door.

In the study, Theo opened his eyes.

Jack was still there.

Chapter Twenty-Five

It turned out that a vacation was the first thing—doubtless one among a long list of reparations Jack would happily pay as long as he was asked—that Theo wanted.

Jack walked around in a daze after that kiss, like he had gotten fantastically lucky and didn't really know why, and Theo rolled his eyes at him, terribly pleased and trying to hide it, and he instructed Jack, "Get it together, Gardner, and book us a hotel somewhere."

They got the bridal suite at the Metropole Hotel.

Cork was different, in some ways, and so similar in others. College kids still crowded into every pub, huddling on the pavement in the December chill, smoking and laughing and making spectacles of themselves, and when they drove past them in the back of a black cab, Theo looked out and grimaced. "Were we ever that young?"

"We're still young. Young enough."

Theo smiled at him, his secret smile not so secret anymore. "I suppose," and he kissed him.

In the hotel room, Theo fell back onto the plush mattress, feet still on the floor, closing his eyes and stretching. Jack stood between his legs, pulled off one of the snug sweaters that Meg had chosen for him.

"Do you wanna go dancing?"

Theo gave him a withering look.

And then his eyes widened as he took in Jack's fitted shirt, trousers with the top button already undone. "I think not."

Jack fell on top of him, breathed a sigh of relief. "Thank God."

They undressed each other, slow and careful like they both might break, and maybe Jack had gotten a little softer (but just a little) and he could practically count the ribs on Theo's torso (he still didn't eat enough, most of the time, and Jack would have to fix that) but fuck, it was still them. Still so rough and tender and perfect, the way they fit, and they slipped into the tub, Theo resting in Jack's arms, and it was overwhelming, and Jack got the giggles, which seemed unfair for a man approaching his forties.

"What are you laughing about, Gardner?"

Jack wrapped his arm around, taking up Theo's cock, moving with just the right amount of pressure. "Just remembering that last time in the bath, when you—"

"Don't say it," and, "I have no idea what you're talking about."

"Of course not."

"But—oh, fuck—you can keep doing that, if you like."

"Still turned on by baths, hmm?"

"Well…" A broken moan. "It might have something to do with you. Maybe."

Jack kissed his ear. "Good."

The towels were fluffier, somehow, and the dark of the night was more profound, and they were slippery with oil, and Jack laid Theo out on the duvet, face against the pillows, drew his hips up and back—

"Oh God." Jack licked, gentle, around Theo's entrance, and pressed his tongue in. "Fuck, Jack."

He had more patience now, and took lots of time, until Theo was drenched, his cock full, heavy between his legs, brushing against the bed. And he was gorgeous, and Jack loved him so much, and how had he ever thought he could live without this, and he breathed so hot against his tender skin, and with this new, scary honesty that had emerged from the deepest parts of him, he blurted out—

"Marry me."

And then kept eating Theo's ass.

"Ahh, oh my God—what the fuck, Jack—" Theo reached around and held Jack's hair. "Have you lost your mind?"

"Totally." Jack slid a finger in. "Completely." He flicked against Theo's prostate. "Without a doubt. Flip over."

Theo did, and stared up at Jack, eyes hazy and mouth sharp. "And were you asking me, or my—" He blushed, voice trailing off.

"Don't know, really." Jack slipped in two fingers, thrusting back and forth. "Both, probably. God, you're beautiful."

"Jack…"

"You. I'm asking you." His heart beat strong and certain. "Of course."

"Hold on." Theo reached down, stilled his hands. "I can't. Not yet. Not after—" His face was pinched but shaded with pleasure, and insecure.

"All right." Jack's voice was low, quiet, and he leaned over, nudging Theo's knees up, kissing him soft and sweet. Long and drawn out and liquid, lingering.

Theo smiled against his mouth. "Are you ever going to get to the fucking?"

"So pushy."

"Yeah, well, I have been waiting for—"

And Jack pressed in.

Once he'd bottomed out—and God, it had been far too long, it was fucking unbelievable—they both stilled, conjoined, and it felt like the years unspooled out from within them, the memories thick, and it was—it was—

"Why do you make me feel this way?" Jack gripped onto Theo's sides, panted the words onto his neck. They were in the half-light of the alley beside their club, and music was playing, and they were crowded on every side by other young people living other secret lives. Jack's back was to the wall, their come still wet and warm in their jeans after rubbing against each other and laughing and crying out, muffled, into the other's neck.

"Because it's us, Jack. This is—" His silvery eyes were guarded but endless like the moon. "It's just—us."

"This is who we are."

"Move," Theo whispered, harsh.

He did.

They stayed up all night, snatches of sleep caught here and there, and Jack couldn't stop touching Theo, like he was terrified that he would wake up without him. He ran his hands over every inch of skin, and he kissed all of those places which were beloved to him, which he had always remembered. And he thought about before, when he'd never been able to be—unguarded.

Throughout his life he felt like he wasn't a real person. He'd tried, with Meg. Tried to mimic her parents, their casual affection, the way they could touch each other. And he must have pretended well enough, and he'd never been stingy with hugs or back pats or kisses on the cheek with his kids. But there was always a part of him which felt like an alien, some kind of Frankenstein's monster who looked human but hadn't quite learned, really, what it meant to be one.

His mother never touched him.

But he wanted this. He—here with Theo—he was ready.

He reached out, shaking, with his right hand, and ran it

down Theo's back, his tattooed skin slick with oil. Theo made a sound, like a great cat purring, and Jack wondered if he could—if maybe he was capable, after all.

He asked a question that had been bothering him for twenty years. "Why wings?"

"Why, Gardner." Theo smiled into the pillow. "I'm shocked to learn that you don't think I'm angelic."

"Oh, right." Jack flicked his ear, then ran his hand down again. "Come on."

"Honestly?" Theo pushed back into Jack's hands, reveling in the touch. "I liked the idea of…flying away. From everything. You know that. And after Father—well. I never wanted to be trapped again. My wings just—remind me. That I have the option."

"It must have hurt a lot." He didn't want to think about Theo being in pain ever again.

"Lots of things hurt, Jack. This was a pain that I chose." Theo looked over Jack's shoulder, a little lost. Not wanting to look at him right then.

"God." Jack kissed his neck, eyes damp. "I'm so sorry."

"I know." But then Theo's gaze sharpened, like he wasn't sure if he could believe it yet, but wanted to try. "But you'd better prove that to me. Many, many times."

Jack did his best.

They greeted the dawn together like it was the first time.

Like it was the first morning of the rest of their lives.

And it was.

When they got back from their vacation, their lives linked up, blended almost seamlessly, as if it had always been that way— them, their families, their whole world. Everyone just called them "Jack 'n' Theo," two individuals made into a single unit, never one without the other.

Theo did move into the apartment Genni had really picked for him, and yes, he did need all that room in the wardrobe, thank you very much, Gardner. He whispered sweet nothings to the espresso machine (and occasionally to Jack, though there was usually profanity involved. And nudity).

Johnny plastered her room with posters of musicians and athletes, jazz singers and footballers, and played music at an entirely unacceptable volume. Jack and Theo were very grateful that he had bought the top-floor apartment—fewer people to bother—and appreciated the well-insulated interior doors. Living in a high-end apartment was…not bad.

"I told you." Theo nudged Jack, after he'd stumbled to Johnny's room to shut the damn door. "Living in luxury is the only way to live."

"Yeah, yeah." He kissed him, rolling them over, crawling down his body and fully taking advantage of their own well-insulated room. "You're always right."

Theo moaned, clutching at Jack's hair. "Absolutely—ah, fuck—glad you agree."

Jasper and Will were thrilled to be roommates, naturally, and they were two peas in a pod—getting into trouble every once in a while, but also earning high grades and being, in general, great kids. It all went very well until that summer after their senior year, when Jack had walked into their room, and—

"Aughh, my eyes!"

"Dad!"

"Jack!"

"Ugh!"

"We weren't—" from Jasper, and, "Jazz, we obviously were, so fuck off, Dad," from Will.

"Well, I guess we should have seen that coming." Theo tried not to laugh as Jack, bright red, flopped onto their pillow-top mattress and groaned into his hands.

Will moved into Johnny's old room.

In theory.

Everybody loved the noise-canceling insulation that summer.

Amy, their fourth Gwynns student, decorated her room in navy and red, mirrors everywhere and gold curtains around her bed, and got on fabulously with Theo—who had way too much fun spoiling her rotten—and together with Daisy and Jules was often planning world domination.

Quinn was a little scared of her, actually.

She was still Jack's little girl.

Beatrice Beaumont popped over with some (uncomfortable) regularity for a glass of whiskey or a pot of tea and Jack had always been anxious until she grabbed him by the face and whispered, Theo out of the room, "You finally got it right. Thank you for loving him back."

"Yeah. I mean—always."

Dare, when he first came over, walked straight up to Theo, a strut still in his step all these years later, with a haughty (and entirely insincere) scowl on his face. Theo actually looked intimidated until Dare cracked, snickering, and gave him one of his signature perfumed hugs. And then he teared up when Quinn, always so intense, kissed his cheek and said, simply, "Welcome home, Theo."

Genni visited often. She still hated Jack. But she'd go all soft and tender at the pure, unreserved contentment on Theo's face when Jack kissed him. Not that she'd admit that, mind.

And that Christmas Eve—the first one they shared as a family, when things were still a little new and a little wobbly but so, so good—Charlie and Meg came over to help them trim the gigantic and mostly tasteful (but rather ostentatious) tree; Deb and Jason piled in, too, with a newly knitted afghan and a hand-carved table and hugs which Jack accepted, finally, as a sign that he was theirs. It was loud and messy and chaotic and it was—it was just right.

They sat on the fluffy velvet couches, recessed lighting off but fairy lights on, and the kids rolled around on the carpet, making a mess, tickling and yelling and coming up with alarming plans, and—

"Ask me again."

Jack paused, fingers sifting through silky strands of hair. "What?"

"What you asked me, in Cork. Ask me again."

"I—" Oh. *Oh.* "Will you—"

"Not now, you lunatic. But—in a year. A year and one day. When you've...stayed with me. Ask me then."

"A year and..."

"One day." Theo looked at him, eyes a little wide. Innocent, almost, like the child he never got to be. "Like Lughnasa."

Jack felt his face soften. He tucked a strand of hair behind Theo's ear. "All right. A year and—next Christmas. All right." Jack looked at Theo's profile as he stared into the fire, an uneven flush on his cheeks. "I love you very much, you know."

Theo raised one delicate eyebrow and scoffed. "I love you too, you abject disaster. Now shut up and grab me some champagne."

Will had been right.

It was good, being all the way happy.

Epilogue

All of our stories have what-ifs. We cannot go through life without them—without the paths we didn't take, without the paths our parents and lovers and friends took. We're strung out on a line, decision after decision tumbling down our lives, triggering the next, the next. We have all of the control and none. Jack and Theo—this has been their story, their choices, their consequences, unalterable as it was told. Lived. But—

This is how it could have been different.

In second grade, Jack's teacher—who was always tired, tasked with caring for children who could barely care for themselves, grading to do and benchmarks to meet and her own burdens to bear—had one extra cup of coffee per day, prepared lovingly by her attentive partner, and she noticed that Jack's clothes were never clean. She considered the way he ate school lunches, the way he tried to take his time, savoring, but how he always finished before the other students and always asked for seconds and never seemed to gain any weight.

And Theo's elementary school counselor called him in for bullying, deciding to stand by the convictions which had brought her to this vocation despite pressure from the school's administration and Theo's parents, and she caught a glimpse of a ring of bruises around Theo's wrist.

In this other world, they were noticed.

And the adults around them stepped in.

In this other world, Jack got adopted by the Daughertys, and Theo's mom was brave, confronted by the reality of her husband's monstrosity, and filed for divorce. Jack met Darius earlier, and they shared all the bits of themselves, and Jack learned how not to be afraid of that secret within him. Theo still read fairy tales—but no longer hiding in his closet, and sometimes his mom read to him, eager to love him and make amends for all she had done to harm him, now that they both were free.

Jack could afford school uniforms, but he willingly picked out some of the used jackets because money meant less to him—he didn't crave it in the same way, and appearances mattered less, and he smiled at the blond boy in the shop because he had no shame. The blond boy smiled back because he knew now what affection felt like.

That first day in the dorms, Theo still went room to room, still competitive, still driven to do well, but no longer cruel. He recognized Jack from that brief meeting a few weeks ago, and he held out his hand. Jack took it.

They were friends. It was—it was good.

That spring day of freshman year after final exams, Jack and Theo stretched out on the grass, side by side, and Meg was there with Charlie, no longer bullied and flirting outrageously, and Dare was still sketching and playing Cuban jazz, and Jack looked over at Theo and his heart pounded and he thought, still terrified even in this better universe, *God, I want him*. And the world wasn't perfect, and it was still so scary and new, but a year later, Theo cradled his face when they were up in the Japanese maple tree and they kissed, and it was sweet.

Long afternoons in the grass with bare chests and the wind blowing and smiles which weren't a secret.

And they went to prom together, even though the school didn't approve—but they didn't hate themselves, and their friends got along, and they all got drunk by the creek and tossed rocks into the water, and Genni took off her heels and Phil laughed and Tom bumped elbows with Quinn as Quinn explained one of their English Literature textbooks. Dare looked at them all and spent hours painting them, black and red and the silver of the moon.

Shots at Pride, dancing filthy, the long glimmering sunshine, the purple-black dark.

When Jack and Theo thought about this undiscovered path, they couldn't be sure, really, if they would have run away—if they would have shared that tiny apartment in Cork, or had a scalding hot bath in a fancy hotel, or fucked with such frenzy against the wall of a nightclub. Theo wondered if he would have learned the value of plain, hard work, scrubbing floors and counting the till. And Jack thought that maybe he wouldn't have his three children—four, now, counting Jazz—whom he loved so completely. Both of them longed so hungrily for a better past, a history which didn't hurt so damned much, and Theo dreamed about a life without the scar on his lip and the heavy press of his father's hand; Jack craved parents who cared.

Nothing could ever excuse that pain, nothing could justify it, and there was no "but" at the end of that sentence. They had been children and they had been wronged. They were the amalgamation, the culmination of all of those things, the hurtful things; could there ever be any justification? Any prize which made that all worth it?

The mystery of those other lives was not for them to know.

Not for us to know about our own.

But there, in the beautiful apartment secured by Franklin's generosity of spirit, his willingness to love an unloved child— there, wrapped up in a new kind of forever, Theo resting in Jack's arms, finally uninjured—they loved each other with all of that history and the sorrow and the ecstasy borne of choices they'd had to make. They were happy, finally, and they didn't take it for granted.

And they loved their children as they should have been loved.

And that was just the way it was.

Acknowledgments

First and foremost, deep gratitude for Mackenzie Walton, my lovely editor, and Carina Press for getting my first novel out there in the world. Eternal thanks to George Shafer, the best friend of my young adulthood, who put up with my insane, manic, irate typing and reminded me to eat and sleep every once in a while. Gratitude always for Jamie MacGillis, my platonic soul mate, who has listened to and believed in me on my best days and my worst. Thanks also to Meredith Shafer, who provided such genuine excitement and support as this novel started pouring out of me at a rapid and alarming pace. To my mother, Julia McCready, words just aren't enough—thank you for being my first reader, and sorry (not sorry) for the naughty bits; and to my father, Richard McCready, thank you for the gifts of David Bowie, Ireland, and true parental love. And finally, thank you to PJ Chwazik, the most demanding partner in the universe, for inspiring my ambition and never letting me get away with being less than who I am. I love you all.

Chapter One

grapevine.us/2024/01/12/the-throne-live-action-cast
10:44 am

BREAKING: Nicholas Madden cast in live-action adaptation of LGBTQ masterpiece *The Throne*

Nicholas Madden was cast this morning as "Frederick" in period piece *The Throne*, confirming rumors to that effect.

Cast alongside him are Sir Reginald Jarrett as "Hubert," Andrée Belfond as "Jehanne" (it's been so long since the French *gamine* has been on our screens!), and Jason Kirkhall as "Ambrose" (an odd choice, as Kirkhall is best known for his superhero franchises, but he can be versatile...if one overlooks his long nights out).

We expect some drama out of so capricious a cast—lest we forget Kirkhall's flighty liaisons with starlets and K-Pop singers, and Sir Reginald Jarrett's infinite on-demand supply of apricot tartlets. But even they are put to shame by Madden's legendary strops, his short-fuse temper, and his rank distaste for misbehaving costars. As the man critics have dubbed the Big Bad Wolf of Hollywood, Madden hits all the stops in the actor bingo, from "extraordinarily talented" to "a proper prick, actually."

Madden's fan base, trusting in their idol's penchant for dramatics, has set up an online clock ticking down to the first on-set breakdown (see it for yourself here).

Despite these apparent drawbacks, *The Throne*—with Priya Chaudhuri set to direct and the Henderson siblings producing—may well turn out a number of award-worthy performances. Chaudhuri, to whom official recognition is long overdue, is a hot bet for Best Director noms next year. *The Throne* might become her golden ticket into Hollywood history...if Kirkhall can keep it in his pants and Madden can keep it together.

Set in turn-of-the-century Paris, *The Throne* was for decades a lost novel. Rediscovered in the early nineties, it was heralded as a masterpiece of LGBTQ literature. The love story at its core is frequently cited by modern critics as a rare early portrayal of a non-tragic gay relationship—though its depiction of bohemian queerness during the Belle Époque is not without its flaws and prejudices.

With Madden cast as one of the two mains, only "Angelo," the novel's most complex and controversial figure, is left to cast.

While Madden will have his work cut out for him as dark, brooding Frederick, Angelo may prove a challenge for the most seasoned actor (as the disastrous stage adaptation from the early oughts has eloquently shown). Whoever bears the brunt of that role and shares the stage with Madden—a man unaccustomed to sharing the spotlight—will have to be an egoistic diva in his own right, or risk being utterly outperformed. With how many times *The Throne* has been in and out of production, those who claim the novel incompatible with the silver screen may well be proven right...

14:01

UPDATE: Cast! In a strange turn of events, *The Throne*'s Angelo will be played by Christian Lavalle, better known for his Calvin Klein and Armani campaigns and his 1.5M Instagram followers than for his acting history. Lavalle, 25, became a Dior mainstay at the tender age of sixteen and has been steadily acquiring modeling gigs ever since; but his experience as an actor is limited to a few appearances in French soaps, television gigs, and international ads.

Casting a newbie to act opposite Nicholas Madden is certainly an odd choice. Can he strike up the right kind of chemistry with the Big Bad Wolf, or will Madden have to carry the movie's huge emotional arc on his shoulders? Will *The Throne* crumple under its own weight?

At least he's French.

Filming is set to begin in June.

June 2024. Paris.

Christian Lavalle was one of two things: a vapid boy-king without the skill and understanding to rival his good looks, or a *devastatingly* talented actor.

Nicholas very much doubted he was the latter.

The Parisian sun in June, warm and soft, spilled like liquid gold over the cobblestones of the Place Colette, the butter-soft columns of the Comédie-Française, and the polished red tables of the café terrace. It was a gorgeous day in Paris. On a late afternoon like this, all one wanted to do was relax in the sun, wear a cool suit of clothes and sip a cocktail.

Nicholas mostly felt hot and overdressed. The sparkling water he had ordered had done nothing to cool him down. It had scattered strange butterflies in his stomach.

He and Lavalle had arrived within minutes of each other to their non-official meet and greet. Lavalle had immediately been waylaid by a horde of fans, and did not seem inclined to put a stop to their fawning.

Nicholas was not a patient man.

But the lean young man who held court in the middle of the Place Colette, surrounded by the gaggle of his devotees, drew his gaze and attracted his attention, inescapably.

Because Christian Lavalle *demanded* attention. His beauty was compelling and undeniable. In a lily-white shirt and black jeans he looked infernally cool; the heat seemed to be beneath his notice. In his ad campaigns he had been merely exqui-site; in motion he was…*distracting*. His hair, made golden by the sun, just touched the corners of his smiling eyes. He was laughing.

"Don't look so offended, Madden," said Madalena, slipping into the seat next to his. She stretched out her arm along the back of his chair and crossed her long legs. "The boy's done nothing to deserve your wrath except land the job. This is a very good look on him. Very *chic*."

"He's twenty-five years old," said Nicholas. "Hardly a boy."

"Then *you* are positively ancient."

Madalena grinned at him. In the Parisian sunshine, she, too, was more beautiful than usual. Her dyed hair was burnished to an auburn sheen; with her white skirt splayed over her crossed legs, her sweetheart neckline betraying a fair amount of brown-skinned cleavage, she looked like an actress right out of the nineteen forties. A shame she had never shown any penchant towards the vocation. She was content to be his PA, to haul him out of bed in the mornings and drink his expensive coffee. Nicholas dreaded the day when she grew tired of him and went off to ru(i)n someone else's life. He suspected her exorbitant pay had something to do with how long she'd stuck by him.

But she *was* beautiful, and he was—even an ocean away from home—famous, and people looked at them, attracted as moths to the flame of recognition and notoriety. The rare few who could tear themselves away from Christian Lavalle were already turning their smartphones on them, daring to take candids and tapping away. He could imagine the tweetstorm.

@somenosyfucker
y'all nicholas madden is in paris and hes not lookin happy about it

@noprivacy
someone dare me i'll totally ask for a selfie

@celebsenlive
c'est qui elle??? depuis quand il a une copine?

@unautreconnard
Nicholas Madden est à Paris? Il tournerait pas un film? 😲

Pictured: a scowling man, hands stuffed in his pockets, glaring at his prospective costar.

It didn't matter. He was in Paris for *The Throne*. The table read was scheduled in less than two days, provided Lavalle could shake off his fans for long enough to make it. Nicholas found the prospect sadly uninspiring. The thrill he'd felt when the script had finally, *finally* landed in his lap had now all but faded. *The Throne* was something real, a period piece with modern sensibilities, a project he could back without feeling that he was giving in to mediocrity. He was an ardent lover of the novel. He'd been waiting for that opportunity for... years. Years. He had made *damn* sure he'd be getting the role.

And then the Henderson siblings had chosen Christian fucking Lavalle, prima donna sublime, to play his Angelo. He was a *fashion model*, for god's sake, an Instagram *influencer* with a reputation for flightiness and barely any acting experience; and nepotism, or beauty, for all Nicholas knew, had landed him the role. It was sacrificing quality to sell tickets. No doubt production had meant to appeal to twin demographics: those who were young and online and celebrity-hungry, and those who were easily distracted by a pretty face. Nicholas had no patience for it.

Madalena tsked at him. "Keep making that face and it'll stick that way. Wind's a-blowing."

"We're supposed to have a—" Nicholas's voice lowered into scorn. "A *meet and greet*. Basic courtesy; the regular fare. I've been here half an hour. He lacks even the professionalism to know when to put away his fans."

Madalena shrugged a smooth shoulder, and produced a tablet from somewhere. "He posted a picture of the Comédie-Française on his Instagram account. Fans flock to him like bees to honey."

Nicholas closed his eyes briefly. "Of course he did."

She turned the tablet. Lavalle's Instagram account was a steady, pastel-colored stream of pictures of Paris, himself, himself and dogs, himself and fans, promo shoots for ad campaigns he was plugging, more dogs, and more Paris. *Amélie*, times ten thousand.

"A disaster," Nicholas said shortly. He doubted Lavalle had even noticed him. Smiling for the cameras must take up the entirety of his cranial activity.

Madalena hummed, scrolling through pictures of honey-gold buildings and bright sun. "Chaudhuri called."

"Pardon me?" Madalena's job was to field his calls and deflect the loonies from his path, not to hit voicemail on the fucking director of the fucking movie.

"Calm down," Madalena said, still not looking at him. "She wanted me to pass on a word, that's all."

Nicholas was only mildly appeased. "Anytime you feel will-ing to share, Madalena—"

"They've chosen a location for the café. There's a neat lit-tle underground bar near Bastille they can convert to Belle Époque aesthetics, whatever that means. She wants you to drop in tonight, get a feel for the place. Food looks good. Very classic. The menu boasts touches of, I quote, 'bistro avant-garde'—whatever *that* means."

Avant-garde food tended to be jelly-colored foam on foal-liver crostini: the sort of thing that was both inedible on the tongue and offensive to good taste. Not a single good medium-rare steak in sight. "Fine." Nicholas glanced away. The gardens of the Palais-Royal glimmered across a plaza of black-and-white marble columns. It was tempting to escape there for a few hours—to stretch out his legs on one of those green iron chairs between the trees, take in the sun, turn off his phone. *Rest.*

"She wants you to bring Lavalle along. Have a private chat. Get to know the guy."

Hell. Well, there went that fucking idea. Nicholas cast her a dark look. "Say that again."

She lifted her eyebrows at him. "Dinner with Chris La-valle." She pointed, helpfully.

"Thank you, Madalena, I know where my damn costar is." So did the rest of the world, apparently. Regrettably.

"And here you are: glaring exquisitely at him, in full sight of every Parisian in the neighborhood, which is doing no good whatsoever for your optics—I say this out of love, not just be-cause your job is also my job. You haven't exchanged a word with the man. Give him a chance," she coaxed, as gentle as with a lion. "Talk to him. He might turn out to be a kinder soul than you think."

Nicholas didn't need a kind soul. He needed a costar—an

equal, a partner, a man he could respect. "He's a diva. An influencer. He isn't an actor. His English is atrocious."

"His accent is lovely. And you barely speak French."

"I know enough." He could say *bonjour, merci*, and *sortez de mon chemin, bordel de merde*, which was usually enough for his purposes.

Madalena brushed sun dust off her skirt. "You keep looking at him."

"The entire blasted world is looking at him. He's making damn sure of it."

"The entire blasted world isn't about to play his lover. And you've been furiously eye-fucking him for half an hour. People are bound to notice." She wriggled her smartphone at him. "I noticed."

"You had better," Nicholas growled, "not be looking up pictures of your employer on that thing."

"I don't need to look you up. You're trending."

"For fuck's sake, Madalena!"

Laughing, she swiped to show him. And there he was—in his expensive sweater, in profile; his elbow was resting on the table next to his coffee cup, one hand covering his mouth. Half in shadow. He looked pensive. Absorbed. Odds were, any one of the morons pointing their expensive smartphones in his direction had caught *who* he was looking at, too. *Goddamn it.*

What the hell *was* wrong with him? Was he a green boy, untrained and inexperienced, so easily distracted by a pretty face and a lithe body that looked as though it had been made for—

He stopped that thought right the fuck there. And handed the phone back, grimacing. "I've been...preoccupied."

"He *is* gorgeous," said Madalena.

"His job description is to look handsome and wear shiny things. Of course he's beautiful."

But Nicholas thought it a weakness. Beauty of that kind meant men like Chris Lavalle could coast by in the world, safe in the knowledge that they would always be loved. Beauty of that kind was too great for this life. Nicholas had worked with good-looking men and women in the past; but never before had it got so much…under his skin. It was an irritant. He disliked it.

"You put too much pressure on yourself, Nicholas," Madalena sighed. "Get a good look at him now; everybody does. He expects it, I suspect. You're gonna get closer to him than anyone else around here ever will," she added. And wasn't that the root of the problem, Nicholas thought, somberly. "Better get over it now, while you're still at arm's length. He might lose some of that attitude once he's in the water with you."

The script had several nude scenes. Nicholas had dismissed them as a regular day's work. Then he had learned whose mouth he would kiss, and who would touch him—so intimately. And things inside his head had gotten a hell of a lot messier.

Theoretically, sex scenes were about the least *sexy* scenes one could film. Nicholas had shot plenty of them in the past. Nudity did not trouble him; he'd kissed enough people on-screen to shrug off the intimacy of it. The technique—the skill—was in looking believably sensual while fighting off the intense foolishness of gooseflesh and wearing a skin-colored sleeve over one's cock. The best way to achieve this, he had found, was to hold himself at a distance from his costar, and manage, however awkwardly, to laugh with them: make the whole thing a day's trip down insanity lane.

He doubted he could laugh with Chris Lavalle.

He was a young Apollo, too lovely and too magnetic to be real. You couldn't laugh with someone like that: you could only worship them or scorn them.

As though summoned by the thought, Lavalle turned across the Place Colette and met his gaze, despite the sunshine in his eyes, despite the distance between them. Nicholas's hand stilled around his coffee cup.

He had remarkable grey eyes. He was a cliché of a Frenchman, charming and remote.

"He's coming over," Madalena observed, chin upon her hand.

"No; is he?" Nicholas muttered.

Christian Lavalle, having at last shaken off his posse—who remained hovering, though thankfully distant—came to a stop beside their table. He gave them a smile: cordial, diplomatic. He met Nicholas's eyes for a moment, then moved on to Madalena with a polite confusion that soon melted into polite disinterest.

"Hello," he said, in a soft voice. "Shall we get on?"

His English was stilted, as with non-native speakers who learned it early on but never fully grasped the measure of the language. His voice was overly formal, and oddly accented, a little deferential.

"Get...on," Nicholas repeated.

Lavalle shrugged. "They have told me to meet Priya at *Le Renard d'Or*."

Priya, Nicholas thought, with vague disbelief. Priya Chaudhuri. Their *director*. He glanced at Madalena, who helpfully said: "The Golden Fox. The bar I told you about."

"We are to have dinner." Lavalle widened his eyes a fraction, smiling. It was a fantastic smile. Nicholas had given the press many a fake, charming grin in the past; this was the best of them all combined. The simmering hatred of them, streamlined, brutally tailored down to an art.

He realized abruptly that Lavalle had no better an opinion of him than *he* had of Lavalle. Hands in his pockets, rocking slightly upon his heels, he looked entirely at ease.

This was his city. His ground.

"Dinner," Nicholas said softly.

Lavalle glanced down, then up again. His lashes were long

and fair against his cheeks. "*Mais bien sûr.* I have made a booking for eight."

Nicholas had assumed Chaudhuri meant for them merely to look about the place. Eight was late for dinner—though not so late for Parisians, who enjoyed eating late into the night; give them a bottle of Beaujolais and a platter of charcuterie, and they would cheerfully wait out the sunrise over the Seine. Lavalle seemed intent on fitting himself to the stereotype as closely as possible. He now turned his lovely smile on Madalena, who—to her credit—neither blinked nor blushed against that frontal attack. "A table only for two, I'm afraid. Although... I am sure I could call...?"

"Oh, no." Her voice was amused. "You two will want to get to know each other." She extended a hand. "I'm Madalena Torres. The PA. Get him home before midnight, yeah?"

Lavalle ducked his head, his smile fading; a flush was just touching his cheekbones. What measure of *control* could the man have on his facial expressions? It was insanity.

"We should go then," said Nicholas shortly, standing. Somewhere to the left of them, someone was snapping pictures. It was grating; yet Lavalle seemed content to linger, presenting his best profile. He was used to it. His job was to look his best for photographs—candids and otherwise.

Nicholas hated amateur paparazzi with the same fervor he hated professional ones. He always visualized the headlines, the tweets, the bloody BuzzFeed captions. "Traffic'll be hell," he grunted, to speed things along. Madalena held his phone hostage on most occasions, or he'd have called his chauffeur.

Lavalle blinked at him. "Traffic? Nobody drives in Paris."

Nicholas looked at the endless flood of cars exiting the arches of the Palais du Louvre, streaming towards the Opéra Garnier.

"Nobody from Paris drives in Paris," Lavalle amended. "*Ah, mais, mes Américains!*" He sounded amused. "We will take the bus. If we walk to the Seine we will find one going directly to Bastille, alongside the river. It will be much more pleasant. Being stuck in traffic is a...a pain in the ass. *Non?*"

Nicholas couldn't remember the last time he'd taken public transportation. His chauffeur would think he'd been kidnapped.

Nevertheless, with Madalena's generous blessing and her kiss burning upon his cheek—a little teaser for the cameras—they found themselves no later than a quarter hour later in one of Paris's green, foul-smelling buses. No seats; these had been optioned by what looked like half the little old lady population in the city. Instead they stood, and swayed.

Lavalle curled both hands around the metal railing, balancing himself with familiar ease, and stared out the window with distinct interest, as though there was something captivating about the view. In profile, he looked abstracted and sad. Did he sweat, or was he utterly unaffected by the heat? Nicholas was mildly impressed. If this was a character he was playing, Lavalle had gone full method.

What the fuck was Chaudhuri thinking? Casting a model who'd never acted in anything much bigger than a late-night soap was courting misery. For a movie that was already heating up next year's award season talk, of all things. Angelo ought to be played by a Frenchman—or at least someone who could speak the language well enough to bluff international audiences—but he was a baroque, interesting character, full of contradictions. He required *talent*. To have him played by a wannabe comedian with his sights on another Dior campaign was nothing short of an imposture.

Lavalle looked the part, at least. In a silken waistcoat, he would be the perfect Belle Époque debauchee. His proud manner, and the haughty curl of his mouth, would suit Angelo's cynical nature to a fault. And he was deeply, notably beautiful—the kind of beauty that was not easily overlooked, not even in Hollywood. His eyes, most remarkably, were grey and clear as still water. All-seeing. Nicholas thought of classical statues, marble-white and merciless and blind.

But Nicholas knew *The Throne* inside and out, and he would not be fooled by appearances.

Angelo was no indifferent torso of Apollo, listless and diffident. He was a man who had been betrayed often, who had loved and who had lost. He did not show emotion easily. He kept his cards close to his chest, an act Nicholas doubted that Lavalle—who did not so much wear his heart on his sleeve as display it prominently on every social media platform known to man—could achieve with any kind of subtlety.

"I don't get tired of it."

"What?" Nicholas, torn from his preoccupations, was brusque. Lavalle didn't seem offended.

He pointed at the view. The bus was coming up to the un-mistakable arches of the Pont Neuf, and beyond it were the tall, dark spires and pale beige buildings of the Conciergerie, holding court above the brown, rushing river. The sun beat down hard, and the sky was a pale, Venetian blue. White slips of cloud were streaming away to the east, towards the hidden towers of Notre-Dame. It was only just the beginning of summer, the longest hours of sunlight in the year, and the days ran long and luminous.

"I've been here a thousand times," said Lavalle. His glance at Nicholas faltered just on the side of charming, as though sharing an intimate moment with a near-stranger was something he wasn't used to; as though he didn't invite intimacy with every picture, every selfie, every #nofilter #homesweethome #liveyourbestlife he posted a couple times an hour. "But I've never grown tired of the view."

Nicholas stared at him. Lavalle held his gaze for a moment, then glanced away. His hair fell softly into his eyes. He'd have to cut it, for the role.

He *had* to be a con. No one was this…this naturally unaffected, to the point that artlessness itself became an affectation. Nicholas could barely figure him out: every second he spent in Lavalle's company troubled him the more.

Lavalle was disconcerting. He kept reinventing himself. He was no longer the elegant, charismatic young man from the Place Colette, who had posed and smiled and allowed his congregation to take an endless stream of selfies. Nicholas had no idea who *this* man was, with that shy smile, those pale sleepy eyes. He only knew that his body was responding in kind—was roused as though from deep slumber into some new state of being, more febrile and more real.

The bus lurched to a stop at a red light—Place du Châtelet, a green plaque said—and with a startled noise Lavalle stumbled against him. He was a sudden, warm weight against Nicholas, who, having wisely braced himself against the railing, captured his elbow in his hand. Muscle and tendon and sheer vitality. Lavalle's eyes lifted to meet his.

They were almost the same height. Nicholas was a touch taller, and broader about the shoulders. He had the sudden urge to slip one arm firmly around Lavalle's waist. Lavalle's hand had landed on his chest, and as the bus resumed its course it remained there, his fingertips tangled in the wool of Nicholas's sweater.

"Pardon," he said. The *n* was softened in his accent, barely there.

"Sure," said Nicholas. His own voice, he realized, was hoarse.

Don't miss Eight Weeks in Paris *by S.R. Lane,*
available wherever books are sold.

www.CarinaPress.com